When Jesus hung dying on his cross, the *volcryn* passed within a year of his agony, headed outward.

When the stardrive transformed Earth into the Federal Empire, the *volcryn* passed the fringes of Hrangan space. War flamed for a thousand years and the *volcryn* passed through it, safe in a place where no fires could ever burn.

When I was a child of three, all the Crey sensitives grew strange and sat staring at the stars with luminous, flickering eyes, as the *volcryn* passed Daronne, heading outward.

Now I am old, and the *volcryn* will soon pierce the Tempter's Veil. And we follow, we follow, through the dark gulfs where no one goes, through the silence that goes on and on, my *Nightflyer* and I give chase, headed outward.

NIGHTFLYERS

NIGHTFLYERS

GEORGE R. R. MARTIN

A TOM DOHERTY ASSOCIATES BOOK

NIGHTFLYERS

Copyright © 1985 by George R.R. Martin

All rights reserved, including the right to reproduce this book or portions thereof in any form.

"Nightflyers" copyright © 1980, 1981 by George R.R. Martin. From *Binary Star 5* (Dell, 1981). A shorter version of this story originally appeared in *Analog*, April 1980, copyright © 1980 by the Condé Nast Publications, Inc.

"A Song for Lya" copyright © 1974 by the Condé Nast Publications, Inc. From *Analog*, June 1974.

"Nor the Many-Colored Fires of a Star Ring" copyright © 1976 by George R.R. Martin. From *Faster Than Light* (Harper & Row, 1976).

"Weekend In A War Zone" copyright © 1977 by Aurora Publishers, Inc. From *Future Pastimes* (Aurora, 1977).

"Override" copyright © 1973 by the Condé Nast Publications, Inc. From *Analog*, September 1973.

"And Seven Times Never Kill Man" copyright © 1975 by the Condé Nast Publications, Inc. From *Analog*, July 1975.

Reprinted by arrangement with Bluejay Books

First Tor printing: February 1987

A TOR Book

Published by Tom Doherty Associates, Inc.
49 West 24 Street
New York, N.Y. 10010

Cover art by Warhola

ISBN: 0-812-54562-1
CAN. ED.: 0-812-54563-X

Printed in the United States of America

0 9 8 7 6 5 4 3 2 1

to Gardner Dozois

Who fished me out of the slush pile
and saved me from those Tubs o'Fun

Contents

Nightflyers

WHEN JESUS OF NAZARETH HUNG DYING ON HIS CROSS, THE *volcryn* passed within a year of his agony, headed outward.

When the Fire Wars raged on Earth, the *volcryn* sailed near Old Poseidon, where the seas were still unnamed and unfished. By the time the stardrive had transformed the Federated Nations of Earth into the Federal Empire, the *volcryn* had moved into the fringes of Hrangan space. The Hrangans never knew it. Like us they were children of the small bright worlds that circled their scattered suns, with little interest and less knowledge of the things that moved in the gulfs between.

War flamed for a thousand years and the *volcryn* passed through it, unknowing and untouched, safe in a place where no fires could ever burn. Afterwards, the Federal Empire was shattered and gone, and the Hrangans vanished in the dark of the Collapse, but it was no darker for the *volcryn*.

When Kleronomas took his survey ship out from Avalon, the *volcryn* came within ten light years of him. Kleronomas found many things, but he did not find the *volcryn*. Not then and not on his return to Avalon, a lifetime later.

When I was a child of three Kleronomas was dust, as distant and dead as Jesus of Nazareth, and the *volcryn* passed close to Daronne. That season all the Crey sensitives grew strange and sat staring at the stars with luminous, flickering eyes.

When I was grown, the *volcryn* had sailed beyond Tara, past the range of even the Crey, still heading outward.

And now I am old and growing older and the *volcryn* will soon pierce the Tempter's Veil where it hangs like a black mist between the stars. And we follow, we follow. Through the dark gulfs where no one goes, through the emptiness, through the silence that goes on and on, my *Nightflyer* and I give chase.

They made their way slowly down the length of the transparent tube that linked the orbital docks to the waiting starship ahead, pulling themselves hand over through weightlessness.

Melantha Jhirl, the only one among them who did not seem clumsy and ill-at-ease in free fall, paused briefly to look at the dappled globe of Avalon below, a stately vastness in jade and amber. She smiled and moved swiftly down the tube, passing her companions with an easy grace. They had boarded starships before, all of them, but never like this. Most ships docked flush against the station, but the craft that Karoly d'Branin had chartered for his mission was too large, and of too singular in design. It loomed ahead; three small eggs side-by-side, two larger spheres beneath and at right angles, the cylinder of the driveroom between, lengths of tube connecting it all. The ship was white and austere.

Melantha Jhirl was the first one through the airlock. The others straggled up one by one until they had all boarded; five women and four men, each an Academy scholar, their backgrounds as diverse as their fields of study. The frail young telepath, Thale Lasamer, was the last to enter. He glanced about nervously as the others chatted and waited for the entry procedure to be completed. "We're being watched," he said.

The outer door was closed behind them, the tube had fallen away; now the inner door slid open. "Welcome to my *Nightflyer*," said a mellow voice from within.

But there was no one there.

Melantha Jhirl stepped into the corridor. "Hello," she said, looking about quizzically. Karoly d'Branin followed her.

"Hello," the mellow voice replied. It was coming from a communicator grill beneath a darkened viewscreen. "This is Royd Eris, master of the *Nightflyer*. I'm pleased to see you again, Karoly, and pleased to welcome the rest of you."

"Where are you?" someone demanded.

"In my quarters, which occupy half of this life-support sphere," the voice of Royd Eris replied amiably. "The other half is comprised of a lounge-library-kitchen, two sanitary stations, one double cabin, and a rather small single. The rest of you will have to rig sleepwebs in the cargo spheres, I'm afraid. The *Nightflyer* was designed as a trader, not a passenger vessel. However, I've opened all the appropriate passageways and locks, so the holds have air and heat and water. I thought you'd find it more comfortable that way. Your equipment and computer system have been stowed in the holds, but there is still plenty of space, I assure you. I suggest you settle in, and then meet in the lounge for a meal."

"Will you join us?" asked the psipsych, a querulous hatchet-faced woman named Agatha Marij-Black.

"In a fashion," Royd Eris said, "in a fashion."

The ghost appeared at the banquet.

They found the lounge easily enough, after they had rigged their sleepwebs and arranged their personal belongings around their sleeping quarters. It was the largest room in this section of the ship. One end of it was a fully equipped kitchen, well stocked with provisions. The opposite end offered several comfortable chairs, two readers, a holotank, and a wall of books and tapes and crystal chips. In the center was a long table with places set for ten.

A light meal was hot and waiting. The academicians helped themselves and took seats at the table, laughing and talking to each other, more at ease now than when they had boarded.

The ship's gravity grid was on, which went a long way towards making them more comfortable; the queasy awkwardness of their weightless transit was soon forgotten.

Finally all the seats were occupied except for one at the head of the table.

The ghost materialized there.

All conservation stopped.

"Hello," said the spectre, the bright shade of a lithe, pale-eyed young man with white hair. He was dressed in clothing twenty years out of date; a loose blue pastel shirt that ballooned at his wrists, clinging white trousers with built-in boots. They could see through him, and his own eyes did not see them at all.

"A hologram," said Alys Northwind, the short, stout xenotech.

"Royd, Royd, I do not understand," said Karoly d'Branin, staring at the ghost. "What is this? Why do you send us a projection? Will you not join us in person?"

The ghost smiled faintly and lifted an arm. "My quarters are on the other side of that wall," he said. "I'm afraid there is no door or lock between the two halves of the sphere. I spend most of my time by myself, and I value my privacy. I hope you will all understand, and respect my wishes. I will be a gracious host nonetheless. Here in the lounge my projection can join you. Elsewhere, if you have anything you need, if you want to talk to me, just use a communicator. Now, please resume your meal, and your conversations. I'll gladly listen. It's been a long time since I had passengers."

They tried. But the ghost at the head of the table cast a long shadow, and the meal was strained and hurried.

From the hour the *Nightflyer* slipped into stardrive, Royd Eris watched his passengers.

Within a few days most of the academicians had grown accustomed to the disembodied voice from the communicators and the holographic spectre in the lounge, but only

Melantha Jhirl and Karoly d'Branin ever seemed really comfortable in his presence. The others would have been even more uncomfortable if they had known that Royd was always with them. Always and everywhere, he watched. Even in the sanitary stations, Royd had eyes and ears.

He watched them work, eat, sleep, copulate; he listened untiringly to their talk. Within a week he knew them, all nine, and had begun to ferret out their tawdry little secrets.

The cyberneticist, Lommie Thorne, talked to her computers and seemed to prefer their company to that of humans. She was bright and quick, with a mobile, expressive face and a small hard boyish body; most of the others found her attractive, but she did not like to be touched. She sexed only once, with Melantha Jhirl. Lommie Thorne wore shirts of softly-woven metal, and had an implant in her left wrist that let her interface directly with her computers.

The xenobiologist, Rojan Christopheris, was a surly, argumentative man, a cynic whose contempt for his colleagues was barely kept in check, a solitary drinker. He was tall and stooped and ugly.

The two linguists, Dannel and Lindran, were lovers in public, constantly holding hands and supporting each other. In private they quarreled bitterly. Lindran had a mordant wit and liked to wound Dannel where it hurt the most, with jokes about his professional competence. They sexed often, both of them, but not with each other.

Agatha Marij-Black, the psipsych, was a hypochrondriac given to black depressions, which worsened in the close confines of the *Nightflyer*.

Xenotech Alys Northwind ate constantly and never washed. Her stubby fingernails were always caked with black dirt, and she wore the same jumpsuit for the first two weeks of the voyage, taking it off only for sex, and then only briefly.

Telepath Thale Lasamer was nervous and temperamental, afraid of everyone around him, yet given to bouts of arrogance in which he taunted his companions with thoughts he had snatched from their minds.

Royd Eris watched them all, studied them, lived with them and through them. He neglected none, not even the ones he found the most distasteful. But by the time the *Nightflyer* had been lost in the roiling flux of stardrive for two weeks, two of his riders had come to engage the bulk of his attention.

"Most of all, I want to know the *why* of them," Karoly d'Branin told him one false night the second week out from Avalon.

Royd's luminescent ghost sat close to d'Branin in the darkened lounge, watching him drink bittersweet chocolate. The others were all asleep. Night and day are meaningless on a starship, but the *Nightflyer* kept the usual cycles and most of the passengers followed them. Old d'Branin, administrator, generalist, and mission leader, was the exception; he kept his own hours, preferred work to sleep, and liked nothing better than to talk about his pet obsession, the *volcryn* he hunted.

"The *if* of them is important as well, Karoly," Royd answered. "Can you truly be certain these aliens of yours exist?"

"*I* can be certain," Karoly d'Branin said, with a broad wink. He was a compact man, short and slender, iron grey hair carefully styled and his tunic almost fussily neat, but the expansiveness of his gestures and the giddy enthusiasms to which he was prone belied his sober appearance. "That is enough. If everyone else were certain as well, we would have a fleet of research ships instead of your little *Nightflyer*." He sipped at his chocolate and sighed with satisfaction. "Do you know the Nor T'alush, Royd?"

The name was strange, but it took Royd only a moment to consult his library computer. "An alien race on the other side of human space, past the Fyndii worlds and the Damoosh. Possibly legendary."

D'Branin chuckled. "No, no, no! Your library is out of date, my friend, you must supplement it the next time you visit Avalon. Not legends, no, real enough, though far away. We have little information about the Nor T'alush, but we are sure they exist, though you and I may never meet one. They were the start of it all."

"Tell me," Royd said. "I am interested in your work, Karoly."

"I was coding some information into the Academy computers, a packet newly arrived from Dam Tullian after twenty standard years in transit. Part of it was Nor T'alush folklore. I had no idea how long that had taken to get to Dam Tullian, or by what route it had come, but it did not matter—folklore is timeless anyway, and this was fascinating material. Did you know that my first degree was in xenomythology?"

"I did not. Please continue."

"The *volcryn* story was among the Nor T'alush myths. It awed me; a race of sentients moving out from some mysterious origin in the core of the galaxy, sailing towards the galactic edge and, it was alleged, eventually bound for intergalactic space itself, meanwhile always keeping to the interstellar depths, no planetfalls, seldom coming within a light year of a star." D'Branin's grey eyes sparkled, and as he spoke his hands swept enthusiastically to either side, as if they could encompass the galaxy. "And doing it all *without a stardrive*, Royd, that is the real wonder! Doing it in ships moving only a fraction of the speed of light! That was the detail that obsessed me! How different they must be, my *volcryn*—wise and patient, long-lived and long-viewed, with none of the terrible haste and passion that consume the lesser races. Think how *old* they must be, those *volcryn* ships!"

"Old," Royd agreed. "Karoly, you said *ships*. More than one?"

"Oh, yes," d'Branin said. "According to the Nor T'alush, one or two appeared first, on the innermost edges of their trading sphere, but others followed. Hundreds of them, each solitary, moving by itself, bound outward, always outward. The direction was always the same. For fifteen thousand standard years they moved among the Nor T'alush stars, and then they began to pass out from among them. The myth said that the last *volcryn* ship was gone three thousand years ago."

"Eighteen thousand years," Royd said, adding. "Are the Nor T'alush that old?"

"Not as star-travellers, no," d'Branin said, smiling. "According to their own histories, the Nor T'alush have only been civilized for about half that long. That bothered me for a while. It seemed to make the *volcryn* story clearly a legend. A wonderful legend, true, but nothing more.

"Ultimately, however, I could not let it alone. In my spare time I investigated, crosschecking with other alien cosmologies to see whether this particular myth was shared by any races other than the Nor T'alush. I thought perhaps I could get a thesis out of it. It seemed a fruitful line of inquiry.

"I was startled by what I found. Nothing from the Hrangans, or the Hrangan slave races, but that made sense, you see. Since they were *out* from human space, the *volcryn* would not reach them until after they had passed through our own sphere. When I looked *in*, however, the *volcryn* story was everywhere." D'Branin leaned forward eagerly. "Ah, Royd, the stories, the *stories*!"

"Tell me," Royd said.

"The Fyndii call them *iy-wivii*, which translates to something like void-horde or dark-horde. Each Fyndii horde tells the same story, only the mindmutes disbelieve. The ships are said to be vast, much larger than any known in their history or ours. Warships, they say. There is a story of a lost Fyndii horde, three hundred ships under *rala-fyn*, all destroyed utterly when they encountered an *iy-wivii*. This was many thousands of years ago, of course, so the details are unclear.

"The Damoosh have a different story, but they accept it as literal truth—and the Damoosh, you know, are the oldest race we've yet encountered. The people of the gulf, they call my *volcryn*. Lovely stories, Royd, lovely! Ships like great dark cities, still and silent, moving at a slower pace than the universe around them. Damoosh legends say the *volcryn* are refugees from some unimaginable war deep in the core of the galaxy, at the very beginning of time. They abandoned the worlds and stars on which they had evolved, sought true peace in the emptiness between.

"The gethsoids of Aath have a similar story, but in their tale that war destroyed all life in our galaxy, and the *volcryn* are gods of a sort, reseeding the worlds as they pass. Other races see them as god's messengers, or shadows out of hell warning us all to flee some terror soon to emerge from the core."

"Your stories contradict each other, Karoly."

"Yes, yes, of course, but they all agree on the essentials— the *volcryn*, sailing out, passing through our short-lived empires and transient glories in their ancient eternal sublight ships. *That* is what matters! The rest is frippery, ornamentation; we will soon know the truth of it. I checked what little was known about the races said to flourish further in still, beyond even the Nor T'alush—civilizations and peoples half legendary themselves, like the Dan'lai and the ullish and the Rohenna'kh—and where I could find anything at all, I found the *volcryn* story once again."

"The legend of the legends," Royd suggested. The spectre's wide mouth turned up in a smile.

"Exactly, exactly," d'Branin agreed. "At that point, I called in the experts, specialists from the Institute for the Study of Non-Human Intelligence. We researched for two years. It was all there, in the libraries and memories and matrices of the Academy. No one had ever looked before, or bothered to put it together.

"The *volcryn* have been moving through the manrealm for most of human history, since before the dawn of spaceflight. While we twist the fabric of space itself to cheat relativity, they have been sailing their great ships right through the heart of our alleged civilization, past our most populous worlds, at stately slow sublight speeds, bound for the Fringe and the dark between the galaxies. Marvelous, Royd, marvelous!''

"Marvelous!" Royd agreed.

Karly d'Branin drained his chocolate cup with a swig, and reached out to catch Royd's arm, but his hand passed through empty light. He seemed disconcerted for a moment, before he began to laugh at himself. "Ah, my *volcryn*. I grow overenthused, Royd. I am so close now. They have preyed on my mind for a dozen years, and within the month I will have them, will behold their splendor with my own weary eyes. Then, *then*, if only I can open communication, if only my people can reach ones so great and strange as they, so different from us—I have hopes, Royd, hopes that at last I will know the *why* of it!"

The ghost of Royd Eris smiled for him, and looked on through calm transparent eyes.

Passengers soon grow restless on a starship under drive, sooner on one as small and spare as the *Nightflyer*. Late in the second week, the speculation began in deadly earnest.

"Who is this Royd Eris, really?" the xenobiologist, Rojan Christopheris, complained one night when four of them were playing cards. "Why doesn't he come out? What's the purpose of keeping himself sealed off from the rest of us?"

"Ask him," suggested Dannel, the male linguist.

"What if he's a criminal of some sort?" Christopheris said. "Do we know anything about him? No, of course not. D'Branin engaged him, and d'Branin is a senile old fool, we all know that."

"It's your play," Lommie Thorne said.

Christopheris snapped down a card. "Setback," he declared, "you'll have to draw again." He grinned. "As for this Eris, who knows that he isn't planning to kill us all."

"For our vast wealth, no doubt," said Lindran, the female

linguist. She played a card on top of the one Christopheris had laid down. "Ricochet," she called softly. She smiled.

So did Royd Eris, watching.

Melantha Jhirl was good to watch.

Young, healthy, active, Melantha Jhirl had a vibrancy about her the others could not match. She was big in every way; a head taller than anyone else on board, large-framed, large-breasted, long-legged, strong, muscles moving fluidly beneath shiny coal-black skin. Her appetites were big as well. She ate twice as much as any of her colleagues, drank heavily without ever seeming drunk, exercised for hours every day on equipment she had brought with her and set up in one of the cargo holds. By the third week out she had sexed with all four of the men on board and two of the other women. Even in bed she was always active, exhausting most of her partners. Royd watched her with consuming interest.

"I am an improved model," she told him once as she worked out on her parallel bars, sweat glistening on her bare skin, her long black hair confined in a net.

"Improved?" Royd said. He could not send his projection down to the holds, but Melantha had summoned him with the communicator to talk while she exercised, not knowing he would have been there anyway.

She paused in her routine, holding her body straight and aloft with the strength of her arms and her back. "Altered, captain," she said. She had taken to calling him captain. "Born on Prometheus among the elite, child of two genetic wizards. Improved, captain. I require twice the energy you do, but I use it all. A more efficient metabolism, a stronger and more durable body, an expected lifespan half again the normal human's. My people have made some terrible mistakes when they try to radically redesign humanity, but the small improvements they do well."

She resumed her exercises, moving quickly and easily, silent until she had finished. When she was done, she vaulted away from the bars and stood breathing heavily for a moment, then crossed her arms and cocked her head and grinned. "Now you know my life story, captain," she said. She pulled off the net to shake free her hair.

"Surely there is more," said the voice from the communicator.

Melantha Jhirl laughed. "Surely," she said. "Do you want to hear about my defection to Avalon, the whys and wherefores of it, the trouble it caused my family on Prometheus? Or are you more interested in my extraordinary work in cultural xenology? Do you want to hear about that?"

"Perhaps some other time," Royd said politely. "What is that crystal you wear?"

It hung between her breasts ordinarily; she had removed it when she stripped for her exercises. She picked it up again and slipped it over her head; a small green gem laced with traceries of black, on a silver chain. When it touched her Melantha closed her eyes briefly, then opened them again, grinning. "It's alive," she said. "Haven't you ever seen one? A whisperjewel, captain. Resonant crystal, etched psionically to hold a memory, a sensation. The touch brings it back, for a time."

"I am familiar with the principle," Royd said, "but not this use. Yours contains some treasured memory, then? Of your family, perhaps?"

Melantha Jhirl snatched up a towel and began to dry the sweat from her body. "Mine contains the sensations of a particularly satisfying session in bed, captain. It arouses me. Or it did. Whisperjewels fade in time, and this isn't as potent as it once was. But sometimes—often when I've come from lovemaking or strenuous exercise—it comes alive on me again, like it did just then."

"Oh," said Royd's voice. "It has made you aroused, then? Are you going off to copulate now?"

Melantha grinned. "I know what part of my life *you* want to hear about, captain—my tumultuous and passionate lovelife. Well, you won't have it. Not until I hear your life story, anyway. Among my modest attributes is an insatiable curiosity. Who are you, captain? Really?"

"One as improved as you," Royd replied, "should certainly be able to guess."

Melantha laughed, and tossed her towel at the communicator grill.

Lommie Thorne spent most of her days in the cargo hold they had designated as the computer room, setting up the system they would use to analyze the *volcryn*. As often as not, the xenotech Alys Northwind came with her to lend a hand. The cyberneticist whistled as she worked; Northwind obeyed her orders in a sullen silence. Occasionally they talked.

"Eris isn't human," Lommie Thorne said one day, as she supervised the installation of a display viewscreen.

Alys Northwind grunted. "What?" A frown broke across her square, flat features. Christopheris and his talk had made her nervous about Eris. She clicked another component into position, and turned.

"He talks to us, but he can't be seen," the cyberneticist said. "This ship is uncrewed, seemingly all automated except for him. Why not entirely automated, then? I'd wager this Royd Eris is a fairly sophisticated computer system, perhaps a genuine Artificial Intelligence. Even a modest program can carry on a blind conversation indistinguishable from a human's. This one could fool you, I'd bet, once it's up and running."

The xenotech grunted and turned back to her work. "Why fake being human, then?"

"Because," said Lommie Thorne, "most legal systems give AIs no rights. A ship can't own itself, even on Avalon. The *Nightflyer* is probably afraid of being seized and disconnected." She whistled. "Death, Alys; the end of self-awareness and conscious thought."

"I work with machines every day," Alys Northwind said

stubbornly. "Turn them off, turn them on, makes no difference. They don't mind. Why should this machine care?"

Lommie Thorne smiled. "A computer is different, Alys," she said. "Mind, thought, life, the big systems have all of that." Her right hand curled around her left wrist, and her thumb began idly rubbing the nubs of her implant. "Sensation, too. I know. No one wants the end of sensation. They are not so different from you and I, really."

The xenotech glanced back and shook her head. "Really," she repeated, in a flat, disbelieving voice.

Royd Eris listened and watched, unsmiling.

Thale Lasamer was a frail young thing; nervous, sensitive, with limp flaxen hair that fell to his shoulders, and watery blue eyes. Normally he dressed like a peacock, favoring the lacy vee-necked shirts and codpieces that were still the fashion among the lower classes of his homeworld. But on the day he sought out Karoly d'Branin in his cramped, private cabin, Lasamer was dressed almost somberly, in an austere grey jumpsuit.

"I feel it," he said, clutching d'Branin by the arm, his long fingernails digging in painfully. "Something is wrong, Karoly, something is very wrong. I'm beginning to get frightened."

The telepath's nails bit, and d'Branin pulled away hard. "You are hurting me," he protested. "My friend, what is it? Frightened? Of what, of whom? I do not understand. What could there be to fear?"

Lasamer raised pale hands to his face. "I don't know, I don't *know*," he wailed. "Yet it's *there*, I feel it. Karoly, I'm picking up something. You know I'm good, I am, that's why you picked me. Just a moment ago, when my nails dug into you, I felt it. I can read you now, in flashes. You're thinking I'm too excitable, that it's the confinement, that I've got to be calmed down." The young man laughed a thin hysterical laugh that died as quickly as it had begun. "No, you see, I am good. Class one, tested, and I tell you I'm afraid. I sense it. Feel it. Dream of it. I felt it even as we were boarding, and it's gotten worse. Something dangerous. Something volatile. And alien, Karoly, *alien!*"

"The *volcryn?*" d'Branin said.

"No, impossible. We're in drive, they're light years away." The edgy laughter sounded again. "I'm not that good, Karoly. I've heard your Crey story, but I'm only a human. No, this is close. On the ship."

"One of us?"

"Maybe," Lassamer said. He rubbed his cheek absently. "I can't sort it out."

D'Branin put a fatherly hand on his shoulder. "Thale, this feeling of yours—could it be that you are just tired? We have all of us been under strain. Inactivity can be taxing."

"Get your hand off me," Lasamer snapped.

D'Branin drew back his hand quickly.

"This is *real*," the telepath insisted, "and I don't need you thinking that maybe you shouldn't have taken me, all that crap. I'm as stable as anyone on this . . . this . . . how *dare* you think I'm unstable, you ought to look inside some of these others, Christopheris with his bottle and his dirty little fantasies, Dannel half sick with fear, Lommie and her machines, with her it's all metal and lights and cool circuits, sick, I tell you, and Jhirl's arrogant and Agatha whines even in her head to herself all the time, and Alys is empty, like a cow. You, you don't touch them, see into them, what do you know of *stable*? Losers, d'Branin, they've given you a bunch of losers, and I'm one of your best, so don't you go thinking that I'm not stable, not sane, you hear." His blue eyes were fevered. "Do you *hear*?"

"Easy," d'Branin said. "Easy, Thale, you're getting excited."

The telepath blinked, and suddenly the wildness was gone. "Excited?" he said. "Yes." He looked around guiltily. "It's hard, Karoly, but listen to me, you must, I'm warning you. We're in danger.''

"I will listen," d'Branin said, "but I cannot act without more definite information. You must use your talent and get it for me, yes? You can do that."

Lasamer nodded. "Yes," he said. "Yes." They talked quietly for more than an hour, and finally the telepath left peacefully.

Afterwards d'Branin went straight to the psipsych, who was lying in her sleepweb surrounded by medicines, complaining bitterly of aches. "Interesting," she said when d'Branin told her. "I've felt something too, a sense of threat, very vague, diffuse. I thought it was me, the confinement, the boredom, the way I feel. My moods betray me at times. Did he say anything more specific?"

"No."

"I'll make an effort to move around, read him, read the others, see what I can pick up. Although, if this is real, he should know it first. He's a one, I'm only a three."

D'Branin nodded. "He seems very receptive," he said. "He told me all kinds of things about the others."

"Means nothing. Sometimes, when a telepath insists he is picking up everything, what it means is that he's picking up nothing at all. He imagines feelings, readings, to make up for those that will not come. I'll keep careful watch on him, d'Branin. Sometimes a talent can crack, slip into a kind of hysteria, and begin to broadcast instead of receive. In a closed environment, that's very dangerous."

Karoly d'Branin nodded. "Of course, of course."

In another part of the ship, Royd Eris frowned.

"Have you noticed the clothing on that holograph he sends us?" Rojan Christopheris asked Alys Northwind. They were alone in one of the holds, reclining on a mat, trying to avoid the wet spot. The xenobiologist had lit a joystick. He offered it to his companion, but Northwind waved it away.

"A decade out of style, maybe more. My father wore shirts like that when he was a boy on Old Poseidon."

"Eris has old-fashioned taste," Alys Northwind said. "So? I don't care what he wears. Me, I like my jumpsuits. They're comfortable. Don't care what people think."

"You don't, do you?" Christopheris said, wrinkling his huge nose. She did not see the gesture. "Well, you miss the point. What if that isn't really Eris? A projection can be anything, can be made up out of whole cloth. I don't think he really looks like that."

"No?" Now her voice was curious. She rolled over and curled up beneath his arm, her heavy white breasts against his chest.

"What if he's sick, deformed, ashamed to be seen the way he really looks?" Christopheris said. "Perhaps he has some disease. The Slow Plague can waste a person terribly, but it takes decades to kill, and there are other contagions—manthrax, new leprosy, the melt, Langamen's Disease, lots of them. Could be that Royd's self-imposed quarantine is just that. A quarantine. Think about it."

Alys Northwind frowned. "All this talk of Eris," she said, "is making me edgy."

The xenobiologist sucked on his joy-stick and laughed. "Welcome to the *Nightflyer*, then. The rest of us are already there."

In the fifth week out, Melantha Jhirl pushed her pawn to the sixth rank and Royd saw that it was unstoppable and resigned. It was his eighth straight defeat at her hands in as many days. She was sitting cross-legged on the floor of the lounge, the chessmen spread out before her in front of a darkened viewscreen. Laughing, she swept them all away. "Don't feel bad, Royd," she told him. "I'm an improved model. Always three moves ahead."

"I should tie in my computer," he replied. "You'd never

know." His ghost materialized suddenly, standing in front of the viewscreen, and smiled at her.

"I'd know within three moves," Melantha Jhirl said. "Try it."

They were the last victims of a chess fever that had swept the *Nightflyer* for more than a week. Initially it had been Christopheris who produced the set and urged people to play, but the others had lost interest quickly when Thale Lasamer sat down and beat them all, one by one. Everyone was certain that he'd done it by reading their minds, but the telepath was in a volatile, nasty mood, and no one dared voice the accusation. Melantha, however, had been able to defeat Lasamer without very much trouble. "He isn't that good a player," she told Royd afterwards, "and if he's trying to lift ideas from me, he's getting gibberish. The improved model knows certain mental disciplines. I can shield myself well enough, thank you." Christopheris and a few of the others then tried a game or two against Melantha, and were routed for their troubles. Finally Royd asked if he might play. Only Melantha and Karoly were willing to sit down with him over the board, and since Karoly could barely recall how the pieces moved from one moment to the next, that left Melantha and Royd as regular opponents. They both seemed to thrive on the games, though Melantha always won.

Melantha stood up and walked to the kitchen, stepping right through Royd's ghostly form, which she steadfastly refused to pretend was real. "The rest of them walk around me," Royd complained.

She shrugged, and found a bulb of beer in a storage compartment. "When are you going to break down and let me behind your wall for a visit, captain?" she asked. "Don't you get lonely back there? Sexually frustrated? Claustrophobic?"

"I have flown the *Nightflyer* all my life, Melantha," Royd said. His projection, ignored, winked out. "If I were subject to claustrophobia, sexual frustration, or loneliness, such a life would have been impossible. Surely that should be obvious to you, being as improved a model as you are?''

She took a squeeze of her beer and laughed her mellow, musical laugh at him. ''I'll solve you yet, captain,'' she warned.

''Meanwhile,'' he said, ''tell me some more lies about your life.''

''Have you ever heard of Jupiter?'' the xenotech demanded of the others. She was drunk, lolling in her sleepweb in the cargo hold.

''Something to do with Earth,'' said Lindran. ''The same myth system originated both names, I believe.''

''Jupiter,'' the xenotech announced loudly, ''is a gas giant in the same solar system as Old Earth. Didn't know that, did you?''

''I've got more important things to occupy my mind than such trivia, Alys,'' Lindran said.

Alys Northwind smiled down smugly. ''Listen, I'm talking to you. They were on the verge of exploring this Jupiter when the stardrive was discovered, oh, way back. After that, course, no one bothered with gas giants. Just slip into drive and find the habitable worlds, settle them, ignore the comets and the rocks and the gas giants—there's another star just a few light years away, and it has *more* habitable planets. But there were people who thought those Jupiters might have life, you know. Do you see?''

''I see that you're blind drunk,'' Lindran said.

Christopheris looked annoyed. ''If there is intelligent life on the gas giants, it shows no interest in leaving them,'' he snapped. ''All of the sentient species we have met up to now have originated on worlds similar to Earth, and most of them are oxygen breathers. Unless you're suggesting that the *volcryn* are from a gas giant?''

The xenotech pushed herself up to a sitting position and smiled conspiratorially. ''Not the *volcryn*,'' she said. ''Royd

Eris. Crack that forward bulkhead in the lounge, and watch the methane and ammonia come smoking out." Her hand made a sensuous waving motion through the air, and she convulsed with giddy laughter.

The system was up and running. Cyberneticist Lommie Thorne sat at the master console, a featureless black plastic plate upon which the phantom images of a hundred keyboard configurations came and went in holographic display, vanishing and shifting even as she used them. Around her rose crystalline data grids, ranks of viewscreens and readout panels upon which columns of figures marched and geometric shapes did stately whirling dances, dark columns of seamless metal that contained the mind and soul of her system. She sat in the semi-darkness happily, whistling as she ran the computer through several simple routines, her fingers moving across the flickering keys with blind speed and quickening tempo. "Ah," she said once, smiling. Later, only, "Good."

Then it was time for the final run-through. Lommie Thorne slid back the metallic fabric of her left sleeve, pushed her wrist beneath the console, found the prongs, jacked herself in. Interface.

Ecstacy.

Inkblot shapes in a dozen glowing colors twisted and melded and broke apart on the readout screens.

In an instant it was over.

Lommie Thorne pulled free her wrist. The smile on her face was shy and satisfied, but across it lay another expression, the merest hint of puzzlement. She touched her thumb to the holes of her wrist jack, and found them warm to the touch, tingling. Lommie shivered.

The system was running perfectly, hardware in good condition, all software systems functioning according to plan, interface meshing well. It had been a delight, as it always was. When she joined with the system, she was wise beyond her years, and powerful, and full of light and electricity and the stuff of life, cool and clean and exciting to touch, and never alone, never small or weak. That was what it was always like when she interfaced, and let herself expand.

But this time something had been different. Something cold had touched her, only for a moment. Something very cold and very frightening, and together she and the system had seen it cleanly for a brief moment, and then it had been gone again.

The cyberneticist shook her head, and drove the nonsense out. She went back to work. After a time, she began to whistle.

During the sixth week, Alys Northwind cut herself badly while preparing a snack. She was standing in the kitchen, slicing a spiced meatstick with a long knife, when suddenly she screamed.

Dannel and Lindran rushed to her, and found her staring down in horror at the chopping block in front of her. The knife had taken off the first joint of the index finger on her left hand, and the blood was spreading in ragged spurts. "The ship lurched," Alys said numbly, staring up at Dannel. "Didn't you feel it jerk? It pushed the knife to the side."

"Get something to stop the bleeding," Lindran said. Dannel looked around in panic. "Oh, I'll do it myself," Lindran finally said, and she did.

The psipsych, Agatha Marij-Black, gave Northwind a tranquilizer, then looked at the two linguists. "Did you see it happen?"

"She did it herself, with the knife," Dannel said.

From somewhere down the corridor, there came the sound of wild, hysterical laughter.

"I dampened him," Marij-Black reported to Karoly d'Branin later the same day. "Psionine-4. It will blunt his receptivity for several days, and I have more if he needs it."

D'Branin wore a stricken look. "We talked several times,

and I could see that Thale was becoming ever more fearful, but he could never tell me the why of it. Did you have to shut him off?''

The psipsych shrugged. ''He was edging into the irrational. Given his level of talent, if he'd gone over the edge he might have taken us all with him. You should never have taken a class one telepath, d'Branin. Too unstable.''

''We must communicate with an alien race. I remind you that is no easy task. The *volcryn* will be more alien than any sentients we have yet encountered. We needed class one skills if we were to have any hope of reaching them. And they have so much to teach us, my friend!''

''Glib,'' she said, ''but you might have no working skills at all, given the condition of your class one. Half the time he's curled up into the foetal position in his sleepweb, half the time he's strutting and crowing and half mad with fear. He insists we're all in real physical danger, but he doesn't know why or from what. The worst of it is that I can't tell if he's really sensing something or simply having an acute attack of paranoia. He certainly displays some classic paranoid symptoms. Among other things, he insists that he's being watched. Perhaps his condition is completely unrelated to us, the *volcryn,* and his talent. I can't be sure.''

''What of your own talent?'' d'Branin said. ''You are an empath, are you not?''

''Don't tell me my job,'' she said sharply. ''I sexed with him last week. You don't get more proximity or better rapport for esping than that. Even under those conditions, I couldn't be sure of anything. His mind is a chaos, and his fear is so rank it stank up the sheets. I don't read anything from the others either, besides the ordinary tensions and frustrations. But I'm only a three, so that doesn't mean much. My abilities are limited. You know I haven't been feeling well, d'Branin. I can barely breathe on this ship. The air seems thick and heavy to me, my head throbs. I ought to stay in bed.''

"Yes, of course," d'Branin said hastily. "I did not mean to criticize. You have been doing all you can under difficult circumstances. How long will it be until Thale is with us again?"

The psipsych rubbed her temple wearily. "I'm recommending we keep him dampened until the mission is over, d'Branin. I warn you, an insane or hysterical telepath is dangerous. That business with Northwind and the knife might have been his doing, you know. He started screaming not long after, remember. Maybe he'd touched her, for just an instant—oh, it's a wild idea, but it's possible. The point is, we don't take chances. I have enough psionine-4 to keep him numb and functional until we're back on Avalon."

"*But*—Royd will take us out of drive soon, and we will make contact with the *volcryn*. We will need Thale, his mind, his talent. Is it vital to keep him dampened? Is there no other way?"

Marij-Black grimaced. "My other option was an injection of esperon. It would have opened him up completely, increased his psionic receptivity tenfold for a few hours. Then, I'd hope, he could focus in on this danger he's feeling. Exorcise it if it's false, deal with it if it's real. But psionine-4 is a lot safer. Esperon is a hell of a drug, with devastating side effects. It raises the blood pressure dramatically, sometimes brings on hyperventilation or seizures, has even been known to stop the heart. Lasamer is young enough so that I'm not worried about that, but I don't think he has the emotional stability to deal with that kind of power. The psionine should tell us something. If his paranoia persists, I'll know it has nothing to do with his telepathy."

"And if it does not persist?" Karoly d'Branin said.

Agatha Marij-Black smiled wickedly at him. "If Lasamer becomes quiescent, and stops babbling about danger? Why, that would mean he was no longer picking up anything, wouldn't it? And *that* would mean there had been something to pick up, that he'd been right all along."

* * *

At dinner that night, Thale Lasamer was quiet and distracted, eating in a rhythmic, mechanical sort of way, with a cloudy look in his blue eyes. Afterwards he excused himself and went straight to bed, falling into exhausted slumber almost immediately.

"What did you do to him?" Lommie Thorne asked Marij-Black.

"I shut off that prying mind of his," she replied.

"You should have done it two weeks ago," Lindran said. "Docile, he's a lot easier to take."

Karoly d'Branin hardly touched his food.

False night came, and Royd's wraith materialized while Karoly d'Branin sat brooding over his chocolate. "Karoly," the apparition said, "would it be possible to tie in the computer your team brought on board with my shipboard system? Your *volcryn* stories fascinate me, and I would like to be able to study them further at my leisure. I assume the details of your investigation are in storage."

"Certainly," d'Branin replied in an offhand, distracted manner. "Our system is up now. Patching it into the *Nightflyer* should present no problem. I will tell Lommie to attend to it tomorrow."

Silence hung in the room heavily. Karoly d'Branin sipped at his chocolate and stared off into the darkness, almost unaware of Royd.

"You are troubled," Royd said after a time.

"Eh? Oh, yes." D'Branin looked up. "Forgive me, my friend. I have much on my mind."

"It concerns Thale Lasamer, does it not?"

Karoly d'Branin looked at the pale, luminescent figure across from him for a long time before he finally managed a stiff nod. "Yes. Might I ask how you knew that?"

"I know everything that occurs on the *Nightflyer*," Royd said.

"You have been watching us," d'Branin said gravely, accusation in his tone. "Then it is so, what Thale says, about us being watched. Royd, how could you? Spying is beneath you."

The ghost's transparent eyes had no life in them, did not see. "Do not tell the others," Royd warned. "Karoly, my friend—if I may call you my friend—I have my own reasons for watching, reasons it would not profit you to know. I mean you no harm. Believe that. You have hired me to take you safely to the *volcryn* and safely back, and I mean to do just that."

"You are being evasive, Royd," d'Branin said. "Why do you spy on us? Do you watch everything? Are you a voyeur, some enemy, is that why you do not mix with us? Is watching all you intend to do?"

"Your suspicions hurt me, Karoly."

"Your deception hurts me. Will you not answer me?"

"I have eyes and ears everywhere," Royd said. "There is no place to hide from me on the *Nightflyer*. Do I see everything? No, not always. I am only human, no matter what your colleagues might think. I sleep. The monitors remain on, but there is no one to observe them. I can only pay attention to one or two scenes or inputs at once. Sometimes I grow distracted, unobservant. I watch everything, Karoly, but I do not see everything."

"*Why*?" D'Branin poured himself a fresh cup of chocolate, steadying his hand with an effort.

"I do not have to answer that question. The *Nightflyer* is my ship."

D'Branin sipped chocolate, blinked, nodded to himself. "You grieve me, my friend. You give me no choice. Thale said we were being watched, I now learn and he was right. He says also that we are in danger. Something alien, he says. You?"

The projection was still and silent.

D'Branin clucked. "You do not answer. Ah, Royd, what

am I to do? I must believe him, then. We are in danger, perhaps from you. I must abort our mission, then. Return us to Avalon, Royd. That is my decision.''

The ghost smiled wanly. ''So close, Karoly? Soon now we will be dropping out of drive.''

Karoly d'Branin made a small sad noise deep in his throat. ''My *volcryn*,'' he said, sighing. ''So close—ah, it pains me to desert them. But I cannot do otherwise, I cannot.''

''You can,'' said the voice of Royd Eris. ''Trust me. That is all I ask, Karoly. Believe me when I tell you that I have no sinister intentions. Thale Lasamer may speak of danger, but no one has been harmed so far, have they?''

''No,'' admitted d'Branin. ''No, unless you count Alys, cutting herself this afternoon.''

''What?'' Royd hesitated briefly. ''Cutting herself? I did not see, Karoly. When did this happen?''

''Oh, early—just before Lasamer began to scream and rant, I believe.''

''I see.'' Royd's voice was thoughtful. ''I was watching Melantha go through her exercises,'' he said finally, ''and talking to her. I did not notice. Tell me how it happened.''

D'Branin told him.

''Listen to me,'' Royd said. ''Trust me, Karoly, and I will give you your *volcryn*. Calm your people. Assure them that I am no threat. And keep Lasamer drugged and quiescent, do you understand? That is very important. He is the problem.''

''Agatha advises much the same thing.''

''I know,'' said Royd. ''I agree with her. Will you do as I ask?''

''I do not know,'' d'Branin said. ''You make it hard for me. I do not understand what is going wrong, my friend. Will you not tell me more?''

Royd Eris did not answer. His ghost waited.

''Well,'' d'Branin said at last, ''you do not talk. How difficult you make it. How soon, Royd? How soon will we see my *volcryn*?''

"Quite soon," Royd replied. "We will drop out of drive in approximately seventy hours."

"Seventy hours," d'Branin said. "Such a short time. Going back would gain us nothing." He moistened his lips, lifted his cup, found it empty. "Go on, then. I will do as you bid. I will trust you, keep Lasamer drugged, I will not tell the others of your spying. Is that enough, then? Give me my *volcryn*. I have waited so long!"

"I know," said Royd Eris. "I know."

Then the ghost was gone, and Karoly d'Branin sat alone in the darkened lounge. He tried to refill his cup, but his hand began to tremble unaccountably, and he poured the chocolate over his fingers and dropped the cup, swearing, wondering, hurting.

The next day was a day of rising tensions and a hundred small irritations. Lindran and Dannel had a "private" argument that could be overheard through half the ship. A three-handed war game in the lounge ended in disaster when Christopheris accused Melantha Jhirl of cheating. Lommie Thorne complained of unusual difficulties in tying her system into the shipboard computers. Alys Northwind sat in the lounge for hours, staring at her bandaged finger with a look of sullen hatred on her face. Agatha Marij-Black prowled through the corridors, complaining that the ship was too hot, that her joints throbbed, that the air was thick and full of smoke, that the ship was too cold. Even Karoly d'Branin was despondent and on-edge.

Only the telepath seemed content. Shot full of psionine-4, Thale Lasamer was often sluggish and lethargic, but at least he no longer flinched at shadows.

Royd Eris made no appearance, either by voice or holographic projection.

He was still absent at dinner. The academicians ate uneasily, expecting him to materialize at any moment, take his accustomed place, and join in the mealtime conversation.

Their expectations were still unfulfilled when the afterdinner pots of chocolate and spiced tea and coffee were set on the table.

"Our captain seems to be occupied," Melantha Jhirl observed, leaning back in her chair and swirling a snifter of brandy.

"We will be shifting out of drive soon," Karoly d'Branin said. "Undoubtedly there are preparations to make." Secretly, he fretted over Royd's absence, and wondered if they were being watched even now.

Rojan Christopheris cleared his throat. "Since we're all here and he's not, perhaps this is a good time to discuss certain things. I'm not concerned about him missing dinner. He doesn't eat. He's a damned hologram. What does it matter? Maybe it's just as well, we need to talk about this. Karoly, a lot of us have been getting uneasy about Royd Eris. What do you know about this mystery man anyway?"

"Know, my friend?" D'Branin refilled his cup with the thick bittersweet chocolate and sipped at it slowly, trying to give himself a moment to think. "What is there to know?"

"Surely you've noticed that he never comes out to play with us," Lindran said drily. "Before you engaged his ship, did anyone remark on this quirk of his?"

"I'd like to know the answer to that one too," said Dannel, the other linguist. "A lot of traffic comes and goes through Avalon. How did you come to choose Eris? What were you told about him?"

"Told about him? Very little, I must admit. I spoke to a few port officials and charter companies, but none of them were acquainted with Royd. He had not traded out of Avalon originally, you see."

"How convenient," said Lindran.

"How suspicious," added Dannel.

"Where *is* he from, then?" Lindran demanded. "Dannel and I have listened to him pretty carefully. He speaks standard very flatly, with no discernible accent, no idiosyncrasies to betray his origins."

"Sometimes he sounds a bit archaic," Dannel put in, "and from time to time one of his constructions will give me an association. Only it's a different one each time. He's travelled a lot."

"Such a deduction," Lindran said, patting his hand. "Traders frequently do, love. Comes of owning a starship."

Dannel glared at her, but Lindran just went on. "Seriously, though, do you know anything about him? Where did this nightflyer of ours come from?"

"I do not know," d'Branin admitted. "I—I never thought to ask."

The members of his research team glanced at each other incredulously. "You never thought to *ask*?" Christopheris said. "How did you come to select this ship?"

"It was available. The administrative council approved my project and assigned me personnel, but they could not spare an Academy ship. There were budgetary constraints as well."

Agatha Marij-Black laughed sourly. "What d'Branin is telling those of you who haven't figured it out is that the Academy was pleased with his studies in xenomyth, with the discovery of the *volcryn* legend, but less than enthusiastic about his plan to seek them out. So they gave him a small budget to keep him happy and productive, assuming this little mission would be fruitless, and they assigned him people who wouldn't be missed back on Avalon." She looked around. "Look at the lot of you. None of us had worked with d'Branin in the early stages, but we were all available for this jaunt. And not a one of us is a first-rate scholar."

"Speak for yourself," Melantha Jhirl said. "I volunteered for this mission."

"I won't argue the point," the psipsych said. "The crux is that the choice of the *Nightflyer* is no large enigma. You just engaged the cheapest charter you could find, didn't you, d'Branin?"

"Some of the available ships would not consider my proposition," d'Branin said. "The sound of it is odd, we must admit. And many ship masters have an almost superstitious fear of dropping out of drive in interstellar space, without a planet near. Of those who would agree to the conditions, Royd Eris offered the best terms, and he was able to leave at once."

"And we *had* to leave at once," said Lindran. "Otherwise the *volcryn* might get away. They've only been passing through this region for ten thousand years, give or take a few thousand."

Someone laughed. D'Branin was nonplussed. "Friends, no doubt I could have postponed departure. I admit I was eager to meet my *volcryn*, to see their great ships and ask them all the questions that have haunted me, to discover the why of them. But I admit also that a delay would have been no great hardship. But why? Royd has been a gracious host, a good pilot. We have been treated well."

"Did you meet him?" Alys Northwind asked. "When you were making your arrangements, did you ever see him?"

"We spoke many times, but I was on Avalon, and Royd in orbit. I saw his face on my viewscreen."

"A projection, a computer simulation, could be anything," Lommie Thorne said. "I can have my system conjure up all sorts of faces for your viewscreen, Karoly."

"No one has ever seen this Royd Eris," Christopheris said. "He has made himself a cipher from the start."

"Our host wishes his privacy to remain inviolate," d'Branin said.

"Evasions," Lindran said. "What is he hiding?"

Melantha Jhirl laughed. When all eyes had moved to her, she grinned and shook her head. "Captain Royd is perfect, a strange man for a strange mission. Don't any of you love a mystery? Here we are flying light years to intercept a hypothetical alien starship from the core of the galaxy that has been outward bound for longer than humanity has been having wars, and all of you are upset because you can't count the warts on Royd's nose." She leaned across the table to refill her brandy snifter. "My mother was right," she said lightly. "Normals are subnormal."

"Maybe we should listen to Melantha," Lommie Thorne said thoughtfully. "Royd's foibles and neuroses are his business, if he does not impose them on us."

"It makes me uncomfortable," Dannel complained weakly.

"For all we know," said Alys Northwind, "we might be travelling with a criminal or an alien."

"*Jupiter*," someone muttered. The xenotech flushed red and there was sniggering around the long table.

But Thale Lasamer looked up furtively from his plate, and giggled. "An *alien*," he said. His blue eyes flicked back and forth in his skull, as if seeking escape. They were bright and wild.

Marij-Black swore. "The drug is wearing off," she said quickly to d'Branin. "I'll have to go back to my cabin to get some more."

"What drug?" Lommie Thorne demanded. D'Branin had been careful not to tell the others too much about Lasamer's ravings, for fear of inflaming the shipboard tensions. "What's going on?"

"Danger," Lasamer said. He turned to Lommie, sitting next to him, and grasped her forearm hard, his long painted fingernails clawing at the silvery metal of her shirt. "We're in danger, I tell you, I'm reading it. Something *alien*. It means us ill. Blood, I see blood." He laughed. "Can you taste it, Agatha? I can almost taste the blood. *It* can, too."

Marij-Black rose. "He's not well," she announced to the others. "I've been dampening him with psionine, trying to hold his delusions in check. I'll get some more." She started towards the door.

"Dampening him?" Christopheris said, horrified. "He's warning us of something. Don't you hear him? I want to know what it *is*."

"Not psionine," said Melantha Jhirl. "Try esperon."

"Don't tell me my job, woman!"

"Sorry," Melantha said. She gave a modest shrug. "I'm one step ahead of you, though. Esperon might exorcise his delusions, no?"

"Yes, but—"

"And it might help him focus on this threat he claims to detect, correct?"

"I know the characteristics of esperon quite well," the psipsych said testily.

Melantha smiled over the rim of her brandy glass. "I'm sure you do. Now listen to me. All of you are anxious about Royd, it seems. You can't stand not knowing whatever it is he's concealing. Rojan has been making up stories for weeks, and he's ready to believe any of them. Alys is so nervous she cut her finger off. We're squabbling constantly. Fears like that won't help us work together as a team. Let's end them. Easy enough." She pointed to Thale. "Here sits a class one telepath. Boost his power with esperon and he'll be able to recite our captain's life history to us, until we're all suitably bored with it. Meanwhile he'll also be vanquishing his personal demons."

"*He's watching us,*" the telepath said in a low, urgent voice.

"No," said Karoly d'Branin, "we must keep Thale dampened."

"Karoly," Christopheris said, "this has gone too far. Several of us are nervous and this boy is terrified. I believe we all need an end to the mystery of Royd Eris. For once, Melantha is right."

"We have no right," d'Branin said.

"We have the need," said Lommie Thorne. "I agree with Melantha."

"Yes," echoed Alys Northwind. The two linguists were nodding.

D'Branin thought regretfully of his promise to Royd. They

were not giving him any choice. His eyes met those of the psipsych, and he sighed. "Do it, then," he said. "Get him the esperon."

"*He's going to kill me*." Thale Lasamer screamed. He leapt to his feet, and when Lommie Thorne tried to calm him with a hand on his arm, he seized a cup of coffee and threw it square in her face. It took three of them to hold him down. "Hurry," Christopheris barked, as the telepath struggled.

Marij-Black shuddered and left the lounge.

When she returned, the others had lifted Lasamer to the table and forced him down, pulling aside his long pale hair to bare the arteries in his neck.

Marij-Black moved to his side.

"Stop that," Royd said. "There is no need."

His ghost shimmered into being in its empty chair at the head of the long dinner table. The psipsych froze in the act of slipping an ampule of esperon into her injection gun, and Alys Northwind startled visibly and released one of Lasamer's arms. The captive did not pull free. He lay on the table, breathing heavily, his pale blue eyes fixed glassily on Royd's projection, transfixed by the vision of his sudden materialization.

Melantha Jhirl lifted her brandy glass in salute. "Boo," she said. "You've missed dinner, captain."

"Royd," said Karoly d'Branin, "I am sorry."

The ghost stared unseeing at the far wall. "Release him," said the voice from the communicators. "I will tell you my great secrets, if my privacy intimidates you so."

"He *has* been watching us," Dannel said.

"We're listening," Northwind said suspiciously. "What are you?"

"I liked your guess about the gas giants," Royd said. "Sadly, the truth is less dramatic. I am an ordinary *homo sapien* in middle age. Sixty-eight standard, if you require precision. The hologram you see before you is the real Royd

Eris, or was so some years ago. I am somewhat older now, but I use computer simulation to project a more youthful appearance to my guests.''

"Oh?" Lommie Thorne's face was red where the coffee had scalded her. "Then why the secrecy?"

"I will begin the tale with my mother," Royd replied. "The *Nightflyer* was her ship originally, custom-built to her design in the Newholme spaceyards. My mother was a freetrader, a notably successful one. She was born trash on a world called Vess, which is a very long way from here, although perhaps some of you have heard of it. She worked her way up, position by position, until she won her own command. She soon made a fortune through a willingness to accept the unusual consignment, fly off the major trade routes, take her cargo a month or a year or two years beyond where it was customarily transferred. Such practices are riskier but more profitable than flying the mail runs. My mother did not worry about how often she and her crews returned home. Her ships were her home. She forgot about Vess as soon as she left it, and seldom visited the same world twice if she could avoid it.''

"Adventurous," Melantha Jhirl said.

"No," said Royd. "Sociopathic. My mother did not like people, you see. Not at all. Her crews had no love for her, nor she for them. Her one great dream was to free herself from the necessity of crew altogether. When she grew rich enough, she had it done. The *Nightflyer* was the result. After she boarded it at Newholme, she never touched a human being again, or walked a planet's surface. She did all her business from the compartments that are now mine, by viewscreen or lasercom. You would call her insane. You would be right." The ghost smiled faintly. "She did have an interesting life, though, even after her isolation. The worlds she saw, Karoly! The things she might have told you would break your heart, but you'll never hear them. She destroyed most of her records for fear that other people might get some use or pleasure from her experiences after her death. She was like that.''

"And you?" asked Alys Northwind.

"She must have touched at least *one* other human being," Lindran put in, with a smile.

"I should not call her my mother," Royd said. "I am her cross-sex clone. After thirty years of flying this ship alone, she was bored. I was to be her companion and lover. She could shape me to be a perfect diversion. She had no patience with children, however, and no desire to raise me herself. After she had done the cloning, I was sealed in a nurturant tank, an embryo linked into her computer. It was my teacher. Before birth and after. I had no birth, really. Long after the time a normal child would have been born, I remained in the tank, growing, learning, on slow-time, blind and dreaming and living through tubes. I was to be released when I had attained the age of puberty, at which time she guessed I would be fit company."

"How horrible," Karoly d'Branin said. "Royd, my friend, I did not know."

"I'm sorry, captain," Melantha Jhirl said. "You were robbed of your childhood."

"I never missed it," Royd said. "Nor her. Her plans were all futile, you see. She died a few months after the cloning, when I was still a fetus in the tank. She had programmed the ship for such an eventuality, however. It dropped out of drive and shut down, drifted in interstellar space for eleven standard years while the computer made me—" He stopped, smiling. "I was going to say *while the computer made me a human being*. Well, while the computer made me whatever I am, then. That was how I inherited the *Nightflyer*. When I was born, it took me some months to acquaint myself with the operation of the ship and my own origins."

"Fascinating," said Karoly d'Branin.

"Yes," said the linguist Lindran, "but it doesn't explain why you keep yourself in isolation."

"Ah, but it does," Melantha Jhirl said. "Captain, perhaps you should explain further for the less improved models?"

"My mother hated planets," Royd said. "She hated stinks and dirt and bacteria, the irregularity of the weather, the sight of other people. She engineered for us a flawless environment, as sterile as she could possibly make it. She disliked gravity as well. She was accustomed to weightlessness from years of service on ancient freetraders that could not afford gravity grids, and she preferred it. These were the conditions under which I was born and raised.

"My body has no immune systems, no natural resistance to anything. Contact with any of you would probably kill me, and would certainly make me very sick. My muscles are feeble, in a sense atrophied. The gravity the *Nightflyer* is now generating is for your comfort, not mine. To me it is agony. At this moment the real me is seated in a floating chair that supports my weight. I still hurt, and my internal organs may be suffering damage. It is one reason why I do not often take on passengers."

"You share your mother's opinion of the run of humanity?" asked Marij-Black.

"I do not. I like people. I accept what I am, but I did not choose it. I experience human life in the only way I can, vicariously. I am a voracious consumer of books, tapes, holoplays, fictions and drama and histories of all sorts. I have experimented with dreamdust. And infrequently, when I dare, I carry passengers. At those times, I drink in as much of their lives as I can."

"If you kept your ship under weightlessness at all times, you could take on more riders," suggested Lommie Thorne.

"True," Royd said politely. "I have found, however, that most planet-born are as uncomfortable weightless as I am under gravity. A ship master who does not have artificial gravity, or elects not to use it, attracts few riders. The exceptions often spend much of the voyage sick or drugged. No. I could also mingle with my passengers, I know, if I kept to my chair and wore a sealed environ-wear suit. I have done so. I find it lessens my participation instead of increasing it. I become a freak, a maimed thing, one who must be treated differently and kept at a distance. These things do not suit my purpose. I prefer isolation. As often as I dare, I study the aliens I take on as riders.''

''Aliens?'' Northwind's voice was confused.

''You are all aliens to me,'' Royd answered.

Silence filled the *Nightflyer*'s lounge.

''I am sorry this has happened, my friend,'' Karoly d'Branin said. ''We ought not have intruded on your personal affairs.''

''Sorry,'' muttered Agatha Marij-Black. She frowned and pushed the ampule of esperon into the injection chamber. ''Well, it's glib enough, but is it the truth? We still have no proof, just a new bedtime story. The hologram could have claimed it was a creature from Jupiter, a computer, or a diseased war criminal just as easily. We have no way of verifying anything that he's said. No—we have *one* way, rather.'' She took two quick steps forward to where Thale Lasamer lay on the table. ''He still needs treatment and we still need confirmation, and I don't see any sense in stopping now after we've gone this far. Why should we live with all this anxiety if we can end it all now?'' Her hand pushed the telepath's unresisting head to one side. She found the artery and pressed the gun to it.

''Agatha,'' said Karoly d'Branin. ''Don't you think . . . perhaps we should forego this, now that Royd . . . ?''

''NO.'' Royd said. ''Stop. I order it. This is my ship. Stop, or . . .''

''. . . or what?'' The gun hissed loudly, and there was a red mark on the telepath's neck when she lifted it away.

Lasamer raised himself to a half-sitting position, supported by his elbows, and Marij-Black moved close to him. ''Thale,'' she said in her best professional tones, ''focus on Royd. You can do it, we all know how good you are. Wait just a moment, the esperon will open it all up for you.''

His pale blue eyes were clouded. "Not close enough," he muttered. "One, I'm one, tested. Good, you know I'm good, but I got to be *close*." He trembled.

The psipsych put an arm around him, stroked him, coaxed him. "The esperon will give you range, Thale," she said. "Feel it, feel yourself grow stronger. Can you feel it? Everything's getting clear, isn't it?" Her voice was a reassuring drone. "You can hear what I'm thinking, I know you can, but never mind that. The others too, push them aside, all that chatter, thoughts, desires, fear. Push it all aside. Remember the danger now? Remember? Go find it, Thale, go find the danger. Look beyond the wall there, tell us what it's like beyond the wall. Tell us about Royd. Was he telling the truth? Tell us. You're good, we all know that, you can tell us." The phrases were almost an incantation.

He shrugged off her support and sat upright by himself. "I can feel it," he said. His eyes were suddenly clearer. "Something—my head hurts—I'm *afraid*!"

"Don't be afraid," said Marij-Black. "The esperon won't make your head hurt, it just makes you better. We're all here with you. Nothing to fear." She stroked his brow. "Tell us what you see."

Thale Lasamer looked at Royd's ghost with terrified little-boy eyes, and his tongue flicked across his lower lips. "He's—"

Then his skull exploded.

Hysteria and confusion.

The telepath's head had burst with awful force, splattering them all with blood and bits of bone and flesh. His body thrashed madly on the tabletop for a long instant, blood spurting from the arteries in his neck in a crimson stream, his limbs twitching in a macabre dance. His head had simply ceased to exist, but he would not be still.

Agatha Marij-Black, who had been standing closest to him, dropped her injection gun and stood slack-mouthed. She

was drenched with his blood, covered with pieces of flesh
and brain. Beneath her right eye, a long sliver of bone had
penetrated her skin, and her own blood was mingling with
his. She did not seem to notice.

Rojan Christopheris fell over backwards, scrambled to his
feet, and pressed himself hard against the wall.

Dannel screamed, and screamed, and screamed, until Lindran
slapped him hard across a blood-smeared cheek and told him
to be quiet.

Alys Northwind dropped to her knees and began to mumble a prayer in a strange tongue.

Karoly d'Branin sat very still, staring, blinking, his chocolate cup forgotten in his hand.

"Do something," Lommie Thorne moaned. "Somebody
do something." One of Lasamer's arms moved feebly, and
brushed against her. She shrieked and pulled away.

Melantha Jhirl pushed aside her brandy snifter. "Control
yourself," she snapped. "He's dead, he can't hurt you."

They all looked at her, but for d'Branin and Marij-Black,
both of whom seemed frozen in shock. Royd's projection had
vanished at some point, Melantha realized suddenly. She
began to give orders. "Dannel, Lindran, Rojan—find a sheet
or something to wrap him in, and get him out of here. Alys,
you and Lommie get some water and sponges. We've got to
clean up." Melantha moved to d'Branin's side as the others
rushed to do as she had told them. "Karoly," she said,
putting a gentle hand on his shoulder, "are you all right,
Karoly?"

He looked up at her, grey eyes blinking. "I—yes, yes, I
am—I told her not to go ahead, Melantha. I told her."

"Yes you did," Melantha Jhirl said. She gave him a
reassuring pat and moved around the table to Agatha Marij-
Black. "Agatha," she called. But the psipsych did not respond, not even when Melantha shook her bodily by the
shoulders. Her eyes were empty. "She's in shock," Melantha
announced. She frowned at the sliver of bone protruding

from Marij-Black's cheek. Sponging off her face with a napkin, she carefully removed the splinter.

"What do we do with the body?" asked Lindran. They had found a sheet and wrapped it up. It had finally stopped twitching, although blood continued to seep out, turning the concealing sheet red.

"Put it in a cargo hold," suggested Christopheris.

"No," Melantha said, "not sanitary. It will rot." She thought for a moment. "Suit up and take it down to the driveroom. Cycle it through and lash it in place somehow. Tear up the sheet if you have to. That section of the ship is vacuum. It will be best there."

Christopheris nodded, and the three of them moved off, the dead weight of Lasamer's corpse supported between them. Melantha turned back to Marij-Black, but only for an instant. Lommie Thorne, who was mopping the blood from the tabletop with a piece of cloth, suddenly began to retch violently. Melantha swore. "Someone help her," she snapped.

Karoly d'Branin finally seemed to stir. He rose and took the blood-soaked cloth from Lommie's hand, and led her away back to his cabin.

"I can't do this alone," whined Alys Northwind, turning away in disgust.

"Help me, then," Melantha said. Together she and Northwind half-led and half-carried the psipsych from the lounge, cleaned her and undressed her, and put her to sleep with a shot of one of her own drugs. Afterwards Melantha took the injection gun and made the rounds. Northwind and Lommie Thorne required mild tranquilizers, Dannel a somewhat stronger one.

It was three hours before they met again.

The survivors assembled in the largest of the cargo holds, where three of them hung their sleepwebs. Seven of eight attended. Agatha Marij-Black was still unconscious, sleeping or in a coma or deep shock; none of them were sure. The rest seemed to have recovered, though their faces were pale and drawn. All of them had changed clothes, even Alys Northwind, who had slipped into a new jumpsuit identical to the old one.

"I do not understand," Karoly d'Branin said. "I do not understand what . . ."

"Royd killed him, is all," Northwind said bitterly. "His secret was endangered so he just—just blew him apart. We all saw it."

"I cannot believe that," Karoly d'Branin said in an anguished voice. "I cannot. Royd and I, we have talked, talked many a night when the rest of you were sleeping. He is gentle, inquisitive, sensitive. A dreamer. He understands about the *volcryn*. He would not do such a thing, could not."

"His projection certainly winked out quick enough when it happened," Lindran said. "And you'll notice he hasn't had much to say since."

"The rest of us haven't been unusually talkative either," said Melantha Jhirl. "I don't know what to think, but my impulse is to side with Karoly. We have no proof that the captain was responsible for Thale's death. There's something here none of us understands yet."

Alys Northwind grunted. "Proof," she said disdainfully.

"In fact," Melantha continued unperturbed, "I'm not even sure *anyone* is responsible. Nothing happened until he was given the esperon. Could the drug be at fault?"

"Hell of a side-effect," Lindran muttered.

Rojan Christopheris frowned. "This is not my field, but I would think, no. Esperon is extremely potent, with both physical and psionic side-effects verging on the extreme, but not *that* extreme."

"What, then?" said Lommie Thorne. "What killed him?"

"The instrument of death was probably his own talent," the xenobiologist said, "undoubtedly augmented by his drug. Besides boosting his principle power, his telepathic sensitivity, esperon would also tend to bring out other psi-talents that might have been latent in him."

"Such as?" Lommie demanded.

"Biocontrol. Telekinesis."

Melantha Jhirl was way ahead of him. "Esperon shoots blood pressure way up anyway. Increase the pressure in his skull even more by rushing all the blood in his body to his brain. Decrease the air pressure around his head simultaneously, using teke to induce a short-lived vacuum. Think about it."

They thought about it, and none of them liked it.

"Who could do such a thing?" Karoly d'Branin said. "It could only have been self-induced, his own talent wild out of control."

"Or turned against him by a greater talent," Alys Northwind said stubbornly.

"No human telepath has talent on that order, to seize control of someone else, body and mind and soul, even for an instant."

"Exactly," the stout xenotech replied. "No *human* telepath."

"Gas giant people?" Lommie Thorne's tone was mocking.

Alys Northwind stared her down. "I could talk about Crey sensitives or *githyanki* soulsucks, name a half-dozen others off the top of my head, but I don't need to. I'll only name one. A Hrangan Mind."

That was a disquieting thought. All of them fell silent and stirred uneasily, thinking of the vast, inimicable power of a Hrangan Mind hidden in the command chambers of the *Nightflyer*, until Melantha Jhirl broke the spell with a short, derisive laugh. "You're frightening yourself with shadows, Alys," she said. "What you're saying is ridiculous, if you stop to think about it. I hope that isn't too much to ask. You're supposed to be xenologists, the lot of you, experts in alien languages, psychology, biology, technology. You don't act the part. We warred with Old Hranga for a thousand years, but we *never* communicated successfully with a Hrangan Mind. If Royd Eris is a Hrangan, they've improved their conversational skills markedly in the centuries since the Collapse.''

Alys Northwind flushed. "You're right," she said. "I'm jumpy.''

"Friends," said Karoly d'Branin, "we must not let our actions be dictated by panic or hysteria. A terrible thing has happened. One of our colleagues is dead, and we do not know why. Until we do, we can only go on. This is no time for rash actions against the innocent. Perhaps, when we return to Avalon, an investigation will tell us what happened. The body is safe for examination, is it not?''

"We cycled it through the airlock into the driveroom," Dannel said. "It'll keep.''

"And it can be studied closely on our return," d'Branin said.

"Which should be immediate," said Northwind. "Tell Eris to turn this ship around!''

D'Branin looked stricken. "But the *volcryn*! A week more and we shall know them, if my figures are correct. To return would take us six weeks. Surely it is worth one additional week to know that they exist? Thale would not have wanted his death to be for nothing.''

"Before he died, Thale was raving about aliens, about danger," Northwind insisted. "We're rushing to meet some aliens. What if they're the danger? Maybe these *volcryn* are even more potent than a Hrangan Mind, and maybe they don't want to be met, or investigated, or observed. What about that, Karoly? You ever think about that? Those stories of yours—don't some of them talk about terrible things happening to the races that meet the *volcryn*?''

"Legends," d'Branin said. "Superstitition.''

"A whole Fyndii horde vanishes in one legend," Rojan Christopheris put in.

"We cannot put credence in these fears of others," d'Branin argued.

"Perhaps there's nothing to the stories," Northwind said,

"but do you care to risk it? *I* don't. For what? Your sources may be fictional or exaggerated or wrong, your interpretations and computations may be in error, or they may have changed course—the *volcryn* may not even be within light years of where we'll drop out."

"Ah," Melantha Jhirl said, "I understand. Then we shouldn't go on because they won't be there, and besides, they might be dangerous."

D'Branin smiled and Lindran laughed. "Not funny," protested Alys Northwind, but she argued no further.

"No," Melantha continued, "any danger we are in will not increase significantly in the time it will take us to drop out of drive and look about for *volcryn*. We have to drop out anyway, to reprogram for the shunt home. Besides, we've come a long way for these *volcryn,* and I admit to being curious." She looked at each of them in turn, but no one spoke. "We continue, then."

"And Royd?" demanded Christopheris. "What do we do about him?"

"What *can* we do?" said Dannel.

"Treat the captain as before," Melantha said decisively. "We should open lines to him and talk. Maybe now we can clear up some of the mysteries that are bothering us, if Royd is willing to discuss things frankly."

"He is probably as shocked and dismayed as we are, my friends," said d'Branin. "Possibly he is fearful that we will blame him, try to hurt him."

"I think we should cut through to his section of the ship and drag him out kicking and screaming," Christopheris said. "We have the tools. That would write a quick end to all our fears."

"It could kill Royd," Melantha said. "Then he'd be justified in anything he did to stop us. He controls this ship. He could do a great deal, if he decided we were his enemies." She shook her head vehemently. "No, Rojan, we can't attack Royd. We've got to reassure him. I'll do it, if no one else wants to talk to him." There were no volunteers. "All right. But I don't want any of you trying any foolish schemes. Go about your business. Act normally."

Karoly d'Branin was nodding agreement. "Let us put Royd and poor Thale from our minds, and concern ourselves with our work, with our preparations. Our sensory instruments must be ready for deployment as soon as we shift out of drive and reenter normal space, so we can find our quarry quickly. We must review everything we know of the *volcryn*." He turned to the linguists and began discussing some of the preliminaries he expected of them, and in a short time the talk had turned to the *volcryn*, and bit by bit the fear drained out of the group.

Lommie Thorne sat listening quietly, her thumb absently rubbing her wrist implant, but no one noticed the thoughtful look in her eyes.

Not even Royd Eris, watching.

Melantha Jhirl returned to the lounge alone.

Someone had turned out the lights. "Captain?" she said softly.

He appeared to her; pale, glowing softly, with eyes that did not see. His clothes, filmy and out-of-date, were all shades of white and faded blue. "Hello, Melantha," the mellow voice said from the communicators, as the ghost silently mouthed the same words.

"Did you hear, captain?"

"Yes," he said, his voice vaguely tinged by surprise. "I hear and I see everything on my *Nightflyer*, Melantha. Not only in the lounge, and not only when the communicators and viewscreens are on. How long have you known?"

"Known?" She smiled. "Since you praised Alys' gas giant solution to the Roydian mystery. The communicators were not on that night. You had no way of knowing. Unless . . ."

"I have never made a mistake before," Royd said. "I told

Karoly, but that was deliberate. I am sorry. I have been under stress."

"I believe you, captain," she said. "No matter. I'm the improved model, remember? I'd guessed weeks ago."

For a time Royd said nothing. Then: "When do you begin to reassure me?"

"I'm doing so right now. Don't you feel reassured yet?"

The apparition gave a ghostly shrug. "I am pleased that you and Karoly do not think I murdered that man. Otherwise, I am frightened. Things are getting out of control, Melantha. Why didn't she listen to me? I told Karoly to keep him dampened. I told Agatha not to give him that injection. I warned them."

"They were afraid, too," Melantha said. "Afraid that you were only trying to frighten them off, to protect some awful plan. I don't know. It was my fault, in a sense. I was the one who suggested esperon. I thought it would put Thale at ease, and tell us something about you. I was curious." She frowned. "A deadly curiosity. Now I have blood on my hands."

Melantha's eyes were adjusting to the darkness in the lounge. By the faint light of the holograph, she could see the table where it had happened, dark streaks of drying blood across its surface among the plates and cups and cold pots of tea and chocolate. She heard a faint dripping as well, and could not tell if it was blood or coffee. She shivered. "I don't like it in here."

"If you would like to leave, I can be with you wherever you go."

"No," she said. "I'll stay. Royd, I think it might be better if you were *not* with us wherever we go. If you kept silent and out of sight, so to speak. If I asked you to, would you shut off your monitors throughout the ship? Except for the lounge, perhaps. It would make the others feel better, I'm sure."

"They don't know."

"They will. You made that remark about gas giants in

everyone's hearing. Some of them have probably figured it out by now."

"If I told you I had cut myself off, you would have no way of knowing whether it was the truth."

"I could trust you," Melantha Jhirl said.

Silence. The spectre stared at her. "As you wish," Royd's voice said finally. "Everything off. Now I see and hear only in here. Now, Melantha, you must promise to control them. No secret schemes, or attempts to breach my quarters. Can you do that?"

"I think so," she said.

"Did you believe my story?" Royd asked.

"Ah," she said. "A strange and wondrous story, captain. If it's a lie, I'll swap lies with you any time. You do it well. If it's true, then you are a strange and wondrous man."

"It's true," the ghost said quietly. "Melantha . . ."

"Yes?"

"Does it bother you that I have . . . watched you? Watched you when you were not aware?"

"A little," she said, "but I think I can understand it."

"I watched you copulating."

She smiled. "Ah," she said, "I'm good at it."

"I wouldn't know," Royd said. "You're good to watch."

Silence. She tried not to hear the steady, faint dripping off to her right. "Yes," she said after a long hesitation.

"Yes? What?"

"Yes, Royd," she said, "I would probably sex with you if it were possible."

"*How did you know what I was thinking*?" Royd's voice was suddenly frightened, full of anxiety and something close to fear.

"Easy," Melantha said, startled. "I'm an improved model. It wasn't so difficult to figure out. I told you, remember? I'm three moves ahead of you."

"You're not a telepath, are you?"

"No," Melantha said. "No."

Royd considered that for a long time. "I believe I'm reassured," he said at last.

"Good," she said.

"Melantha," he added, "one thing. Sometimes it is not wise to be too many moves ahead. Do you understand?"

"Oh? No, not really. You frighten me. Now reassure me. Your turn, captain Royd"

"Of what?"

"What happened in here? Really?"

Royd said nothing.

"I think you know something," Melantha said. "You gave up your secret to stop us from injecting Lasamer with esperon. Even after your secret was forfeit, you ordered us not to go ahead. Why?"

"Esperon is a dangerous drug," Royd said.

"More than that, captain," Melantha said. "You're evading. What killed Thale Lasamer? Or is it *who*?"

"*I* didn't."

"One of us? The *volcryn*?"

Royd said nothing.

"Is there an alien aboard your ship, captain?"

Silence.

"Are we in danger? Am *I* in danger, captain? I'm not afraid. Does that make me a fool?"

"I like people," Royd said at last. "When I can stand it, I like to have passengers. I watch them, yes. It's not so terrible. I like you and Karoly especially. I won't let anything happen to you."

"What might happen?"

Royd said nothing.

"And what about the others, Royd? Christopheris and Northwind, Dannel and Lindran, Lommie Thorne? Are you taking care of them, too? Or only Karoly and I?"

No reply.

"You're not very talkative tonight," Melantha observed.

"I'm under strain," his voice replied. "And certain things

you are safer not to know. Go to bed, Melantha Jhirl. We've talked long enough.''

''All right, captain,'' she said. She smiled at the ghost and lifted her hand. His own rose to meet it. Warm dark flesh and pale radiance brushed, melded, were one. Melantha Jhirl turned to go. It was not until she was out in the corridor, safe in the light once more, that she began to tremble.

False midnight.

The talks had broken up, and one by one the academicians had gone to bed. Even Karoly d'Branin had retired, his appetite for chocolate quelled by his memories of the lounge.

The linguists had made violent, noisy love before giving themselves up to sleep, as if to reaffirm their life in the face of Thale Lasamer's grisly death. Rojan Christopheris had listened to music. But now they were all still.

The *Nightflyer* was filled with silence.

In the darkness of the largest cargo hold, three sleepwebs hung side by side. Melantha Jhirl twisted occasionally in her sleep, her face feverish, as if in the grip of some nightmare. Alys Northwind lay flat on her back, snoring loudly, a reassuring wheeze of noise from her solid, meaty chest.

Lommie Thorne lay awake, thinking.

Finally she rose and dropped to the floor, nude, quiet, light and careful as a cat. She pulled on a tight pair of pants, slipped a wide-sleeved shirt of black metallic cloth over her head, belted it with a silver chain, shook out her short hair. She did not don her boots. Barefoot was quieter. Her feet were small and soft, with no trace of callous.

She moved to the middle sleepweb and shook Alys Northwind by her shoulder. The snoring stopped abruptly. ''Huh?'' the xenotech said. She grunted in annoyance.

''Come,'' whispered Lommie Thorne. She beckoned.

Northwind got heavily to her feet, blinking, and followed the cyberneticist through the door, out into the corridor. She'd been sleeping in her jumpsuit, its seam open nearly to her crotch. She frowned and sealed it. "What the hell," she muttered. She was disarrayed and unhappy.

"There's a way to find out if Royd's story was true," Lommie Thorne said carefully. "Melantha won't like it, though. Are you game to try?"

"What?" Northwind asked. Her face betrayed her interest.

"Come," the cyberneticist said.

They moved silently through the ship, to the computer room. The system was up, but dormant. They entered quietly; all empty. Currents of light ran silkily down crystalline channels in the data grids, meeting, joining, splitting apart again; rivers of wan multi-hued radiance crisscrossing a black landscape. The chamber was dim, the only noise a buzz at the edge of human hearing, until Lommie Thorne moved through it, touching keys, tripping switches, directing the silent luminescent currents. Bit by bit the machine woke.

"What are you *doing*?" Alys Northwind said.

"Karoly told me to tie in our system with the ship," Lommie Thorne replied as she worked. "I was told Royd wanted to study the *volcryn* data. Fine, I did it. Do you understand what that means?" Her shirt whispered in soft metallic tones when she moved.

Eagerness broke across the flat features of xenotech Alys Northwind. "The two systems are tied together!"

"Exactly. So Royd can find out about the *volcryn*, and we can find out about Royd." She frowned. "I wish I knew more about the *Nightflyer*'s hardware, but I think I can feel my way through. This is a pretty sophisticated system d'Branin requisitioned."

"Can you take over from Eris?"

"Take over?" Lommie sounded puzzled. "You been drinking again, Alys?"

"No, I'm serious. Use your system to break into the ship's control, overwhelm Eris, countermand his orders, make the *Nightflyer* respond to us, down here. Wouldn't you feel safer if we were in control?"

"Maybe," the cyberneticist said doubtfully. "I could try, but why do that?"

"Just in case. We don't have to use the capacity. Just so we have it, if an emergency arises."

Lommie Thorne shrugged. "Emergencies and gas giants. I only want to put my mind at rest about Royd, whether he had anything to do with killing Lasamer." She moved over to a readout panel, where a half-dozen meter-square viewscreens curved around a console, and brought one of them to life. Long fingers ghosted through holographic keys that appeared and disappeared as she used them, the keyboard changing shape again and yet again. The cyberneticist's pretty face grew thoughtful and serious. "We're in," she said. Characters began to flow across a viewscreen, red flickerings in glassy black depths. On a second screen, a schematic of the *Nightflyer* appeared, revolved, halved; its spheres shifted size and perspective at the whim of Lommie's fingers, and a line of numerals below gave the specifications. The cyberneticist watched, and finally froze both screens.

"Here," she said, "here's my answer about the hardware. You can dismiss your takeover idea, unless those gas giant people of yours are going to help. The *Nightflyer*'s bigger and smarter than our little system here. Makes sense, when you stop to think about it. Ship's all automated, except for Royd."

Her hands moved again, and two more display screens stirred. Lommie Thorne whistled and coaxed her search program with soft words of encouragement. "It looks as though there *is* a Royd, though. Configurations are all wrong for a robot ship. Damn, I would have bet anything." The characters began to flow again, Lommie watching the figures as they drifted by. "Here's life support specs, might tell us something." A finger jabbed, and one screen froze yet again.

"Nothing unusual," Alys Northwind said in disappointment.

"Standard waste disposal. Water recycling. Food processor, with protein and vitamin supplements in stores." She began to whistle. "Tanks of Renny's moss and neograss to eat up the CO_2. Oxygen cycle, then. No methane or ammonia. Sorry about that."

"Go sex with a computer!"

The cyberneticist smiled. "Ever tried it?" Her fingers moved again. "What else should I look for? You're the tech, what would be a giveaway? Give me some ideas."

"Check the specs for nurturant tanks, cloning equipment, that sort of thing," the xenotech said. "That would tell us whether he was lying."

"I don't know," Lommie Thorne said. "Long time ago. He might have junked that stuff. No use for it."

"Find Royd's life history," Northwind said. "His mother's. Get a readout on the business they've done, all this alleged trading. They must have records. Account books, profit-and-loss, cargo invoices, that kind of thing." Her voice grew excited, and she gripped the cyberneticist from behind by her shoulders. "A log, a ship's log! There's got to be a log. Find it!"

"All right." Lommie Thorne whistled, happy, at ease with her system, riding the data winds, curious, in control. Then the screen in front of her turned a bright red and began to blink. She smiled, touched a ghost key, and the keyboard melted away and reformed under her. She tried another tack. Three more screens turned red and began to blink. Her smile faded.

"What is it?"

"Security," said Lommie Thorne. "I'll get through it in a second. Hold on." She changed the keyboard yet again, entered another search program, attached on a rider in case it was blocked. Another screen flashed red. She had her machine chew the data she'd gathered, sent out another feeler. More red. Flashing. Blinking. Bright enough to hurt the eyes. All the screens were red now. "A good security program," she said with admiration. "The log is well protected."

Alys Northwind grunted. "Are we blocked?"

"Response time is too slow," Lommie Thorne said, chewing on her lower lip as she thought. "There's a way to fix that." She smiled, and rolled back the soft black metal of her sleeve.

"What are you doing?"

"Watch," she said. She slid her arm under the console, found the prongs, jacked in.

"Ah," she said, low in her throat. The flashing red blocks vanished from her readout screens, one after the other, as she sent her mind coursing into the *Nightflyer*'s system, easing through all the blocks. "Nothing like slipping past another system's security. Like slipping onto a man." Log entries were flickering past them in a whirling, blurring rush, too fast for Alys Northwind to read. But Lommie read them.

Then she stiffened. "Oh," she said. It was almost a whimper. "Cold," she said. She shook her head and it was gone, but there was a sound in her ears, a terrible whooping sound. "Damn," she said, "that'll wake everyone." She glanced up when she felt Alys's fingers dig painfully into her shoulder, squeezing, hurting.

A grey steel panel slid almost silently across the access to the corridor, cutting off the whooping cry of the alarm. "What?" Lommie Thorne said.

"That's an emergency airseal," said Alys Northwind in a dead voice. She knew starships. "It closes where they're about to load or unload cargo in vacuum."

Their eyes went to the huge curving outer airlock above their heads. The inner lock was almost completely open, and as they watched it clicked into place, and the seal on the outer door cracked, and now it was open half a meter, sliding, and beyond was twisted nothingness so burning-bright it seared the eyes.

"Oh," said Lommie Thorne, as the cold coursed up her arm. She had stopped whistling.

* * *

Alarms were hooting everywhere. The passengers began to stir. Melantha Jhirl tumbled from her sleepweb and darted into the corridor, nude, frantic, alert. Karoly d'Branin sat up drowsily. The psipsych muttered fitfully in drug-induced sleep. Rojan Christopheris cried out in alarm.

Far away metal crunched and tore, and a violent shudder ran through the ship, throwing the linguists out of their sleepwebs, knocking Melantha from her feet.

In the command quarters out of the *Nightflyer* was a spherical room with featureless white walls, a lesser sphere—a suspended control console—floating in its center. The walls were always blank when the ship was in drive; the warped and glaring underside of spacetime was painful to behold.

But now darkness woke in the room, a holoscope coming to life, cold black and stars everywhere, points of icy unwinking brilliance, no up and no down and no direction, the floating control sphere the only feature in the simulated sea of night.

The *Nightflyer* had shifted out of drive.

Melantha Jhirl found her feet again and thumbed on a communicator. The alarms were still hooting, and it was hard to hear. "Captain," she shouted, "what's happening?"

"I don't know," Royd's voice replied. "I'm trying to find out. Wait."

Melantha waited. Karoly d'Branin came staggering out into the corridor, blinking and rubbing his eyes. Rojan Christopheris was not long behind him. "What is it? What's wrong?" he demanded, but Melantha just shook her head. Lindran and Dannel soon appeared as well. There was no sign of Marij-Black, Alys Northwind, or Lommie Thorne. The academicians looked uneasily at the seal that blocked cargo hold three. Finally Melantha told Christopheris to go look. He returned a few minutes later. "Agatha is still unconscious," he said, talking at the top of his voice to be heard over the alarms. "The drugs still have her. She's moving around, though. Crying out."

"Alys and Lommie?"

Christopheris shrugged. "I can't find them. Ask your friend Royd."

The communicator came back to life as the alarms died. "We have returned to normal space," Royd's voice said, "but the ship is damaged. Hold three, your computer room, was breached while we were under drive. It was ripped apart by the flux. The computer dropped us out of drive automatically, fortunately for us, or the drive forces might have torn my entire ship apart."

"Royd," said Melantha, "Northwind and Thorne are missing."

"It appears your computer was in use when the hold was breached," Royd said carefully. "I would presume them dead, although I cannot say that with certainty. At Melantha's request I have deactivated most of my monitors, retaining only the lounge input. I do not know what transpired. But this is a small ship, and if they are not with you, we must assume the worst." He paused briefly. "If it is any consolation, they died swiftly and painlessly."

"You killed them," Christopheris said, his face red and angry. He started to say more, but Melantha slipped her hand firmly over his mouth. The two linguists exchanged a long, meaningful look. "Do we know how it happened, captain?" Melantha asked.

"Yes," he said, reluctantly.

The xenobiologist had taken the hint, and Melantha took away her hand to let him breathe. "Royd?" she prompted.

"It sounds insane, Melantha," his voice replied, "but it appears your colleagues opened the hold's loading lock. I doubt they did so deliberately, of course. They were using the system interface to gain entry to the *Nightflyer*'s data storage and controls, and they shunted aside all the safeties."

"I see," Melantha said. "A terrible tragedy."

"Yes. Perhaps more terrible than you think. I have yet to discover the extent of damage to my ship."

"We should not keep you if you have duties to perform," Melantha said. "All of us are shocked, and it is difficult to talk now. Investigate the condition of your ship, and we'll continue our discussion at a more opportune time. Agreed?"

"Yes," said Royd.

Melantha turned off the communicator. Now, in theory, the device was dead; Royd could neither see nor hear them.

"Do you believe him?" Christopheris snapped.

"I don't know," Melantha Jhirl said, "but I do know that the other cargo holds can all be flushed just as hold three was. I'm moving my sleepweb into a cabin. I suggest that those of you who are living in hold two do the same."

"Clever," Lindran said, with a sharp nod of her head. "We can crowd in. It won't be comfortable, but I doubt that I'd sleep the sleep of angels in the holds after this."

"We should also get our suits out of storage in four," Dannel suggested. "Keep them close at hand. Just in case."

"If you wish," Melantha said. "It's possible that all the locks might pop open simultaneously. Royd can't fault us for taking precautions." She flashed a grim smile. "After today we've earned the right to act irrationally."

"This is no time for your damned jokes, Melantha," Christopheris said. He was still red-faced, and his tone was full of fear and anger. "Three people are dead, Agatha is perhaps deranged or catatonic, the rest of us are endangered—"

"Yes. And we still have no idea what is happening," Melantha pointed out.

"*Royd Eris is killing us!*" Christopheris shrieked. "I don't know who or what he is and I don't know if that story he gave us is true and I don't *care*. Maybe he's a Hrangan Mind or the avenging angel of the *volcryn* or the second coming of Jesus Christ. What the hell difference does it make? He's *killing* us!" He looked at each of them in turn. "Any one of us could be next," he added. "Any one of us. Unless . . .

we've got to make plans, *do* something, put a stop to this once and for all."

"You realize," Melantha said gently, "that we cannot actually know whether the good captain has turned off his sensory inputs down here. He could be watching and listening to us right now. He isn't, of course. He said he wouldn't and I believe him. But we have only his word on that. Now, Rojan, you don't appear to trust Royd. If that's so, you can hardly put any faith in his promises. It follows therefore that from your own point of view it might not be wise to say the things that you're saying." She smiled slyly. "Do you understand the implications of what I'm saying?"

Christopheris opened his mouth and closed it again, looking very like a tall, ugly fish. He said nothing, but his eyes moved furtively, and his flush deepened.

Lindran smiled thinly. "I think he's got it," she said.

"The computer is gone, then," Karoly d'Branin said suddenly in a low voice.

Melantha looked at him. "I'm afraid so, Karoly."

D'Branin ran his fingers through his hair, as if half aware of how untidy he looked. "The *volcryn*," he muttered. "How will we work without the computer?" He nodded to himself. "I have a small unit in my cabin, a wrist model, perhaps it will suffice. It *must* suffice, it must. I will get the figures from Royd, learn where we have dropped out. Excuse me, my friends. Pardon, I must go." He wandered away in a distracted haze, talking to himself.

"He hasn't heard a word we've said," Dannel said, incredulous.

"Think how distraught he'd be if *all* of us were dead," added Lindran. "Then he'd have no one to help him look for *volcryn*."

"Let him go," Melantha said. "He is as hurt as any of us, maybe more so. He wears it differently. His obsessions are his defense."

"Ah. And what is *our* defense?"

"Patience, maybe," said Melantha Jhirl. "All of the dead were trying to breach Royd's secret when they died. We haven't tried. Here we are discussing their deaths."

"You don't find that suspicious?" asked Lindran.

"Very," Melantha said. "I even have a method of testing my suspicions. One of us can make yet another attempt to find out whether our captain told us the truth. If he or she dies, we'll know." She shrugged. "Forgive me, however, if I'm not the one who tries. But don't let me stop you if you have the urge. I'll note the results with interest. Until then, I'm going to move out of the cargo hold and get some sleep." She turned and strode off, leaving the others to stare at each other.

"Arrogant bitch," Dannel observed almost conversationally after Melantha had left.

"Do you really think he can hear us?" Christopheris whispered to the two linguists.

"Every pithy word," Lindran said. She smiled at his discomfiture. "Come, Dannel, let's get to a safe area and back to bed."

He nodded.

"But," said Christopheris, "we have to *do* something. Make plans. Defenses."

Lindran gave him a final withering look, and pulled Dannel off behind her down the corridor.

"Melantha? Karoly?"

She woke quickly, alert at the mere whisper of her name, fully awake almost at once, and sat up in the narrow single bed. Squeezed in beside her, Karoly d'Branin groaned and rolled over, yawning.

"Royd?" she asked. "Is it morning?"

"We are drifting in interstellar space three light years from the nearest star, Melantha," replied the soft voice from the walls. "In such a context, the term *morning* has no meaning. But, yes, it is morning."

Melantha laughed. "*Drifting*, you said? How bad is the damage?"

"Serious, but not dangerous. Hold three is a complete ruin, hanging from my ship like half of a broken egg, but the damage was confined. The drives themselves are intact, and the *Nightflyer*'s computers did not seem to suffer from your system's destruction. I feared they might. I have heard of phenomena like electronic death traumas."

D'Branin said, "Eh? Royd?"

Melantha stroked him affectionately. "I'll tell you later, Karoly," he said. "Go back to sleep. Royd, you sound serious. Is there more?"

"I am worried about our return flight, Melantha," Royd said. "When I take the *Nightflyer* back into drive, the flux will be playing directly on portions of the ship that were never engineered to withstand it. Our configurations are askew now; I can show you the mathematics of it, but the question of the flux forces is the vital one. The airseal across the access to hold three is a particular concern. I've run some simulations, and I don't know if it can take the stress. If it bursts, my whole ship will split apart in the middle. My engines will go shunting off by themselves, and the rest— Even if the life support sphere remains intact, we will all soon be dead."

"I see. Is there anything we can do?"

"Yes. The exposed areas would be easy enough to reinforce. The outer hull is armored to withstand the warping forces, of course. We could mount it in place, a crude shield, but according to my projections it would suffice. If we do it correctly, it will help correct our configurations as well Large portions of the hull were torn loose when the locks opened, but they are still out there, most within a kilometer or two, and could be used."

At some point Karoly d'Branin had finally come awake. "My team has four vacuum sleds," he said. "We can retrieve those pieces for you, my friend."

"Fine, Karoly, but that is not my primary concern. My ship is self-repairing within certain limits, but this exceeds those limits by an order of magnitude. I will have to do this myself."

"You?" D'Branin was startled. "Royd, you said—that is, your muscles, your weakness—this work will be too much for you. Surely we can do this for you!"

Royd's reply was tolerant. "I am only a cripple in a gravity field, Karoly. Weightless, I am in my element, and I will be killing the *Nightflyer*'s gravity grid momentarily, to try to gather my own strength for the repair work. No, you misunderstand. I am capable of the work. I have the tools, including my own heavy-duty sled."

"I think I know what you are concerned about, captain," Melantha said.

"I'm glad," Royd said. "Perhaps then you can answer my question. If I emerge from the safety of my chambers to do this work, can you keep your colleagues from harming me?"

Karoly d'Branin was shocked. "Oh, Royd, Royd, how could you think such a thing? We are scholars, scientists, not—not criminals, or soldiers, or—or animals, we are human, how can you believe we would threaten you or do you harm?"

"Human," Royd repeated, "but alien to me, suspicious of me. Give me no false assurances, Karoly."

He sputtered. Melantha took him by the hand and bid him quiet. "Royd," she said, "I won't lie to you. You'd be in some danger. But I'd hope that, by coming out, you'd make our friends joyously happy. They'd be able to see that you told the truth, see that you were only human." She smiled. "They *would* see that, wouldn't they?"

"They would," Royd said, "but would it be enough to offset their suspicions? They believe I am responsible for the deaths of the other three, do they not?"

"Believe is too strong a word. They suspect it, they fear

it. They are frightened, captain, and with good cause. *I* am frightened.''

"No more than I.''

"I would be less frightened if I knew what *did* happen. Will you tell me?''

Silence.

"Royd, if—''

"I have made mistakes, Melantha,'' Royd said gravely. "But I am not alone in that. I did my best to stop the esperon injection, and I failed. I might have saved Alys and Lommie if I had seen them, heard them, known what they were about. But you made me turn off my monitors, Melantha. I cannot help what I cannot see. Why? If you saw three moves ahead, did you calculate these results?''

Melantha Jhirl felt briefly guilty. "*Mea culpa*, captain, I share the blame. I know that. Believe me, I know that. It is hard to see three moves ahead when you do not know the rules, however. Tell me the rules.''

"I am blind and deaf,'' Royd said, ignoring her. "It is frustrating. I cannot help if I am blind and deaf. I am going to turn on the monitors again, Melantha. I am sorry if you do not approve. I want your approval, but I must do this with or without it. I have to *see*.''

"Turn them on,'' Melantha said thoughtfully. "I was wrong, captain. I should never have asked you to blind yourself. I did not understand the situation, and I overestimated my own power to control the others. A failing of mine. Improved models too often think they can do anything.'' Her mind was racing, and she felt almost sick; she had miscalculated, misled, and there was more blood on her hands. "I think I understand better now.''

"Understand what?'' Karoly d'Branin said, baffled.

"You do *not* understand,'' Royd said sternly. "Don't pretend that you do, Melantha Jhirl. Don't! It is not wise or safe to be too many moves ahead.'' There was something disturbing in his tone.

Melantha understood that too.

"What?" Karoly said. "I do not understand."

"Neither do I," Melantha said carefully. "Neither do I, Karoly." She kissed him lightly. "None of us understand, do we?"

"Good," said Royd.

She nodded, and put a reassuring arm around Karoly. "Royd," she said, "to return to the question of repairs, it seems to me you must do this work, regardless of what promises we can give you. You won't risk your ship by slipping back into drive in your present condition, and the only other option is to drift out here until we all die. What choice do we have?"

"I have a choice," Royd said with deadly seriousness. "I could kill all of you, if that were the only way to save myself and my ship."

"You could try," Melantha said.

"Let us have no more talk of death," d'Branin said.

"You are right, Karoly," Royd said. "I do not wish to kill any of you. But I must be protected."

"You will be," Melantha said. "Karoly can set the others to chasing your hull fragments. I'll be your protection. I'll stay by your side. If anyone tries to attack you, they'll have to deal with me. They won't find that easy. And I can assist you. The work will be done three times as fast."

Royd was polite. "It is my experience that most planet-born are clumsy and easily tired in weightlessness. It would be more efficient if I worked alone, although I will gladly accept your services as a bodyguard."

"I remind you that I'm the improved model, captain," Melantha said. "Good in free fall as well as in bed. I'll help."

"You are stubborn. As you will, then. In a few moments I shall depower the gravity grid. Karoly, go and prepare your people. Unship your vacuum sleds and suit up. I will exit the *Nightflyer* in three standard hours, after I have recovered from the pains of your gravity. I want all of you outside the ship before I leave. Is that condition understood?''

"Yes," said Karoly. "All except Agatha. She has not regained consciousness, friend, she will not be a problem.''

"No," said Royd, "I meant *all* of you, including Agatha. Take her outside with you.''

"But Royd!" protested d'Branin.

"You're the captain," Melantha Jhirl said firmly. "It will be as you say; all of us outside. Including Agatha.''

Outside. It was as though some vast animal had taken a bite out of the stars.

Melantha Jhirl waited on her sled close by the *Nightflyer*, and looked at stars. It was not so very different out here in the depths of interstellar space. The stars were cold, frozen points of light; unwinking, austere, more chill and uncaring somehow than the same suns made to dance and twinkle by an atmosphere. Only the absense of a landmark primary reminded her of where she was: in the places between, where men and women and their ships do not stop, where the *volcryn* sail crafts impossibly ancient. She tried to pick out Avalon's sun, but she did not know where to search. The configurations were strange to her and she had no idea of how she was oriented. Behind her, before her, above, all around, the starfields stretched endlessly. She glanced down, or what seemed like down just then, beyond her feet and her sled and the *Nightflyer,* expecting still more alien stars. And the *bite* hit her with an almost physical force.

Melantha fought off a wave of vertigo. She was suspended above a pit, a yawning chasm in the universe, black, starless, vast.

Empty.

She remembered then: the Tempter's Veil. Just a cloud of dark gases, nothing really, galactic pollution that obscured the light from the stars of the Fringe. But this close at hand, it seemed immense, terrifying, and she had to break her gaze when she began to feel as if she were falling. It was a gulf beneath her and the frail silver-white shell of the *Nightflyer*, a gulf about to swallow them.

Melantha touched one of the controls on the sled's forked handle, swinging around so the Veil was to her side instead of beneath her. That seemed to help somehow. She concentrated on the *Nightflyer*, ignoring the looming wall of blackness beyond. It was the largest object in her universe, bright amid the darkness, ungainly, its shattered cargo sphere giving the whole craft an unbalanced cast.

She could see the other sleds as they angled through the black, tracking the missing pieces of hull, grappling with them, bringing them back. The linguistic team worked together, as always, sharing a sled. Rojan Christopheris was alone, working in a sullen silence. Melantha had almost had to threaten him with physical violence before he agreed to join them. The xenobiologist was certain that it was all another plot, that once they were outside the *Nightflyer* would slip into drive without them and leave them to lingering deaths. His suspicions were inflamed by drink, and there had been alcohol on his breath when Melantha and Karoly had finally forced him to suit up. Karoly had a sled too, and a silent passenger; Agatha Marij-Black, freshly drugged and asleep in her vacuum suit, safely locked into place.

While her colleagues labored, Melantha Jhirl waited for Royd Eris, talking to the others occasionally over the comm link. The two linguists, unaccustomed to weightlessness, were complaining a good deal, and bickering as well. Karoly tried to soothe them frequently. Christopheris said little, and his few comments were edged and biting. He was still angry. Melantha watched him flit across her field of vision, a stick figure in form-fitting black armor standing erect at the controls of his sled.

Finally the circular airlock atop the foremost of the *Nightflyer*'s major spheres, dilated, and Royd Eris emerged.

She watched him approach, curious, wondering what he

would look like. In her mind were a half-dozen contradictory pictures. His genteel, cultured, too-formal voice sometimes reminded her of the dark aristocrats of her native Prometheus, the wizards who toyed with human genes and played baroque status games. At other times his naivete made her imagine him as an inexperienced youth. His ghost was a tired-looking thin young man, and he was supposed to be considerably older than that pale shadow, but Melantha found it difficult to hear an old man talking when he spoke.

Melantha felt a nervous tingle as he neared. The lines of his sled and his suit were different than theirs, disturbingly so. Alien, she thought, and quickly squelched the thought. Such differences meant nothing. Royd's sled was large, a long oval plate with eight jointed grappling arms bristling from its underside like the legs of a metallic spider. A heavy-duty cutting laser was mounted beneath the controls, its snout jutting threateningly forward. His suit was far more massive than the carefully engineered Academy worksuits they wore, with a bulge between its shoulder blades that was probably powerpack, and rakish radiant fins atop shoulders and helmet. It made him seem hulking; hunched and deformed.

But when he finally came near enough for Melantha to see his face, it was just a face.

White, very white, that was the predominant impression she got; white hair cropped very short, a white stubble around the sharply chiseled lines of his jaw, almost invisible eyebrows beneath which his eyes moved restlessly. His eyes were large and vividly blue, his best feature. His skin was pale and unlined, scarcely touched by time.

He looked wary, she thought. And perhaps a bit frightened.

Royd stopped his sled close to hers, amid the twisted ruin that had been cargo hold three, and surveyed the damage, the pieces of floating wreckage that had once been flesh, blood, glass, metal, plastic. Hard to distinguish now, all of them fused and burned and frozen together. "We have a good deal of work to do," he said. "Shall we begin?"

"First let's talk," she replied. She shifted her sled closer and reached out to him, but the distance was still too great, the width of the bases of the two vacuum sleds keeping them apart. Melantha backed off and turned herself over completely, so that Royd stood upside down in her world and she upside down in his. She moved to him again, positioning her sled directly over/under his. Their gloved hands met, brushed, parted. Melantha adjusted her altitude. Their helmets touched.

"Now I have touched you," Royd said, with a tremor in his voice. "I have never touched anyone before, or been touched."

"Oh, Royd. This isn't touching, not really. The suits are in the way. But I will touch you, *really* touch you. I promise you that."

"You can't. It's impossible."

"I'll find a way," she said firmly. "Now, turn off your comm. The sound will carry through our helmets."

He blinked and used his tongue controls and it was done.

"Now we can talk," she said. "Privately."

"I do not like this, Melantha," he said. "This is too obvious. This is dangerous."

"There is no other way. Royd, I *do* know."

"Yes," he said. "I knew you did. Three moves ahead, Melantha. I remember the way you play chess. But this is a more serious game, and you are safer if you feign ignorance."

"I understand that, captain. Other things I'm less sure about. Can we talk about them?"

"No. Don't ask me to. Just do as I tell you. You are in peril, all of you, but I can protect you. The less you know, the better I can protect you." Through the transparent faceplates, his expression was somber.

She stared into his upside-down eyes. "It might be a second crew member, someone else hidden in your quarters, but I don't believe that. It's the ship, isn't it? Your ship is killing us. Not you. It. Only that doesn't make sense. You command the *Nightflyer*. How can it act independently? And why? What motive? And how was Thale Lasamer killed? The business with Alys and Lommie, that was easy, but a psionic murder? A starship with psi? I can't accept that. It can't be the ship. Yet it can't be anything else. Help me, captain.''

He blinked, anguish behind his eyes. ''I should never have accepted Karoly's charter, not with a telepath among you. It was too risky. But I wanted to see the *volcryn*, and he spoke of them so movingly.'' He sighed. ''You understand too much already, Melantha. I can't tell you more, or I would be powerless to protect you. The ship is malfunctioning, that is all you need to know. It is not safe to push too hard. As long as I am at the controls, I think I can keep you and the others from harm. Trust me.''

''Trust is a two-way bond,'' Melantha said.

Royd lifted his hand and pushed her away, then tongued his communicator back to life. ''Enough gossip,'' he announced. ''We have work to do. Come. I want to see just how improved you actually are.''

In the solitude of her helmet, Melantha Jhirl swore softly.

With an irregular twist of metal locked beneath him in his sled's magnetic grip, Rojan Christopheris sailed back towards the *Nightflyer*. He was watching from a distance when Royd Eris emerged on his oversized work sled. He was closer when Melantha Jhirl moved to him, inverted her sled, and pressed her faceplate to Royd's. Christopheris listened to their soft exchange, heard Melantha promise to touch him, Eris, the *thing*, the killer. He swallowed his rage. Then they cut him out, cut all of them out, went off the open circuit. But still she hung there, suspended by that cipher in the hunchbacked spacesuit, faces pressed together like two lovers kissing.

Christopheris swept in close, unlocked his captive plate so it would drift towards them. ''Here,'' he announced. ''I'm off to get another.'' He tongued off his own comm and swore, and his sled slid around the spheres and tubes of the *Nightflyer*.

Somehow they were all in it together, Royd and Melantha and possibly old d'Branin as well, he thought sourly. She had protected Eris from the first, stopped them when they might have taken action together, found out who or what he was. He did not trust her. His skin crawled when he remembered that they had been to bed together. She and Eris were the same, whatever they might be. And now poor Alys was dead, and that fool Thorne and even that damned telepath, but still Melantha was with *him*, against them. Rojan Christopheris was deeply afraid, and angry, and half drunk.

The others were out of sight, off chasing spinning wedges of half-slagged metal. Royd and Melantha were engrossed in each other, the ship abandoned and vulnerable. This was his chance. No wonder Eris had insisted that all of them precede him into the void; outside, isolated from the controls of the *Nightflyer*, he was only a man. A weak one at that.

Smiling a thin hard smile, Christopheris brought his sled curling around the cargo spheres, hidden from sight, and vanished into the gaping maw of the driveroom. It was a long tunnel, everything open to vacuum, safe from the corrosion of an atmosphere. Like most starships, the *Nightflyer* had a triple propulsion system: the gravfield for landing and lifting, useless away from a gravity well, the nukes for deep space sublight maneuverings, and the great stardrives themselves. The lights of his sled flickered past the encircling ring of nukes and sent long bright streaks along the sides of the closed cylinders of the stardrives, the huge engines that bent the stuff of spacetime, encased in webs of metal and crystal.

At the end of the tunnel was a great circular door, reinforced metal, closed: the main airlock.

Christopheris set the sled down, dismounted—pulling his boots free of the sled's magnetic grip with an effort—and moved to the airlock. This was the hardest part, he thought. The headless body of Thale Lasamer was tethered loosely to a massive support strut by the lock, like a grisly guardian of the way. The xenobiologist had to stare at it while he waited for the lock to cycle. Whenever he glanced away, somehow he would find his eyes creeping back to it. The body looked almost natural, as if it had never had a head. Christopheris tried to remember what Lasamer had looked like, but the features would not come to mind. He moved uncomfortably, but then the lock door slid open and he gratefully entered the chamber to cycle through.

He was alone in the *Nightflyer*.

A cautious man, Christopheris kept his suit on, though he collapsed the helmet and yanked loose the suddenly-limp metallic fabric so it fell behind his back like a hood. He could snap it in place quickly enough if the need arose. In cargo hold four, where they had stored their equipment, the xenobiologist found what he was looking for; a portable cutting laser, charged and ready. Low power, but it would do.

Slow and clumsy in weightlessness, he pulled himself down the corridor into the darkened lounge.

It was chilly inside, the air cold on his cheeks. He tried not to notice. He braced himself at the door and pushed off across the width of the room, sailing above the furniture, which was all safely bolted into place. As he drifted towards his objective, something wet and cold touched his face. It startled him, but it was gone before he could quite make out what it was.

When it happened again, Christopheris snatched at it, caught it, and felt briefly sick. He had forgotten. No one had cleaned the lounge yet. The—the *remains* were still there, floating now, blood and flesh and bits of bone and brain. All around him.

He reached the far wall, stopped himself with his arms, pulled himself down to where he wanted to go. The bulk-head. The wall. No doorway was visible, but the metal couldn't be very thick. Beyond was the control room, the computer access, safety, power. Rojan Christopheris did not think of himself as a vindictive man. He did not intend to harm Royd Eris, that judgment was not his to make. He would take control of the *Nightflyer*, warn Eris away, make certain the man stayed sealed in his suit. He would take them all back without any more mysteries, any more killings. The Academy arbiters could listen to the story, and probe Eris, and decide the right and wrong of it, guilt and innocence, what should be done.

The cutting laser emitted a thin pencil of scarlet light. Christopheris smiled and applied it to the bulkhead. It was slow work, but he had patience. They would not have missed him, quiet as he'd been, and if they did they would assume he was off sledding after some hunk of salvage. Eris' repairs would take hours, maybe days, to finish. The bright blade of the laser smoked where it touched the metal. Christopheris applied himself diligently.

Something moved on the periphery of his vision, just a little flicker, barely seen. A floating bit of brain, he thought. A sliver of bone. A bloody piece of flesh, hair still hanging from it. Horrible things, but nothing to worry about. He was a biologist, he was used to blood and brains and flesh. And worse, and worse; he had dissected many an alien in his day, cutting through chitin and mucous, pulsing stinking food sacs and poisonous spines, he had seen and touched it all.

Again the motion caught his eye, teased at it. Not wanting to, Christopheris found himself drawn to look. He could not *not* look, somehow, just as he had been unable to ignore the headless corpse near the airlock. He looked.

It was an eye.

Christopheris trembled and the laser slipped sharply off to one side, so he had to wrestle with it to bring it back to the channel he was cutting. His heart raced. He tried to calm himself. Nothing to be frightened of. No one was home, and if Royd should return, well, he had the laser as a weapon and he had his suit on if an airlock blew.

He looked at the eye again, willing away his fear. It was just an eye, Thale Lasamer's eye, pale blue, bloody but intact, the same watery eye the boy had when alive, nothing supernatural. A piece of dead flesh, floating in the lounge amid other pieces of dead flesh. Someone should have cleaned up the lounge, Christopheris thought angrily. It was indecent to leave it like this, it was uncivilized.

The eye did not move. The other grisly bits were drifting on the air currents that flowed across the room, but the eye was still. It neither bobbed nor spun. It was fixed on him. Staring.

He cursed himself and concentrated on the laser, on his cutting. He had burned an almost straight line up the bulkhead for about a meter. He began another at right angles.

The eye watched dispassionately. Christopheris suddenly found he could not stand it. One hand released its grip on the laser, reached out, caught the eye, flung it across the room. The action made him lose balance. He tumbled backward, the laser slipping from his grasp, his arms flapping like the wings of some absurd heavy bird. Finally he caught an edge of the table and stopped himself.

The laser hung in the center of the room, floating amid coffee pots and pieces of human debris, still firing, turning slowly. That did not make sense. It should have ceased fire when he released it. A malfunction, Christopheris thought nervously. Smoke was rising where the thin line of the laser traced a path across the carpet.

With a shiver of fear, Christopheris realized that the laser was turning towards him.

He raised himself, put both hands flat against the table, pushed up out of the way, bobbing towards the ceiling.

The laser was turning more swiftly now.

He pushed away from the ceiling hard, slammed into a wall, grunted in pain, bounced off the floor, kicked. The laser was spinning quickly, chasing him. Christopheris soared, braced himself for another ricochet off the ceiling. The beam swung around, but not fast enough. He'd get it while it was still firing off in the other direction.

He moved close, reached, and saw the eye.

It hung just above the laser. Staring.

Rojan Christopheris made a small whimpering sound low in his throat, and his hand hesitated—not long, but long enough—and the scarlet beam came up and around.

Its touch was a light, hot caress across his neck.

It was more than an hour later before they missed him. Karoly d'Branin noticed his absence first, called for him over the comm link, and got no answer. He discussed it with the others.

Royd Eris moved his sled back from the armor plate he had just mounted, and through his helmet Melantha Jhirl could see the lines around his mouth grow hard.

It was just then that the noises began.

A shrill bleat of pain and fear, followed by moans and sobbing. Terrible wet sounds, like a man choking on his own blood. They all heard. The sounds filled their helmets. And almost clear amid the anguish was something that sounded like a word; "Help."

"That's Christopheris," a woman's voice said. Lindran.

"He's hurt," Dannel added. "He's crying for help. Can't you hear it?"

"Where—?" someone started.

"The ship," Lindran said. "He must have returned to the ship."

Royd Eris said, "The fool. No. I warned—"

"We're going to check," Lindran announced. Dannel cut free the hull fragment they had been bringing in, and it spun away, tumbling. Their sled angled down towards the *Nightflyer*.

"Stop," Royd said. "I'll return to my chambers and check from there, if you wish, but you may not enter the ship. Stay outside until I give you clearance."

The terrible sounds went on and on.

"Go to hell," Lindran snapped at him over the open circuit.

Karoly d'Branin had his sled in motion too, hastening after the linguists, but he had been further out and it was a long way back to the ship. "Royd, what can you mean, we must help, don't you see? He is hurt, listen to him. Please, my friend."

"No," Royd said. "Karoly, stop! If Rojan went back to the ship alone, he is dead."

"How do you know that?" Dannel demanded. "Did you arrange it? Set traps in case we disobeyed you?"

"No," Royd said, "listen to me. You can't help him now. Only I could have helped him, and he did not listen to me. Trust me. Stop." His voice was despairing.

In the distance, d'Branin's sled slowed. The linguists did not. "We've already listened to you too damn much, I'd say," Lindran said. She almost had to shout to be heard above the noises, the whimpers and moans, the awful wet sucking sounds, the distorted pleas for help. Agony filled their universe. "Melantha," Lindran continued, "keep Eris right where he is. We'll go carefully, find out what is happening inside, but I don't want him getting back to his controls. Understood?"

Melantha Jhirl hesitated. The sounds beat against her ears. It was hard to think.

Royd swung his sled around to face her, and she could feel the weight of his stare. "Stop them," he said. "Melantha, Karoly, order it. They will not listen to me. They do not know what they are doing." He was clearly in pain.

In his face Melantha found decision. "Go back inside quickly, Royd. Do what you can. I'm going to try to intercept them."

"Whose side are you on?" Lindran demanded.

Royd nodded to her across the gulf, but Melantha was already in motion. Her sled backed clear of the work area, congested with hull fragments and other debris, then accelerated briskly as she raced around the exterior of the *Nightflyer* towards the driveroom.

But even as she approached, she knew it was too late. The linguists were too close, and already moving much faster than she was.

"*Don't,*" she said, authority in her tone. "Christopheris is dead."

"His ghost is crying for help, then," Lindran replied. "When they tinkered you together, they must have damaged the genes for hearing, bitch."

"The ship isn't safe."

"Bitch," was all the answer she got.

Karoly's sled pursued vainly. "Friends, you must stop, please, I beg it of you. Let us talk this out together."

The sounds were his only reply.

"I am your superior," he said. "I order you to wait outside. Do you hear me? I order it, I invoke the authority of the Academy of Human Knowledge. Please, my friends, please."

Melantha watched helplessly as Lindran and Dannel vanished down the long tunnel of the driveroom.

A moment later she halted her own sled near the waiting black mouth, debating whether she should follow them on into the *Nightflyer*. She might be able to catch them before the airlock opened.

Royd's voice, hoarse counterpoint to the sounds, answered her unvoiced question. "Stay, Melantha. Proceed no further."

She looked behind her. Royd's sled was approaching.

"What are you doing here? Royd, use your own lock. You have to get back inside!"

"Melantha," he said calmly, "I cannot. The ship will not respond to me. The lock will not dilate. The main lock in the driveroom is the only one with manual override. I am trapped outside. I don't want you or Karoly inside the ship until I can return to my console."

Melantha Jhirl looked down the shadowed barrel of the driveroom, where the linguists had vanished.

"What will—"

"Beg them to come back, Melantha. Plead with them. Perhaps there is still time."

She tried. Karoly d'Branin tried as well. The twisted symphony of pain and pleading went on and on, but they could not raise Dannel or Lindran at all.

"They've cut out their comm," Melantha said furiously. "They don't want to listen to us. Or that . . . that sound."

Royd's sled and d'Branin's reached her at the same time. "I do not understand," Karoly said. "Why can you not enter, Royd? What is happening?"

"It is simple, Karoly," Royd replied. "I am being kept outside until—until—"

"Yes?" prompted Melantha.

"—until Mother is done with them."

The linguists left their vacuum sled next to the one that Christopheris had abandoned, and cycled through the airlock in unseemly haste, with hardly a glance for the grim headless doorman.

Inside they paused briefly to collapse their helmets. "I can still hear him," Dannel said. The sounds were faint inside the ship.

Lindran nodded. "It's coming from the lounge. Hurry."

They kicked and pulled their way down the corridor in less than a minute. The sounds grew steadily louder, nearer. "He's in there," Lindran said when they reached the doorway.

"Yes," Dannel said, "but is he alone? We need a weapon. What if . . . Royd had to be lying. There *is* someone else on board. We need to defend ourselves."

Lindran would not wait. "There are two of us," she said. "Come *on*!" She launched herself through the doorway, calling Christopheris by name.

It was dark inside. What little light there was spilled through the door from the corridor. Her eyes took a long moment to adjust. Everything was confused; walls and ceilings and floor were all the same, she had no sense of direction. "Rojan," she called, dizzily. "Where are you?" The lounge seemed empty, but maybe it was only the light, or her sense of unease.

"Follow the sound," Dannel suggested. He hung in the door, peering warily about for a minute, and then began to feel his way cautiously down a wall, groping with his hands.

As if in response to his comment, the sobbing sounds grew suddenly louder. But they seemed to come first from one corner of the room, than from another.

Lindran, impatient, propelled herself across the chamber, searching. She brushed against a wall in the kitchen area, and that made her think of weapons, and Dannel's fears. She knew where the utensils were stored. "Here," she said a moment later, turning towards him, "Here, I've got a knife, that should thrill you." She flourished it, and brushed against a floating bubble of liquid as big as her fist. It burst and reformed into a hundred smaller globules. One moved past her face, close, and she tasted it. Blood.

But Lasamer had been dead a long time. His blood ought to have dried by now, she thought.

"Oh, merciful god," said Dannel.

"What?" Lindran demanded. "Did you find him?"

Dannel was fumbling his way back towards the door, creeping along the wall like an oversized insect, back the way he had come. "Get out, Lindran," he warned. "*Hurry!*"

"Why?" She trembled despite herself. "What's wrong?"

"The screams," he said. "The wall, Lindran, the wall. The sounds."

"You're not making sense," she snapped. "Get a hold of yourself."

He gibbered. "Don't you see? The sounds are coming from the *wall*. The communicator. Faked. Simulated." Dannel reached the door, and dove through it, sighing audibly. He did not wait for her. He bolted down the corridor and was gone, pulling himself hand over hand wildly, his feet thrashing and kicking behind him.

Lindran braced herself and moved to follow.

The sounds came from in front of her, from the door. "Help me," it said, in Rojan Christopheris' voice. She heard moaning and that terrible wet choking sound, and she stopped.

From her side came a wheezing ghastly death rattle. "Ahhhh," it moaned, loudly, building in a counterpoint to the other noise. "Help me."

"Help me, help me, help me," said Christopheris from the darkness behind her.

Coughing and a weak groan sounded under her feet.

"Help me," all the voices chorused, "help me, help me, help me." Recordings, she thought, recordings being played back. "Help me, help me, help me, help me." All the voices rose higher and louder, and the words turned into a scream, and the scream ended in wet choking, in wheezes and gasps and death. Then the sounds stopped. Just like that; turned off.

Lindran kicked off, floated towards the door, knife in hand.

Something dark and silent crawled from beneath the dinner table and rose to block her path. She saw it clearly for a moment, as it emerged between her and the light. Rojan Christopheris, still in his vacuum suit, but with the helmet pulled off. He had something in his hand that he raised to point at her. It was a laser, Lindran saw, a simple cutting laser.

She was moving straight towards him, coasting, helpless. She flailed and tried to stop herself, but she could not.

When she got quite close, she saw that Rojan had a second mouth below his chin, a long blackened slash, and it was grinning at her, and little droplets of blood flew from it, wetly, as he moved.

*   *   *

Dannel rushed down the corridor in a frenzy of fear, bruising himself as he smashed off walls and doorways. Panic and weightlessness made him clumsy. He kept glancing over his shoulder as he fled, hoping to see Lindran coming after him, but terrified of what he might see in her stead. Every time he looked back, he lost his sense of balance and went tumbling again.

It took a long, *long* time for the airlock to open. As he waited, trembling, his pulse began to slow. The sounds had dwindled behind him, and there was no sign of pursuit. He steadied himself with an effort. Once inside the lock chamber, with the inner door sealed between him and the lounge, he began to feel safe.

Suddenly Dannel could barely remember why he had been so terrified.

And he was ashamed; he had run, abandoned Lindran. And for what? What had frightened him so? An empty lounge? Noises from the walls? A rational explanation for that forced itself on him all at once. It only meant that poor Christopheris was somewhere else in the ship, that's all, just somewhere else, alive and in pain, spilling his agony into a comm unit.

Dannel shook his head ruefully. He'd hear no end of this, he knew. Lindran liked to taunt him. She would never let him forget it. But at least he would return, and apologize. That would count for something. Resolute, he reached out and killed the cycle on the airlock, then reversed it. The air that had been partially sucked out came gusting back into the chamber.

As the inner door rolled back, Dannel felt his fear return briefly, an instant of stark terror when he wondered what might have emerged from the lounge to wait for him in the corridors of the *Nightflyer*. He faced the fear and willed it away. He felt strong.

When he stepped out, Lindran was waiting.

He could see neither anger nor disdain in her curiously calm features, but he pushed himself towards her and tried to frame a plea for forgiveness anyway. "I don't know why I—"

With languid grace, her hand came out from behind her back. The knife flashed up in a killing arc, and that was when Dannel finally noticed the hole burned in her suit, still smoking, just between her breasts.

"Your *mother*?" Melantha Jhirl said incredulously as they hung helpless in the emptiness beyond the ship.

"She can hear everything we say," Royd replied. "But at this point it no longer makes any difference. Rojan must have done something very foolish, very threatening. Now she is determined to kill you all."

"She, she, what do you mean?" D'Branin's voice was puzzled. "Royd, surely you do not tell us that your mother is still alive. You said she died even before you were born."

"She did, Karoly," Royd said. "I did not lie to you."

"No," Melantha said. "I didn't think so. But you did not tell us the whole truth either."

Royd nodded. "Mother is dead, but her—her spirit still lives, and animates my *Nightflyer*." He sighed. "Perhaps it would be more fitting to say her *Nightflyer*. My control has been tenuous at best."

"Royd," d'Branin said, "spirits do not exist. They are not real. There is no survival after death. My *volcryn* are more real than any ghosts."

"I don't believe in ghosts either," said Melantha curtly.

"Call it what you will, then," Royd said. "My term is as good as any. The reality is unchanged by the terminology. My mother, or some part of my mother, lives in the *Nightflyer*, and she is killing all of you as she has killed others before."

"Royd, you do not make sense," d'Branin said.

"Quiet, Karoly. Let the captain explain."

"Yes," Royd said. "The *Nightflyer* is very—very ad-

vanced, you know. Automated, self-repairing, large. It had
to be, if mother were to be freed from the necessity of crew.
It was built on Newholme, you will recall. I have never been
there, but I understand that Newholme's technology is quite
sophisticated. Avalon could not duplicate this ship, I suspect.
There are few worlds that could.''

"The point, captain?"

"The point—the point is the computers, Melantha. They
had to be extraordinary. They are, believe me, they are.
Crystal-matrix cores, lasergrid data retrieval, full sensory
extension, and other—features.''

"Are you trying to tell us that the *Nightflyer* is an Artificial Intelligence? Lommie Thorne suspected as much.''

"She was wrong,'' Royd said. "My ship is not an Artificial Intelligence, not as I understand it. But it is something
close. Mother had a capacity for personality impress built in.
She filled the central crystal with her own memories, desires,
quirks, her loves and her—her hates. That was why she could
trust the computer with my education, you see? She knew it
would raise me as she herself would, had she the patience.
She programmed it in certain other ways as well.''

"And you cannot deprogram, my friend?'' Karoly asked.

Karoly's voice was despairing. "I have *tried*, Karoly. But
I am a weak hand at systems work, and the programs are
very complicated, the machines very sophisticated. At least
three times I have eradicated her, only to have her surface
once again. She is a phantom program, and I cannot track
her. She comes and goes as she will. A ghost, do you see?
Her memories and her personality are so intertwined with the
programs that run the *Nightflyer* that I cannot get rid of her
without destroying the central crystal, wiping the entire system. But that would leave me helpless. I could never reprogram, and with the computers down the entire ship would
fail, drivers, life support, everything. I would have to leave
the *Nightflyer*, and that would kill me.''

"You should have told us, my friend,'' Karoly d'Branin

said. "On Avalon, we have many cyberneticists, some very great minds. We might have aided you. We could have provided expert help. Lommie Thorne might have helped you."

"Karoly, I have *had* expert help. Twice I have brought systems specialists on board. The first one told me what I have just told you; that it was impossible without wiping the programs completely. The second had trained on Newholme. She thought she might be able to help me. Mother killed her."

"You are still holding something back," Melantha Jhirl said. "I understand how your cybernetic ghost can open and close airlocks at will and arrange other accidents of that nature. But how do you explain what she did to Thale Lasamer?"

"Ultimately I must bear the guilt," Royd replied. "My loneliness led me to a grievous error. I thought I could safeguard you, even with a telepath among you. I have carried other riders safely. I watch them constantly, warn them away from dangerous acts. If mother attempts to interfere, I countermand her directly from the master control console. That usually works. Not always. Usually. Before this trip she had killed only five times, and the first three died when I was quite young. That was how I learned about her, about her presence in my ship. That party included a telepath too.

"I should have known better, Karoly. My hunger for life has doomed you all to death. I overestimated my own abilities, and underestimated her fear of exposure. She strikes out when she is threatened, and telepaths are always a threat. They sense her, you see. A malign, looming presence, they tell me, something cool and hostile and inhuman."

"Yes," Karoly d'Branin said, "yes, that was what Thale said. An alien, he was certain of it."

"No doubt she feels alien to a telepath used to the familiar contours of organic minds. Hers is not a human brain, after all. What it is I cannot say—a complex of crystallized memories, a hellish network of interlocking programs, a meld of circuitry and spirit. Yes, I can understand why she might feel alien."

"You still haven't explained how a computer program could explode a man's skull," Melantha said.

"You wear the answer between your breasts, Melantha."

"My whisperjewel?" she said, puzzled. She felt it then, beneath her vacuum suit and her clothing; a touch of cold, a vague hint of eroticism that made her shiver. It was as if his mention had been enough to make the gem come alive.

"I was not familiar with whisperjewels until you told me of yours," Royd said, "but the principle is the same. Esper-etched, you said. Then you know that psionic power can be stored. The central core of my computer is resonant crystal, many times larger than your tiny jewel. I think mother impressed it as she lay dying."

"Only an esper can etch a whisperjewel," Melantha said.

"You never asked the *why* of it, either of you," Royd said. "You never asked why mother hated people so. She was born gifted, you see. On Avalon she might have been a class one, tested and trained and honored, her talent nurtured and rewarded. I think she might have been very famous. She might have been stronger than a class one, but perhaps it is only after death that she acquired such power, linked as she is to the *Nightflyer*.

"The point is moot. She was not born on Avalon. On Vess, her ability was seen as a curse, something alien and fearful. So they cured her of it. They used drugs and electro-shock and hypnotraining that made her violently ill whenever she tried to use her talent. They used other, less savory methods as well. She never lost her power, of course, only the ability to use it effectively, to control it with her conscious mind. It remained part of her, suppressed, erratic, a source of shame and pain, surfacing violently in times of great emotional stress. And half a decade of institutional care almost drove her insane. No wonder she hated people.''

''What was her talent? Telepathy?''

''No. Oh, some rudimentary ability perhaps. I have read that all psi talents have several latent abilities in addition to their one developed strength. But mother could not read minds. She had some empathy, although her cure had twisted it curiously, so that the emotions she felt literally sickened her. But her major strength, the talent they took five years to shatter and destroy, was teke.''

Melantha Jhirl swore. ''Of *course* she hated gravity! Telekinesis under weightlessness is—''

''Yes,'' Royd finished. ''Keeping the *Nightflyer* under gravity tortures me, but it limits mother.''

In the silence that followed that comment, each of them looked down the dark cylinder of the driverrom. Karoly d'Branin moved awkwardly on his sled. ''Dannel and Lindran have not returned,'' he said.

''They are probably dead,'' Royd said dispassionately.

''What will we do, then? We must plan. We cannot wait here indefinitely.''

''The first question is what *I* can do,'' Royd Eris replied. ''I have talked freely, you'll note. You deserved to know. We have passed the point where ignorance was a protection. Obviously things have gone too far. There have been too many deaths and you have been witness to all of them. Mother cannot allow you to return to Avalon alive.''

''True,'' said Melantha. ''But what shall she do with you? Is your own status in doubt, captain?''

''The crux of the problem,'' Royd admitted. ''You are still three moves ahead, Melantha. I wonder if it will suffice. Your opponent is four ahead in this game, and most of your pawns are already captured. I fear checkmate is imminent.''

''Unless I can persuade my opponent's king to desert, no?''

She could see Royd's wan smile. ''She would probably

kill me too if I choose to side with you. She does not need me.''

Karoly d'Branin was slow to grasp the point. "But—but what else could—"

"My sled has a laser. Yours do not. I could kill you both, right now, and thereby earn my way back into the *Nightflyer*'s good graces."

Across the three meters that lay between their sleds, Melantha's eyes met Royd's. Her hands rested easily on the thruster controls. "You could try, captain. Remember, the improved model isn't easy to kill."

"I would not kill you, Melantha Jhirl," Royd said seriously. "I have lived sixty-eight standard years and I have never lived at all. I am tired, and you tell grand gorgeous lies. Will you really touch me?"

"Yes."

"I risk a lot for that touch. Yet in a way it is no risk at all. If we lose, we will all die together. If we win, well, I shall die anyway when they destroy the *Nightflyer*, either that or live as a freak in an orbital hospital, and I would prefer death."

"We will build you a new ship, captain," Melantha promised.

"Liar," Royd replied. But his tone was cheerful. "No matter. I have not had much a life anyway. Death does not frighten me. If we win, you must tell me about your *volcryn* once again, Karoly. And you, Melantha, you must play chess with me, and find a way to touch me, and . . ."

"And sex with you?" she finished, smiling.

"If you would," he said quietly. He shrugged. "Well, mother has heard all of this. Doubtless she will listen carefully to any plans we might make, so there is no sense making them. Now there is no chance that the control lock will admit me, since it is keyed directly into the ship's computer. So we must follow the others through the driveroom, and enter through the main lock, and take what small chances we are given. If I can reach my console and restore gravity, perhaps we can win. If not—''

He was interrupted by a low groan.

For an instant Melantha thought the *Nightflyer* was wailing at them again, and she was surprised that it was so stupid as to try the same tactic twice. Then the groan sounded once more, and in the back of Karoly d'Branin's sled, the forgotten fourth member of their company struggled against the bonds that held her down. D'Branin hastened to free her, and Agatha Marij-Black tried to rise to her feet and almost floated off the sled, until he caught her hand and pulled her back. ''Are you well?'' he asked. ''Can you hear me? Have you pain?''

Imprisoned beneath a transparent faceplate, wide frightened eyes flicked rapidly from Karoly to Melantha to Royd, and then to the broken *Nightflyer*. Melantha wondered whether the woman was insane, and started to caution d'Branin, when Marij-Black spoke.

''The *volcryn*!'' was all she said. ''Oh. The *volcryn*!''

Around the mouth of the driveroom, the ring of nuclear engines took on a faint glow. Melantha Jhirl heard Royd suck in his breath sharply. She gave the thruster controls of her sled a violent twist. ''Hurry,'' she said loudly. ''The *Nightflyer* is preparing to move.''

A third of the way down the long barrel of the driveroom, Royd pulled abreast of her, stiff and menacing in his black, bulky armor. Side by side they sailed past the cylindrical stardrives and the cyberwebs; ahead, dimly lit, was the main airlock and its ghastly sentinel.

''When we reach the lock, jump over to my sled,'' Royd said. ''I want to stay armed and mounted, and the chamber is not large enough for two sleds.''

Melantha Jhirl risked a quick glance behind her. ''Karoly,'' she called. ''Where are you?''

"Outside, my love, my friend," the answer came. "I cannot come. Forgive me."

"We have to stay together!"

"No," d'Branin said, "no, I could not risk it, not when we are so close. It would be so tragic, so futile, Melantha. To come so close and fail. Death I do not mind, but I must see them first, finally, after all these years."

"My mother is going to move the ship," Royd cut in. "Karoly, you will be left behind, lost."

"I will wait," d'Branin replied. "My *volcryn* come, and I must wait for them."

Then the time for conversation was gone, for the airlock was almost upon them. Both sleds slowed and stopped, and Royd Eris reached out and began the cycle while Melantha Jhirl moved to the rear of his huge oval worksled. When the outer door moved aside, they glided through into the lock chamber.

"When the inner door opens it will begin," Royd told her evenly. "The permanent furnishings are either built in or welded or bolted into place, but the things that your team brought on board are not. Mother will use those things as weapons. And beware of doors, airlocks, any equipment tied into the *Nightflyer*'s computer. Need I warn you not to unseal your suit?"

"Hardly," she replied.

Royd lowered the sled a little, and its grapplers made a metallic sound as they touched against the floor of the chamber.

The inner door hissed open, and Royd applied his thrusters.

Inside Dannel and Lindran waited, swimming in a haze of blood. Dannel had been slit from crotch to throat and his intestines moved like a nest of pale, angry snakes. Lindran still held the knife. They swam closer, moving with a grace they had never possessed in life.

Royd lifted his foremost grapplers and smashed them to the side as he surged forward. Dannel caromed off a bulkhead, leaving a wide wet mark where he struck, and more of his guts came sliding out. Lindran lost control of the knife. Royd accelerated past them, driving up the corridor through the cloud of blood.

"I'll watch behind," Melantha said. She turned and put her back to his. Already the two corpses were safely behind them. The knife was floating uselessly in the air. She started to tell Royd that they were all right when the blade abruptly shifted and came after them, gripped by some invisible force.

"*Swerve!*" she cried.

The sled shot wildly to one side. The knife missed by a full meter, and glanced ringingly off a bulkhead.

But it did not drop. It came at them again.

The lounge loomed ahead. Dark.

"The door is too narrow," Royd said. "We will have to abandon—" As he spoke, they hit; he wedged the sled squarely into the doorframe, and the sudden impact jarred them loose.

For a moment Melantha floated clumsily in the corridor, her head whirling, trying to sort up from down. The knife slashed at her, opening her suit and her shoulder clear through to the bone. She felt sharp pain and the warm flush of bleeding. "Damn," she shrieked. The knife came around again, spraying droplets of blood.

Melantha's hand darted out and caught it.

She muttered something under her breath and wrenched the blade free of the hand that had been gripping it.

Royd had regained the controls of his sled and seemed intent on some manipulation. Beyond him, in the dimness of the lounge, Melantha glimpsed a dark semi-human form rise into view.

"*Royd!*" she warned. The thing activated its small laser. The pencil beam caught Royd square in the chest.

He touched his own firing stud. The sled's heavy-duty laser came alive, a shaft of sudden brilliance. It cindered Christopheris' weapon and burned off his right arm and part of his chest. The beam hung in the air, throbbing, and smoked against the far bulkhead.

Royd made some adjustments and began cutting a hole. "We'll be through in five minutes or less," he said curtly.

"Are you all right?" Melantha asked.

"I'm uninjured," he replied. "My suit is better armored than yours, and his laser was a low-powered toy."

Melantha turned her attention back to the corridor.

The linguists were pulling themselves toward her, one on each side of the passage, to come at her from two directions at once. She flexed her muscles. Her shoulder stabbed and screamed. Otherwise she felt strong, almost reckless. "The corpses are coming after us again," she told Royd. "I'm going to take them."

"Is that wise?" he asked. "There are two of them."

"I'm an improved model," Melantha said, "and they're dead." She kicked herself free of the sled and sailed towards Dannel in a high, graceful trajectory. He raised his hands to block her. She slapped them aside, bent one arm back and heard it snap, and drove her knife deep into his throat before she realized what a useless gesture that was. Blood oozed from his neck in a spreading cloud, but he continued to flail at her. His teeth snapped grotesquely.

Melantha withdrew her blade, seized him, and with all her considerable strength threw him bodily down the corridor. He tumbled, spinning wildly, and vanished into the haze of his own blood.

Melantha flew in the opposite direction, revolving lazily.

Lindran's hands caught her from behind.

Nails scrabbled against her faceplate until they began to bleed, leaving red streaks on the plastic.

Melantha whirled to face her attacker, grabbed a thrashing arm, and flung the woman down the passageway to crash into her struggling companion. The reaction sent her spinning like a top. She spread her arms and stopped herself, dizzy, gulping.

"I'm through," Royd announced.

Melantha turned to see. A smoking meter-square opening had been cut through one wall of the lounge. Royd killed the laser, gripped both sides of the doorframe, and pushed himself towards it.

A piercing blast of sound drilled through her head. She doubled over in agony. Her tongue flicked out and clicked off the comm; then there was blessed silence.

In the lounge it was raining. Kitchen utensils, glasses and plates, pieces of human bodies all lashed violently across the room, and glanced harmlessly off Royd's armored form. Melantha—eager to follow—drew back helplessly. That rain of death would cut her to pieces in her lighter, thinner vacuun suit. Royd reached the far wall and vanished into the secret control section of the ship. She was alone.

The *Nightflyer* lurched, and sudden acceleration provided a brief semblance of gravity. Melantha was thrown to one side. Her injured shoulder smashed painfully against the sled.

All up and down the corridor doors were opening.

Dannel and Lindran were moving toward her once again.

The *Nightflyer* was a distant star sparked by its nuclear engines. Blackness and cold enveloped them, and below was the unending emptiness of the Tempter's Veil, but Karoly d'Branin did not feel afraid. He felt strangely transformed.

The void was alive with promise.

"They *are* coming," he whispered. "Even I, who have no psi at all, even I can feel it. The Crey story must be so, even from light years off they can be sensed. Marvelous!"

Agatha Marij-Black seemed small and shrunken. "The *volcryn*," she muttered. "What good can they do us. I hurt. The ship is gone. D'Branin, my head aches." She made a small frightened noise. "Thale said that, just after I injected him, before—before—you know. He said that his head hurt. It aches so terribly."

"Quiet, Agatha. Do not be afraid. I am here with you.

Wait. Think only of what we shall witness, think only of that!''

"I can sense them," the psipsych said.

D'Branin was eager. "Tell me, then. We have our little sled. We shall go to them. Direct me."

"Yes," she agreed. "Yes. Oh, yes."

Gravity returned; in a flicker, the universe became almost normal.

Melantha fell to the deck, landed easily and rolled, and was on her feet cat-quick.

The objects that had been floating ominously through the open doors along the corridor all came clattering down.

The blood was transformed from a fine mist to a slick covering on the corridor floor.

The two corpses dropped heavily from the air, and lay still.

Royd spoke to her from the communicators built into the walls. "I made it," he said.

"I noticed," she replied.

"I'm at the main control console. I have restored the gravity with a manual override, and I'm cutting off as many computer functions as possible. We're still not safe, though. Mother will try to find a way around me. I'm countermanding her by sheer force, as it were. I cannot afford to overlook anything, and if my attention should lapse, even for a moment . . . Melantha, was your suit breached?"

"Yes. Cut at the shoulder."

"Change into another one. *Immediately.* I think the counter programming I'm doing will keep the locks sealed, but I can't take any chances."

Melantha was already running down the corridor, toward the cargo hold where the suits and equipment were stored.

"When you have changed," Royd continued, "dump the corpses into the mass conversion unit. You'll find the appropriate hatch near the driveroom airlock, just to the left of the lock controls. Convert any other loose objects that are not indispensible as well; scientific instruments, books, tapes, tableware—"

"Knives," suggested Melantha.

"By all means."

"Is teke still a threat, captain?"

"Mother is vastly weaker in a gravity field," Royd said. "She has to fight it. Even boosted by the *Nightflyer*'s power, she can only move one object at a time, and she has only a fraction of the lifting force she wields under weightless conditions. But the power is still there, remember. Also, it is possible she will find a way to circumvent me and cut out the gravity again. From here I can restore it in an instant, but I don't want any likely weapons lying around even for that brief period of time."

Melantha reached the cargo area. She stripped off her vacuum suit and slipped into another one in record time, wincing at the pain in her shoulder. It was bleeding badly, but she had to ignore it. She gathered up the discarded suit and a double armful of instruments and dumped them into the conversion chamber. Afterwards she turned her attention to the bodies. Dannel was no problem. Lindran crawled down the corridor after her as she pushed him through, and thrashed weakly when it was her own turn, a grim reminder that the *Nightflyer*'s powers were not all gone. Melantha easily overcame her feeble struggles and forced her through.

Christopheris' burned, ruined body writhed in her grasp and snapped its teeth at her, but Melantha had no real trouble with it. While she was cleaning out the lounge, a kitchen knife came spinning at her head. It came slowly, though, and Melantha just batted it aside, then picked it up and added it to the pile for conversion. She was working through the cabins, carrying Agatha Marij-Black's abandoned drugs and injection gun under her arm, when she heard Royd cry out.

A moment later a force like a giant invisible hand wrapped

itself around her chest and squeezed and pulled her, struggling, to the floor.

Something was moving across the stars.

Dimly and far off, d'Branin could see it, though he could not yet make out details. But it was there, that was unmistakable, some vast shape that blocked off a section of the starscape. It was coming at them dead on.

How he wished he he had his team with him now, his computer, his telepath, his experts, his instruments.

He pressed harder on the thrusters, and rushed to meet his *volcryn*.

Pinned to the floor, hurting, Melantha Jhirl risked opening her suit's comm. She had to talk to Royd. "Are you there?" she asked. "What's happen . . . happening?" The pressure was awful, and it was growing steadily worse. She could barely move.

The answer was pained and slow in coming. ". . . outwitted . . . me," Royd's voice managed. ". . . hurts . . . to . . . talk."

"Royd—"

". . . she . . . teked . . . the . . . dial . . . up . . . two . . . gees . . . three . . . higher . . . right . . . here . . . on . . . the . . . board . . . all . . . I . . . have to . . . to do . . . turn it . . . back . . . back . . . let me."

Silence. Then, finally, when Melantha was near despair, Royd's voice again. One word:

". . . can't . . ."

Melantha's chest felt as if it were supporting ten times her own weight. She could imagine the agony Royd must be in; Royd, for whom even one gravity was painful and dangerous. Even if the dial was an arm's length away, she knew his feeble musculature would never let him reach it. "Why," she started. Talking was not as hard for her as it seemed to be

for him. "Why would . . . she turn *up* the . . . the gravity
. . . it . . . weakens her, too . . . yes?"

". . . yes . . . but . . . in a . . . a time . . . hour . . .
minute . . . my . . . my heart . . . will burst . . . and . . .
and then . . . you alone . . . she . . . will . . . kill gravity
. . . kill you . . ."

Painfully Melantha reached out her arm and dragged herself half a length down the corridor. "Royd . . . hold on . . .
I'm coming . . ." She dragged herself forward again. Agatha's
drug kit was still under her arm, impossibly heavy. She eased
it down and started to shove it aside. It felt as if weighed a
hundred kilos. She reconsidered. Instead she opened its lid.

The ampules were all neatly labeled. She glanced over
them quickly, searching for adrenaline or synthastim, anything that might give her the strength she needed to reach
Royd. She found several stimulants, selected the strongest,
and was loading it into the injection gun with awkward,
agonized slowness when her eyes chanced on the supply of
esperon.

Melantha did not know why she hesitated. Esperon was
only one of a half-dozen psionic drugs in the kit, none of
which could do her any good, but something about seeing it
bothered her, reminded her of something she could not quite
lay her finger on. She was trying to sort it out when she
heard the noise.

"Royd," she said, "your mother . . . could she move . . .
she couldn't move anything . . . teke it . . . in this high a
gravity . . . could she?"

"Maybe," he answered, ". . . if . . . concentrate . . . all
her . . . power . . . hard . . . maybe possible . . . why?"

"Because," Melantha Jhirl said grimly, "because something . . . some*one* . . . is cycling through the airlock."

"It is not truly a ship, not as I thought it would be," Karoly
d'Branin was saying. His suit, Academy-designed, had a
built-in encoding device, and he was recording his comments

for posterity, strangely secure in the certainty of his impending death. "The scale of it is difficult to imagine, difficult to estimate. Vast, vast. I have nothing but my wrist computer, no instruments, I cannot make accurate measurements, but I would say, oh, a hundred kilometers, perhaps as much as three hundred, across. Not solid mass, of course, not at all. It is delicate, airy, no ship as we know ships, no city either. It is—oh, beautiful—it is crystal and gossamer, alive with its own dim lights, a vast intricate kind of spiderwebby craft—it reminds me a bit of the old starsail ships they used once, in the days before drive, but this great construct, it is not solid, it cannot be driven by light. It is no ship at all, really. It is all open to vacuum, it has no sealed cabins or life-support spheres, none visible to me, unless blocked from my line of sight in some fashion, and no, I cannot believe that, it is too open, too fragile. It moves quite rapidly. I would wish for the instrumentation to measure its speed, but it is enough to be here. I am taking the sled at right angles to it, to get clear of its path, but I cannot say that I will make it. It moves so much faster than we. Not at light speed, no, far below light speed, but still faster than the *Nightflyer* and its nuclear engines, I would guess . . . only a guess.

"The *volcryn* craft has no visible means of propulsion. In fact, I wonder how—perhaps it is a light-sail, laser-launched millenia ago, now torn and rotted by some unimaginable catastrophe—but no, it is too symmetrical, too beautiful, the webbings, the great shimmering veils near the nexus, the beauty of it.

"I must describe it, I must be more accurate, I know. It is difficult, I grow too excited. It is large, as I have said, kilometers across. Roughly—let me count—yes, roughly octagonal in shape. The nexus, the center, is a bright area, a small darkness surrounded by a much greater area of light, but only the dark portion seems entirely solid—the lighted areas are translucent, I can see stars through them, though discolored, shifted towards the purple. Veils, I call those the veils. From the nexus and the veils eight long—oh, vastly long—spurs project, not quite spaced evenly, so it is not a true geometric octagon—ah, I see better now, one of the spurs is shifting, oh, very slowly, the veils are rippling—they are mobile then, those projections, and the webbing runs from one spur to the next, around and around, but there are—patterns, odd patterns, it is not at all the simple webbing of a spider. I cannot quite see order in the patterns, in the traceries of the webs, but I feel sure the order is there, the meaning is waiting to be found.

"There are lights. Have I mentioned the lights? The lights are brightest around the center nexus, but they are nowhere very bright, a dim violet. Some visible radiation then, but not much. I would like to take an ultraviolet reading of this craft, but I do not have the instrumentation. The lights move. The veils seem to ripple, and lights run constantly up and down the length of the spurs, at differing rates of speed, and sometimes other lights can be seen transversing the webbing, moving across the patterns. I do not know what the lights are. Some form of communication, perhaps. I cannot tell whether they emanate from inside the craft or outside. I—oh! There was another light just then. Between the spurs, a brief flash, a starburst. It is gone now, already. It was more intense than the others, indigo. I feel so helpless, so ignorant. But they are beautiful, my *volcryn* . . .

"The myths, they—this is really not much like the legends, not truly. The size, the lights. The *volcryn* have often been linked to lights, but those reports were so vague, they might have meant anything, described anything from a laser propulsion system to simple exterior lighting. I could not know it meant this. Ah, what mystery! The ship is still too far away to see the finer detail. It is so large, I do not think we shall get clear of it. It seems to have turned towards us, I think, yet I may be mistaken, it is only an impression. My instruments, if I only had my instruments. Perhaps the darker area in the center is a craft, a life capsule. The *volcryn* must be inside it. I wish my team were with me, and Thale, poor Thale. He was a class one, we might have made contact, might have communicated with them. The things we would learn! The things they have seen! To think how old this craft is, how ancient the race, how long they have been outbound . . . it fills me with awe. Communication would be such a gift, such an impossible gift, but they are so alien."

"*D'Branin*," Agatha Marij-Black said in a low, urgent voice. "Can't you feel?"

Karoly d'Branin looked at her as if seeing her for the first time. "Can *you* feel them? You are a three, can you sense them now, strongly?"

"Long ago," the psipsych said, "long ago."

"Can you project? Talk to them, Agatha. Where are they? In the center area? The dark?"

"Yes," she replied, and she laughed. Her laugh was shrill and hysterical, and d'Branin had to recall that she was a very sick woman. "Yes, in the center, d'Branin, that's where the pulses come from. Only you're wrong about them. It's not a *them* at all, your legends are all lies, lies, I wouldn't be surprised if we were the first ever to see your *volcryn*, to come this close. The others, those aliens of yours, they merely *felt*, deep and distantly, sensed a bit of the nature of the *volcryn* in their dreams and visions, and fashioned the rest to suit themselves. Ships, and wars, and a race of eternal travellers, it is all—all—"

"Yes. What do you mean, Agatha, my friend? You do not make sense. I do not understand."

"No," Marij-Black said, "you do not, do you?" Her voice was suddenly gentle. "You cannot feel it, as I can. So clear now. This must be how a one feels, all the time. A one full of esperon."

"What do you feel? *What*?"

"It's not a *them*, Karoly. It's an *it*. Alive, Karoly, and quite mindless, I assure you."

"Mindless?" d'Branin said. "No, you must be wrong,

you are not reading correctly. I will accept that it is a single
creature if you say so, a single great marvelous star-traveller,
but how can it be mindless? You sensed it, its mind, its
telepathic emanations. You and the whole of the Crey sensitives and all the others. Perhaps its thoughts are too alien for
you to read.''

"Perhaps. But what I do read is not so terribly alien at all.
Only animal. Its thoughts are slow and dark and strange,
hardly thoughts at all, faint. Stirrings cold and distant. The
brain must be huge all right, I grant you that, but it can't be
devoted to conscious thought.''

"What do you mean?''

"The propulsion system, d'Branin. Don't you *feel*? The
pulses? They are threatening to rip off the top of my skull.
Can't you guess what is driving your damned *volcryn* across
the galaxy? And why they avoid gravity wells? Can't you
guess how it is moving?''

"No,'' d'Branin said, but even as he denied it a dawn of
comprehension broke across his face, and he looked away
from his companion, back at the swelling immensity of the
volcryn, its lights moving, its veils a-ripple as it came on and
on, across light years, light centuries, across eons.

When he looked back at her, he mouthed only a single
word: "Teke,'' he said.

She nodded.

Melantha Jhirl struggled to lift the injection gun and press
it against an artery. It gave a single loud hiss, and the drug
flooded her system. She lay back and gathered her strength
and tried to think. Esperon, esperon, why was that important? It had killed Lasamer, made him a victim of his own
latent abilities, multiplied his power and his vulnerability.
Psi. It all came back to psi.

The inner door of the airlock opened. The headless corpse
came through.

It moved with jerks, unnatural shufflings, never lifting its legs from the floor. It sagged as it moved, half-crushed by the weight upon it. Each shuffle was crude and sudden; some grim force was literally yanking one leg forward, then the next. It moved in slow motion, arms stiff by its sides.

But it moved.

Melantha summoned her own reserves and began to squirm away from it, never taking her eyes off its advance.

Her thoughts went round and round, searching for the piece out of place, the solution to the chess problem, finding nothing.

The corpse was moving faster than she was. Clearly, visibly, it was gaining.

Melantha tried to stand. She got to her knees with a grunt, her heart pounding. Then one knee. She tried to force herself up, to lift the impossible burden on her shoulders as if she were lifting weights. She was strong, she told herself. She was the improved model.

But when she put all her weight on one leg, her muscles would not hold her. She collapsed, awkwardly, and when she smashed against the floor it was as if she had fallen from a building. She heard a sharp *snap*, and a stab of agony flashed up her arm, her good arm, the arm she had tried to use to break her fall. The pain in her shoulder was terrible and intense. She blinked back tears and choked on her own scream.

The corpse was halfway up the corridor. It must be walking on two broken legs, she realized. It didn't care. A force greater than tendons and bone and muscle was holding it up.

"Melantha . . . heard you . . . are . . . you . . . Melantha?"

"*Quiet*," she snarled at Royd. She had no breath to waste on talk.

Now she used all the disciplines she had ever learned, willed away the pain. She kicked feebly, her boots scraping for purchase, and she pulled herself forward with her unbroken arm, ignoring the fire in her shoulder.

The corpse came on and on.

She dragged herself across the threshold of the lounge, worming her way under the crashed sled, hoping it would delay the cadaver. The thing that had been Thale Lasamer was a meter behind her.

In the darkness, in the lounge, where it had all begun, Melantha Jhirl ran out of strength.

Her body shuddered and she collapsed on the damp carpet, and she knew that she could go no further.

On the far side of the door, the corpse stood stiffly. The sled began to shake. Then, with the scrape of metal against metal, it slid backwards, moving in tiny sudden increments, jerking itself free and out of the way.

Psi. Melantha wanted to curse it, and cry. Vainly she wished for a psi power of her own, a weapon to blast apart the teke-driven corpse that stalked her. She was improved, she thought despairingly, but not improved enough. Her parents had given her all the genetic gifts they could arrange, but psi was beyond them. The genes were astronomically rare, recessive, and—

—and suddenly it came to her.

"Royd," she said, putting all of her remaining will into her words. She was weeping, wet, frightened. "The dial . . . *teke it*. Royd, teke it!"

His reply was faint, troubled. ". . . can't . . . I don't . . . Mother . . . only . . . her . . . not me . . . no . . . Mother . . ."

"Not Mother," she said, desperate. "You always . . . say . . . *Mother*. I forgot . . . forgot. Not your Mother . . . listen . . . you're a *clone* . . . same genes . . . you have it too . . . power."

"Don't," he said. "Never . . . must-be . . . sex-linked."

"No! It *isn't*. I know . . . Promethean, Royd . . . don't tell a Promethean . . . about genes . . . turn it!"

The sled jumped a third of a meter, and listed to the side. A path was clear.

The corpse came forward.

". . . trying," Royd said. "Nothing . . . I *can't*!"

"She *cured* you," Melantha said bitterly. "Better than . . . she . . . was cured . . . pre-natal . . . but it's only . . . suppressed . . . you *can*!"

"I . . . don't . . . know . . . how."

The corpse stood above her. Stopped. Its pale-fleshed hands trembled, spasmed, jerked upward. Long painted fingernails. Made claws. Began to rise.

Melantha swore. "*Royd*!"

". . . sorry . . ."

She wept and shook and made a futile fist.

And all at once the gravity was gone. Far, far away, she heard Royd cry out and then fall silent.

"The flashes come more frequently now," Karoly d'Branin dictated, "or perhaps it is simply that I am closer, that I can see them better. Bursts of indigo and deep violet, short, and fast-fading. Between the webbing. A field, I think. The flashes are particles of hydrogen, the thin ethereal stuff of the reaches between the stars. They touch the field, between the webbing, the spurs, and shortly flare into the range of visible light. Matter to energy, yes, that is what I guess. My *volcryn* feeds.

"It fills half the universe, comes on and on. We shall not escape it, oh, so sad. Agatha is gone, silent, blood on her faceplate. I can almost see the dark area, almost, almost. I have a strange vision, in the center is a face, small, rat-like, without mouth or nose or eyes, yet still a face somehow, and it stares at me. The veils move so sensuously. The webbing looms around us.

"Ah, the light, the light!"

The corpse bobbed awkwardly into the air, its hands hanging limply before it. Melantha, reeling in the weightlessness, was suddenly violently sick. She ripped off the helmet, collapsed it, and pushed away from her own nausea, trying to ready herself for the *Nightflyer*'s furious assault.

But the body of Thale Lasamer floated dead and still, and nothing else moved in the darkened lounge. Finally Melantha recovered, and she moved to the corpse, weakly, and pushed it, a small and tentative shove. It sailed across the room.

"Royd?" she said uncertainly.

There was no answer.

She pulled herself through the hole into the control chamber.

And found Royd Eris suspended in his armored suit. She shook him, but he did not stir. Trembling, Melantha Jhirl studied his suit, and then began to dismantle it. She touched him. "Royd," she said, "here. Feel, Royd, here, I'm here, feel it." His suit came apart easily, and she flung the pieces of it away. "Royd, *Royd*."

Dead. Dead. His heart had given out. She punched it, pummeled it, tried to pound it into new life. It did not beat. Dead. Dead.

Melantha Jhirl moved back from him, blinded by her own tears, edged into the console, glanced down.

Dead. Dead.

But the dial on the gravity grid was set on zero.

"Melantha," said a mellow voice from the walls.

I have held the *Nightflyer*'s crystalline soul within my hands.

It is deep red and multi-faceted, large as my head, and icy to the touch. In its scarlet depths, two small sparks of smoky light burn fiercely, and sometimes seem to whirl.

I have crawled through the consoles, wound my way carefully past safeguards and cybernets, taking care to damage nothing, and I have laid rough hands on that great crystal, knowing it is where *she* lives.

And I cannot bring myself to wipe it.

Royd's ghost has asked me not to.

Last night we talked about it once again, over brandy and

chess in the lounge. Royd cannot drink, of course, but he sends his spectre to smile at me, and he tells me where he wants his pieces moved.

For the thousandth time he offered to take me back to Avalon, or any world of my choice, if only I would go outside and complete the repairs we abandoned so many years ago, so the *Nightflyer* might safely slip into stardrive.

For the thousandth time I refused.

He is stronger now, no doubt. Their genes are the same, after all. Their power is the same. Dying, he too found the strength to impress himself upon the great crystal. The ship is alive with both of them, and frequently they fight. Sometimes she outwits him for a moment, and the *Nightflyer* does odd, erratic things. The gravity goes up or down or off completely. Blankets wrap themselves around my throat when I sleep. Objects come hurtling out of dark corners.

Those times have come less frequently of late, though. When they do come, Royd stops her, or I do. Together, the *Nightflyer* is ours.

Royd claims he is strong enough alone, that he does not really need me, that he can keep her under check. I wonder. Over the chessboard, I still beat him nine games out of ten.

And there are other considerations. Our work, for one. Karoly would be proud of us. The *volcryn* will soon enter the mists of the Tempter's Veil, and we follow close behind. Studying, recording, doing all that old d'Branin would have wanted us to do. It is all in the computer, and on tape and paper as well, should the system ever be wiped. It will be interesting to see how the *volcryn* thrives in the Veil. Matter is so thick there, compared to the thin diet of interstellar hydrogen on which the creature has fed so many endless eons.

We have tried to communicate with it, with no success. I do not believe it is sentient at all. And lately Royd has tried to imitate its ways, gathering all his energies in an attempt to move the *Nightflyer* by teke. Sometimes, oddly, his mother even joins with him in those efforts. So far they have always failed, but we will keep trying.

So goes our work. We know our results will reach humanity. Royd and I have discussed it, and we have a plan. Before I die, when my time is near, I will destroy the central crystal and clear the computers, and afterwards I will set course manually for the close vicinity of an inhabited world. The *Nightflyer* will become a true ghost ship then. It will work. I have all the time I need, and I am an improved model.

I will not consider the other option, although it means much to me that Royd suggests it again and again. No doubt I could finish the repairs, and perhaps Royd could control the ship without me, and go on with the work. But that is not important.

I was wrong so many times. The esperon, the monitors, my control of the others; all of them my failures, payment for my *hubris*. Failure hurts. When I finally touched him, for the first and last and only time, his body was still warm. But *he* was gone already. He never felt my touch. I could not keep that promise.

But I can keep my other.

I will not leave him alone with her.

Ever.

Dubuque, Iowa
November 1978

Override

DUSK WAS SETTLING SOFTLY OVER THE HIGH LAKES AS KABA-raijian and his crew made their way home from the caves. It was a calm, quiet dusk; a twilight blended of green waters, and mellow night winds, and the slow fading of Grotto's gentle sun. From the rear of his launch Kabaraijian watched it fall, and listened to the sounds of twilight over the purring of the engine.

Grotto was a quiet world, but the sounds were there, if you knew how to listen. Kabaraijian knew. He sat erect in the back of the boat, a slight figure with swarthy skin, and long black hair, and brown eyes that drifted dreamy. One thin hand rested on his knee, the other, forgotten, on the motor. And his ears listened to the bubbling of the water in the wake of the launch, and the swish-splash of the lakeleapers breaking surface, and the wind moving the trailing green branches of the trees along the near shore. In time, he'd hear the nightflyers, too, but they were not yet up.

There were four in the boat, but only Kabaraijian listened or heard. The others, bigger men with pasty faces and vacant eyes, were long past hearing. They wore the dull gray coveralls of deadmen, and there was a steel plate in the back of each man's skull. Sometimes, when his corpse controller was on, Kabaraijian could listen with their ears, and see with their eyes. But that was work, hard work, and not worth it. The sights and sounds a corpse handler felt through his crew were pale echoes of real sensation, seldom useful and never pleasurable.

And now, Grotto's cooling dusk, was an off-time. So Kabaraijian's corpse controller was off, and his mind, disengaged from the dead men, rested easy in its own body. The launch moved purposefully along the lake shore, but Kabaraijian's thoughts wandered lazily, when he thought at all. Mostly he just sat, and watched the water and the trees, and listened. He'd worked the corpse crew hard that day, and now he was drained and empty. Thought—thought especially— was more effort than he was prepared to give. Better to just linger with the evening.

It was a long, quiet voyage, across two big lakes and one small one, through a cave, and finally up a narrow and swift-running river. Kabaraijian turned up the power then, and the trip grew noisier as the launch sliced a path through the river's flow. Night had settled before he reached the station, a rambling structure of blue-black stone set by the river's edge. But the office windows still glowed with a cheery yellow light.

A long dock of native silverwood fronted the river, and a dozen launches identical to Kabaraijian's were already tied up for the night. But there were still empty berths. Kabaraijian took one of them, and guided the boat into it.

When the launch was secure, he slung his collection box under one arm, and hopped out onto the dock. His free hand went to his belt, and thumbed the corpse controller. Vague sense blurs drifted into his mind, but Kabaraijian shunted them aside, and shook the dead men alive with an unheard shout. The corpses rose, one by one, and stepped out of the launch. Then they followed Kabaraijian to the station.

Munson was waiting inside the office—a fat, scruffy man with gray hair, and wrinkles around his eyes, and a fatherly manner. He had his feet up on his desk and was reading a novel. When Kabaraijian entered, he smiled and sat up and put down the book, inserting his leather placemark carefully. " 'Lo, Matt," he said. "Why are you always the last one in?"

"Because I'm usually the last one out," Kabaraijian said, smiling. It was his newest line. Munson asked the same question every night, and always expected Kabaraijian to come up with a fresh answer. He seemed only moderately pleased by this one.

Kabaraijian set the collection box down on Munson's desk and opened it. "Not a bad day," he said. "Four good stones, and twelve smaller ones."

Munson scooped a handful of small, grayish rocks from inside the padded metal box and studied them. Right now they weren't much to look at. But cut and polished they'd be something else again: swirlstones. They were gems without fire, but they had their own beauty. Good ones looked like crystals of moving fog, full of soft colors and softer mysteries and dreams.

Munson nodded, and dropped the stones back into the box. "Not bad," he said. "You always do good, Matt. You know where to look."

"The rewards of coming back slow and easy," Kabaraijian said. "I look around me."

Munson put the box under his desk, and turned to his computer console, a white plastic intruder in the wood-paneled room. He entered the swirlstones into the records, and looked back up. "You want to wash down your corpses?"

Kabaraijian shook his head. "Not tonight. I'm tired. I'll just flop them for now."

"Sure," said Munson. He rose, and opened the door behind his desk. Kabaraijian followed him, and the three dead men followed Kabaraijian. Behind the office were barracks, long and low-roofed, with row on row of simple wooden bunks. Most of them were full. Kabaraijian guided his dead men to three empty ones and maneuvered them in. Then he thumbed his controller off. The echoes in his head blinked out, and the corpses sagged heavily into the bunks.

Afterwards, he chatted with Munson for a few minutes back in the office. Finally, the old man went back to his novel, and Kabaraijian back to the cool night.

A row of company scooters sat in back of the station, but Kabaraijian left them alone, preferring the ten-minute walk from the river to the settlement. He covered the forest road with an easy, measured pace, pausing here and there to brush aside vines and low branches. It was always a pleasant walk. The nights were calm, the breezes fragrant with the fruity scent of local trees and heavy with the songs of the nightflyers.

The settlement was bigger and brighter and louder than the river station; a thick clot of houses and bars and shops built alongside the spaceport. There were a few structures of wood and stone, but most of the settlers were still content with the plastic prefabs the company had given them free.

Kabaraijian drifted through the new-paved streets, to one of the outnumbered wooden buildings. There was a heavy wooden sign over the tavern door, but no lights. Inside he found candles and heavy, stuffed chairs, and a real log fire. It was a cozy place, the oldest bar on Grotto, and still the favorite watering hole for corpse handlers and hunters and other river station personnel.

A loud shout greeted him when he entered. "Hey! Matt! Over here!"

Kabaraijian found the voice, and followed it to a table in the corner, where Ed Cochran was nursing a mug of beer. Cochran, like Kabaraijian, wore the blue-and-white tunic of a corpse handler. He was tall and lean, with a thin face that grinned a lot and a mass of tangled red-blond hair.

Kabaraijian sank gratefully into the chair opposite him. Cochran grinned. "Beer?" he asked. "We could split a pitcher."

"No thanks. I feel like wine tonight. Something rich and mellow and slow."

"How'd it go?" said Cochran.

Kabaraijian shrugged. "O.K.," he said. "Four nice stones,

a dozen little ones. Munson gave me a good estimate. To-morrow should be better. I found a nice new place." He turned toward the bar briefly, and gestured. The bartender nodded, and the wine and glasses arrived a few minutes later.

Kabaraijian poured and sipped while Cochran discussed his day. It hadn't gone well; only six stones, none of them very big.

"You've got to range farther," Kabaraijian told him. "The caves around here have been pretty well worked out. But the High Lakes go on and on. Find someplace new."

"Why bother?" Cochran said, frowning. "Don't get to keep them anyway. What's the percentage in knocking yourself out?"

Kabaraijian twirled the wine glass slowly in a thin, dark hand, and watched the dream-red depths. "Poor Ed," he said, in a voice half-sadness and half-mockery. "All you see is the work. Grotto is a pretty planet. I don't *mind* the extra miles, Ed, I enjoy them. I'd probably travel in my off-time if they didn't pay me to do it. The fact that I get bigger swirlstones and my estimates go up—well, that's extra gravy."

Cochran smiled and shook his head. "You're crazy, Matt," he said affectionately. "Only corpse handler in the universe who'd be happy if they paid him off with scenery."

Kabaraijian smiled too, a slight lifting at the corners of his mouth. "Philistine," he said accusingly.

Cochran ordered another beer. "Look, Matt, you've got to be practical. Sure, Grotto is O.K., but you're not gonna be here all your life." He set down his beer, and pulled up the sleeve of his tunic, to flash his heavy wristlet. The gold shone softly in the candlelight, and the sapphires danced with dark blue flame. "Junk like this was valuable once," Cochran said, "before they learned how to synthesize it. They'll crack swirlstones, too, Matt. You know they will. They already have people working on it. So maybe you've got two years left, or three. But what then? Then they won't need corpse handlers anymore. So you'll move on, no better off than when you first landed."

"Not really," said Kabaraijian. "The station pays pretty good, and my estimates haven't been bad. I've got some money put away. Besides, maybe I won't move on. I like Grotto. Maybe I'll stay, and join the colonists, or something."

"Doing what? Farming? Working in an office? Don't give me that crap, Matt. You're a corpse handler, always will be. And in a couple years Grotto won't need corpses."

Kabaraijian sighed. "So?" he said. "So?"

Cochran leaned forward. "So have you thought about what I told you?"

"Yes," Kabaraijian said. "But I don't like it. I don't think it would work, first of all. Spaceport security is tight to keep people from smuggling out swirlstones, and you want to do just that. And even if it would work, I don't want any part of it. I'm sorry, Ed."

"I think it *would* work," Cochran said stubbornly. "The spaceport people are human. They can be tempted. Why should the company get all the swirlstones when we do all the work?"

"They've got the concession," Kabaraijian said.

Cochran waved him silent. "Yeah, sure. So what? By what right? We *deserve* some, for ourselves, while the damn things are still valuable."

Kabaraijian sighed again, and poured himself another glass of wine. "Look," he said, lifting the glass to his lips, "I don't quarrel with that. Maybe they should pay us more, or give us an interest in the swirlstones. But it's not worth the risk. We'll lose our crews if they catch us. *And* we'll get expelled.

"I don't want that, Ed, and I won't risk it. Grotto is too good to me, and I'm not going to throw it away. You know, some people would say we're pretty lucky. Most corpse handlers never get to work a place like Grotto. They wind up on the assembly lines of Skrakky, or in the mines of New Pittsburg. I've seen those places. No thanks. I'm not going to risk returning to *that* sort of life."

Cochran threw imploring eyes up to the ceiling, and spread his hands helplessly. "Hopeless," he said, shaking his head. "Hopeless." Then he returned to his beer. Kabaraijian was smiling.

But his amusement died short minutes later, when Cochran suddenly stiffened and grimaced across the table. "Damn," he said. "Bartling. What the hell does *he* want here?"

Kabaraijian turned toward the door, where the newcomer was standing and waiting for his eyes to adjust to the dim light. He was a big man, with an athletic frame that had gone to pot over the years and now sported a considerable paunch. He had dark hair streaked with white and a bristling black beard, and he was wearing a fashionable multicolored tunic.

Four others had entered behind him, and now stood flanking him on either side. They were younger men than he was, and bigger, with hard faces and impressive builds. The bodyguards made sense. Lowell Bartling was widely known for his dislike of corpse handlers, and the tavern was full of them.

Bartling crossed his arms, and looked around the room slowly. He was smirking. He started to speak.

Almost before he got the first word out of his mouth, he was interrupted. One of the men along the bar emitted a loud, rude noise, and laughed. "Hiya, Bartling," he said. "What are you doing down here? Thought you didn't associate with us low-lifes?"

Bartling's face tightened, but his smirk was untouched. "Normally I don't, but I wanted the pleasure of making this announcement personally."

"You're leaving Grotto!" someone shouted. There was laughter all along the bar. "I'll drink to that," another voice added.

"No," said Bartling. "No, friend, *you* are." He looked around, savoring the moment. "Bartling Associates has just acquired the swirlstone concession, I'm happy to tell you. I take over management of the river station at the end of the month. And, of course, my first act will be to terminate the employment of all the corpse handlers currently under contract.''

Suddenly the room was very silent, as the implications of that sank in. In the corner in the back of the room, Cochran rose slowly to his feet. Kabaraijian remained seated, stunned.

"You can't do that," Cochran said belligerently. "We've got contracts."

Bartling turned to face him. "Those contracts can be broken," he said, "and they will be."

"You son of a bitch," someone said.

The bodyguard tensed. "Watch who you call names, meatmind," one of them answered. All around the room, men started getting to their feet.

Cochran was livid with anger. "Damn you, Bartling," he said. "Who the hell do you think you are? You've got no right to run us off the planet."

"I have every right," Bartling said. "Grotto is a good, clean, beautiful planet. There's no place here for your kind. It was a mistake to bring you in, and I've said so all along. Those *things* you work with contaminate the air. And you're even worse. You work with those things, those corpses, *voluntarily,* for money. You disgust me. You don't belong on Grotto. And now I'm in a position to see that you leave." He paused, then smiled. "Meatmind," he added, spitting out the word.

"Bartling, I'm going to knock your head off," one of the handlers bellowed. There was a roar of agreement. Several men started forward at once.

And jerked to a sudden stop when Kabaraijian interjected a soft, "No, wait," over the general hubbub. He hardly raised his voice at all, but it still commanded attention in the room of shouting men.

He walked through the crowd and faced Bartling, looking much calmer than he felt. "You realize that without corpse labor your costs will go way up," he said in a steady, reasonable voice, "and your profits down."

Bartling nodded. "Of course I realize it. I'm willing to take the loss. We'll use *men* to mine the swirlstones. They're too beautiful for corpses, anyway."

"You'll be losing money for nothing," Kabaraijian said.

"Hardly. I'll get rid of your stinking corpses."

Kabaraijian cracked a thin smile. "Maybe some. But not all of us, Mr. Bartling. You can take away our jobs, perhaps, but you can't throw us off Grotto. I for one refuse to go."

"Then you'll starve."

"Don't be so melodramatic. I'll find something else to do. You don't own all of Grotto. And I'll keep my corpses. Dead men can be used for a lot of things. It's just that we haven't thought of them all yet."

Bartling's smirk had vanished suddenly. "If you stay," he said, fixing Kabaraijian with a hard stare, "I promise to make you very, very sorry."

Kabaraijian laughed. "Really? Well, personally, I promise to send one of my deadmen by your house every night after you go to bed, to make hideous faces at the window and moan." He laughed again, louder. Cochran joined him, then others. Soon the whole tavern was laughing.

Bartling turned red and began a slow burn. He came here to taunt his enemies, to crow his triumph, and now they were laughing at him. Laughing in the face of victory, cheating him. He seethed a long minute, then turned and walked furiously out the door. His bodyguards followed.

The laughter lingered a while after his exit, and several of the other handlers slapped Kabaraijian on the back as he made his way back to his seat. Cochran was happy about it too. "You really took the old man apart," he said when they reached the corner table.

But Kabaraijian wasn't smiling anymore. He slumped down into his seat heavily, and reached almost immediately for the wine. "I sure did," he said slowly, between sips. "I sure did."

Cochran looked at him curiously "You don't seem too happy."

"No," said Kabaraijian. He studied his wine. "I'm having second thoughts. That insufferable bigot riled me, made me want to get to him. Only I wonder if I can pull it off. What *can* corpses do on Grotto?"

His eyes wandered around the tavern, which had suddenly become very somber. "It's sinking in," he told Cochran. "I'll bet they're all talking about leaving . . ."

Cochran had stopped grinning. "Some of us will stay," he said uncertainly. "We can farm with the corpses, or something."

Kabaraijian looked at him. "Uh-uh. Machinery is more efficient for farming. And deadmen are too clumsy for anything but the crudest kind of labor, much too slow for hunting." He poured more wine, and mused aloud. "They're O.K. for cheap factory labor, or running an automole in a mine. But Grotto doesn't have any of that. They can hack out swirlstones with a vibrodrill, only Bartling is taking that away from us." He shook his head.

"I don't know, Ed," he continued. "It's not going to be easy. And maybe it'll be impossible. With the swirlstone concession under his belt, Bartling is bigger than the settlement company now."

"That was the idea. The company sets us up, and we buy it out as we grow."

"True. But Bartling grew a little too fast. He can really start throwing his weight around now. It wouldn't surprise me if he amended the charter, to keep corpses off-planet. That *would* force us out."

"Can he get away with that?" Cochran was getting angry again, and his voice rose slightly.

"Maybe," Kabaraijian said, "if we let him. I wonder . . ." He sloshed his wine thoughtfully. "You think this deal of his is final?"

Cochran looked puzzled. "He said he had it."

"Yes. I don't suppose he'd crow about it if it wasn't in his pocket. Still, I'm curious what the company would do if someone made them a better offer."

"Who?"

"Us, maybe?" Kabaraijian sipped his wine and considered that. "Get all the handlers together, everybody puts in whatever they have. That should give us a fair sum. Maybe we could buy out the river station ourselves. Or something else, if Bartling has the swirlstones all locked up. It's an idea."

"Nah, it'd never work," Cochran said. "Maybe you've got some money, Matt, but I sure as hell don't. Spent most of it here. Besides, even the guys that have money, you'd never be able to get them together."

"Maybe not," Kabaraijian said. "But it's worth trying. Organizing against Bartling is the only way we're going to be able to keep ourselves on Grotto in the long run."

Cochran drained his beer, and signaled for another. "Nah," he said. "Bartling's too big. He'll slap you down hard if you bother him too much. I got a better idea."

"Swirlstone smuggling," Kabaraijian said, smiling.

"Yeah," Cochran said with a nod. "Maybe now you'll reconsider. If Bartling's gonna throw us off-planet, at least we can take some of his swirlstones with us. That'd set us up good wherever we go."

"You're incorrigible," Kabaraijian said. "But I'll bet half the handlers on Grotto will try the same thing now. Bartling will expect that. He'll have the spaceport screwed up tight when we start leaving. He'll catch you, Ed. And you'll lose your crew, or worse. Bartling might even try to force through deadman laws, and start exporting corpses."

Cochran looked uneasy at that. Corpse handlers saw too much of deadmen to relish the idea of becoming one. They tended to cluster on planets without deadman laws, where capital crimes still drew prison terms or "clean" executions. Grotto was a clean planet now, but laws can change.

"I might lose my crew anyway, Matt," Cochran said. "If Bartling throws us out, I'll have to sell some of my corpses for passage money."

Kabaraijian smiled. "You still have a month, even with

the worst. And there are pleny of swirlstones out there for the finding.'' He raised his glass. "Come. To Grotto. It's a lovely planet, and we may stay here yet."

Cochran shrugged and lifted his beer. "Yeah," he said. But his grin didn't hide his worry.

Kabaraijian reported to the station early the next morning, when Grotto's sun was fighting to dispel the river mists. The row of empty launches was still tied to the dock, bobbing up and down in the rapidly thinning fog.

Munson was inside the office, as always. So, surprisingly, was Cochran. Both of them looked up when Kabaraijian entered.

"Morning, Matt," Munson said gravely. "Ed's been telling me about last night." Today, for some reason, he looked his age. "I'm sorry, Matt. I didn't know anything about it."

Kabaraijian smiled. "I never thought you did. If you *do* hear anything, though, let me know. We're not going to go without a fight." He looked at Cochran. "What are you doing here so early? Usually you're not up until the crack of noon."

Cochran grinned. "Yeah. Well, I figured I'd start early. I'm going to need good estimates this month, if I want to save my crew."

Munson had dug two collection boxes out from under his desk. He handed them to the two corpse handlers, and nodded. "Back room's open," he said. "You can pick up your deadmen whenever you like."

Kabaraijian started to circle the desk, but Cochran grabbed his arm. "I think I'll try way east," he said. "Some caves there that haven't really been hit yet. Where you going?"

"West," said Kabaraijian. "I found a good new place, like I told you."

Cochran nodded. They went to the back room together, and thumbed their controllers. Five deadmen stumbled from their bunks and followed them, shuffling, from the office.

Kabaraijian thanked Munson before he left. The old man had washed down his corpses anyway, and fed them.

The mists were just about gone when they reached the dock. Kabaraijian marched his crew into the boat and got set to cast off. But Cochran stopped him, looking troubled.

"Uh—Matt," he said, standing on the dock and staring down into the launch. "This new place—you say it's real good?"

Kabaraijian nodded, squinting. The sun was just clearing the treetops, and framing Cochran's head.

"Can I talk you into splitting?" Cochran said, with difficulty. It was an unusual request. The practice was for each handler to range alone, to find and mine his own swirlstone cave. "I mean, with only a month left, you probably won't have time to get everything, not if the place is as good as you say. And I need good estimates, I really do."

Kabaraijian could see that it wasn't an easy favor to ask. He smiled. "Sure," he said. "There's plenty there. Get your launch and follow me."

Cochran nodded and forced a grin. He walked down the dock to his launch, his dead men trailing behind.

Going downriver was easier than going up, and faster. Kabaraijian hit the lake in short order, and sent his launch surging across the sparkling green surface in a spray of foam. It was an exhilarating morning, with a bright sun, and a brisk wind that whipped the water into tiny waves. Kabaraijian felt good, despite the events of the previous night. Grotto did that to him. Out on the High Lakes, somehow, he felt that he could beat Bartling.

He'd run into similar problems before, on other worlds. Bartling wasn't alone in his hatred. Ever since the first time they'd ripped a man's brain from his skull and replaced it with a dead man's synthabrain, there had been people screaming that the practice was a perversion and the handlers tainted and unclean. He'd gotten used to the prejudice; it was part of corpse handling. And he'd beaten it before. He could beat Bartling now.

The first part of the voyage was the quickest. The two launches streaked over two big local lakes, past shores lined thickly with silverwood trees and vine-heavy danglers. But then they began to slow, as the lakes grew smaller and choked with life, and the country wilder. Along the banks, the stately silverwoods and curious danglers began to give way to the dense red and black chaos of firebriar brambles, and a species of low, gnarled tree that never had received a proper name. The vegetation grew on ground increasingly hilly and rocky, and finally mountainous.

Then they began to pass through the caves.

There were hundreds of them, literally, and they honey-combed the mountains that circled the settlement on all sides. The caves had never been mapped thoroughly. There were far too many of them, and they all seemed to connect with each other, forming a natural maze of incredible complexity. Most of them were still half-full of water; they'd been carved from the soft mountain rock by the streams and rivers that still ran through them.

A stranger could easily get lost in the caves, but strangers never came there. And the corpse handlers never got lost. This was their country. This was where the swirlstones waited, cloaked in rock and darkness.

The launches were all equipped with lights. Kabaraijian switched his on as soon as they hit the first cave, and slowed. Cochran, following close behind, did likewise. The channels that ran through the nearer caves were well known, but shallow, and it didn't pay to risk tearing out the bottom of your boat.

The channel was narrow at first, and the glistening, damp walls of soft greenish stone seemed to press in on them from either side. But gradually the walls moved farther and farther back, finally peeling away entirely as the stream carried the two launches into a great vaulted underground chamber. The cavern was as big as a spaceport, its ceiling lost in the gloom overhead. Before long the walls vanished into the dark too,

and the launches traveled in two small bubbles of light across
the gently stirring surface of a cold black lake.

Then, ahead of them, the walls took form again. But this
time, instead of one passage, there were many. The stream
had carved one entrance, but a good half-dozen exits.

Kabaraijian knew the cave, however. Without hesitating,
he guided his boat into the widest passage, on the extreme
right. Cochran followed in his wake. Here the waters flowed
down an incline, and the boats began to pick up speed again.
"Be careful," Kabaraijian warned Cochran at one point.
"The ceiling comes down here." Cochran acknowledged the
shout with a wave of his hand.

The warning came barely in time. While the walls were
increasingly farther apart, the stone roof above them was
moving steadily closer, giving the illusion that the waters
were rising. Kabaraijian remembered the way he'd sweated
the first time he'd taken this passage; the boat had been going
too fast, and he'd feared getting pinched in by the ceiling,
and overwhelmed by the climbing waters.

But it was an idle fear. The roof sank close enough to
scrape their heads, but no closer. And then it began to rise
again to a decent height. Meanwhile, the channel widened
still more, and soft sand shelves appeared along either wall.

Finally there was a branching in the passage, and this time
Kabaraijian chose the left-hand way. It was small and dark
and narrow, with barely enough room for the launch to
squeeze through. But it was also short, and after a brief
journey, it released them to a second great cavern.

They moved across the chamber quickly, and entered its
twin under a grotesque stone arch. Then came yet another
twisting passage, and more forks and turns. Kabaraijian led
them calmly, hardly thinking, hardly *having* to think. These
were his caves; this particular section of undermountain was
his domain, where he'd worked and mined for months. He
knew where he was going. And finally he got there.

The chamber was big, and haunting. Far above the shallow

waters, the roof had been eaten through by erosion, and light poured in from three great gashes in the rock. It gave the cavern a dim greenish glow, as it bounced off the pale green walls and the wide shallow pool.

The launches spilled from a thin crack in the cave wall, carried by rushes of cold black water. The water turned green when it hit the light, and tumbled and warmed and slowed. The boats slowed, too, and moved leisurely across the huge chamber toward the white sand beaches that lined the sides.

Kabaraijian pulled up by one such beach, and hopped out into the shallow water, dragging his launch up onto the sand. Cochran followed his example, and they stood side by side when both boats were safely beached.

"Yeah," said Cochran, looking around. "It's nice. And it figures. Leave it to you to find a pretty place to work, while the rest of us are up to our ankles in water, clutching lights."

Kabaraijian smiled. "I found it yesterday," he said. "Completely unworked. Look." He pointed at the wall. "I barely started." There was a pile of loose stones in a rough semicircle around the area he'd been working, and a large bite missing from the rock. But most of the wall was untouched, stretching away from them in sheets of shimmering green.

"You sure no one else knows about this place?" Cochran asked.

"Reasonably. Why?"

Cochran shrugged. "When we were coming through the caves, I could have sworn I heard another launch behind us somewhere."

"Probably echoes," Kabaraijian said. He looked toward his launch. "Anyway, we better get going." He hit his corpse controller, and the three still figures in the boat began to move.

He stood stock-still on the sand, watching them. And as he watched, somewhere in the back of his head, he was also watching himself with their eyes. They rose stiffly, and two of them climbed out onto the sand. The third walked to the chest in the front of the launch, and began unloading the equipment; vibrodrills and picks and shovels. Then, his arms full, he climbed down and joined the others.

None of them were really moving, of course. It was all Kabaraijian. It was Kabaraijian who moved their legs, and made their hands clasp and their arms reach. It was Kabaraijian, his commands picked up by controller and magnified by synthabrain, who put life into the bodies of the dead men. The synthabrains kept the automatic functions going, but it was the corpse handler who gave the corpse its will.

It wasn't easy, and it was far from perfect. The sense impressions thrown back to the handler were seldom useful; mostly he had to watch his corpses to know what they were doing. The manipulation was seldom graceful; corpses moved slowly and clumsily, and fine work was beyond them. A corpse could swing a mallet, but even the best handler couldn't make a deadman thread a needle, or speak.

With a bad handler, a corpse could hardly move at all. It took coordination to run even one deadman, if the handler was doing anything himself. He had to keep the commands to the corpse separate from the commands to his own muscles. That was easy enough for most, but the task grew increasingly complex as the crew grew larger. The record for one handler was twenty-six corpses; but all *he'd* done was march them, in step. When the dead men weren't all doing the same thing, the corpse handler's work became much more challenging.

Kabaraijian had a three-crew; all top meat, corpses in good condition. They'd been big men, and they still were; Kabaraijian paid premiums for food to keep his property in good condition. One had dark hair and a scar along a cheek, another was blond and young and freckled, the third had mousy brown locks. Other than that, they were interchangeable; all about the same height and weight and build. Corpses don't have personality. They lose that with their minds.

Cochran's crew, climbing out onto the sand in compliance

with his work orders, was less impressive. There were only two of them, and neither was a grade-one specimen. The first corpse was brawny enough, with wide shoulders and rippling muscles. But his legs were twisted matchsticks, and he stumbled often and walked more slowly than even the average corpse. The second deadman was reedy and middle-aged, bald and under-muscled. Both were grimy. Cochran didn't believe in taking care of his crew the way Kabaraijian did. It was a bad habit. Cochran had started as a paid handler working somebody else's corpses; upkeep hadn't been his concern.

Each of Kabaraijian's crew bent and picked up a vibrodrill from the stack of equipment on the sand. Then, parallel to each other, they advanced on the cave wall. The drills sank humming holes into the porous rock, and from each drill bite a network of thin cracks branched and grew.

The corpses drilled in unison until each drill was sunk nearly to its hilt and the cracks had grown finger wide. Then, almost as one, they withdrew the drills and discarded them in favor of picks. Work slowed. Crack by crack, the corpses attacked the wall, laboriously peeling off a whole layer of greenish stone. They swung the picks carefully, but with bone-jarring force, untiring, relentless. Incapable of pain, their bones could scarely feel jars.

The deadmen did all the work. Kabaraijian stood behind, a slight, dark statue in the sand, with hands on hips and eyes hooded. He did nothing but watch. Yet he did all. Kabaraijian *was* the corpses; the corpses were Kabaraijian. He was one man in four bodies, and it was his hand that guided each blow, though he did not touch a tool.

Forty feet down the cave, Cochran and his crew had unpacked and set to work. But Kabaraijian was barely conscious of them, though he could hear the hum of their vibrodrills and the hammering of their picks. His mind was with his corpses, chipping at his wall, alert for the telltale grayish glitter of a swirlstone node. It was draining work;

demanding work; tense and nervous. It was a labor only corpse crews could do with real efficiency.

They'd tried other methods a few short years before, when men had first found Grotto and its caves. The early settlers went after swirlstones with automoles, tractorlike rockeaters that could chew up mountains. Problem was, they also chewed up the fragile, deep-buried swirlstones, which often went unrecognized until too late. The company discovered that careful hand labor was the only way to keep from chipping or shattering an excessive number of stones. And corpse hands were the cheapest hands you could buy.

Those hands were busy now, tense and sweating as the crew peeled whole sections of rock off the broken wall. The natural cleavage of the stone was vertical, which sped the work. Find a crack—force in a pick—lean back and pull—and, with a snap, a flat chunk of rock came with you. Then find a new crack, and begin again.

Kabaraijian watched unmoving as the wall came down, and the pile of green stone accumulated around the feet of his deadmen. Only his eyes moved, flicking back and forth over the rock restlessly, alert for swirlstones but finding nothing. Finally he pulled the corpses back, and approached the wall himself. He touched it, stroked the stone, and frowned. The crew had ripped down an entire layer of rock, and had come up empty.

But that was hardly unusual, even in the best of caves. Kabaraijian walked back to the sand's edge, and sent his crew back to work. They picked up vibrodrills and attacked the wall again.

Abruptly he was conscious of Cochran standing beside him, saying something. He could hardly make it out. It isn't easy to pay close attention when you're running three dead men. Part of his mind detached itself and began to listen.

Cochran was repeating himself. He knew that a handler at work wasn't likely to hear what he said the first time. "Matt," he was saying, "listen. I think I heard something. Faintly, but I heard it. It sounded like another launch."

That was serious. Kabaraijian wrenched his mind loose from the deadmen, and turned to give Cochran his full attention. The three vibrodrills died, one by one, and suddenly the soft slap of water against sand echoed loudly around them.

"A launch?"

Cochran nodded.

"You sure?" Kabaraijian said.

"Uh—no," said Cochran. "But I *think* I heard something. Same thing as before, when we were moving through the caves."

"I don't know," Kabaraijian said, shaking his head. "Don't think it's likely, Ed. Why would anyone follow us? The swirlstones are everywhere, if you bother to look."

"Yeah," Cochran said. "But I heard something, and I thought I should tell you."

Kabaraijian nodded. "All right," he said. "Consider me told. If anyone shows up, I'll point out a section of wall and let him work it."

"Yeah," Cochran said again. But somehow he didn't look satisfied. His eyes kept jumping back and forth, agitated. He wheeled and walked back down the sand, to the section of wall where his own corpses stood frozen.

Kabaraijian turned back toward the rock, and his crew came alive again. The drills started humming, and once more the cracks spread out. Then, when the cracks were big enough, picks replaced drills, and another layer of stone started coming down.

But this time, something was behind it.

The corpses were ankle deep in splinters of stone when Kabaraijian saw it; a fist-sized chunk of gray nestled in the green. He stiffened at the sight of it, and the corpses froze in mid-swing. Kabaraijian walked around them, and studied the swirlstone node.

It was a beauty; twice the size of the largest stone he'd ever brought in. Even damaged, it would be worth a fortune.

But if he could pry it loose intact, his estimate would set a record. He was certain of that. They'd cut it as one stone. He could almost see it. An egg of crystalline fog, smoky and mysterious, where drifting veils of mist shrouded half-seen colors.

Kabaraijian thought about it, and smiled. He touched the node lightly, and turned to call to Cochran.

That saved his life.

The pick sliced through the air where his head had been and smashed against the wall with awful impact, barely missing the swirlstone node. Sparks and rock chips flew together. Kabaraijian stood frozen. The corpse drew the pick back over its head for another swing.

Within, Kabaraijian reeled, staggered. The pick swung down. Not at the wall; at him.

Then he moved, barely in time, throwing himself to one side. The blow missed by inches, and Kabaraijian landed in the sand and scrambled quickly to his feet. Crouched and wary, he began to back away.

The corpse advanced on him, the pick held over his head.

Kabaraijian could hardly think. He didn't understand. The corpse that moved on him was dark-haired and scarred; *his* corpse.

The corpse moved slowly. Kabaraijian kept a safe distance. Then he looked behind him. His other two dead men were advancing from other directions. One held a pick. The other had a vibrodrill.

Kabaraijian swallowed nervously, and stopped dead. The ring of corpses tightened around him. He screamed.

Down the beach, Cochran was looking at the tableau. He took one step toward Kabaraijian. From behind him, there was a blur of something being swung, and a dull thud. Cochran spun with the blow, and landed face down in the sand. He did not get up. His barrel-chested, gimpy corpse stood over him, pick in hand, swinging again and again. His other corpse was moving down the cave, toward Kabaraijian.

The scream was still echoing in the cave, but now Kabaraijian was silent. He watched Cochran go down, and suddenly he moved, throwing himself at the dark-haired dead man. The pick descended, vicious but clumsy. Kabaraijian dodged it. He bowled into the corpse, and both of them went down. The corpse was much slower getting up. By the time he did rise, Kabaraijian was behind him.

The corpse handler moved back, step by slow step. His own crew was in front of him now, stumbling toward him with weapons raised. It was a chilling sight. Their arms moved, and they walked. But their eyes were blank and their faces were dead—*DEAD!* For the first time, Kabaraijian understood the horror some people felt near deadmen.

He looked over his shoulder. Both of Cochran's corpses were heading his way, armed. Cochran still had not risen. He lay with his face in the sand and the waters lapping at his boots.

His mind began to work again, in the short breather he was granted. His hand went to his belt. The controller was still on, still warm and humming. He tested it. He reached out, to his corpses, into them. He told them to stand still, to drop their tools, to freeze.

They continued to advance.

Kabaraijian shivered. The controller was still working; he could still feel the echoes in his head. But somehow, the corpses weren't responding. He felt very cold.

And colder when it finally hit him, like ice water. Cochran's corpses hadn't responded either. Both crews had turned on their handlers.

Override!

He'd heard of such things. But he'd never seen one, or dreamt of seeing one. Override boxes were very expensive and even more, illegal, contraband on any planet where corpse handling was allowed.

But now he was seeing one in action. Someone wanted to kill him. Someone was trying to do just that. Someone was using his own corpses against him, by means of an override box.

He threw himself at his corpses mentally, fighting for control, grappling for whatever had taken them over. But there was no struggle, nothing to come to grips with. The deadmen simply failed to respond.

Kabaraijian bent and picked up a vibrodrill.

He straightened quickly, spinning around to face Cochran's two corpses. The big one with the matchstick legs moved in, swinging its pick. Kabaraijian checked the blow with the vibrodrill, holding it above him as a shield. The dead man brought the pick back again.

Kabaraijian activated the drill and drove it into the corpse's gut. There was an awful second of spurting blood and tearing flesh. There should have been a scream too, and agony. But there wasn't.

And the pick came down anyway.

Kabaraijian's thrust had thrown the corpse's aim off, and the blow was a glancing one, but it still ripped his tunic half off his chest and clawed a bloody path from shoulder to stomach. Reeling, he staggered back against the wall, empty-handed.

The corpse came on, pick swinging up again, eyes blank. The vibrodrill transfixed it, still humming, and the blood came in wet red spurts. But the corpse came on.

No pain, Kabaraijian thought, with the small part of his mind not frozen with terror. The blow wasn't immediately fatal, and the corpse can't feel it. It's bleeding to death, but it doesn't know it, doesn't care. It won't stop till it's dead. *There's no pain!*

The corpse was nearly on top of him. He dropped to the sand, grabbed a hunk of rock, and rolled.

Dead men are slow, woefully slow; their reflexes are long-distance ones. The blow was late and off-target. Kabaraijian rolled into the corpse and knocked it down. Then he was on top of it, the rock clutched in his fist, hammering at the thing's skull, smashing it again and again, breaking through to the synthabrain.

Finally, the corpse stopped moving. But the others had reached him. Two picks swung almost simultaneously. One missed entirely. The other took a chunk out of his shoulder.

He grabbed the second pick, and twisted, fighting to stop it, losing. The corpses were stronger than he was, much stronger. The deadman wrenched the pick free and brought it back for another try.

Kabaraijian got to his feet, smashing into the corpse and sending it flailing. The others swung at him, grabbed at him. He didn't stay to fight. He ran. They pursued, slow and clumsy but somehow terrifying.

He reached the launch, seized it with both hands, and shoved. It slid reluctantly across the sand. He shoved again, and this time it moved more easily. He was drenched in blood and sweat, and his breath came in short gasps, but he kept shoving. His shoulder shrieked agony. He let it shriek, putting it to the side of the launch and finally getting the boat clear of the sand.

Then the corpses were on him again, swinging at him even as he climbed into the launch. He started the motor and flipped it to top speed. The boat responded. It took off in a sudden explosion of foam, slicing across the green waters toward the dark slit of safety in the far cavern wall. Kabaraijian sighed . . . and the corpse grabbed him.

It was in the boat. Its pick was buried uselessly in the wood, but it still had its hands, and those were enough. It wrapped those hands around his neck, and squeezed. He swung at it madly, smashing at its calm, empty face. It made no effort to ward off the blows. It ignored them. Kabaraijian hit it again and again, poked at the vacant eyes, hammered at its mouth until its teeth shattered.

But the fingers on his neck grew tighter and tighter, and not all his struggling could pry one loose. Choking, he stopped kicking the corpse, and kicked the rudder control.

The launch veered wildly, leaning from side to side. The cave rushed past in a blur, and the walls moved in on them. Then came sudden impact, the shriek of tearing wood, and the short tumble from launch to water. Kabaraijian landed on top, but they both went under. The corpse held its grip through everything, dragging Kabaraijian down with it, still choking the life from his throat.

But Kabaraijian took a deep breath before the green closed over him. The corpse tried to breathe underwater. Kabaraijian helped it. He stuck both hands into its mouth and kept it open, making sure it got a good lungful of water.

The deadman died first. And its fingers weakened.

Finally, his lungs near bursting, Kabaraijian forced his way free, and kicked to the surface. The water was only chest high. He stood on the unmoving corpse, keeping it under while he sucked in great draughts of air.

The launch had impaled itself on a crest of jagged rocks that rose from the water off to one side of the exit. The passage from the cave was still at hand, outlined in shadow a few short feet away. But now, was it safe? Without a launch? Kabaraijian considered making his way out on foot, and gave up the idea instantly. There were too many miles to go before he reached simple daylight, let alone the safety of the river station. It would mean being hunted in the darkness by whatever remained of his corpse crew. The prospect sent a chill down his back. No, better to stay and face his attacker.

He kicked free of the corpse, and moved to the debris of his launch, still hung up on the rocks that had caught it. Shielded by the wreck, he'd be difficult to find, or at least to see. And if his enemy couldn't see him, it would be hard to send the corpses against him.

Meanwhile, maybe he could find his enemy.

His enemy. Who? Bartling, of course. It had to be Bartling, or one of his hirelings. Who else?

But *where?* They had to be close, within sight of the beach. You can't run a corpse by remote control; the sense feedback isn't good enough. The only senses you get are vision and hearing, and then dimly. You have to *see* the corpse, see what it's doing, and what you want it to do. So Bartling's man was around here somewhere. In the cave. But where?

And how? Kabaraijian considered that. It must be the other launch that Cochran had heard. Someone must have been following them, someone with an override box. Maybe Bartling had a tracer put on his launch during the night.

Only how'd he know *which* launch to trace?

Kabaraijian bent slightly so only his head showed above the water, and looked out around the end of the ruined launch. The beach was a white sand smear across the dim green length of the huge cavern. There was no noise but the water slapping the side of the boat. But there was motion. The second launch had been pulled free of the sand, and one of the corpses was climbing on board. The others, moving slowly, were wading out into the underground pool. Their picks rested on their shoulders.

They were coming for him. The enemy suspected he was still here. The enemy was hunting for him. Again, he was tempted to dive toward the exit, to run and swim back toward daylight, out of this awful dimness where his own corpses stalked him with cold faces and colder hands.

He squelched the impulse. He might get a head start while they searched the cavern. But, with the launch, they'd make it up in no time. He could try to lose them in the intricacies of the caves. But if they got ahead of him, they could just wait at caves' ends. No, no. He had to stay there and find his enemy.

But *where?* He scanned the cave, and saw nothing. It was a great expanse of murky green, stone and water and beaches. The pool was dotted by a few large rocks rising from the water. A man might be hiding behind them. But not a launch. There was nothing big enough to hide a launch. Maybe the enemy wore aquagear? But Cochran had heard a launch . . .

The corpse boat was halfway across the cavern, heading for the exit. It was his dead man seated at the controls, the brown-haired one. The other two corpses trailed, as they walked slowly across the shallow pool in the wake of the launch.

Three dead men, stalking. But somewhere their handler was hiding. The man with the override box. Their mind and their will. But where?

The launch was coming closer. Was it leaving? Maybe they thought he'd run for it? Or . . . no, probably the enemy was going to blockade the exit, and *then* search the cave.

Did they see him? Did they know where he was?

Suddenly he remembered his corpse controller, and his hand fumbled under water to make sure it was still intact. It was. And working; controllers were watertight. It no longer controlled. But it still might be useful . . .

Kabaraijian closed his eyes, and tried to shut off his ears. He deliberately blotted his senses, and concentrated on the distant sensory echoes that still murmured in his mind. They were there. Even vaguer than usual, but less confused; there were only two sets of images now. His third corpse floated a few feet from him, and it wasn't sending anything.

He twisted his mind tight, and listened, and tried to see. The blurs began to define themselves. Two pictures, both wavering, took form, superimposed over each other. A sense tangle, but Kabaraijian pulled at the threads. The pictures resolved.

One corpse was waist deep in green water, moving slowly, holding a pick. It could see the shaft of the tool, and the hand wrapped around it, and the gradually deepening water. But it wasn't even looking in Kabaraijian's direction.

The second dead man was in the launch, one hand resting on the controls. It wasn't looking either. It was staring down, at the instruments. It took a lot of concentration for a corpse to run any sort of machine. So the handler was having it keep a firm eye on the engine.

Only it could see more than just the engine. It had a very good view of the entire launch.

And suddenly everything fell into place. Certain now that the wrecked launch hid him from view, Kabaraijian moved farther back into its shadow, then threw a hand over the side and pulled himself on board, crouching so he wouldn't be found. The rocks had torn a hole in the bottom of the boat. But the tool chest was intact. He crawled to it, and flipped it open. The corpses had unpacked most of the mining equipment, but there was still a repair kit. Kabaraijian took out a heavy wrench and a screwdriver. He shoved the screwdriver into his belt, and gripped the wrench tightly. And waited.

The other launch was nearly on top of him, and he could hear the purr of its motor and the water moving around it. He waited until it was next to his boat. Then he stood up suddenly, and jumped.

He landed smack in the middle of the other boat, and the launch rocked under the impact. Kabaraijian didn't give the enemy time to react—at least not the time it takes a corpse. He took a single short step, and brought the wrench around in a vicious backhanded blow to the deadman's head. The corpse slumped back. Kabaraijian bent, grabbed its legs, and lifted. And suddenly the deadman was no longer in the launch.

And Kabaraijian, wheeling, was looking down at the stunned face of Ed Cochran. He hefted the wrench with one hand even as his other reached for the controls, and upped the speed. The boat accelerated, and dove toward the exit. Cave and corpses vanished behind, and darkness closed in with the rocky walls. Kabaraijian switched on the lights.

"Hello, Ed," he said, hefting the wrench again. His voice was very steady and very cold.

Cochran breathed a noisy sigh of relief. "Matt," he said. "Thank God, I just came to. My corpses—they—"

Kabaraijian shook his head. "No, Ed, it won't wash.

Don't bother me with that, please. Just give me the override box.''

Cochran looked scared. Then, fighting, he flashed his grin. ''Heh. You gotta be kiddin', right? I don't have no override box. I told you I heard another launch.''

''There was no other launch. That was a set-up, in case you failed. So was that blow you took on the beach. I'll bet that was tricky—having your corpse swing the pick so you got hit with the side instead of the point. But it was very well done. My compliments, Ed. That was good corpse handling. As was the rest. It isn't easy to coordinate a five-crew doing different things simultaneously. Very nice, Ed. I underestimated you. Never thought you were that good a handler.''

Cochran stared at him from the floor of the launch, his grin gone. Then his gaze broke, and his eyes went back and forth between the walls that pressed around them.

Kabaraijian waved the wrench again, his palm sweaty where he gripped it. His other hand touched his shoulder briefly. The bleeding had stopped. He sat slowly, and rested his hand on the motor.

''Aren't you going to ask me how I knew, Ed?'' Kabaraijian said. Cochran, sullen, said nothing. ''I'll tell you anyway,'' Kabaraijian continued. ''I saw you. I looked through the eyes of my corpse, and I saw you huddled here in the boat, lying on the floor and peeking over the side to try and spot me. You didn't look dead at all, but you looked very guilty. And suddenly I got it. *You* were the only one with a clear view of that stuff on the beach. *You* were the only one in the cave.''

He paused, awkward. His voice broke a little, and softened. ''Only—why? *Why*, Ed?''

Cochran looked up at him again. He shrugged. ''Money,'' he said. ''Only money, Matt. What else?'' He smiled; not his usual grin, but a strained, tight smile. ''I like you, Matt.''

''You've got a peculiar way of showing it,'' Kabaraijian told him. He couldn't help smiling as he said it. ''Whose money?''

"Bartling's," said Cochran. "I needed money real bad. My estimates were low, I didn't have anything saved. If I had to leave Grotto, that would've meant selling my crew just for passage money. Then I'd be a hired handler again. I didn't want that. I needed money fast."

He shrugged. "I was going to try smuggling some swirlstones, but you didn't make that sound good. And last night I got another idea. I didn't think that crap about organizing us and outbidding Bartling would work, but I figured he'd be interested. So I went to see him after I left the tavern. Thought he might pay a little for the information, and maybe even make an exception, let me stay."

He shook his head dourly. Kabaraijian stayed silent. Finally Cochran resumed. "I got to see him, him with three bodyguards. When I told him, he got hysterical. You'd humilated him already, and now he thought you were on to something. He—he made me an offer. A lot of money, Matt. A *lot* of money."

"I'm glad I didn't come cheap."

Cochran smiled. "Nah, he said. "Bartling really wanted you, and I made him pay. He gave me the override box. Wouldn't touch it himself. He said he'd had it made in case the 'meatminds' and their 'zombies' ever attacked him." Cochran reached into the pocket of his tunic, and look out a small, flat cartridge. It looked like a twin for the controller on his belt. He flipped it lightly through the air at Kabaraijian.

But Kabaraijian made no effort to catch it. The box sailed past his shoulder, and hit the water with a splash.

"Hey," said Cochran. "You shoulda got that. Your corpses won't respond till you turn it off."

"My shoulder's stiff," Kabaraijian started. He stopped abruptly.

Cochran stood up. He looked at Kabaraijian as if he were seeing him for the first time. "Yeah," he said. His fists clenched. "Yeah." He was a full head taller than Kabaraijian, and much heavier. And suddenly he seemed to notice the extent of the other's injuries.

The wrench seemed to grow heavier in Kabaraijian's hand. "Don't," he warned.

"I'm sorry," Cochran said. And he dove forward.

Kabaraijian brought the wrench around at his head, but Cochran caught the blow before it connected. His other hand reached up and wrapped itself around Kabaraijian's wrist, and twisted. He felt his fingers going numb.

There was no thought of fair play, or mercy. He was fighting for his life. His free hand went to his waist and grabbed the screwdriver. He pulled it out, and stabbed. Cochran gasped, and his grip suddenly loosened. Kabaraijian stabbed again, and twisted up and out, ripping a gash in tunic and flesh.

Cochran reeled back, clutching at his stomach. Kabaraijian followed him and stabbed a third time, savagely. Cochran fell.

He tried to rise once, and gave it up, falling heavily back to the floor of the launch. Then he lay there, bleeding.

Kabaraijian went back to the motor, and kept the boat clear of the walls. He guided them down the passages smoothly, through the caves and the tunnels and the deep green pools. And in the harsh boat light, he watched Cochran.

Cochran never moved again, and he spoke only once. Just after they had left the caves and come out into the early afternoon sun of Grotto, he looked up briefly. His hands were wet with blood. And his eyes were wet too. "I'm sorry, Matt," he said. "I'm damn sorry."

"Oh, *God!*" Kabaraijian said, his voice thick. And suddenly he stopped the boat dead in the water, and bent to the supply cache. Then he went to Cochran and dressed and bandaged his injuries.

When he reached the controls again, he flipped the speed up to maximum. The launch streaked across the glittering green lakes.

But Cochran died before they reached the river.

Kabaraijian stopped the boat then, and let it float dead in the water. He listened to the sounds of Grotto around him; the rush of river water pouring into the great lake, the songbirds and the daywings, the ever-active lakeleapers arcing through the air. He sat there until dusk fell, staring upriver, and thinking.

He thought of tomorrow and the day after. Tomorrow he must return to the swirlstone caves. His corpses should have frozen when he moved out of range; they should be salvageable. And one of Cochran's crew was still there, too. Maybe he could still piece together a three-crew, if the corpse he'd pushed overboard hadn't drowned.

And there were swirlstones there, big ones. He'd get that egg of dancing fog, and turn it in, and get a good estimate. Money. He had to have money, all he could scrape together. Then he could start talking to the others. And then . . . and then Bartling would have a fight on his hands. Cochran was one casualty, the first. But not the last. He'd tell the others that Bartling had sent a man out with an override box, and that Cochran had been killed because of it. It was true. It was all true.

That night Kabaraijian returned with only one corpse in his launch, a corpse that was strangely still and unmoving. Always his corpses had walked behind him into the office. That night the corpse rode on his shoulder.

Chicago
December, 1972

Weekend In A War Zone

SATURDAY DAWN, WITH THE SUN JUST A DIM LIGHT BEHIND the clouds. They're passing out the guns. We're outside, in the ready base on the edge of the war zone, standing in line and shuffling through an inch of slush. I don't understand why they make us stand in line. They could have given us the guns inside, with the uniforms. It's cold out here.

The armorer is the same guy that ran the credit check. Reed-thin, sallow complexion, squinty little eyes. Bored before and bored now, taking his own sweet time about everything. While we stand here and go shuffle-shuffle through the slush. He writes down the serial number of every rifle he hands over. I guess there is an extra charge if you lose the damn thing. They charge for everything. This weekend will cost a fortune. I wonder, again, what the hell I'm doing here. Tennis is a hell of a lot cheaper. And you come back alive. Always. Every time.

My turn. The armorer squints at me, checks the serial number on the gun he's holding, writes it down, hands it over. Name, he asks for. "Birch," I say. "Andrew Birch." He writes that down, too. I take the gun and move off. The next guy shuffles up to the table.

The gun is smooth black plastic, long as my arm, contours all flowing graceful towards the snout at the business end. It feels slick and cold in my hand, and there's a smell of oil about it. It's unloaded. I take a cartridge chamber from my belt and slip it in, and it clicks as it locks in place. Now I'm ready. Like the guys in the ads. My first patrol. An armed soldier. A man. Right.

What bullshit.

I don't think I'm much of a soldier. I hold the gun awkwardly, despite the company hypnotraining. I don't know quite what to do with it. If I knew, I wouldn't want to do it. I play tennis on weekends. I don't belong here. I was an idiot to come. What if they shoot me? The Concoms have guns, too.

I turn the gun over, examine it. There's a rough spot on the underside of the barrel. Lettering. A serial number and a legend: PROPERTY OF MANEUVER, INC.

Stancato drifts over, his gun under his arm, flipping up the nightvisor on his helmet. He's got the helmet tilted to one side. Rakishly, I suppose. That's Stancato. What's worse, it looks good on him. In combat boots and helmet and this mess of green and brown that Maneuver tries to pass off as a uniform, he manages to look good. Rugged, masculine. He's at home out here, his stance says. He shouldn't be. It's his first time, too. I know that.

Stancato always looks natural. He's taller than I am, and he's all lean muscle and dark good looks. I'm short and moon-faced, with wishy-washy brown hair. Stancato eats like a horse and it doesn't disturb his chic body at all. I turn to flab the second I'm not paying attention. Stancato wears all the latest at the office. Now it's flare-necks and half-capes, last month it was something else. He looks cool and fashionable. I wear the same stuff and I look like an overdressed moron.

I suspect I look like a moron now, in this uniform. It doesn't fit. It bunches in all the wrong places, and it's tight where it shouldn't be. It's not even warm. The wind cuts right through it. You think we'd get better, with the fee they make us pay. I've got half a mind to report them to Consumer Protection. If I come back alive.

Stancato fondles his gun, and smiles at me. "A nice piece of hardware," he says. "It'll do good by us." How the hell does he know? His first trip, he talks like a vet already. But he's probably right. It'll do good by him.

The drop-chopper is revving up across the ready-base, but it's not time to go yet. The others are still shuffling through the muck. I feel called upon to say something. I often feel that way, especially around Stancato. He's got a way of coming up to me and saying something that almost forces me to stick my foot in my mouth.

This time I think. I don't want him to know how nervous I am. "You think old man Dolecek will notice us?" I say, finally. Dolecek is our boss. The reason I'm here. The fucker maneuvers every weekend, been doing it for twenty years. Says a man isn't really a man until he's been blooded. Sounds just like a war zone commercial. But the fucker has a promotion to give, and I haven't had a promotion in two years. This had better impress him.

Stancato is here for the same reason, only he won't admit it. He says he got bored with tennis and golf and hiking, wants more excitement. Stancato is a greedy bastard. He's two years younger than me, but we're the same grade already. Now he wants to pass me by.

"Dolecek signed up to be a major this time out," Stancato says, grinning. "He's not going to see us, Andy boy. He won't even know you're here. So just relax and enjoy it."

Everybody has their guns now. The sarge lets out a bark, and we all trot towards the drop-chopper. It's a big noisy thing, all green metal and roaring rotors whapping the air, with the Maneuver trademark on its side. There are long benches along either wall, and the platoon fills them quickly. I wind up between Stancato and an older man with a smashed-in nose and an immense gut. Just a grunt, like the rest of us poor slobs, but I notice he's got vet marks on his sleeve.

He's done this before, and he's got lots of killpoints in his time. I study his face, try to figure out what makes him a killer, instead of a killee. Nothing shows, though.

The pilot takes us up. The faces around me are a little tense, but happy. A lot of smiles, some joking. What the hell are they so happy about? Don't they know they might get killed? I feel slightly sick myself. This was a dumb idea.

Stancato is one of the smilers. "You okay, Andy?" he says to me over the noise of the copter. "You don't look so good." He's grinning so I know that he's just kidding around. But he doesn't fool me. He likes to put me down.

"I'm all right." I'm not going to throw up, no matter how much I want to. That would give Stancato too much pleasure. If I can't hold back, I'll throw up on him. "I'm just a little nervous," I say.

"Scared, you mean." He laughs at me. "C'mon, Andy, admit it. We're all scared. Nothing to be ashamed of. I'm terrified. You'd be stupid if you weren't scared. The Concoms will be shooting real bullets at us." Again that laugh. "But that's what makes it interesting, right?"

"Right." Believe it.

The Gut looks over. "You got it," he says. Deep, gravelly voice, half his teeth missing. A real prole. "I been going out for ten years, scared every time. But that's *living*."

"A man hasn't lived until he's seen death," Stancato says, in his smooth, witty voice. It was one of Maneuver's slogans.

"A man ain't a man till he's *maneuvered*," I say, providing the other catchphrase from the ads. Instantly I feel inane. Stancato's quote somehow sounded appropriate to the conversation. Mine sounded stupid. Too late, though. I said it.

Now the Gut laughs at me. "Yeah. And I bet you boys are just now getting to be men, hey?" He nods at his own pronouncement. "Yeah. You're both green as hell. I can tell."

"A perceptive man," Stancato says. Some perception. If we weren't green, we'd be wearing vet marks.

"Damn straight," says the Gut. "I know my way around, too. Stick close to me. I'll show you how it's done. Make sure the Concoms don't get any killpoints off my buddies."

I can't think of anyone I'd want less as a buddy, unless it's Stancato. But maybe I should do like the Gut says. He doesn't seem to have any holes in him, and I don't want any in me.

There's a loud thud, and the copter shakes around us. The rotors die whining. We've arrived. The middle of the war zone. We'll be alone out here. The platoon we're replacing was on a sweep through the forested countryside. Looking for Concoms. I hope the Concoms aren't looking for us. What ever happened to old-fashioned wars where everybody met on a battlefield and shot at each other?

We spill out of the chopper into a sea of mud. The sun is higher in the sky now, a corner of it peeking through the overcast. Most of the slush has dissolved. But the wind is still blowing, and it's as cold as ever.

We're in a rocky, nondescript clearing, surrounded by evergreens, with barely enough room for the drop-chopper to set down. The other Maneuver platoon is all lined up, ready to board. They swear a lot, but most of them seem to be grinning. Dirt they have plenty of, but no blood. And I don't see any wounded. Maybe this will be easier than I thought.

The Gut waves to one of the others, gets a grin in return. "How's it go?" the Gut shouts.

"Oughta get our money back. Laying down good credit for a hike." He shakes his head, looks towards his sarge, glances at me with disdain as his eyes sweep by. Smartass. Probably has money pouring out of his ears. Either that or enough killpoints to rate him a big discount. Otherwise how could he afford to buy a whole week of war at Maneuver's rates? Probably looks down on us weekenders.

Once we're all out, they start piling in, then the chopper sets its rotors to whapping again and they're off, home free. Back to the offices and the suburbs, or wherever. The Concoms don't shoot at drop-choppers, thanks to the free substitution rule. But they've been known to wipe out a new platoon as soon as it's landed. I recall that nervously, and look around.

The sarge snaps an order, and we assemble like good little soldiers. He looks us over, obviously not pleased. "Awright," he begins, in his best sarge-talk. Like something out of an old war movie. He doesn't look the part though. He's more like a misplaced accountant. He wears glasses and he's too young and he smiles too damn much. Not a bit intimidating. I notice he isn't wearing any vet marks either. Another strike against me. Andy Birch, you're a real winner.

"We're gonna cover ground," our green sarge tells us. "Those bastards were told to find the Concoms, and they farted around for a week. So we find 'em. Assholes and elbows time, kiddies. We're gonna find out how you punks handle action. And it better be good, or I'll give you more misery than the Concoms ever dreamed of. Remember, we get position-points if we find a camp, plus killpoints for every Concom we take care of. That means discounts next time around."

I find myself evaluating his performance. The first part sounded good, but maybe a little overdone. Rock Fury and all that. But those closing lines jarred. Wonder if he gets special training, or a manual, or what? Or do they just take his money and let him wing it?

He's giving us orders now. We split into smaller groups, and fan out into the forest. Why split up, I wonder? Why not just march along in a line, or something? I suppose there's a reason. He must be going by the book, or by orders from some smartass who bought himself a weekend commission.

I wind up with Stancato and the Gut. I stood close to the Gut when we got split up, so I'd be teamed with him. A vet can't do me any harm, I figure, and he might make a difference. Stancato, damn him, figures the same way.

So we're scrambling through forest tangle, guns in hand. Heading upcountry, towards the mountains. The others are around us somewhere, but I can't see them. The air is cold and the ground wet. I hope the sarge lets us stop for lunch.

I'm exhausted. This is worse than tennis, much worse, and I can't take it. I'm sucking down icy air in great draughts, and that fucking Gut doesn't let up. He just plows on ahead, pushing aside the greenery, tramping through the muck. He's like a flabby mack truck, and he wants to run me into the ground. Stancato isn't even breathing hard, but I'm going to collapse. The gun weighs a ton.

We've covered a lot of territory. No doubt we're in a war zone by now. I can hear firing in the distance, very dimly, big guns going boom-boom. And a Concom skimmer flight went overhead awhile ago. Way up, but the Gut told us to flatten ourselves in the mud all the same. The stuff soaked right through the uniform. I'm colder than ever, but luckily the wind's died some.

Near noon we stop to eat in a small clearing against the side of a cliff. Just the three of us. I don't know where the others have got off to. I don't understand any of this. Shouldn't we be staying with the others? Where are they? Wouldn't it be better if the whole platoon was together? I paid good money for this weekend. I wish I knew what was going on.

We sit with our backs to the moss-slick stone, guns across our laps, eating rations from hotpaks. It's good to get the load off my back and sit down for a while. And I'm hungry. But the food is terrible. You'd think Maneuver would do better for the prices we're paying. How do they ever keep a customer?

Stancato isn't bothered, though. He eats quickly, almost ravenous, then smiles at me as I poke at my food. "Eat up, Andy," he says. "We'll need all our strength. Day's just begun." Then he stands and stretches, still smiling. "This is life," he tells me. "This is exhilarating. Out beyond the city, with enemies around you and a gun in your hand. Yes, I do believe Maneuver's right. Life is sweeter when death is close.''

The Gut looks up from his pak, grimaces. "Sid down. And don't talk so loud. You wanna bring the Concoms down on us? You won't live long that way.''

Stancato sits, grinning. "You know a lot about this, eh?''

The Gut nods. "Damn straight. I could sarge if I wanted to, y'know. Even buy a weekend commission. I got lots of killpoints. But that isn't for me. This is better, out here. Before I go, I'm going to get more killpoints than anyone. That's what I want, not to fight no war from an office, like the leadbutts with the big credit who sign on as weekend commanders.''

I look at him, shoving aside my food half-eaten. An ugly man with an ugly nose and a huge pot and a small brain. Yet he's killed men, better men than him probably, and he comes back when others die. Why? I start to ask the question.

But Stancato talks first. "You like killing,'' he says, eyes hard and eager. He'll like it, I know. He likes hurting, likes to put people down, to humiliate them. Shooting holes in them is just his speed.

"It's war,'' the Gut says. "Here, in the zone, yeah, but out there too. We just don't call it war, but it still is. There are guys after you every minute, after your woman, after your job, pushing shit on your kids, trying to stick it to you. You have to fight back, and this is one way. Yeah, I like it. Why not? Those Concoms—'' he jerks his head towards the shrubbery, savagely, "most of them are niggers, y'know. The Concoms do a lot of advertising down there where they live. They hate us anyway. Why shouldn't I enjoy getting a few of them?'' He looks belligerent, as if he dares us to challenge him. I'm certainly not going to. He's a fool, but I might need him.

Maneuver must like men like him. They hate, they kill, and they come back weekend after weekend. Sure they get discounts. But they make money for the company all the same. Pile up those points, get enough of them, and finally Maneuver wins the war and Consolidated Combat has to hand over a big chunk of credit, instead of the other way around.

War after war, the Gut is there, I bet. Says something about man, something disgusting. No real war for over fifty years, so we invent bloodgames so animals like the Gut can play them and get their rocks off.

Stancato is going to be good at this, yes. Maybe he'll turn into the Gut in time. That would be nice. He deserves a fate like that. Not me, though. I get out, after this weekend.

The Gut gets to his feet and gestures. We pick up our guns and follow, back into the forest.

Late afternoon. The war is all around us and the mud has turned back to slush and snow. But there are rocks underfoot, so we're making better time.

There is a horrible smell in the woods. And noises, firing, somewhere close. We crouch low and head towards it, scrambling silent as we can. I breathe easier now. I'm scared, but I've gotten my second wind. And my muscles don't ache anymore. I can't feel them at all.

Ahead, a fallen tree is rotting, with a dead body draped across it, face buried in bloody snow. Like a tableau from a movie. It doesn't touch me until I realize that it's real. Then I start.

It's been dead a while. The smell gets stronger as we approach. Near, I can see the swollen flesh, and choke on the decay. The visor on its helmet is down. It died at night, then. Its uniform is grayish, its skin black. A Concom. My first sight of the enemy. I hope all the Concoms I see are dead.

The Gut goes by without comment, smiling just a little. Stancato walks around it, swiftly, barely looking, unmoved. Just another part of the scenery for calm, cool Stancato. I stop as they go on ahead.

I can't see the eyes through the visor. I realize I don't want to. Who the hell was it? How much did *he* have to pay for the dubious privilege of rotting out here? I feel a sudden urge to touch the body, the dead flesh. Revolted at myself, I stifle it. Yet I stare.

Something *moves* on the body. I watch in fascination. Then suddenly, with a rush, I'm sick. I turn away, retching, vomiting all over the ground. For some reason, I avoid throwing up on the body.

When I stop, Stancato is there, smiling his tight little smile. "Take it easy, Andy," he says. He puts an arm around me, the big man. "It's only a maggot. It won't hurt you."

Only a maggot. Only a maggot. God, but I hate him. I grit my teeth, wrench free of him violently, and stalk back into the forest.

We ran into three others from our platoon, and now we're together. I hardly remember them from the chopper, but I'm sure they must have been there. Don't know that we've gained much. Two beefy oafs and a gawk is what we've got now. But the gawk has vet marks.

He talks with the Gut now, all low whispers, and he keeps looking around. They look absurd, like a military Mutt 'n Jeff. The Gawk and the Gut. These are the people I'm relying on to get me through? Shit. The Gawk looks like he'd have trouble getting across the street. A long pinched-in face and acne scars. He doesn't look like a warrior. But maybe soldiers don't look like in the movies. Maybe the ugly guys kill best. Hell. Stancato will be pissed when he finds that out. He wants to be best at everything.

The Gut looks our way and gestures. "We got something," he says. "Grenade blasts over on the east. Rifle fire. Jim says some of our boys are pinned down by the Concoms. Let's go get'em out." He grins.

We run, a jogging trot, shoving aside the branches and sloshing through patches of snow. The Gut looks eager. I'm terrified. What have I gotten myself into? Where are we going? I want out. This is madness. My hand trembles where I hold the gun. I'm going to throw up again.

The war sweeps over us.

One of the beef boys ahead of me stumbles suddenly, and the firing begins all around us. He falls, his head twisting grotesquely, his rifle spinning into a snowbank, a flower of blood blossoming from his chest. Dead, dead, I think. We don't know where the shot came from.

"A sniper!" the Gut yells. "Cover! Take cover!"

Then he's gone, faded away, down somewhere. The others fade, too. Only I remain, standing over the body, blinking down at it, frozen, indecisive. Another shot rings out, a stream of shots. I hear them hiss around me, and I feel strangely safe. You never hear the bullet that kills you, they say.

Then someone grabs me, pulls me, yanks me off my feet and knocks me into the trees. Stancato, of course. He falls down beside me, eyes sweeping alertly, rifle in hand, ready. I've dropped my rifle. It's out there, near the body. And I'm crying. At least my cheeks are wet.

Stancato ignores me. He lifts his gun and fires, and the black snout spits a rapid burst of death towards the trees. Was that where the shots were coming from? I don't know. I didn't notice. But he seems to. Other people are firing too. Our guys, I think. But not me. Not me. I lost my gun.

Then, for a long time, breathless silence. Stancato waits, hands tight on gun, eyes moving all the time the others are waiting too. No one moves. No one fires.

It's dusk now. That comes on me suddenly as I watch the twilight creep around the evergreens, and wrap the woods in folds of grayness. A lot of time is gone. But we don't move. We don't know if we've gotten the sniper, or if he's gone, or if he's waiting out there, lurking, gun hungry for one of us to move. So Stancato stays put. Me too. I'm not going to be the target. Besides, I can't do much else. I lost my gun.

Finally, with the darkness all but complete, someone moves. A quick dart from here to there in the trees. Then another. Then a sudden burst of fire raking over the sniper's position, in the rocks upslope from us. At last a head pokes out of the black. Nightvisor down, half-crouched, the Gawk edges out into the open. Nothing happens. The Concom is dead, or gone.

The Gut appears suddenly, a ponderous shadow in the dark. He bends over the body, touches it, shakes his head. Is he really sorry, I wonder? Or just pissed that the enemy got a killpoint off a buddy? The latter. He's not the caring sort.

Stancato stands, and strides back into the open, confident, smiling. I hesitate and follow. "You think we got him?" Stancato asks.

The Gut shrugs. "Dunno. We gotta look. Maybe, maybe not. He might've just taken off."

They look, Stancato and the Gut, going over towards the place the shots had come from. The rest of us wait. The Gawk eyes me with distaste. I squirm under his gaze, look at the other man, look away quickly when I find him ignoring me. They both dislike me. I can tell. I froze. I'm a coward to them. I have to prove myself. But not Stancato, no, not him. He did everything right, as usual. I wipe my hands on my jacket, nervously. Then, flushing, I bend to pick up my gun. Why didn't I do that sooner? Why didn't I fight? Dammit, Birch, why do you always do everything wrong?

Stancato and the Gut come back. Stancato slaps me on the back. Always hale and hearty, yes sir. Even nice to cowards, the patronizing bastard. He smiles at me. "Looks like he got away," he says. "We must've scared him off."

"Look," I say, falteringly, "I didn't mean to drop—"

Stancato cuts me off. "Don't worry about it. Getting to cover was the important thing." He gestures at the body.

"He kept his gun. Didn't do us much good, did it? Better to have you alive, we don't need dead heroes, right?"

The Gut had been listening. He nods now, reluctantly. "Yeah, maybe you got something." Then he looks at me. "But watch it, kid. Freeze again, and you get us all wiped out. You could've got your buddy killed then, y'know."

I smiled faintly. I can't do anything else. So they forgive me. How goddam fucking big of them. And it's all Stancato's doing, of course. He likes to do this to me. He knows how much I loathe him, and he knows it embarrasses me when I have to feel grateful to him. The bastard. Not enough showing me up all the time, making me feel like a fool, he wants me to be a thankful fool, happy over his interest in li'l ol' me. Shit, shit, shit.

Dark is draping the forest. The others have lowered their nightvisors. I pull mine down, and the trees turn to stiff black shadows outlined against a field of red. Only the branches show. The needles are invisible for some reason. I shiver briefly, or maybe just tremble. The forest has become a murky hell, full of charcoal skeletons and half-seen shapes. I think I preferred the darkness. But I keep the visor down.

We move off, the Gut leading, the rest of us strung out behind. I don't know where we're going, or why. I don't care. I just want this to be over with. Only a handful of hours to midnight now. Then another day, and another midnight, and the weekend's over. And the drop-chopper returns to collect us. Me. I made it this far. Maybe I can make it all the way.

Next weekend, back to tennis. I don't need this. Maybe Stancato does, but he's sick. I don't. This is where Birch gets out.

Yes. I can do it. The thought soothes me. I clutch my gun and walk more quickly.

We march for hours, silent except for heavy breathing and the crunch of new-formed ice underfoot as it gets colder. I forget about the war, Stancato, everything. Except my feet and the cold. My boots have been soaked through and through, and the wetness has seeped in. My feet hurt for a long time, but now they've stopped. Numb. But tomorrow there will be blisters. I hate blisters. I'll bet Stancato never gets blisters. I'll bet never had a blister in his life. Or a pimple, for that matter. He'd be a lot more bearable if he'd grown up with a face full of pimples like any normal person.

The wind is blowing very loudly, shrieking around the pines, slicing through this shitty little uniform something awful. In a world of red and black, the biting cold is strangely out of place. Blue and white are the colors of cold. This is all wrong. But I feel it all the same.

We walk. Aimlessly? Probably not. But aimless to me. Tramp, tramp, tramp, the boys are marching. This is war. What an overrated gyp.

The thought comes, goes. Then my mind wanders back to my feet and the cold. As always. Nothing else can hold me. The gun is very cold now, the plastic almost freezing. Maybe it's frozen to my hand. That should keep me from dropping it when they start shooting again.

More walking. All in silence. Breathing and footsteps ahead and behind me. But I don't know what's going on. It must be past midnight now. It must be. The war seems to have stopped for the night. I can't hear anything. But maybe my ears are tired, like the rest of me.

Fuck it all. Who cares. I'm cold. Fuck you, Stancato. And you, Dolecek. And you, Gut. All of you. Idiots.

Maybe it's near dawn. We've been walking a long time.

The idea excites me. I halt, very briefly, lift my visor. But there's no light to the east. The stars are still up. Orion riding high, his dogs at his heels. Brilliant points in the black. I can see his sword. I can never see his sword in the city.

The stars look cold. With the visor up, I can see the cold as well as feel it. I suck in a chunk of ice, feeling strangely restful.

Something shoves me from behind Stancato. "C'mon, Andy," he says, voice urgent. "Don't give up. We don't want to fall behind and get lost."

I growl at him and stumble ahead. Give up, hell. I wasn't giving up. I just stopped to see if it was dawn. That fucker. Doesn't he give me any credit?

We walk some more, through woods and mountains that look much like the woods and mountains we've already walked through. Through an icewater creek that wakes up my feet to sudden screaming pain. Then back into the woods. We walk. The night is silent, but far away a flight of skimmers flame across the sky and drip fire. Black fire, to us. We watch. We walk.

Finally, finally, rest. The Gut has found a cave. No, not a real cave. Just a small hollow in a wall of rock. But shelter. He slings off his pack, growls something to the Gawk, spreads out his groundcloth, and lays down. Instantly he is asleep, snoring. I'm exhausted. I lay down next to him. The others drop to their cloths, and stretch out.

The Gawk tells me I have the first watch.

I get up and watch, my muscles protesting, my mind blank. When the others are asleep, I slip up my visor and watch the stars. And the skimmers. The western horizon is the one that's light, shining with orange flame and bright white flashes that grow and die against the mountains. A battle somewhere. I listen for the sound of the guns. Dimly, far off. I can hear it.

They're all asleep now. The Gut looks like a sack of laundry, and he snores like a bellows. The Gawk is all curled up in the corner, a frightened little boy. The other guy, the hunk of cannonfodder, sleeps with his mouth hanging open. But Stancato looks good. He's stretched out sort of casual, as if the cold doesn't touch him, his face composed, breathing light and regular. Alert, I'll bet. He won't be taken by surprise if the Concoms come at us.

Briefly, I consider that. What would happen if I left here?

Maybe the Concoms would come. Wipe them out. Get some killpoints. It'd be easy.

No. I wouldn't be able to find my way back. Besides, what if the Concoms *didn't* get them? Then I'd be in trouble good. Besides, I can't leave men to die. Not even Stancato. Can I?

Well, maybe Stancato.

If I'd played tennis, I'd be home now, asleep probably, in a warm bed with Miriam. Not that she's that exciting. I married her on the rebound anyway, after Glenda left me for Stancato. Tall, blond Glenda. Always so nice until *he* came along, then turning on me, siding with him, cutting me down when I tried to keep her. She made a big mistake. I would've married her. Stancato just digs her body.

So Glenda lost. And me too, I wound up with fat, dull Miriam. Only Stancato wins.

I could shoot him. I wonder if he knows that. I could kill him right here, as he sleeps. They'd never suspect. He'd be just another casualty of the war.

Or would he? They must have some way to tell who shot who. Else how could they keep track of the killpoints? I could let him have it from behind, but they'd find me out. Concom bullets must be different, or something like that. I'm sure it has something to do with the guns. I know they can find you when your time is up, if you've still got the gun. Maybe the same gadget keeps track of who you shoot.

I kill Stancato, and he gets me from beyond the grave. Shit. A final victory. I'm not going to give him that too.

I shove the thought aside. I'm not going to kill Stancato. I'll be lucky if I kill anybody. I'll probably freeze again. One way or the other.

I stand there and think on that and watch the night. Hours pass. Finally, I wake the Gawk to relieve me, and sleep comes. On a bed of ice-slick stone.

*   *   *

Awareness returns with a backache and a scream. I jerk up, groggy, confused. Someone is screaming. I look at the entrance, blink. Bullets whine around me.

The Concoms are outside.

We're trapped, locked in. Dead men. They're going to kill me. Fear comes in great waves. I stare, shake.

Stancato is on his stomach near the front of the hollow, sweeping his gun back and forth, laying down withering fire in great moving arcs. They are bodies outside. And one half-inside. The nameless beef boy. He got more than one slug. His body is in two parts. The bottom half is near the exit. The rest is all over the cave.

There's blood on my clothes. I study it, sick. I want to go to sleep again.

Something explodes just outside our shelter, and fragments tear into the cave and bounce off the rock. Nobody buys it, though. There's a lot of screaming going on, outside and in. I can't make any sense of all the noise.

The Gawk is lying next to Stancato, his back to the door, clicking a new cartridge chamber into his gun. He looks at me, snarls. Then he gets up, grabs my gun, shoves it into my stomach. "Shoot. Fight, you fucking green asshole—*shoot!*"

He turns back to the door, drops to his knees.

And catches a bullet right in the neck. Spurting blood, screaming, he falls back onto me.

He's dropped his gun. I pick it up and hand it to him, but he won't take it.

"Andy," Stancato says. "Down. Down before they get you." He fires as he talks, never stopping. So efficient, so calm. He doesn't look frightened. The killing machine, the hero, the great warrior.

I decide to show him. I drop the Gawk to lie in his own blood, lie down next to Stancato, bring up my gun, wrap my finger round the trigger.

Outside, dawn breaks. Sunday dawn. Halfway home now, but they're after me. I can't see them, though. Just points of light from two-three spots, where their fire rakes the cave mouth. And the positions move.

I fire. Bullets spray out in a steady stream. There's no kick. The gun just warms slightly. I shoot, not at anything, just wiping out the trees. Maybe I'll hit something, but I don't especially want to.

My firing has given Stancato his chance. He stops to reload, sliding back in the cave a little, keeping low, taking the cartridge chamber from his belt and calmly fitting it into the gun. No fumbling, no hurry. No mistakes. In a second he's next to me again, and we rake the trees together.

Somebody screams. "We got one," I say, and stop firing.

"Maybe they want us to think so," Stancato says. "Want us to come out. They can't get in, but they know we're trapped."

Trapped. Yes. I remember that. We're trapped. The Gut, the great vet, our fearless buddy, he got us trapped, probably got us killed. I'm furious. Stancato is firing alone.

Then I realize that the Gut isn't in the cave.

"Where is he?" I demanded of Stancato. I don't know the Gut's name. Strange. I thought I did. Stancato seems to.

He doesn't answer. He's stopped firing, too. He waits for someone to move.

We wait a good five minutes in silence. Hoping they'll come out to see if we're dead. They don't buy it. Instead they let their guns play over the rock, again and again, and bullets whine around us. Finally someone lobs a grenade. We have to give ourselves away. While I stare, Stancato grabs it and lobs it back. Right where it came from. He pitches for the office softball team, that Stancato. Good, of course. Very good.

The grenade explodes, tearing a gout out of the forest and the mud. Almost simultaneously, someone else opens up from the side. Screams. We got them.

A Concom staggers from behind a rock, bleeding from a hole in his chest the size of a fist. He gets two feet before the fire from the side cuts him down, hammering him ruthlessly as he tumbles and lays twitching. I watch with sick fascination as he screams and dies and clutches at the air. A thin, short black man, he dies hard. Ashamed, I realize that I have a hard-on. God. I'm sick. As bad as *they* are.

The Gut steps from the side, gun under his arm. "All clear," he shouts. "We got all of them."

Stancato rises and goes to him. "How many were there?"

"Eight," he says. He laughs. "Eight killpoints now. How's our side?"

I leave the cave, the blood-filled cave. Stancato and the Gut watch me approach, wordlessly. The answer to the Gut's question.

"Damn." That's all he says. He wanted me dead. Just like Stancato. I'm a coward, a sick coward, no good to them. The better men are dead. That's what the Gut's thinking.

"How—?" I say feebly. I can hardly think.

"I was coming on guard," the Gut says. "They opened fire on both of us. Got him, but I dropped down real quick-like and got into the bushes. And by then your buddy here was up and shooting at them, so they couldn't all go looking for me." He grins. "You shoot good," he says to Stancato. "You got a couple right off, and that's what saved us."

Saved us? Stancato saved us? Does he always have to be the hero? Something tightens within me. I turn away from the two of them, leaving them there to smile at each other, to grin and congratulate themselves on the blood they've spilled. The butchers.

The body of the black man lies near a clump of bare bushes and the branch of an evergreen. It's stopped moving now, but blood still drains slowly into the mud. His hands are old—lined leather hands too small for his great, baggy gray uniform.

I bend to him, to the man whose death I enjoyed. Nearby, half under the tree, I see his gun. I drop my own and reach for it.

The Concom guns are molded from greenish plastic, but otherwise they're the same. Of course. The weapons have to be the same, or the war wouldn't be fair. Underneath, there's a serial number, and a legend that says PROPERTY OF CONSOLIDATED COMBAT, INC.

You pays your money and you takes your choice. Fight in the mountains, Maneuver against Consolidated Combat! Try a *jungle* war, General Warfare versus Battlemaster! Slug it out in the streets of the city, Tactical League against Risk, Ltd. There are thirty-four war zones and ten fighting clubs. You pays your money and you takes your choice. But all the choices are the same.

I stand, the Concom gun in hand. And something comes at me.

He jumps out of the dim-lit dawn greenery, and I take him in in a blink. Gray uniform, black face, young—younger than me. A kid, a bloody, wounded kid. We didn't get them all. This one just lost his gun. He comes at me with a upraised knife.

I watch him come. He must cover several yards to get me. He comes swiftly, but not swiftly enough. I raise the gun.

And I can't fire. I can't fire. I can't fire.

When he's almost on me, Stancato guns him down from the side. Very efficiently. He curls slowly, drops gently into the mud. No screaming for this one. His knife falls near my foot.

Stancato has saved my life again.

I turn and look at him. He's smiling, and his gun smokes. Another killpoint. He's good at this. He'll get a big discount next time. Me? No. No way. They'll take away my license. They won't let me play. I get hard-ons from watching men die, but I can't kill them.

Stancato steps towards me, starts to say something. I look at my gun, avoiding his eyes. It's a Concom gun. Shoots Concom bullets. Maybe they can't tell who shot who except for the bullets. Stancato has saved my life twice. I can't stand it. He'll tell everyone.

As he walks toward me, I raise the gun, quite calmly, and shoot him. I think I do it very well.

He doesn't have time to look surprised. The Concom gun shoots a stream of bullets, real fast. His chest just explodes, and I turn the nozzle up, and the bullets keep coming, and his dark handsome calm smiling efficient face disintegrates into bloody meat.

The Gut is standing there, mouth open, screaming. "You shot your buddy!" he screams. "You shot your buddy!" I turn the gun and shoot him too. The hell with his vet marks. He isn't so hard to kill.

I've been marching all day, alone, through the woods. My feet are cold, but I don't mind. I have a Maneuver gun under one arm and a Concom gun under the other. I'm piling up killpoints. If I get enough, maybe next week I can sarge it.

Chicago
April, 1973

And Seven Times
Never Kill Man

Ye may kill for yourselves,
and your mates,
and your cubs as they need,
and ye can;

But kill not for pleasure of killing,
and seven times never kill Man!

—Rudyard Kipling

OUTSIDE THE WALLS THE JAENSHI CHILDREN HUNG, A ROW of small gray-furred bodies still and motionless at the ends of long ropes. The oldest among them, obviously, had been slaughtered before hanging; here a headless male swung upside down, the noose around the feet, while there dangled the blast-burned carcass of a female. But most of them, the dark hairy infants with the wide golden eyes, most of them had simply been hung. Toward dusk, when the wind came swirling down out of the ragged hills, the bodies of the lighter children would twist at the ends of their ropes and bang against the city walls, as if they were alive and pounding for admission.

But the guards on the walls paid the thumping no mind as they walked their relentless rounds, and the rust-streaked metal gates did not open.

"Do you believe in evil?" Arik neKrol asked Jannis Ryther as they looked down on the City of the Steel Angels from the crest of a nearby hill. Anger was written across every line of his flat yellow-brown face, as he squatted among the broken shards of what once had been a Jaenshi worship pyramid.

"Evil?" Ryther murmured in a distracted way. Her eyes never left the redstone walls below, where the dark bodies of the children were outlined starkly. The sun was going down, the fat red globe that the Steel Angels called the Heart of Bakkalon, and the valley beneath them seemed to swim in bloody mists.

"Evil," neKrol repeated. The trader was a short, pudgy man, his features decidedly mongoloid except for the flame-red hair that fell nearly to his waist. "It is a religious concept, and I am not a religious man. Long ago, when I was a very child growing up on ai-Emerel, I decided that there was no good or evil, only different ways of thinking." His small, soft hands felt around in the dust until he had a large, jagged shard that filled his fist. He stood and offered it to Ryther. "The Steel Angels have made me believe in evil again," he said.

She took the fragment from him wordlessly and turned it over in her hands. Ryther was much taller than neKrol, and much tinner; a hard bony woman with a long face, short black hair, and eyes without expression. The sweat-stained coveralls she wore hung loosely on her spare frame.

"Interesting," she said finally, after studying the shard for several minutes. It was as hard and smooth as glass, but stronger; colored a translucent red, yet so very dark it was almost black. "A plastic?" she asked, throwing it back to the ground.

NeKrol shrugged. "That was my very guess, but of course it is impossible. The Jaenshi work in bone and wood and sometimes metal, but plastic is centuries beyond them."

"Or behind them," Ryther said. "You say these worship pyramids are scattered all through the forest?"

"Yes, as far as I have ranged. But the Angels have smashed all those close to their valley, to drive the Jaenshi away. As they expand, and they *will* expand, they will smash others."

Ryther nodded. She looked down into the valley again, and as she did the last sliver of the Heart of Bakkalon slid below the western mountains and the city lights began to come on. The Jaenshi children swung in pools of soft blue illumination, and just above the city gates two stick figures could be seen working. Shortly they heaved something outward, a rope uncoiled, and then another small dark shadow jerked and twitched against the wall. "Why?" Ryther said, in a cool voice, watching.

NeKrol was anything but cool. "The Jaenshi tried to defend one of their pyramids. Spears and knives and rocks against the Steel Angels with lasers and blasters and screech-guns. But they caught them unaware, killed a man. The Proctor announced it would not happen again." He spat. "Evil. The children trust them, you see."

"Interesting," Ryther said.

"Can you do anything?" neKrol asked, his voice agitated. "You have your ship, your crew. The Jaenshi need a protector, Jannis. They are helpless before the Angels."

"I have four men in my crew," Ryther said evenly. "Perhaps four hunting lasers as well." That was all the answer she gave.

NeKrol looked at her helplessly. *"Nothing?"*

"Tomorrow, perhaps, the Proctor will call on us. He has surely seen the *Lights* descend. Perhaps the Angels wish to trade." She glanced again into the valley. "Come, Arik, we must go back to your base. The trade goods must be loaded."

Wyatt, Proctor of the Children of Bakkalon on the World of Corlos, was tall and red and skeletal, and the muscles stood out clearly on his bare arms. His blue-black hair was cropped very short, his carriage was stiff and erect. Like all

the Steel Angels, he wore a uniform of chameleon cloth (a
pale brown now, as he stood in the full light of day on the
edge of the small, crude spacefield), a mesh-steel belt with
hand-laser and communicator and screechgun, and a stiff red
Roman collar. The tiny figurine that hung on a chain about
his neck—the pale child Bakkalon, nude and innocent and
bright-eyed, but holding a great black sword in one small
fist—was the only sign of Wyatt's rank.

Four other Angels stood behind him: two men, two women,
all dressed identically. There was a sameness about their
faces, too; the hair always cropped tightly, whether it was
blond or red or brown, the eyes alert and cold and a little
fanatic, the upright posture that seemed to characterize members of the military-religious sect, the bodies hard and fit.
NeKrol, who was soft and slouching and sloppy, disliked
everything about the Angels.

Proctor Wyatt had arrived shortly after dawn, sending one
of his squad to pound on the door of the small gray prefab
bubble that was neKrol's trading base and home. Sleepy and
angry, but with a guarded politeness, the trader had risen to
greet the Angels, and had escorted them out to the center of
the spacefield, where the scarred metal teardrop of the *Lights
of Jolostar* squatted on three retractable legs.

The cargo ports were all sealed now; Ryther's crew had
spent most of the evening unloading neKrol's trade goods
and replacing them in the ship's hold with crates of Jaenshi
artifacts that might bring good prices from collectors of
extraterrestrial art. No way of knowing until a dealer looked
over the goods; Ryther had dropped neKrol only a year ago,
and this was the first pickup.

"I am an independent trader, and Arik is my agent on this
world," Ryther told the proctor when she met him on the
edge of the field. "You must deal through him."

"I see," Proctor Wyatt said. He still held the list he had
offered Ryther, of goods the Angels wanted from the indus-

trialized colonies on Avalon and Jamison's World. "But neKrol will not deal with us."

Ryther looked at him blankly.

"With good reason," neKrol said. "I trade with the Jaenshi, you slaughter them."

The Proctor had spoken to neKrol often in the months since the Steel Angels had established their city-colony, and the talks had all ended in arguments; now he ignored him. "The steps we took were needed," Wyatt said to Ryther. "When an animal kills a man, the animal must be punished, and other animals must see and learn, so that beasts may know that man, the seed of Earth and child of Bakkalon, is the lord and master of them all."

NeKrol snorted. "The Jaenshi are not beasts, Proctor, they are an intelligent race, with their own religion and art and customs, and they . . ."

Wyatt looked at him. "They have no soul. Only the children of Bakkalon have souls, only the seed of Earth. What mind they may have is relevant only to you, and perhaps them. Soulless, they are beasts."

"Arik has shown me the worship pyramids they build," Ryther said. "Surely creatures that build such shrines must have souls."

The Proctor shook his head. "You are in error in your belief. It is written clearly in the Book. We, the seed of Earth, are truly the children of Bakkalom, and no others. The rest are animals, and in Bakkalon's name we must assert our dominion over them."

"Very well," Ryther said. "But you will have to assert your dominion without aid from the *Lights of Jolostar*, I'm afraid. And I must inform you, Proctor, that I find your actions seriously disturbing, and intend to report them when I return to Jamison's World."

"I expected no less," Wyatt said. "Perhaps by next year you will burn with love of Bakkalon, and we may talk again. Until then, the world of Corlos will survive." He saluted her, and walked briskly from the field, followed by the four Steel Angels.

"What good will it do to report them?" neKrol said bitterly, after they had gone.

"None," Ryther said, looking off toward the forest. The wind was kicking up the dust around her, and her shoulders slumped, as if she were very tired. "The Jamies won't care, and if they did, what could they do?"

NeKrol remembered the heavy red-bound book that Wyatt had given him months ago. "And Bakkalon the pale child fashioned his children out of steel," he quoted, "for the stars will break those of softer flesh. And in the hand of each new-made infant He placed a beaten sword, telling them, 'This is the Truth and the Way.' " He spat in disgust. "That is their very creed. And we can do nothing?"

Her face was empty of expression now. "I will leave you two lasers. In a year, make sure the Jaenshi know how to use them. I believe I know what sort of trade goods I should bring."

The Jaenshi lived in clans (as neKrol thought of them) of twenty to thirty, each clan divided equally between adults and children, each having its own home-forest and worship pyramid. They did not build; they slept curled up in trees around their pyramid. For food, they foraged; juicy blue-black fruits grew everywhere, and there were three varieties of edible berries, a hallucinogenic leaf, and a soapy yellow root the Jaenshi dug for. NeKrol had found them to be hunters as well, though infrequently. A clan would go for months without meat, while the snuffling brown bushogs multiplied all around them, digging up roots and playing with the children. Then suddenly, when the bushog population had reached some critical point, the Jaenshi spearmen would walk among them calmly, killing two out of every three, and that week great hog roasts would be held each night around the pyramid. Similar patterns could be discerned with the white-bodied tree slugs that sometimes covered the fruit trees like a plague, until the Jaenshi gathered them for a stew, and with the fruit-stealing pseudomonks that haunted the higher limbs.

So far as neKrol could tell, there were no predators in the forests of the Jaenshi. In his early months on their world, he had worn a long force-knife and a hand-laser as he walked from pyramid to pyramid on his trade route. But he had never encountered anything even remotely hostile, and now the knife lay broken in his kitchen, while the laser was long lost.

The day after the *Lights of Jolostar* departed, neKrol went armed into the forest again, with one of Ryther's hunting lasers slung over his shoulder.

Less than two kilometers from his base, neKrol found the camp of the Jaenshi he called the waterfall folk. They lived up against the side of a heavy-wooded hill, where a stream of tumbling blue-white water came sliding and bouncing down, dividing and rejoining itself over and over, so the whole hillside was an intricate glittering web of waterfalls and rapids and shallow pools and spraying wet curtains. The clan's worship pyramid sat in the bottommost pool, on a flat gray stone in the middle of the eddies; taller than most Jaenshi, coming up to neKrol's chin, looking infinitely heavy and solid and immovable, a three-sided block of dark, dark red.

NeKrol was not fooled. He had seen other pyramids sliced to pieces by the lasers of the Steel Angels and shattered by the flames of their blasters; whatever powers the pyramids might have in Jaenshi myth, whatever mysteries might lie behind their origin, it was not enough to stay the swords of Bakkalon.

The glade around the pyramid-pool was alive with sunlight when neKrol entered, and the long grasses swayed in the light breeze, but most of the waterfall folk were elsewhere. In the trees perhaps, climbing and coupling and pulling down fruits, or ranging through the forests on their hill. The trader found only a few small children riding on a bushog in the clearing when he arrived. He sat down to wait, warm in the sunlight.

Soon the old talker appeared.

He sat down next to neKrol, a tiny shriveled Jaenshi with only a few patches of dirty gray-white fur left to hide the wrinkles in his skin. He was toothless, clawless, feeble; but his eyes, wide and golden and pupilless as those of any Jaenshi, were still alert, alive. He was the talker of the waterfall folk, the one in closest communication with the worship pyramid. Every clan had a talker.

"I have something new to trade," neKrol said, in the soft slurred speech of the Jaenshi. He had learned the tongue before coming here, back on Avalon. Tomas Chung, the legendary Avalonian linguesp, had broken it centuries before, when the Kleronomas Survey brushed by this world. No other human had visited the Jaenshi since, but the maps of Kleronomas and Chung's language-pattern analysis both remained alive in the computers at the Avalon Institute for the Study of Non-Human Intelligence.

"We have made you more statues, have fashioned new woods," the old talker said. "What have you brought? Salt?"

NeKrol undid his knapsack, laid it out, and opened it. He took out one of the bricks of salt he carried, and laid it before the old talker. "Salt," he said. "And more." He laid the hunting rifle before the Jaenshi.

"What is this?" the old talker asked.

"Do you know of the Steel Angels?" neKrol asked.

The other nodded, a gesture neKrol had taught him. "The godless who run from the dead valley speak of them. They are the ones who make the gods grow silent, the pyramid breakers."

"This is a tool like the Steel Angels use to break your pyramids," neKrol said. "I am offering it to you in trade."

The old talker sat very still. "But we do not wish to break pyramids," he said.

"This tool can be used for other things," neKrol said. "In

time, the Steel Angels may come here, to break the pyramid of the waterfall folk. If by then you have tools like this, you can stop them. The people of the pyramid in the ring-of-stone tried to stop the Steel Angels with spears and knives, and now they are scattered and wild and their children hang dead from the walls of the City of the Steel Angels. Other clans of the Jaenshi were unresisting, yet now they too are godless and landless. The time will come when the waterfall folk will need this tool, old talker.''

The Jaenshi elder lifted the laser and turned it curiously in his small withered hands. ''We must pray on this,'' he said. ''Stay, Arik. Tonight we shall tell you, when the god looks down on us. Until then, we shall trade.'' He rose abruptly, gave a swift glance at the pyramid across the pool, and faded into the forest, still holding the laser.

NeKrol sighed. He had a long wait before him; the prayer assemblies never came until sundown. He moved to the edge of the pool and unlaced his heavy boots to soak his sweaty, calloused feet in the crisp cold waters.

When he looked up, the first of the carvers had arrived; a lithe young Jaenshi female with a touch of auburn in her body fur. Silent (they were all silent in neKrol's presence, all save the talker), she offered him her work.

It was a statuette no larger than his fist, a heavy-breasted fertility goddess fashioned out of the fragrant, thin-veined blue wood of the fruit trees. She sat cross-legged on a triangular base, and three thin slivers of bone rose from each corner of the triangle to meet above her head in a blob of clay.

NeKrol took the carving, turned it this way and that, and nodded his approval. The Jaenshi smiled and vanished, taking the salt brick with her. Long after she was gone, neKrol continued to admire his acquisition. He had traded all his life, spending ten years among the squid-faced gethsoids of Aath and four with the stick-thin Fyndii, traveling a trader's circuit to a half-dozen stone age planets that had once been slaveworlds of the broken Hrangan Empire; but nowhere had he found artists like the Jaenshi. Not for the first time, he wondered why neither Kleronomas nor Chung had mentioned the native carvings. He was glad they hadn't, though, and fairly certain that once the dealers saw the crates of wooden gods he had sent back with Ryther, the world would be overrun by traders. As it was, he had been sent here entirely on speculation, in hopes, of finding a Jaenshi drug or herb or liquor that might move well in stellar trade. Instead he'd found the art, like an answer to a prayer.

Other workmen came and went as the morning turned to afternoon and the afternoon to dusk, setting their craft before him. He looked over each piece carefully, taking some and declining others, paying for what he took in salt. Before full darkness had descended, a small pile of goods sat by his right hand; a matched set of redstone knives, a gray deathcloth woven from the fur of an elderly Jaenshi by his widow and friends (with his face wrought upon it in the silky golden hairs of a pseudomonk), a bone spear with tracings that reminded neKrol of the runes of Old Earth legend; and statues. The statues were his favorites, always; so often alien art was alien beyond comprehension, but the Jaenshi work-men touched emotional chords in him. The gods they carved, each sitting in a bone pyramid, wore Jaenshi faces, yet at the same time seemed archetypically human: stern-faced war gods, things that looked oddly like satyrs, fertility goddesses like the one he had bought, almost-manlike warriors and nymphs. Often neKrol had wished that he had a formal education in extee anthropology, so that he might write a book on the universals of myth. The Jaenshi surely had a rich mythology, though the talkers never spoke of it; nothing else could explain the carvings. Perhaps the old gods were no longer worshipped, but they were still remembered.

By the time the Heart of Bakkalon went down and the last reddish rays ceased to filter through the looming trees, neKrol had gathered as much as he could carry, and his salt was all but exhausted. He laced up his boots again, packed his acquisitions with painstaking care, and sat patiently in the poolside grass, waiting. One by one, the waterfall folk joined him. Finally the old talker returned.

The prayers began.

The old talker, with the laser still in his hand, waded carefully across the night-dark waters, to squat by the black bulk of the pyramid. The others, adults and children together, now some forty strong, chose spots in the grass near the banks, behind neKrol and around him. Like him, they looked out over the pool, at the pyramid and the talker outlined clearly in the light of a new-risen, oversized moon. Setting the laser down on the stone, the old talker pressed both palms flat against the side of the pyramid, and his body seemed to go stiff, while all the other Jaenshi also tensed and grew very quiet.

NeKrol shifted restlessly and fought a yawn. It was not the first time he'd sat through a prayer ritual, and he knew the routine. A good hour of boredom lay before him; the Jaenshi did silent worship, and there was nothing to be heard but their steady breathing, nothing to be seen but forty impassive faces. Sighing, the trader tried to relax, closing his eyes and concentrating on the soft grass beneath him and the warm breeze that tossed his wild mane of hair. Here, briefly, he found peace. How long would it last, he mused, should the Steel Angels leave their valley . . .

The hour passed, but neKrol, lost in meditation, scarce felt the flow of time. Until suddenly he heard the rustlings and chatter around him, as the waterfall folk rose and went back into the forest. And then the old talker stood in front of him, and laid the laser at his feet.

"No," he said simply.

NeKrol started. "What? But you *must*. Let me show you what it can do . . ."

"I have had a vision, Arik. The god has shown me. But

also he has shown me that it would not be a good thing to take this in trade."

"Old Talker, the Steel Angels will come . . ."

"If they come, our god shall speak to them," the Jaenshi elder said, in his purring speech, but there was finality in the gentle voice, and no appeal in the vast liquid eyes.

"For our food, we thank ourselves, none other. It is ours because we worked for it, ours because we fought for it, ours by the only right that is: the right of the strong. But for that strength—for the might of our arms and the steel of our swords and the fire in our hearts—we thank Bakkalon, the pale child, who gave us life and taught us how to keep it."

The Proctor stood stiffly at the centermost of the five long wooden tables that stretched the length of the great mess hall, pronouncing each word of the grace with solemn dignity. His large veined hands pressed tightly together as he spoke, against the flat of the upward-jutting sword, and the dim lights had faded his uniform to an almost-black. Around him, the Steel Angels sat at attention, their food untouched before them; fat boiled tubers, steaming chunks of bushog meat, black bread, bowls of crunchy green neograss. Children below the fighting age of ten, in smocks of starchy white and the omnipresent mesh-steel belts, filled the two outermost tables beneath the slit-like windows; toddlers struggled to sit still under the watchful eyes of stern nine-year-old houseparents with hardwood batons in their belts. Further in, the fighting brotherhood sat, fully armed, at two equally long tables, men and women alternating, leather-skinned veterans sitting next to ten-year-olds who had barely moved from the children's dorm to the barracks. All of them wore the same chameleon cloth as Wyatt, though without his collar, and a few had buttons of rank. The center table, less than half the length of the others, held the cadre of the Steel Angels; the squadfathers and squadmothers, the weaponsmasters, the healers, the four fieldbishops, all those who wore the high, stiff crimson collar. And the Proctor, at its head.

"Let us eat," Wyatt said at last. His sword moved above his table with a whoosh, describing the slash of blessing, and he sat to his meal. The Proctor, like all the others, had stood single-file in the line that wound past the kitchen to the mess hall, and his portions were no larger than the least of the brotherhood.

There was a clink of knives and forks, and the infrequent clatter of a plate, and from time to time the thwack of a baton, as a houseparent punished some transgression of discipline by one of his charges; other than that, the hall was silent. The Steel Angels did not speak at meals, but rather meditated on the lessons of the day as they consumed their spartan fare.

Afterwards, the children—still silent—marched out of the hall, back to their dormitory. The fighting brotherhood followed, some to chapel, most to the barracks, a few to guard duty on the walls. The men they were relieving would find late meals still warm in the kitchen.

The officer core remained; after the plates were cleared away, the meal became a staff meeting.

"At ease," Wyatt said, but the figures along the table relaxed little, if at all. Relaxation had been bred out of them by now. The Proctor found one of them with his eyes. "Dhallis," he said, "you have the report I requested?"

Fieldbishop Dhallis nodded. She was a husky middle-aged woman with thick muscles and skin the color of brown leather. On her collar was a small steel insignia, an ornamental memory-chip that meant Computer Services. "Yes, Proctor," she said, in a hard, precise voice. "Jamison's World is a fourth-generation colony, settled mostly from Old Poseidon. One large continent, almost entirely unexplored, and more than twelve thousand islands of various sizes. The human population is concentrated almost entirely on the islands, and makes its living by farming sea and land, aquatic husbandry, and heavy industry. The oceans are rich in food and metal. The total population is about seventy-nine million. There are two large cities, both with spaceports: Port Jamison and Jolostar.'' She looked down at the computer printout on the table. ''Jamison's World was not even charted at the time of the Double War. It has never known military action, and the only Jamie armed forces are their planetary police. It has no colonial program and has never attempted to claim political jurisdiction beyond its own atmosphere.''

The Proctor nodded. ''Excellent. Then the trader's threat to report us is essentially an empty one. We can proceed. Squadfather Walman?''

''Four Jaenshi were taken today, Proctor, and are now on the walls,'' Walman reported. He was a ruddy young man with a blond crewcut and large ears. ''If I might, sir, I would request discussion of possible termination of the campaign. Each day we search harder for less. We have virtually wiped out every Jaenshi youngling of the clans who originally inhabited Sword Valley.''

Wyatt nodded. ''Other opinions?''

Fieldbishop Lyon, blue-eyed and gaunt, indicated dissent. ''The adults remain alive. The mature beast is more dangerous than the youngling, Squadfather.''

''Not in this case,'' Weaponsmaster C'ara DaHan said. DaHan was a giant of a man, bald and bronze-colored, the chief of Psychological Weaponry and Enemy Intelligence. ''Our studies show that once the pyramid is destroyed, neither full-grown Jaenshi nor the immature pose any threat whatsoever to the children of Bakkalon. Their social structure virtually disintegrates. The adults either flee, hoping to join some other clan, or revert to near-animal savagery. They abandon the younglings, most of whom fend for themselves in a confused sort of way and offer no resistance when we take them. Considering the number of Jaenshi on our walls, and those reported slain by predators or each other, I strongly feel that Sword Valley is virtually clean of the animals.

Winter is coming, Proctor, and much must be done. Squad-father Walman and his men should be set to other tasks.''

There was more discussion, but the tone had been set; most of the speakers backed DaHan. Wyatt listened carefully, and all the while prayed to Bakkalon for guidance. Finally he motioned for quiet.

"Squadfather," he said to Walman, "tomorrow collect all the Jaenshi—both adults and children—that you can, but do not hang them if they are unresisting. Instead, take them to the city, and show them their clanmates on our walls. Then cast them from the valley, one in each direction of the compass." He bowed his head. "It is my hope that they will carry a message, to all the Jaenshi, of the price that must be paid when a beast raises hand or claw or blade against the seed of Earth. Then, when the spring comes and the children of Bakkalon move beyond Sword Valley, the Jaenshi will peacefully abandon their pyramids and quit whatever lands men may require, so the glory of the pale child might be spread."

Lyon and DaHan both nodded, among others. "Speak wisdom to us," Fieldbishop Dhallis said then.

Proctor Wyatt agreed. One of the lesser-ranking squad-mothers brought him the Book, and he opened it to the Chapter of Teachings.

"In those days much evil had come upon the seed of Earth," the Proctor read, "for the children of Bakkalon had abandoned Him to bow to softer gods. So their skies grew dark and upon them from above came the Sons of Hranga with red eyes and demon teeth, and upon them from below came the vast Horde of Fyndii like a cloud of locusts that blotted out the stars. And the worlds flamed, and the children cried out, 'Save us! Save us!'

"And the pale child came and stood before them, with His great sword in His hand, and in a voice like thunder He rebuked them. 'You have been weak children,' He told them, 'for you have disobeyed. Where are your swords? Did I not set swords in your hands?'

"And the children cried out, 'We have beaten them into plowshares, oh Bakkalon!'

"And He was sore angry. 'With plowshares, then, shall you face the Sons of Hranga! With plowshares shall you slay the Horde of Fyndii?'' And He left them, and heard no more their weeping, for the Heart of Bakkalon is a Heart of Fire.

"But then one among the seed of Earth dried his tears, for the skies did burn so bright that they ran scalding on his cheeks. And the bloodlust rose in him and he beat his plow-share back into a sword, and charged the Sons of Hranga, slaying as he went. The others saw, and followed, and a great battle-cry rang across the worlds.

"And the pale child heard, and came again, for the sound of battle is more pleasing to his ears than the sound of wails. And when He saw, He smiled. 'Now you are my children again,' He said to the seed of Earth. 'For you had turned against me to worship a god who calls himself a lamb, but did you not know that lambs go only to the slaughter? Yet now your eyes have cleared, and again you are the Wolves of God!'

"And Bakkalon gave them all swords again, all His children and all the seed of Earth, and He lifted his great black blade, the Demon-Reaver that slays the soulless, and swung it. And the Sons of Hranga fell before His might, and the great Horde that was the Fyndii burned beneath His gaze. And the children of Bakkalon swept across the worlds.''

The Proctor lifted his eyes. "Go, my brothers-in-arms, and think on the Teachings of Bakkalon as you sleep. May the pale child grant you visions!"

They were dismissed.

The trees on the hill were bare and glazed with ice, and the snow—unbroken except for their footsteps and the stirrings of the bitter-sharp north wind—gleamed a blinding white in the noon sun. In the valley beneath, the City of the Steel

Angels looked preternaturally clean and still. Great snow-drifts had piled against the eastern walls, climbing halfway up the stark scarlet stone; the gates had not opened in months. Long ago, the children of Bakkalon had taken their harvest and fallen back inside the city, to huddle around their fires. But for the blue lights that burned late into the cold black night, and the occasional guard pacing atop the walls, neKrol would hardly have known that the Angels still lived.

The Jaenshi that neKrol had come to think of as the bitter speaker looked at him out of eyes curiously darker than the soft gold of her brothers. "Below the snow, the god lies broken," she said, and even the soothing tones of the Jaenshi tongue could not hide the hardness in her voice. They stood at the very spot where neKrol had once taken Ryther, the spot where the pyramid of the people of the ring-of-stone once stood. NeKrol was sheathed head to foot in a white thermosuit that clung too tightly, accenting every unsightly bulge. He looked out on Sword Valley from behind a dark blue plastifilm in the suit's cowl. But the Jaenshi, the bitter speaker, was nude, covered only by the thick gray fur of her winter coat. The strap of the hunting laser ran down between her breasts.

"Other gods beside yours will break unless the Steel Angels are stopped," neKrol said, shivering despite his thermosuit.

The bitter speaker seemed hardly to hear. "I was a child when they came, Arik. If they had left our god, I might be a child still. Afterwards, when the light went out and the glow inside me died, I wandered far from the ring-of-stone, beyond our own home forest; knowing nothing, eating where I could. Things are not the same in the dark valley. Bushogs honked at my passing, and charged me with their tusks, other Jaenshi threatened me and each other. I did not understand and I could not pray. Even when the Steel Angels found me, I did not understand, and I went with them to their city, knowing nothing of their speech. I remember the walls, and the children, many so much younger than me. Then I screamed and struggled; when I saw those on the ropes, something wild and godless stirred to life inside me." Her eyes regarded him, her eyes like burnished bronze. She shifted in the ankle-deep snow, curling a clawed hand around the strap of her laser.

NeKrol had taught her well since the day she had joined him, in the late summer when the Steel Angels had cast her from Sword Valley. The bitter speaker was by far the best shot of his six, the godless exiles he had gathered to him and trained. It was the only way; he had offered the lasers in trade to clan after clan, and each had refused. The Jaenshi were certain that their gods would protect them. Only the godless listened, and not all of them; many—the young children, the quiet ones, the first to flee—many had been accepted into other clans. But others, like the bitter speaker, had grown too savage, had seen too much; they fit no longer. She had been the first to take the weapon, after the old talker had sent her away from the waterfall folk.

"It is often better to be without gods," neKrol told her. "Those below us have a god, and it has made them what they are. And so the Jaenshi have gods, and because they trust, they die. You godless are their only hope."

The bitter speaker did not answer. She only looked down on the silent city, besieged by snow, and her eyes smoldered.

And neKrol watched her, and wondered. He and his six were the hope of the Jaenshi, he had said; if so, was there hope at all? The bitter speaker, and all his exiles, had a madness about them, a rage that made him tremble. Even if Ryther came with the lasers, even if so small a group could stop the Angels' march, even if all that came to pass—what then? Should all the Angels die tomorrow, where would his godless find a place?

They stood, all quiet, while the snow stirred under their feet and the north wind bit at them.

The chapel was dark and quiet. Flameglobes burned a dim, eerie red in either corner, and the rows of plain wooden benches were empty. Above the heavy altar, a slab of rough black stone, Bakkalon stood in hologram, so real he almost breathed; a boy, a mere boy, naked and milky white, with the wide eyes and blond hair of innocent youth. In his hand, half again taller than himself, was the great black sword.

Wyatt knelt before the projection, head bowed and very still. All through the winter his dreams had been dark and troubled, so each day he would kneel and pray for guidance. There was none else to seek but Bakkalon; he, Wyatt, was the Proctor, who led in battle and in faith. He alone must riddle his visions.

So daily he wrestled with his thoughts, until the snows began to melt and the knees of his uniform had nearly worn through from long scraping on the floor. Finally, he had decided, and this day he had called upon the senior collars to join him in the chapel.

Alone they entered, while the Proctor knelt unmoving, and chose seats on the benches behind him, each apart from his fellows. Wyatt took no notice; he prayed only that his words would be correct, his vision true. When they were all there, he stood and turned to face them.

"Many are the worlds on which the children of Bakkalon have lived," he told them, "but none so blessed as this, our Corlos. A great time is on us, my brothers-in-arms. The pale child has come to me in my sleep, as once he came to the first Proctors in the years when the brotherhood was forged. He has given me visions."

They were quiet, all of them, their eyes humble and obedient; he was their Proctor, after all. There could be no questioning when one of higher rank spoke wisdom or gave orders. That was one of the precepts of Bakkalon, that the chain of command was sacred and never to be doubted. So all of them kept silence.

"Bakkalon Himself has walked upon this world. He has walked among the soulless and the beasts of the field and told them our dominion, and this he has said to me: that when the spring comes and the seed of Earth moves from Sword Valley to take new land, all the animals shall know their place and retire before us. This I do prophesy!

"More, we shall see miracles. That too the pale child has promised me, signs by which we will know His truth, signs that shall bolster our faith with new revelation. But so too shall our faith be tested, for it will be a time of sacrifices, and Bakkalon will call upon us more than once to show our trust in Him. We must remember His Teachings and be true, and each of us must obey Him as a child obeys the parent and a fighting man his officer: that is, swiftly and without question. For the pale child knows best.

"These are the visions He has granted me, there are the dreams that I have dreamed. Brothers, pray with me."

And Wyatt turned again and knelt, and the rest knelt with him, and all the heads were bowed in prayer save one. In the shadows at the rear of the chapel where the flameglobes flickered but dimly, C'ara DaHan stared at his Proctor from beneath a heavy beetled brow.

That night, after a silent meal in the mess hall and a short staff meeting, the Weaponsmaster called upon Wyatt to go walking on the walls. "Proctor, my soul is troubled," he told him. "I must have counsel from he who is closest to Bakkalon." Wyatt nodded, and both donned heavy nightcloaks of black fur and oil-dark metal cloth, and together they walked the redstone parapets beneath the stars.

Near the guardhouse that stood above the city gates, DaHan paused and leaned out over the ledge, his eyes searching the slow-melting snow for long moments before he turned them on the Proctor. "Wyatt," he said at last, "my faith is weak."

The Proctor said nothing, merely watched the other, his face concealed by the hood of his nightcloak. Confession was not a part of the rites of the Steel Angels; Bakkalon had said that a fighting man's faith ought never to waver.

"In the old days," C'ara DaHan was saying, "many

weapons were used against the children of Bakkalon. Some, today, exist only in tales. Perhaps they never existed. Perhaps they are empty things, like the gods the soft men worship. I am only a Weaponsmaster; such knowledge is not mine.

"Yet there is a tale, my Proctor—one that troubles me. Once, it is said, in the long centuries of war, the Sons of Hranga loosed upon the seed of Earth foul vampires of the mind, the creatures men called soul-sucks. Their touch was invisible, but it crept across kilometers, farther than a man could see, farther than a laser could fire, and it brought madness. Visions, my Proctor, visions! False gods and foolish plans were put in the minds of men, and . . ."

"Silence," Wyatt said. His voice was hard, as cold as the night air that crackled around them and turned his breath to steam.

There was a long pause. Then, in a softer voice, the Proctor continued. "All winter I have prayed, DaHan, and struggled with my visions, I am the Proctor of the Children of Bakkalon on the World of Corlos, not some new-armed child to be lied to by false gods. I spoke only after I was sure. I spoke as your Proctor, as your father in faith and your commanding officer. That you would question me, Weaponsmaster, that you would doubt—this disturbs me greatly. Next will you stop to argue with me on the field of battle, to dispute some fine point of my orders?"

"Never, Proctor," DaHan said, kneeling in penance in the packed snow atop the walkway.

"I hope not. But, before I dismiss you, because you are my brother in Bakkalon, I will answer you, though I need not and it was wrong of you to expect it. I will tell you this; the Proctor Wyatt is a good officer as well as a devout man. The pale child has made prophecies to me, and has predicted that miracles will come to pass. All these things we shall see with our very eyes. But if the prophecies should fail us, and if no signs appear, well, our eyes will see that too. And then I will know that it was not Bakkalon who sent the visions, but only a false god, perhaps a soul-suck of Hranga. Or do you think a Hrangan can work miracles?"

"No," DaHan said, still on his knees, his great bald head downcast. "That would be heresy."

"Indeed," said Wyatt. The Proctor glanced briefly beyond the walls. The night was crisp and cold and there was no moon. He felt transfigured, and even the stars seemed to cry the glory of the pale child, for the constellation of the Sword was high upon the zenith, the Soldier reaching up toward it from where he stood on the horizon.

"Tonight you will walk guard without your cloak," the Proctor told DaHan when he looked down again. "And should the north wind blow and the cold bite at you, you will rejoice in the pain, for it will be a sign that you submit to your Proctor and your god. As your flesh grows bitter numb, the flame in your heart must burn hotter."

"Yes, my Proctor," DaHan said. He stood and removed his nightcloak, handing it to the other. Wyatt gave him the slash of blessing.

On the wallscreen in his darkened living quarters the taped drama went through its familiar measured paces, but neKrol, slouched in a large cushioned recliner with his eyes half-closed, hardly noticed. The bitter speaker and two of the other Jaenshi exiles sat on the floor, golden eyes rapt on the spectacle of humans chasing and shooting each other amid the vaulting tower cities of ai-Emerel; increasingly they had begun to grow curious about other worlds and other ways of life. It was all very strange, neKrol thought; the waterfall folk and the other clanned Jaenshi had never shown any such interest. He remembered the early days, before the coming of the Steel Angels in their ancient and soon-to-be-dismantled warship, when he had set all kinds of trade goods before the Jaenshi talkers; bright bolts of glittersilk from Avalon, glowstone jewelry from High Kavalaan, duralloy knives and solar generators and steel powerbows, books from a dozen worlds, medicines and wines—he had come with a little of everything. The talkers took some of it, from time to time, but never with any enthusiasm; the only offering that excited them was salt.

It was not until the spring rains came and the bitter speaker began to question him that neKrol realized, with a start, how seldom any of the Jaenshi clans had ever asked him *anything*. Perhaps their social structure and their religion stifled their natural intellectual curiosity. The exiles were certainly eager enough, especially the bitter speaker. NeKrol could answer only a small portion of her questions of late, and even then she always had new ones to puzzle him with. He had begun to grow appalled with the extent of his own ignorance.

But then, so had the bitter speaker; unlike the clanned Jaenshi—did the religion make *that* much difference?—she would answer questions as well, and neKrol had tried quizzing her on many things that he'd wondered at. But most of the time she would only blink in bafflement, and begin to question herself.

"There are no stories about our gods," she said to him once, when he'd tried to learn a little of Jaenshi myth. "What sort of stories could there be? The gods live in the worship pyramids, Arik, and we pray to them and they watch over us and light our lives. They do not bounce around and fight and break each other like your gods seem to do."

"But you had other gods once, before you came to worship the pyramids," neKrol objected. "The very ones your carvers did for me." He had even gone so far as to unpack a crate and show her, though surely she remembered, since the people of the pyramid in the ring-of-stone had been among the finest craftsmen.

Yet the bitter speaker only smoothed her fur, and shook her head. "I was too young to be a carver, so perhaps I was not told," she said. "We all know that which we need to know, but only the carvers need to do these things, so perhaps only they know the stories of these old gods."

Another time he had asked her about the pyramids, and had gotten even less. "Build them?" she had said. "We did not build them, Arik. They have always been, like the rocks and the trees." But then she blinked. "But they are *not* like the rocks and the trees, are they?" And, puzzled, she went away to talk to the others.

But if the godless Jaenshi were more thoughtful than their brothers in the clans, they were also more difficult, and each day neKrol realized more and more the futility of their enterprise. He had eight of the exiles with him now—they had found two more, half dead from starvation, in the height of winter—and they all took turns training with the two lasers and spying on the Angels. But even should Ryther return with the weaponry, their force was a joke against the might the Proctor could put in the field. The *Lights of Jolostar* would be carrying a full arms shipment in the expectation that every clan for a hundred kilometers would now be roused and angry, ready to resist the Steel Angels and overwhelm them by sheer force of numbers; Jannis would be blank-faced when only neKrol and his ragged band appeared to greet her.

If in fact they did. Even that was problematical; he was having much difficulty keeping his guerrilas together. Their hatred of the Steel Angels still bordered on madness, but they were far from a cohesive unit. None of them liked to take orders very well, and they fought constantly, going at each other with bared claws in struggles for social dominance. If neKrol had not warned them, he suspected they might even duel with the lasers. As for staying in good fighting shape, that too was a joke. Of the three females in the band, the bitter speaker was the only one who had not allowed herself to be impregnated. Since the Jaenshi usually gave birth in litters of four to eight, neKrol calculated that late summer would present them with an exile population explosion. And there would be more after that, he knew; the godless seemed to copulate almost hourly, and there was no such thing as

Jaenshi birth control. He wondered how the clans kept their population so stable, but his charges didn't know that either."

"I suppose we sexed less," the bitter speaker said when he asked her, "but I was a child, so I would not really know. Before I came here, there was never the urge. I was just young, I would think." But when she said it, she scratched herself and seemed very unsure.

Sighing, neKrol eased himself back in the recliner and tried to shut out the noise of the wall-screen. It was all going to be very difficult. Already the Steel Angels had emerged from behind their walls, and the powerwagons rolled up and down Sword Valley turning forest into farmland. He had gone up into the hills hmself, and it was easy to see that the spring planting would soon be done. Then, he suspected, the children of Bakkalon would try to expand. Just last week one of them—a giant "with no head fur," as his scout had described him—was seen up in the ring-of-stone, gathering shards from the broken pyramid. Whatever that meant, it could not be for the good.

Sometimes he felt sick at the forces he had set in motion, and almost wished that Ryther would forget the lasers. The bitter speaker was determined to strike as soon as they were armed, no matter what the odds. Frightened, neKrol reminded her of the hard Angel lesson the last time a Jaenshi had killed a man; in his dreams he still saw children on the walls.

But she only looked at him, with the bronze tinge of madness in her eyes, and said, "Yes, Arik. I remember."

Silent and efficient, the white-smocked kitchen boys cleared away the last of the evening's dishes and vanished. "At ease," Wyatt said to his officers. Then: "The time of miracles is upon us, as the pale child foretold.

"This morning I sent three squads into the hills to the southeast of Sword Valley, to disperse the Jaenshi clans on lands that we require. They reported back to me in early afternoon, and now I wish to share their reports with you. Squadmother Jolip, will you relate the events that transpired when you carried out your orders?''

''Yes, Proctor.'' Jolip stood, a white-skinned blond with a pinched face, her uniform hanging slightly loose on a lean body. ''I was assigned a squad of ten to clear out the so-called cliff clan, whose pyramid lies near the foot of a low granite cliff in the wilder part of the hills. The information provided by our intelligence indicated that they were one of the smaller clans, with only twenty-odd adults, so I dispensed with heavy armor. We did take a class five blastcannon, since the destruction of the Jaenshi pyramids is slow work with sidearms alone, but other than that our armament was strictly standard issue.

''We expected no resistance, but recalling the incident at the ring-of-stone, I was cautious. After a march of some twelve kilometers through the hills to the vicinity of the cliff, we fanned out in a semi-circle and moved in slowly, with screechguns drawn. A few Jaenshi were encountered in the forest, and these we took prisoner and marched before us, for use as shields in the event of an ambush or attack. That, of course, proved unnecessary.

''When we reached the pyramid by the cliff, they were waiting for us. At least twelve of the beasts, sir. One of them sat near the base of the pyramid with his hands pressed against its side, while the others surrounded him in a sort of a circle. They all looked up at us, but made no other move.''

She paused a minute, and rubbed a thoughtful finger up against the side of her nose. ''As I told the Proctor, it was all very odd from that point forward. Last summer, I twice led squads against the Jaenshi clans. The first time, having no idea of our intentions, none of the soulless were there; we simply destroyed the artifact and left. The second time, a crowd of the creatures milled around, hampering us with their bodies while not being actively hostile. They did not disperse until I had one of them screeched down. And, of course, I studied the reports of Squadfather Allor's difficulties at the ring-of-stone.

"This time, it was all quite different. I ordered two of my men to set the blastcannon on its tripod, and gave the beasts to understand that they must get out of the way. With hand signals, of course, since I know none of their ungodly tongue. They complied at once, splitting into two groups and, well, lining up, on either side of the line-of-fire. We kept them covered with our screechguns, of course, but everything seemed very peaceful.

"And so it was. The blaster took the pyramid out neatly, a big ball of flame and then sort of a thunder as the thing exploded. A few shards were scattered, but no one was injured, as we had all taken cover and the Jaenshi seemed unconcerned. After the pyramid broke, there was a sharp ozone smell, and for an instant a lingering bluish fire—perhaps an afterimage. I hardly had time to notice them, however, since that was when the Jaenshi all fell to their knees before us. All at once, sirs. And then they pressed their heads against the ground, prostrating themselves. I thought for a moment that they were trying to hail us as gods, because we had shattered their god, and I tried to tell them that we wanted none of their animal worship, and required only that they leave these lands at once. But then I saw that I had misunderstood, because that was when the other four clan members came forward from the trees atop the cliff, and climbed down, and gave us the statue. Then the rest got up. The last I saw, the entire clan was walking due east, away from Sword Valley and the outlying hills. I took the statue and brought it back to the Proctor." She fell silent but remained standing, waiting for questions.

"I have the statuette here," Wyatt said. He reached down beside his chair and set it on the table, then pulled off the white cloth covering he had wrapped around it.

The base was a triangle of rockhard blackbark, and three long splinters of bone rose from the corners to make a pyramid-frame. Within, exquisitely carved in every detail from soft blue wood, Bakkalon the pale child stood, holding a painted sword.

"What does this mean?" Fieldbishop Lyon asked, obviously startled.

"Sacrilege!" Fieldbishop Dhallis said.

"Nothing so serious," said Gorman, Fieldbishop for Heavy Armor. "The beasts are simply trying to ingratiate themselves, perhaps in the hope that we will stay our swords."

"None but the seed of Earth may bow to Bakkalon," Dhallis said. "It is written in the Book! The pale child will not look with favor on the soulless!"

"Silence, my brothers-in-arms!" the Proctor said, and the long table abruptly grew quiet again. Wyatt smiled a thin smile. "This is the first of the miracles of which I spoke this winter in the chapel, the first of the strange happenings that Bakkalon told to me. For truly He has walked this world, our Corlos, so even the beasts of the fields know His likeness! Think on it, my brothers. Think on this carving. Ask yourselves a few simple questions. Have any of the Jaenshi animals ever been permitted to set foot in this holy city?"

"No, of course not," someone said.

"Then clearly none of them have seen the holograph that stands above our altar. Nor have I often walked among the beasts, as my duties keep me here within the walls. So none could have seen the pale child's likeness on the chain of office that I wear, for the few Jaenshi who have seen my visage have not lived to speak of it—they were those I judged, who hung upon our city walls. The animals do not speak the language of the Earthseed, nor have any among us learned their simple beastly tongue. Lastly, they have not read the Book. Remember all this, and wonder; how did their carvers know what face and form to carve?"

Quiet; the leaders of the children of Bakkalon looked back and forth among themselves in wonderment.

Wyatt quietly folded his hands. "A miracle. We shall have

no more trouble with the Jaenshi, for the pale child has come to them.''

To the Proctor's right, Fieldbishop Dhallis sat rigidly. ''My Proctor, my leader in faith,'' she said, with some difficulty, each word coming slowly, ''surely, *surely*, you do not mean to tell us that these, these *animals*—that they can worship the pale child, that He accepts their worship!''

Wyatt seemed calm, benevolent; he only smiled. ''You need not trouble your soul, Dhallis. You wonder whether I commit the First Fallacy, remembering perhaps the Sacrilege of G'hra when a captive Hrangan bowed to Bakkalon to save himself from an animal's death, and the False Proctor Gibrone proclaimed that all who worship the pale child must have souls.'' He shook his head. ''You see, I read the Book. But no, Fieldbishop, no sacrilege has transpired. Bakkalon *has* walked among the Jaenshi, but surely has given them only truth. They have seen Him in all His armed dark glory, and heard Him proclaim that they are animals, without souls, as surely He would proclaim. Accordingly, they accept their place in the order of the universe, and retire before us. They will never kill a man again. Recall that they did not bow to the statue they carved, but rather gave the statue to *us,* the seed of Earth, who alone can rightfully worship it. When they did prostrate themselves, it was at *our* feet, as animals to men, and that is as it should be. You see? They have been given truth.''

Dhallis was nodding. ''Yes, my Proctor. I am enlightened. Forgive my moment of weakness.''

But halfway down the table, C'ara DaHan leaned forward and knotted his great knuckled hands, frowning all the while. ''My Proctor,'' he said heavily.

''Weaponsmaster?'' Wyatt returned. His face grew stern.

''Like the Fieldbishop, my soul has flickered briefly with worry, and I too would be enlightened, if I might?''

Wyatt smiled. ''Proceed,'' he said, in a voice without humor.

"A miracle this thing may be indeed," DaHan said, "but first we must question ourselves, to ascertain that it is not the trick of a soulless enemy. I do not fathom their strategem, or their reasons for acting as they have, but I do know of one way that the Jaenshi might have learned the features of our Bakkalon."

"Oh?"

"I speak of the Jamish trading base, and the red-haired trader Arik neKrol. He is an Earthseed, an Emereli by his looks, and we have given him the Book. But he remains without a burning love of Bakkalon, and goes without arms like a godless man. Since our landing he has opposed us, and he grew most hostile after the lesson we were forced to give the Jaenshi. Perhaps he put the cliff clan up to it, told them to do the carving, to some strange ends of his own. I believe that he *did* trade with them."

"I believe you speak truth, Weaponsmaster. In the early months after landing, I tried hard to convert neKrol. To no avail, but I did learn much of the Jaenshi beasts and of the trading he did with them." The Proctor still smiled. "He traded with one of the clans here in Sword Valley, with the people of ring-of-stone, with the cliff clan and that of the far fruit tangle, with the waterfall folk, and sundry clans further east."

"Then it is his doing," DaHan said. "A trick!"

All eyes moved to Wyatt. "I did not say that. NeKrol, whatever intentions he might have, is but a single man. He did not trade with all the Jaenshi, nor even know them all." The Proctor's smile grew briefly wider. "Those of you who have seen the Emereli know him for a man of flab and weakness; he could hardly walk as far as might be required, and he has neither aircar nor power sled."

"But he *did* have contact with the cliff clan," DaHan said. The deep-graven lines on his bronze forehead were set stubbornly.

"Yes, he did," Wyatt answered. "But Squadmother Jolip

did not go forth alone this morning. I also sent out Squadfather Walman and Squadfather Allor, to cross the waters of the White Knife. The land there is dark and fertile, better than that to the east. The cliff clan, who are southeast, were between Sword Valley and the White Knife, so they had to go. But the other pyramids we moved against belonged to far-river clans, more than thirty kilometers south. They have never seen the trader Arik neKrol, unless he has grown wings this winter.''

Then Wyatt bent again, and set two more statues on the table, and pulled away their coverings. One was set on a base of slate, and the figure was carved in a clumsy broad manner; the other was finely detailed soaproot, even to the struts of the pyramid. But except for the materials and the workmanship, the later statues were identical to the first.

"Do you see a trick, Weaponsmaster?" Wyatt asked.

DaHan looked, and said nothing, for Fieldbishop Lyon rose suddenly and said, "I see a miracle," and others echoed him. After the hubbub had finally quieted, the brawny Weaponsmaster lowered his head and said, very softly, "My Proctor. Read wisdom to us."

"The lasers, speaker, the *lasers*!" There was a tinge of hysterical desperation in neKrol's tone. "Ryther is not back yet, and that is the very point. We must wait."

He stood outside the bubble of the trading base, bare-chested and sweating in the hot morning sun, with the thick wind tugging at his tangled hair. The clamor had pulled him from a troubled sleep. He had stopped them just on the edge of the forest, and now the bitter speaker had turned to face him, looking fierce and hard and most unJaenshi-like with the laser slung across her shoulders, a bright blue glittersilk scarf knotted around her neck, and fat glowstone rings on all eight of her fingers. The other exiles, but for the two that were heavy with child, stood around her. One of them held the other laser, the rest carried quivers and powerbows. That had been the speaker's idea. Her newly-chosen mate was down on one knee, panting; he had run all the way from the ring-of-stone.

"No, Arik," the speaker said, eyes bronze-angry. "Your lasers are now a month overdue, by your own count of time. Each day we wait, and the Steel Angels smash more pyramids. Soon they may hang children again."

"Very soon," neKrol said. "Very soon, if you attack them. Where is your very hope of victory? Your watcher says they go with two squads and a powerwagon—can you stop them with a pair of lasers and four powerbows? Have you learned to think here, or not?"

"Yes," the speaker said, but she bared her teeth at him as she said it. "Yes, but that cannot matter. The clans do not resist, so we must."

From one knee, her mate looked up at neKrol. "They . . . they march on the waterfall," he said, still breathing heavily.

"The waterfall!" the bitter speaker repeated. "Since the death of winter, they have broken more than twenty pyramids, Arik, and their powerwagons have crushed the forest and now a great dusty road scars the soil from their valley to the riverlands. But they had hurt no Jaenshi yet this season, they had let them go. And all those clans-without-a-god have gone to the waterfall, until the home forest of the waterfall folk is bare and eaten clean. Their talkers sit with the old talker and perhaps the waterfall god takes them in, perhaps he is a very great god. I do not know these things. But I *do* know that now the bald Angel has learned of the twenty clans together, of a grouping of half-a-thousand Jaenshi adults, and he leads a powerwagon against them. Will he let them go so easy this time, happy with a carved statue? Will *they* go, Arik, will they give up a second god as easily as a first?" The speaker blinked. "I fear they will resist with their silly claws. I fear the bald Angel will hang them even if they do not resist, because so many in union throws suspicion in him. I fear many things and know little, but I know *we* must be there. You will not stop us, Arik, and we cannot wait for your long-late lasers.''

And she turned to the others and said, "Come, we must run," and they had faded into the forest before neKrol could even shout for them to stay. Swearing, he turned back to the bubble.

The two female exiles were leaving just as he entered. Both were close to the end of their term, but they had powerbows in their hands. NeKrol stopped short. "You too!" he said furiously, glaring at them. "Madness, it is the very stuff of madness!" They only looked at him with silent golden eyes, and moved past him toward the trees.

Inside, he swiftly braided his long red hair so it would not catch on the branches, slipped into a shirt, and darted toward the door. Then he stopped. A weapon, he must have a weapon! He glanced around frantically and ran heavily for his storeroom. The powerbows were all gone, he saw. What then, what? He began to rummage, and finally settled for a duralloy machete. It felt strange in his hand and he must have looked most unmartial and ridiculous, but somehow he felt he must take something.

Then he was off, toward the place of the waterfall folk.

NeKrol was overweight and soft, hardly used to running, and the way was nearly two kilometers through lush summer forest. He had to stop three times to rest, and quiet the pains in his chest, and it seemed an eternity before he arrived. But still he beat the Steel Angels; a powerwagon is ponderous and slow, and the road from Sword Valley was longer and more hilly.

Jaenshi were everywhere. The glade was bare of grass and twice as large as neKrol remembered it from his last trading trip, early that spring. Still the Jaenshi filled all of it, sitting on the ground, staring at the pool and the waterfall, all silent, packed together so there was scarcely room to walk among them. More sat above, a dozen in every fruit tree, some of the children even ascending to the higher limbs where the pseudomonks usually ruled alone.

On the rock at the center of the pool, with the waterfall behind them as a backdrop, the talkers pressed around the pyramid of the waterfall folk. They were closer together than even those in the grass, and each had his palms flat against the sides. One, thin and frail, sat on the shoulders of another so that he too might touch. NeKrol tried to count them and gave up; the group was too dense, a blurred mass of gray-furred arms and golden eyes, the pyramid at their center, dark and unmovable as ever.

The bitter speaker stood in the pool, the waters ankle-deep around her. She was facing the crowd and screeching at them, her voice strangely unlike the usual Jaenshi purr; in her scarf and rings, she looked absurdly out of place. As she talked, she waved the laser rifle she was holding in one hand. Wildly, passionately, hysterically, she was telling the gathered Jaenshi that the Steel Angels were coming, that they must leave at once, that they should break up and go into the forest and regroup at the trading base. Over and over again she said it.

But the clans were stiff and silent. No one answered, no one listened, no one heard. In full daylight, they were praying.

NeKrol pushed his way through them, stepping on a hand here and a foot there, hardly able to set down a boot without crunching Jaenshi flesh. He was standing next to the bitter speaker, who still gestured wildly, before her bronze eyes seemed to see him. Then she stopped. "Arik," she said, "the Angels are coming, and *they will not listen*."

"The others," he panted, still short on breath. "Where are they?"

"The trees," the bitter speaker replied, with a vague gesture. "I sent them up in the trees. Snipers, Arik, such as we saw upon your wall."

"Please," he said. "Come back with me. Leave them,

leave them. You told them. I told them. Whatever happens, it is their doing, it is the fault of their fool religion.''

"I cannot leave," the bitter speaker said. She seemed confused, as so often when neKrol had questioned her back at the base. "It seems I should, but somehow I know I must stay here. And the others will *never* go, even if I did. They feel it much more strongly. We must be here. To fight, to talk." She blinked. "I do not know *why*, Arik, but we must."

And before the trader could reply, the Steel Angels came out of the forest.

There were five of them at first, widely spaced; then shortly five more. All afoot, in uniforms whose mottled dark greens blended with the leaves, so that only the glitter of the mesh-steel belts and matching battle helmets stood out. One of them, a gaunt pale woman, wore a high red collar; all of them had hand-lasers drawn.

"You!" the blond woman shouted, her eyes finding Arik at once, as he stood with his braid flying in the wind and the machete dangling uselessly in his hand. "Speak to these animals! Tell them they must leave! Tell them that no Jaenshi gathering of this size is permitted east of the mountains, by order of the Proctor Wyatt, and the pale child Bakkalon. Tell them!" And then she saw the bitter speaker, and started. "And take the laser from the hand of that animal before we burn both of you down!"

Trembling neKrol dropped the machete from limp fingers into the water. "Speaker, drop the gun," he said in Jaenshi, "*please*. If you ever hope to see the far stars. Let loose the laser, my friend, my child, this very now. And I will take you when Ryther comes, with me to ai-Emerel and further places." The trader's voice was full of fear; the Steel Angels held their lasers steady, and not for a moment did he think the speaker would obey him.

But strangely, meekly, she threw the laser rifle into the pool. NeKrol could not see to read her eyes.

The Squadmother relaxed visibly. "Good," she said. "Now, talk to them in their beastly talk, tell them to leave. If not, we shall crush them. A powerwagon is on its way!" And now, over the roar and tumble of the nearby waters, neKrol could hear it; a heavy crunching as it rolled over trees, rending them into splinters beneath wide duramesh treads. Perhaps they were using the blastcannon and the turret lasers to clear away boulders and other obstacles.

"We have told them," neKrol said desperately. "Many times we have told them, but they do not hear!" He gestured all about him; the glade was still hot and close with Jaenshi bodies and none among the clans had taken the slightest notice of the Steel Angels or the confrontation. Behind him, the clustered talkers still pressed small hands against their god.

"Then we shall bare the sword of Bakkalon to them," the Squadmother said, "and perhaps they will hear their own wailing!" She holstered her laser and drew a screechgun, and neKrol, shuddering, knew her intent. The screechers used concentrated high-intensity sound to break down cell walls and liquefy flesh. Its effects were psychological as much as anything; there was no more horrible death.

But then a second squad of the Angels were among them, and there was a creak of wood straining and snapping, and from behind a final grove of fruit trees, dimly, neKrol could see the black flanks of the powerwagon, its blastcannon seemingly trained right at him. Two of the newcomers wore the scarlet collar—a red-faced youth with large ears who barked orders to his squad, and a huge, muscular man with a bald head and lined bronze skin. NeKrol recognized him; the Weaponsmaster C'ara DaHan. It was DaHan who laid a heavy hand on the Squadmother's arm as she raised her screechgun. "No," he said. "It is not the way."

She holstered the weapon at once. "I hear and obey."

DaHan looked at neKrol. "Trader," he boomed, "is this your doing?"

"No," neKrol said.

"They will not disperse," the Squadmother added.

"It would take us a day and a night to screech them down," DaHan said, his eyes sweeping over the glade and the trees, and following the rocky twisted path of the waterwall up to its summit. "There is an easier way. Break the pyramid and they go at once." He stopped then, about to say something else; his eyes were on the bitter speaker.

"A Jaenshi in rings and cloth," he said. "They have woven nothing but deathcloth up to now. This alarms me."

"She is one of the people of the ring-of-stone," neKrol said quickly. "She has lived with me."

DaHan nodded. "I understand. You are truly a godless man, neKrol, to consort so with soulless animals, to teach them to ape the ways of the seed of Earth. But it does not matter." He raised his arm in signal; behind him, among the trees, the blastcannon of the powerwagon moved slightly to the right. "You and your pet should move at once," DaHan told neKrol. "When I lower my arm, the Jaenshi god will burn and if you stand in the way, you will never move again."

"The *talkers!*" neKrol protested, "the blast will—" and he started to turn to show them. But the talkers were crawling away from the pyramid, one by one.

Behind him, the Angels were muttering. "A miracle!" one said hoarsely. "Our child! Our Lord!" cried another.

NeKrol stood paralyzed. The pyramid on the rock was no longer a reddish slab. Now it sparkled in the sunlight, a canopy of transparent crystal. And below that canopy, perfect in every detail, the pale child Bakkalon stood smiling, with his Demon-Reaver in his hand.

The Jaenshi talkers were scrambling from it now, tripping in the water in their haste to be away. NeKrol glimpsed the old talker, running faster than any despite his age. Even he seemed not to understand. The bitter speaker stood open-mouthed.

The trader turned. Half of the Steel Angels were on their knees, the rest had absent-mindedly lowered their arms and they froze in gaping wonder. The Squadmother turned to DaHan. "It *is* a miracle," she said. "As Proctor Wyatt has foreseen. The pale child walks upon this world."

But the Weaponsmaster was unmoved. "The Proctor is not here and this is no miracle," he said in a steely voice. "It is a trick of some enemy, and I will not be tricked. We will burn the blasphemous thing from the soil of Corlos." His arm flashed down.

The Angels in the powerwagon must have been lax with awe; the blastcannon did not fire. DaHan turned in irritation. "It is no miracle!" he shouted. He began to raise his arm again.

Next to neKrol, the bitter speaker suddenly cried out. He looked over with alarm, and saw her eyes flash a brilliant yellow-gold. "The god!," she muttered softly. "The light returns to me!"

And the whine of powerbows sounded from the trees around them, and two long bolts shuddered almost simultaneously in the broad back of C'ara DaHan. The force of the shots drove the Weaponsmaster to his knees, smashed him against the ground.

"RUN!" neKrol screamed, and he shoved the bitter speaker with all his strength, and she stumbled and looked back at him briefly, her eyes dark bronze again and flickering with fear. Then, swiftly, she was running, her scarf aflutter behind her as she dodged toward the nearest green.

"Kill her!" the Squadmother shouted. "Kill them all!" And her words woke Jaenshi and Steel Angels both; the children of Bakkalon lifted their lasers against the suddenly-surging crowd, and the slaughter began. NeKrol knelt and scrabbled on the moss-slick rocks until he had the laser rifle in his hands, then brought it to his shoulder and commenced to fire. Light stabbed out in angry bursts; once, twice, a third time. He held the trigger down and the bursts became a beam, and he sheared through the waist of a silver-helmeted Angel before the fire flared in his stomach and he fell heavily into the pool.

For a long time he saw nothing; there was only pain and noise, the water gently slapping against his face, the sounds of high-pitched Jaenshi screaming, running all around him. Twice he heard the roar and crackle of the blastcannon, and more than twice he was stepped on. It all seemed unimportant. He struggled to keep his head on the rocks, half out of the water, but even that seemed none too vital after a while. The only thing that counted was the burning in his gut.

Then, somehow, the pain went away, and there was a lot of smoke and horrible smells but not so much noise, and neKrol lay quietly and listened to the voices.

"The pyramid, Squadmother?" someone asked.

"It *is* a miracle," a woman's voice replied. "Look, Bakkalon stands there yet. And see how he smiles! We have done right here today!"

"What should we do with it?"

"Lift it aboard the powerwagon. We shall bring it back to Proctor Wyatt."

Soon after the voices went away, and neKrol heard only the sound of the water, rushing down endlessly, falling and tumbling. It was a very restful sound. He decided he would sleep.

The crewman shoved the crowbar down between the slats and lifted. The thin wood hardly protested at all before it gave. "More statues, Jannis," he reported, after reaching inside the crate and tugging loose some of the packing material.

"Worthless," Ryther said, with a brief sigh. She stood in the broken ruins of neKrol's trading base. The Angels had ransacked it, searching for armed Jaenshi, and debris lay everywhere. But they had not touched the crates.

The crewman took his crowbar and moved on to the next stack of crated artifacts. Ryther looked wistfully at the three

Jaenshi who clustered around her, wishing they could communicate a little better. One of them, a sleek female who wore a trailing scarf and a lot of jewelry and seemed always to be leaning on a powerbow, knew a smattering of Terran, but hardly enough. She picked up things quickly, but so far the only thing of substance she had said was, "Jamson' World. Arik take us. Angels kill." That she had repeated endlessly until Ryther had finally made her understand that, yes, they would take them. The other two Jaenshi, the pregnant female and the male with the laser, never seemed to talk at all.

"Statues again," the crewman said, having pulled a crate from atop the stack in the ruptured storeroom and pried it open.

Ryther shrugged; the crewman moved on. She turned her back on him and wandered slowly outside, to the edge of the spacefield where the *Lights of Jolostar* rested, its open ports bright with yellow light in the gathering gloom of dusk. The Jaenshi followed her, as they had followed her since she arrived; afraid, no doubt, that she would go away and leave them if they took their great bronze eyes off her for an instant.

"Statues," Ryther muttered, half to herself and half to the Jaenshi. She shook her head. "Why did he do it?" she asked them, knowing they could not understand. "A trader of his experience? You could tell me, maybe, if you knew what I was saying. Instead of concentrating on deathcloths and such, on real Jaenshi art, why did Arik train you people to carve alien versions of human gods? He should have known no dealer would accept such obvious frauds. Alien art is *alien*." She sighed. "My fault, I suppose. We should have opened the crates." She laughed.

The bitter speaker stared at her. "Arik deathcloth. Gave."

Ryther nodded, abstractly. She had it now, hanging just above her bunk; a strange small thing, woven partly from Jaenshi fur and mostly from long silken strands of flame red hair. On it, gray against the red, was a crude but recognizable caricature of Arik neKrol. She had wondered at that, too. The tribute of the widow? A child? Or just a friend? What *had* happened to Arik during the year the *Lights* had been away? If only she had been back on time, then . . . but she'd lost three months on Jamison's World, checking dealer after dealer in an effort to unload the worthless statuettes. It had been middle autumn before the *Lights of Jolostar* returned to Corlos, to find neKrol's base in ruins, the Angels already gathering in their harvests.

And the Angels—when she'd gone to them, offering the hold of unwanted lasers, offering to trade, the sight on those blood-red city walls had sickened even her. She had thought she'd gone prepared, but the obscenity she encountered was beyond any preparation. A squad of Steel Angels found her, vomiting, beyond the tall rusty gates, and had escorted her inside, before the Proctor.

Wyatt was twice as skeletal as she remembered him. He had been standing outdoors, near the foot of a huge platform-altar that had been erected in the middle of the city. A startlingly lifelike statue of Bakkalon, encased in a glass pyramid and set atop a high redstone plinth, threw a long shadow over the wooden altar. Beneath it, the squads of Angels were piling the newly-harvested neograss and wheat and the frozen carcasses of bushogs.

"We do not need your trade," the Proctor told her. "The World of Corlos is many-times-blessed, my child, and Bakkalon lives among us now. He has worked vast miracles, and shall work more. Our faith is in Him." Wyatt getured toward the altar with a thin hand. "See? In tribute we burn our winter stores, for the pale child has promised that this year winter will not come. And He has taught us to cull ourselves in peace as once we were culled in war, so the seed of Earth grows ever stronger. It is a time of great new revelation!" His eyes had burned as he spoke to her; eyes darting and fanatic, vast and dark yet strangely flecked with gold.

As quickly as she could, Ryther had left the City of the
Steel Angels, trying hard not to look back at the walls. But
when she had climbed the hills, back toward the trading base,
she had come to the ring-of-stone, to the broken pyramid
where Arik had taken her. Then Ryther found that she could
not resist, and powerless she had turned for a final glance out
over Sword Valley. The sight had stayed with her.

Outside the walls the Angel children hung, a row of small
white-smocked bodies still and motionless at the end of long
ropes. They had gone peacefully, all of them, but death is
seldom peaceful; the older ones, at least, died quickly, necks
broken with a sudden snap. But the small pale infants had the
nooses round their waists, and it had seemed clear to Ryther
that most of them had simply hung there till they starved.

As she stood, remembering, the crewman came from inside neKrol's broken bubble. "Nothing," he reported. "All
statues." Ryther nodded.

"Go?" the bitter speaker said. "Jamson' World?"

"Yes," she replied, her eyes staring past the waiting
Lights of Jolostar, out toward the black primal forest. The
Heart of Bakkalon was sunk forever. In a thousand thousand
woods and a single city, the clans had begun to pray.

Chicago
October, 1974

Nor the Many-Colored Fires of a Star Ring

OUTSIDE THE WINDOW THE STORMFIRES RAGED ON.

The view filled an entire wall in the monitoring room, a tapestry of ever-moving flame, a flowing pattern of liquid light of every color and shape. Great swirls of molten gold slid by, sinuous and snakelike. Lances of orange and scarlet flashed into view and then were gone again. Bluegreen bolts hammered against the window like raindrops, tendrils of amber smoke whirled past, streaks of pure white burned their lingering impressions into the eyes of the watchers.

Dancing, moving, changing; all the colors of nullspace shrieked a silent random song. At least they thought it was random. For five long standard months the vortex had turned in the void of Nowhere, and still the computers had not found a repetition.

Inside, a long room awash with the lights of the maelstrom, five monitors sat at their consoles facing the window and kept watch on the vortex. Each console was a maze of tiny lights and glowing control studs, and in the center of each were four readout screens where numbers chased by endlessly and thin red lines traced graphs. There was also a small digital timer, where the hundredths of seconds piled up relentlessly on top of the five months already registered.

The monitors changed shifts every eight hours. Now there were three women and two men on duty. All of them wore the pale blue smocks of techs and dark-lensed safety glasses. But the months had made them careless; only Trotter, at the central console, wore the glasses over his eyes. The rest of them had them up, around their foreheads or tangled in their hair.

Behind the monitors were the two horseshoe-shaped control consoles and the wall of computer banks. Al Swiderski, a big raw-boned blond in a white lab coat, was tending the computers. Jennifer Gray held down one of the control chairs. The other was empty, but that did not matter. At the moment they were only places to sit; everything was locked on automatic, and the nullspace engines of the Nowhere Star Ring burned in constant fury.

Swiderski, a sheaf of computer printout in his hand, drifted over to where Jennifer was writing on a clipboard. "We're nearing critical, I think," he said in a hard flat voice.

Jennifer looked up at him, all business. She was a beautiful woman, tall and slim, with bright green eyes and long straight red-blond hair. She wore a severe white lab coat and a gold ring. "Roughly eight hours," she told Swiderski with a shake of her head. "If my calculations are correct. Then we can kill the engines and see what we have."

Swiderski looked out at the swirling stormfires. "Five layers of transparent duralloy," he said softly. "Four buffers of refrigerated air, and a triple layer of glass. And still the inner window is warm to the touch, Jennifer." He nodded. "I wonder what we'll have."

The watch went on.

A mile down the ring, on another deck, Kerin daVittio entered the old control room alone.

The others seldom came here. The room was his alone. Once, years ago, it had been the nerve center of the Nowhere

Star Ring; from here, a single man had at his fingertips all the awesome powers of a thousand nullspace engines. From here, he could stir the vortex to life and watch it spin.

But no longer. The Nowhere Star Ring had been deserted for nearly six years, and when Jennifer and her team had come they'd found the old control room far too small for their purposes. So they abandoned it. Now the engines responded to the twin consoles in the monitoring room. The control room belonged to Kerin, to his spidermechs and the ghosts of his shadowed ring.

The room was a tiny cube, immaculate and white. The familiar horseshoe console was its center. Kerin sat within it, the controls around him, a reflective look on his face. He was a short, wiry man, with a mop of black hair and restless dark eyes; often he was intense, often dreamy. Long ago he'd discarded his blue tech smock for civilian clothes; now he wore black trousers and a dark red V-necked shirt.

Practiced hands moved over the controls, and the walls melted.

He was outside, in blackness, the star ring beneath him.

The holographic projection gave him a view of the ring and the vortex that the monitoring room window could not match. There was nothing left in the room but him and the console, floating in vacuum miles above the action. The section of the ring that held the control room loomed large under his feet; the rest curved slowly away in both directions, finally dwindling to a metal ribbon that went out and out and out before looping back to join itself in the far dim distance. A silver circlet a hundred miles in diameter; the Nowhere Star Ring was built to standard specifications.

Within the ring, bound by its dampers and its armor, kept alive by the furious power of a thousand fusion reactors, the nullspace vortex turned in mindless glory. This was the multicolored maelstrom that had given man the stars.

Kerin glanced at it briefly, until the light began to hurt his eyes. Then he looked down to his console. The bend of the horseshoe, immediately before him, was all dark; his hands moved restlessly over the disconnected studs that once controlled the vortex. But the studs along either arm still glowed softly; to his left, the holo controls, to his right, the spidermech command. Banks and banks of buttons, all lit a soft pale green. No reason to move those, Swiderski had said; so the old control room was half alive, and Kerin worked alone.

His left hand reached out to the controls, and the holograms spun around him; now he was thirty miles down the ring, getting visual input from another set of projectors. The view was much the same, the five-month old firestorm still turned below. But this was the trouble spot.

He swiveled to his right, and touched some other studs. Below, a panel slid open in the skin of the star ring, and a spider-mech emerged.

It was, in fact, much like a metal spider: eight legs, a fat silver body of shining duralloy that reflected the vortex colors in streaks along its flanks, a familiar, scurrying gait. It used all eight legs to cling to the star ring as Kerin sent it running to the problem.

Once there, he slid back another panel, and switched to his spidereyes. The holos fractured; the illusion of being outside vanished. The spidermech had a lot of eyes, most of them in its stomach. Now it stood above the opening in the ring, reaching down with four legs while the other, alternate four clung to the sides of the panel, and all its eyes studied the troublesome engine. The wall before Kerin gave him visual input; normal range, infrared, ultraviolet. The wall to his right measured radioactivity and saw with X-rays, the one to his left printed out the latest input the computer was getting from the monitors on this particular engine.

With four hands at work, things went quickly. Kerin shut down the engine briefly, traced the problem to its source, pulled a part and replaced it from a storage cavity within the spidermech. Then he withdrew his metal arms and leaned back. The panel slid shut. He jumped from his spidereyes back to the holos.

The spidermech stood frozen; the vortex burned. Kerin looked at them without seeing. His hand moved left, and again the holos shifted. No longer was he looking in at the spinning fires; now he stared out, beyond the circle of the ring.

At the infinite empty darkness of Nowhere.

For a second after he turned around, as always, he thought he was going blind. But then his eyes adjusted, and he could see the console dimly. And that was all. He slouched back in his chair, put his boots up on the console, and sighed. Familiar fear washed over him. And awe.

Brooding, he watched the emptiness.

He'd seen holos of the other dozen star rings; but this ring, *this* was singular. Cerberus, the first, floats six million miles beyond Pluto, surrounded by a sea of stars. They may be small and cold and distant, but they *are* stars, proof that Cerberus and its men are safe within the home system and the comforting sanity of the known universe. The same is true for Black Door, adrift in a Trojan position behind Jupiter. And Vulcan, which burns black and broken in the shadow of the sun.

On the flip side of Cerberus spins another ring, surrounded by strange stars, yet snug for all that. So what if the stars are not the stars of human history? Who cares what galaxy they might be in? Nearby is Second Chance, a warm green world under a bright yellow sun, with fast-rising cities and people.

And Vulcan? So? It opens on an inferno, yes; its hellish vortex is the gateway to the inside of a star. But that too Kerin could understand.

Black Door was more frightening; enter here, and find

yourself in the yawning gulf between galaxies. No single stars here, no nearby planets. Only distant spirals, far off, in configurations utterly unknown to man. And, luckily, a second hole, around which they'd built a second star ring, to the lush bright system of Dawn.

But on the far side of the Hole to Nowhere was the darkest realm of all. Here blackness rules, immense and empty. There are no stars. There are no planets. There are no galaxies. No light races through this void; no matter mars its perfection. As far as man can see, as far as his machines can sense, in all directions; only nothingness and vacuum. Infinite and silent and more terrible than anything Kerin had ever known.

Nowhere. The place beyond the universe, they called it.

Kerin, alone among the Nowhere crew, still used the old control room. Kerin alone had work that took him *outside*. Early on, he had hardly minded. It gave him time alone, time to think and dream and fiddle with the poems that were his hobby. He had taken to studying Nowhere the way he had Jenny once had studied stars, back in their days on Earth. But something had caught him, and now he could not stop. Obsessed, possessed, he paused after every job.

Like a moth and a flame, so Kerin and the darkness.

Sometimes it was like blindness. He convinced himself that he was sitting in a pitch-black room, that there were walls only a few feet away from him. He could feel the walls, almost. He knew they were there.

But at other times the void opened before him. Then he could see and sense the *depth* of the darkness, he could feel the cold grip of infinity, and he knew, he *knew*, that if he traveled away from the star ring he would fall forever through empty space.

And there were still other times, when his eyes played tricks. He would see stars then. Or perhaps a dim pinprick of light—the universe expanding toward them? Sometimes nightmare shapes struggled on the canvas of night. Sometimes Jennifer danced there, slim and seductive.

For five long months they had lived in Nowhere, in a place where the only reality was them. But the rest of them, facing inward toward the flames, lived all untouched.

While Kerin the displaced poet fought the primal dark alone.

Where were they?
Nowhere.
But where is *that?*
No one is sure.

Kerin considered the question, hard, in their first days out here. And before that, on the long voyage to Nowhere and during the months of preparation. He knew something of Nowhere, and of the star rings—as much as any layman. Now he read more. And he and Jenny stayed up late more nights than one, talking it out in bed.

He got most of his answers from her. He was hardly stupid, Kerin, but his interests lay elsewhere. He was the poet of their partnership; the humanist, the lover, the barroom philosopher, born in the undercity and bred to a world of corridor stickball and slidewalks and elevator races. Jenny was the scientist, the practical one, born on a religious farming commune and raised to be a serious adult. She found her lost innocence in Kerin. They were utterly unalike, yet each brought strength to the relationship.

Kerin taught her poetry, literature, love. She taught him science—and gave him star rings he could never have grabbed by himself.

She answered his questions. But this time neither she nor anyone had the answer. In his memory all his talks and readings and study had blended into one blurred conversation with Jenny.

"It depends on what the star rings are," she said.

"Gateways through space, no?"

"That's the accepted theory, the most popular one, but it's not established fact yet. Call it the space warp theory. It says that the universe is warped, that the fabric of the space-time continuum has holes in it, places you can punch through to come out someplace else. Black holes, for example . . ."

"The so-called natural star rings?" he interrupted.

"So the theory says. If we could reach a black hole, we'd find out. We can't, though, not with sub-light ships. Luckily, we don't need to. We found a second kind of warp, the nullspace anomalies. The accidental discovery of a spot six million miles beyond Pluto where matter seemed to be leaking into space from nowhere—the later discovery that, with enough energy the warp could be widened temporarily so that a ship could slip through—that was the breakthrough. Thusly, Cerberus, the first of the star rings. We went through the nullspace vortex, and found ourselves deep within another system, near Second Chance.

"Fine. But *where* was Second Chance in relation to Earth? At first, astronomers guessed it was simply somewhere else in our galaxy. Now they're not so sure. The stars in a Second Chance sky are completely unfamiliar, and the local configuration can't be found. So it looks as though the space warp—if that's what it was—threw us a long, long way."

"You don't sound convinced."

"I'm not. The discovery of the Hole to Nowhere twenty-odd years ago badly shook the space warp theory. If we simply jump to another portion of space when we go through a star ring, then *where* was Nowhere? The only feasible answer that's been suggested is Whitfield's Hypothesis. He said that Nowhere is beyond the expanding universe—at a spot in the space-time continuum so far from everything else that even the light of the Big Bang hasn't reached it yet. The only problem with this is that it disagrees with the established belief that matter defines space. If Whitfield is correct, then either space can exist without matter—picture a pre-creation universe of infinite hard vacuum—or, alternatively, Nowhere never existed at all until the first probe ship came through the vortex and created it."

"Wild," he said. "Is he right?"

She laughed. "You think *I* know? The space warp theory, modified by Whitfield's Hypothesis, is still accepted by the vast majority of nullspace theoreticians. But there are two other contenders, at least."

"Such as?"

"Such as the alternate universe theory. Accept that, and you buy a cosmic picture where the star rings are gates between alternate realities that occupy the same space. History is different in each reality, stellar geography is changed, even the natural laws might not be the same."

"Hmmmm," said Kerin. "I see. Then Nowhere is a reality where creation has never taken place, a universe that was utterly without matter or energy—until we entered."

"Right. Except the theory is generally discredited nowadays, except by mystics. We've opened a good dozen star rings, and so far we have yet to come upon any alternate Earths, or even the tiniest modification in the speed of light. Excepting Nowhere, all these side-by-side continuums seem pretty much like our own.

"The time travel theory is a more serious one. It's got a good bit of support. Its adherents claim the star rings throw us backwards or forwards in time, to periods when different stars occupied the same cosmic space now occupied by Sol, the colony systems, and such."

"In which case ships to Nowhere either go back before the Big Bang, or forward in time, after the universe has fallen in on itself," Kerin said.

"*If* it's going to fall in," Jenny replied, grinning. "They're not so sure of that anymore. You should keep up with the latest theories, love. But you do have the general drift. The hypothesis is a lot more sophisticated than that, of course. It has to account for the fact that the nullspace anomalies stay put, relative to the solar system, even though Sol and the galaxy and the universe are all moving. Foster modified the original time travel theory by postulating that the nullspace vortex moves ships through both time *and* space, and nowadays most of the scientists who don't buy the space warp theory line up with him.''

''And you?''

She shrugged. ''I don't know. When they discovered Nowhere and punched through to build a ring on this side, they thought they'd find the answer. Nowhere was a very singular place. Figure it out, and you figure out the star rings, and maybe the cosmos. They tried, for a long time. The Nowhere Star Ring used to be a full-time research base, but finally it was abandoned. Robot probes launched in fifty different directions twenty years ago are still reporting back, and their reports are still the same—vast unending nothingness. Absolute vacuum. Not much you can do with findings like that.''

''No,'' he said, thoughtful.

''Anyway, it doesn't matter. I'll leave Nowhere for someone else to crack. My own research has a more practical thrust.''

He was there because of Jenny.

Oh, he had a job, and it was a fairly important one. On an ordinary star ring, the spidermechs were seldom used, but the Nowhere experiment put an unheard-of-strain on the nullspace engines. Kerin filled a function. But others could have filled it just as well. It was Jennifer who had gotten him the post, over Swiderski's protests; it was because of Jennifer that Kerin had taken it.

They shared a cabin, a large one with a mock window at the foot of their king-sized bed. Outside the window were the stars of home; a comforting holo. Bookcases ran along either wall. Hers held obscure texts on nullspace, most of them full of math; his held poetry and fiction, equally obscure. At night, they lit the room dimly, and talked for hours in the tender after-time.

"It's strange," he said to her during the first week, as she lay warm against him with her head on his chest. "I don't know why it fascinates me so much, but it does. I've got to do a poem about it, Jenny. I've got to make someone else feel what I feel when I'm out there. You understand? It's the ultimate symbol of death, really. You know?"

She kissed him. "Mmm," she mumbled in a drowsy voice. "Can't say. I've thought about it much. I suppose it is. It all depends on how you look at it." She laughed. "Back when this was still a research station, they had more than one crack-up. The place does something to people. Some people, anyway. Others are utterly unaffected. Al, for example. He calls it a lot of nothing."

Kerin snorted. He and Swiderski had disliked each other from the instant they met. "He would say that. He stays down in the monitoring room and avoids the whole issue."

"He loves you too. Just the other day he told me that I was a brilliant theoretician, but my taste in men was revolting." Jenny laughed. Kerin fought briefly, and wound up joining her.

But things changed.

"Kerin," she said to him two months afterwards, and he answered with a questioning look.

"You've been very quiet lately," she said. "Is something wrong?"

"I don't know," he said. He ran his fingers idly through her hair as he stared at the ceiling.

"Talk about it," she urged.

"It's hard to put into words," he said. Then he laughed. "Maybe that's why I can't write any poems about it." There was a quiet. "You remember that time, back in college, when we picnicked in the forest preserve?"

Jenny nodded. "Uh-huh," she said, puzzled.

"Remember what we talked about?"

She hesitated. "I don't know. Love? We used to talk about love a lot. That was right when we met." She smiled. "No, wait, now I remember. That was the day I tried to convert you. All that business about the apple."

"Yeah," he said, "only God could make an apple, you said. The existence of apples somehow proved the existence of God. I never quite understood that argument, by the way. And I didn't even *like* apples."

Jenny smiled, gave him a quick kiss. "I remember. That night you dragged me down to that pizza place of yours in the undercity. In the middle of a big pepperoni pizza you said that if God really existed, and if he had any class, he would have created a world where pizza grew on trees instead of apples. I should have been furious, but it was all too funny."

"I guess," he said. "But I meant it, too. Apples never awed me; man could do better. Nothing really awed me, when I stop to think about it. I never bought your God, Jenny, you know that. But I had something else."

"I should have pointed to the stars," Jenny said. "A lot more impressive than any apple."

"Admittedly. But I would have answered with the star rings. Man-made, very beautiful, very powerful. And think of what they mean. Even the vast gulfs between the suns, even those, man has beaten."

He fell silent. Jenny cuddled against him, but she did not break the spell. Finally he resumed, in a slow serious voice.

"Nowhere is something else, Jenny. For the first time,

I've run up against something I can't get a grip on. I don't understand it, I don't like it, and I don't like the thoughts it's making me think. Every time I run a check or do a repair, I wind up staring at it and shivering."

"Kerin?" Jenny said, concern in her voice. There was something very strange in his.

Sensing her worry, he turned to her and smiled. "Um," he said. "I'm getting entirely too serious. Comes of reading too much Matthew Arnold. Forget about it." He kissed her.

But *he* did not forget.

And as time passed, he got steadily more sober. His duties kept him away from Jennifer on-shift, and more and more he seemed to be avoiding people during the off-shift. Even in the cafeteria he seemed a little too solemn, too preoccupied, for the rest of the crew to be comfortable. Some of the others started to avoid him; Kerin never seemed to notice.

One night he said he felt sick. Jennifer found him in bed, staring at the ceiling again. She sat down next to him. "Kerin, we have to talk. I don't understand. You've been positively morbid lately. What's going on?"

He sighed. "Yeah." A pause. "I went down to the fourth deck today, and found the old probe room."

Jennifer said nothing.

"It's still there," he continued, "still functioning after six years. The lights were out, and there was a layer of dust. And ghosts. I could hear my footsteps and something else, sort of a thin whine coming from the control consoles.

"I watched the readout screens for a long time. They were all the same, just straight blue lines moving slowly across a black screen. Nothing, Jenny. They've found nothing. Twenty years now, accelerating steadily to near light speed, and they've yet to find a single particle, an atom, a ray of light. Then I thought I knew what the whine was. The robots were crying, Jenny. For twenty years they've been falling through night, and the only island of light and sound and sanity is far behind, lost in the void. That's too much, even for machines. They're alone and they're scared and they're crying. And the whole probe room was alive with their whispers and their wails. No wonder the researchers went away. The dark beat them, Jenny. Nowhere is beyond human understanding." He trembled.

"Kerin," she said. "They're only probes. They don't have emotions."

"Tell me about it," he said. "I work with those spidermechs every day, and every damned one of them is different. Moodiest damned machines I've ever seen. Nowhere is getting to them too. For the probes, it's a thousand times worse. So, all right, they are only machines. But they don't belong out here."

He looked at her. "And neither do we, Jenny, at least not now. We'll be there soon enough. Every day I watch it, and I know. Whatever we have, whatever we believe in, it doesn't matter. Nothing matters, except the void out there. *That's* real, *that's* forever. We're just for a brief meaningless little time, and nothing makes sense. And the time will come when we'll be out there, wailing, in a sea of never-ending night.

"*Invictus* is a child's joke. We can't make a mark on *that*, out there. It's not a symbol of death, Jenny. What a fool I was. It's the reality.

"Maybe we're dead already. And this is hell."

There was nothing she could say; she did not understand.

He was floating high above the ring, surveying his dark domain, when the intercom buzzed. The noise startled him, yet brought a smile to his face. He leaned forward and flicked open the channel. "You have just disturbed the silence of infinity with your intercom buzz," he said.

"I always was irreverent," Jennifer's voice replied. "You sound cheerful, Kerin."

"I'm trying, what can I say? We're all doomed and everything we do is meaningless, but maybe we have to fight." He said it lightly, in a guarded half-mocking tone. He had given up being serious about it; he and Jenny had been arguing entirely too much, and his gloom had driven her into spending more and more time with Swiderski.

"We're close, Kerin. Come up. I want you to be here when it happens."

Kerin stretched stiff muscles. "All right," he said. "I'll be right up. Don't think I'll be much help, though."

"Just so you're there," she answered.

He flicked off, quickly ran the spidermech back to its lair, urging it on under his breath, then banished the darkness with a snap of his thumb. Back in the bright white control room, he unstrapped, exited through a sliding door. Then he moved down the corridor to an interdeck ladder, climbed to a shuttle, and rode to the monitoring room.

Where all the folk of Nowhere had gathered to watch the colors dance. The third shift was on, attentive at the monitor consoles, restless, watching the seconds pile up. But the two off-shifts were there too, prowling the room, hands shoved into pockets, pale blue smocks rumpled. This was a moment no one wanted to miss.

Swiderski, sitting in one of the control chairs, glanced up when Kerin entered. "Aha," he said. "Our black philosopher lives! To what do we owe this singular pleasure?"

Jenny was in the second lighted throne. Kerin moved behind her, and rested a hand on her shoulder. He stared at Swiderski. "You know, Al, I've got spidermechs with a better personality than you." One of the techs guffawed.

"Quiet," Jennifer said. She studied her clipboard, ignoring Swiderski's puzzled frown. The rest kept impatient eyes on the window.

Out there, bright-burning shadows raced from right to left, caught in the unending flow. Yellow, silver, blue, crimson, orange, green, purple. Gushes and spears, swirls and tendrils, firedrops and roaring floods. In the airless starless empty they turned and mingled and mixed and turned. The window, as always, drenched the room with shifting light. The many-colored flames of the star ring flickered in the eyes of the watchers.

"Five minutes," Trotter announced in a loud voice. A short, stout man, the head of the tech crew; off duty now, but still here to officiate.

"Safety lenses," Jennifer said suddenly, looking up from her chair. "In case something goes wrong."

Around the room, one by one, the watchers lowered their dark goggles until all the eyes were hidden. All but Kerin's. His glasses were forgotten, somewhere back in his room.

A short brown-haired woman drifted up to his side, offering him a pair. He tried to remember her name, failed. A tech. "Thanks," he said, taking the goggles and covering his eyes.

She shrugged. "Sure. A big moment, isn't it?"

He looked back toward the window, where the colors now were muted. "I suppose."

She refused to go away. "We don't see much of you anymore, Kerin. Is everything all right "

"Sure," he said. But his face stayed somber.

"Two minutes," Trotter announced. Kerin fell silent, and his hand tightened on Jenny's shoulder. She looked up at him, and smiled. They watched the window.

Over a year ago she had found the key. He'd shared that moment, the start, as she waved her battered clipboard in his face and whooped. Now he could share the finish. Somehow, despite everything he had said, that still mattered.

"One minute," Trotter said. Then the seconds peeled off one by one. The next voice was Jennifer's. It was her right. She'd started it all. "Now," she said. She hit the controls before her. And all around the star ring, the nullspace engines died.

Dead silence in the monitoring room; a hush of indrawn

breath. Long seconds. Then, with a rush, explosion. Laughter, tears, papers flying, techs hugging each other.

Beyond the window, the colors were still spinning.

Swiderski was suddenly there, standing at Jennifer's side, grinning. "You did it!" he said. "*We* did it. A self-sustaining vortex."

Jenny permitted herself a brief smile, immune to the riot around her. "It hasn't been a minute yet," she said, cautiously. "The vortex may fade, after all. Before we celebrate too much, let's see how long the thing sustains itself without the engines."

Swiderski shook his head, laughing. "Ah, Jenny. It doesn't matter. A second is time enough, shows that it's possible. It's a big breakthrough. Now maybe we can even generate a vortex without an anomaly, anywyere—think of it! A hundred star rings in orbit around Earth!"

Jennifer rose. Swiderski, still dripping enthusiasm, grabbed her, hugged her hard. She accepted the hug calmly, disengaged as soon as he released her. "That's still a long way off, Al," she told him. "We may not see it in our lifetimes. Let's just wait to make sure *all* my calculations work out, okay? You take the next watch."

She glanced toward Kerin. He grinned. They left the monitoring room together. Out in the corridor, she took him by the hand.

An anomaly is not a gate; it is too small. But it can be opened. The price—energy.

Thus the star rings, built around the holes. A thousand fusion engines provide a lot of energy.

Wake them, and in the center of the ring a bright-colored star flares to sudden brilliance. The star becomes a disc, the colors changing, spinning. The disc grows with each flicker of the eye. In seconds it spans the ring; the nullspace vortex, the colored maelstrom of space. Kept alive by energy, it is itself a creature of awful power.

The armored ringships tear into its center, and suddenly are gone, to reappear on the flip side of the hole. Elsewhere, far elsewhere.

Then the ring man kills the engines. And—in an instant— the vortex is gone. It blinks out. Like a light, turned off.

It works. But why? How?

Dr. Jennifer Gray made the first big advance in the field. A leading nullspace theoretician, she got permission for a series of controlled experiments with the Black Door Star Ring. Her first step was to let the vortex burn for a full day; previously no vortex had been kept alive for much over an hour. The costs in terms of fuel and energy were too great.

At Black Door, Dr. Gray discovered that the vortex, some- how, gains energy.

Her measurements were very precise. A certain amount of energy is poured into the ring center by the engines; enough to create the vortex, to keep it alive. But the energy of the vortex itself was greater than what was being pumped in. A minute difference at first. But it builds, the longer the vortex turns.

There followed the Gray Equations; run a star ring long enough, her figures said, and the vortex will be self-sustaining. Then the ring can possibly be a power source, instead of a drain. More importantly, her work provided the first real insight into the nature of the nullspace vortex. It was hoped that in time, enough understanding might be acquired so that star rings could be constructed anywhere.

Further experimentation was called for. Since Black Door was a busy gateway, and since the work might possibly be dangerous, the government gave Dr. Gray and her team access to the abandoned Nowhere Star Ring.

They had been saving a special bottle of wine. They broke it out and took it back to their room. Kerin poured two glasses, and they drank a toast to the Gray Equations.

"I'd like to give Swiderski a hit in the face," Kerin said, sitting on the bed. He sipped his wine thoughtfully.

Jenny smiled. "Al is all right. And you sound better."

Kerin sighed. "Ah, so that's why we haven't been arguing." He set down his glass on a night table, rose, and shook his head. "Maybe I'm getting resigned to it," he said. "Or maybe I'm just getting better at hiding it. I don't know."

"And I thought my triumph had put you in a good mood."

"I wonder," he mused. He walked across their room to the mock window, and stared out at the starscape. "I think maybe it was more that buzz you gave me. That never happened before. I mean, there I am in the midst of infinite darkness, and suddenly there's this big raucous noise." He tapped the window glass lightly with his fist. "It's a lie," he said. "There's only darkness and death, Jenny, and nothing we can do to change it. Except . . ."

He turned to face her. "Except make noises? I don't know."

"Oh, Kerin. Why do you let it obsess you? Just let it be."

He shook his head violently. "No, that's no answer. We can avoid thinking about it, but it still won't go away. No, I've got to beat it somehow, face it down and beat it. Only I don't have anything to beat it with. Not even the vortex, not even the star rings. But that noise . . . that doesn't do it either, of course, but, but . . ."

Jenny smiled. "Our black philosopher. Al is right. I really don't understand you, love. I'm afraid I'm like Swiderski in that. To me it's just a lot of nothing. Oh, I get hints of what's bothering you, but it's all an intellectual exercise. To you it's more than that."

He nodded.

"I wish I could help more, help you work it out. Whatever it is."

"Maybe you can," Kerin said. "Maybe you have. I've got to think this through." He stared at nothing and rubbed his chin.

And suddenly the intercom buzzed. Jenny shook off her

musings, put down her glass, and reached over to the bedside. "Yes," she said.

Swiderski's voice. "Jennifer, you'd better get up here at once."

"What's wrong? Is the vortex fading already?" Kerin, across the room, stood frozen.

"No," Swiderski said. "There's something wrong. It's not fading at all, Jenny. It's gaining energy, from no place. Even faster than before."

"That can't be," she said.

"It is."

Outside, winds of scarlet flame shrieked by in silent fury.

Jenny sat in one of the control chairs, clutching her talisman clipboard, and cleared a computer screen. "Give me the figures," she said to Ahmed, on the central monitor.

He nodded, hit a stud, and the figures from one of his readout screens blinked into life on hers. Jennifer studied them in silence, looking up every once in a while at the raging fire outside. Behind her, Swiderski stood near the computers, scratching his head. The monitors, goggles down, tended to their screens.

Her fingers went to a console, tentatively, thoughtfully. She punched in an equation, paused, tugged absently at her hair. Then she nodded firmly, and set to work.

Forty-five minutes later she looked up at Swiderski. "The Gray Equations are wrong," she said, emotionless. "According to my predictions, the vortex was supposed to maintain itself for five months at least, the energy level gradually tapering off, until finally booster shots from the nullspace engines were required. That's not what's happening."

"An error somewhere," Swiderski started.

She dismissed him with an impatient toss of her head. "No. The whole equation's worthless. I made a fundamental mistake somewhere, I misunderstood something key about the nature of the vortex. Otherwise this wouldn't be going on.''

"You're too hard on yourself."

"We have to start all over. Bleed all the monitors into the main computer, Ahmed. I don't want to miss a thing." Her fingers raced over the keys of the console. The monitor crew set to their tasks, exchanging puzzled looks. Swiderski, frowning, sat in the second throne.

And up against the door Kerin stood quietly, his arms crossed, watching the racing fires. Then, unnoticed, he turned and left.

One by one, the others drifted into the control room. The watch changed in silence; those going off stayed in the monitoring room, drinking coffee and exchanging whispers. Once in a while someone laughed. Jennifer never looked up, but Swiderski glared at them.

As hours passed, he got up, fidgeting, and went over to Jennifer. "You ought to get some sleep," he told her. "Been up too long. Something like twenty straight hours now, isn't it?"

Annoyance flashed across her face. "So have you, Al. This can't wait."

Defeated, he turned to his chair, and ran through some equations of his own.

More hours of silent waiting, while the fires screamed a few feet away.

Finally Jennifer leaned back, frowning. Her long fingers drummed on the console. She looked to the central monitor, where Sandy Lindagan had replaced Ahmed. "Call Trotter," Jennifer said. "Tell him to wake up the off-shifts"—glancing around—"the ones who aren't loitering around here, anyway."

Lindagan gave her a questioning look, shrugged, and did it. "What are you doing?" Swiderski said.

"Clear your screen," Jennifer told him. "Have the computer graph the rate of increase prior to switch-off."

He did it. A red line traced a slow-ascending curve across

his console face. They'd known the rate of increase for months, though. "So?" Swiderski said.

"Now, let it draw on the monitors. Plot the increase *since* we reached s-point."

Swiderski punched some more studs, bit his lip, wiped the screen, and did it again. The answer was the same. The line soared. A row of blinking figures underneath told the story.

"Not just an increase in the arithmetic rate of energy gain," he said.

"No," snapped Jennifer. "Geometric. S-point was some sort of point of no return. Somehow we've got a chain reaction in nullspace itself."

Sandy Lindagan looked over, her face pale. "Jennifer," she said. "Then you want Trotter so . . . ."

"So he can get the ship ready," Jennifer said, standing abruptly. "We've got to get out. Al, you take over here. I'm going for Kerin." She started toward the door.

One of the off-duty monitors had wandered over to the window. He touched it lightly with his fingertips, and yowled, spilling a cup of coffee.

When he took his fingers away, they were red and burned.

Their bedroom was empty.

She went to the old control room. That too was deserted.

She stood in the white cubicle, puzzled. Where?

Then she remembered.

In the sealed-off portion of the ring she found him, pacing slowly back and forth in the gloom and dusty darkness of the probe room. It was the first time she had ever been there. The only light was the glow of the console buttons, and the straight blue tracery of the lines on the readout screens. But a ghostly half-heard whine came from the instrument panels.

"You hear them, Jenny?" Kerin said. "My lost souls? Wailing in the darkness?"

"A minor malfunction somewhere," she said, watching him as he stalked restlessly through the shadows. Then swiftly she told him what had happened. Halfway through she began to sob.

And Kerin came to her, wrapped her in his arms, pressed her hard against him. Wordless.

"I *failed*, Kerin," she said, and all the disappointment she had hidden from the others, all the agony, came out now. "All my equations, the whole *theory* . . ."

"It's all right," he told her. He stroked her hair. Then, despite himself, he shivered. "Jenny," he said, "what now? I mean, is the ring going to short-circuit or something? And we'll be stuck here?"

She shook her head. "No, we're going back, as soon as the ship is ready. The vortex *will* overload the ring, but not the engines, no. They're not even in the picture. It's the dampers we have to worry about, and the armor. The vortex is self-sustaining now, building energy fast, God knows how or from where, but it's happening. Have you ever seen what a vortex does to an unarmored ship, Kerin? It'll do that to us soon. It'll generate so much power that the star ring can't hold it in any longer. Then it'll melt free. An explosion, Kerin, and an unbound vortex, expanding at the speed of light, generating more and more energy all the while. But by that time, hopefully, we'll be through the hole, safe on the flip side. I don't think it will break through the continuum. I hope not."

Her voice faded, and there was only the whine. Kerin shook his head, as if to clear it. And then, wildly, he began to laugh.

Of course, he was the last one to the ship.

They left within seventy-two hours, over Swiderski's protests. "You were wrong before, Jenny," the big blond kept saying, "you might be wrong now. Besides, I ran through your calculations. The ring walls will hold for at least another week *minimum*, and we could make valuable observations. And still get clear before the ring starts to melt."

Jennifer overruled him. "We can't take the chance. It's hot in here already. The risk isn't worth it, Al. We're leaving."

An hour before departure, Kerin vanished.

Jennifer grabbed a shuttle and went searching. She checked their bedroom, deserted now; the stars in the holo beamed on a bare metal cabin. She tried the old control room, and found that he'd been there. The door slid back on the fracture visions of his spidereyes. But the chair was vacant. Next the probe room. Still no Kerin.

She flipped on the shuttle intercom and called back to the ring port where the ship lay waiting. Trotter answered. "He's here," he said quickly. "Came running up about ten seconds after you went off after him. Hurry back."

She did.

The departure was all confusion. Jenny did not find Kerin until the ship had boosted free of the Nowhere Star Ring and was circling out into the yawning vacuum before turning back toward the vortex. He was sitting in the ship's main lounge.

All the lights were out when she entered. But the viewscreen was on, filling one long wall, and Kerin and a half-dozen others watched in silence. Ahead of them a spinning multi-colored hell howled in the midst of virgin blackness. The ring, binding the fires, was a tiny glint of silver thread, all but lost in the immense fury of the stormfires.

Jennifer sat down beside him.

"Look," Kerin said. "Look at those ripples, the bulges. Like a thunderhead, all bunched up with lightning, getting ready to explode. It's always been flat before, Jenny, you know? Sort of two-dimensional? Not now. When she blows, she'll blow in all directions." He took her hand, squeezed hard, grinned at her. "My poor probes, they'll be delighted. After twenty years of darkness, light, coming up behind them fast. Think of it. Something at last, in an infinity of noth-ing." Kerin looked at her, still smiling. "You broke the quiet in my little dark room with your intercom buzz. This will be a much bigger noise, in a much bigger quiet.''

The vortex loomed larger and larger ahead, filling the screen. The ringship was nearing and picking up speed.

"Where did you go?" Jennifer said.

"To the control room," he said, and the ghosts were all gone from his voice. "I yanked two of my spiders out of their hidey-holes.''

"But *why*?"

"They're sitting in the monitoring room now, love. Perched on top of the control chairs, right where you and Al used to sit. I keyed in the computer, a timed command. An hour after we're safe on the other side of space, my spiders are going to lean forward and punch all your pretty studs and turn back on the engines.''

She whistled. "That'll speed up the explosion something fierce. The energy level was increasing fast enough anyway. Why give it more energy to multiply?''

He squeezed her hand again. "To make the noise bigger, love. Call it a gesture. How much energy would you say is out there, spinning around like a big pinwheel, eh?''

"A lot. The explosion will begin with the force of a supernova, easily. It'd take that much power to melt down the ring.''

"Hmmm. Except that this time, the explosion doesn't damp out, right? It keeps going, the vortex expands and expands and—''

"—expands. Yes. Geometrically.''

The viewscreen was alive with the colors of the vortex. For an instant it almost seemed as if they were back in the monitoring room on the Nowhere Star Ring. Tongues of fire leaped up at them, and bluish demon shapes whipped by, shrieking.

Then the ship shuddered, and there were stars again.

Jennifer smiled. "You look smug," she told Kerin.

He put his arm around her. "*We* look smug. We have a

right to be. We just beat that fucking darkness. There's only one thing we did wrong.''

She blinked. ''What?''

''We put apples on the trees, instead of pizza.''

A Song for Lya

THE CITIES OF THE SHKEEN ARE OLD, OLDER FAR THAN MAN'S, and the great rust-red metropolis that rose from their sacred hill country had proved to be the oldest of them all. The Shkeen city had no name. It needed none. Though they built cities and towns by the hundreds and the thousands, the hill city had no rivals. It was the largest in size and population, and it was alone in the sacred hills. It was their Rome, Mecca, Jerusalem; all in one. It was *the* city, and all Shkeen came to it at last, in the final days before Union.

That city had been ancient in the days before Rome fell, had been huge and sprawling when Babylon was still a dream. But there was no feel of age to it. The human eye saw only miles and miles of low, red-brick domes; small hummocks of dried mud that covered the rolling hills like a rash. Inside they were dim and nearly airless. The rooms were small and the furniture crude.

Yet it was not a grim city. Day after day it squatted in those scrubby hills, broiling under a hot sun that sat in the sky like a weary orange melon; but the city teemed with life: smells of cooking, the sounds of laughter and talk and children running, the bustle and sweat of brickmen repairing the domes, the bells of the Joined ringing in the streets. The Shkeen were a lusty and exuberant people, almost childlike. Certainly there was nothing about them that told of great age or ancient wisdom. This is a young race, said the signs, this is a culture in its infancy.

But that infancy had lasted more than fourteen thousand years.

The human city was the real infant, less than ten Earth years old. It was built on the edge of the hills, between the Shkeen metropolis and the dusty brown plains where the spaceport had gone up. In human terms, it was a beautiful city; open and airy, full of graceful archways and glistening fountains and wide boulevards lined by trees. The buildings were wrought of metal and colored plastic and native woods, and most of them were low in deference to Shkeen architecture. Most of them . . . the Administration Tower was the exception, a polished blue steel needle that split a crystal sky.

You could see it for miles in all directions. Lyanna spied it even before we landed, and we admired it from the air. The gaunt skyscrapers of Old Earth and Baldur were taller, and the fantastic webbed cities of Arachne were far more beautiful—but that slim blue Tower was still imposing enough as it rose unrivaled to its lonely dominance above the sacred hills.

The spaceport was in the shadow of the Tower, easy walking distance. But they met us anyway. A low-slung scarlet aircar sat purring at the base of the ramp as we disembarked, with a driver lounging against the stick. Dino Valcarenghi stood next to it, leaning on the door and talking to an aide.

Valcarenghi was the planetary administrator, the boy wonder of the sector. Young, of course, but I'd known that. Short, and good-looking, in a dark, intense way, with black hair that curled thickly against his head and an easy, genial smile.

He flashed us that smile then, when we stepped off the ramp, and reached to shake hands. "Hi," he began, "I'm glad to see you." There was no nonsense with formal introductions. He knew who we were, and we knew who he was, and Valcarenghi wasn't the kind of man who put much stock in ritual.

Lyanna took his hand lightly in hers, and gave him her vampire look: big, dark eyes opened wide and staring, thin mouth lifted in a tiny faint smile. She's a small girl, almost waiflike, with short brown hair and a child's figure. She can look very fragile, very helpless. When she wants to. But she rattles people with that look. If they know Lya's a telepath, they figure she's poking around amid their innermost secrets. Actually she's playing with them. When Lyanna is *really* reading, her whole body goes stiff and you can almost see her tremble. And those big, soul-sucking eyes get narrow and hard and opaque.

But not many people know that, so they squirm under her vampire eyes and look the other way and hurry to release her hand. Not Valcarenghi, though. He just smiled and stared back, then moved on to me.

I *was* reading when I took his hand—my standard operating procedure. Also a bad habit, I guess, since it's put some promising friendships into an early grave. My talent isn't equal to Lya's. But it's not as demanding, either. I read emotions. Valcarenghi's geniality came through strong and genuine. With nothing behind it, or at least nothing that was close enough to the surface for me to catch.

We also shook hands with the aide, a middle-aged blond stork named Nelson Gourlay. Then Valcarenghi ushered everybody into the aircar and we took off. "I imagine you're tired," he said after we were airborne, "so we'll save the tour of the city and head straight for the Tower. Nelse will show you your quarters, then you can join us for a drink, and we'll talk over the problem. You've read the materials I sent?"

"Yes," I said. Lya nodded. "Interesting background, but I'm not sure why we're here."

"We'll get to that soon enough," Valcarenghi replied. "I ought to be letting you enjoy the scenery." He gestured toward the window, smiled, and fell silent.

So Lya and I enjoyed the scenery, or as much as we could enjoy during the five-minute flight from spaceport to tower. The aircar was whisking down the main street at treetop level, stirring up a breeze that whipped the thin branches as we went by. It was cool and dark in the interior of the car, but outside the Shkeen sun was riding toward noon, and you could see the heat waves shimmering from the pavement. The population must have been inside huddled around their air-conditioners, because we saw very little traffic.

We got out near the main entrance to the Tower and walked through a huge, sparkling-clean lobby. Valcarenghi left us then to talk to some underlings. Gourlay led us into one of the tubes and we shot up fifty floors. Then we waltzed past a secretary into another, private tube, and climbed some more.

Our rooms were lovely; carpeted in cool green, and paneled with wood. There was a complete library there, mostly Earth classics bound in synthaleather, with a few novels from Baldur, our home world. Somebody had been researching our tastes. One of the walls of the bedroom was tinted glass, giving a panoramic view of the city far below us, with a control that could darken it for sleeping.

Gourlay showed it to us dutifully, like a dour bellhop. I read him briefly though, and found no resentment. He was nervous, but only slightly. There was honest affection there for someone. Us? Valcarenghi?

Lya sat down on one of the twin beds. "Is someone bringing our luggage?" she asked.

Gourlay nodded. "You'll be well taken care of," he said. "Anything you want, ask."

"Don't worry, we will," I said. I dropped to the second bed, and gestured Gourlay to a chair. "How long have you been here?"

"Six years," he said, taking the chair gratefully and sprawling out all over it. "I'm one of the veterans. I've worked under four administrators now. Dino, and Stuart before him, and Gustaffson before *him*. I was even under Rockwood a few months.''

Lya perked up, crossing her legs under her and leaning forward. "That was all Rockwood lasted, wasn't it?"

"Right," Gourlay said. "He didn't like the planet, took a quick demotion to assistant administrator someplace else. I didn't care much, to tell the truth. He was the nervous type, always giving orders to prove who was boss."

"And Valcarenghi?" I asked.

Gourlay made a smile look like a yawn. "Dino? Dino's OK, the best of the lot. He's good, knows he's good. He's only been here two months, but he's gotten a lot done, and he's made a lot of friends. He treats the staff like people, calls everybody by his first name, all that stuff. People like that."

I was reading, and I read sincerity. It was Valcarenghi that Gourlay was affectionate toward, then. He believed what he was saying.

I had more questions, but I didn't get to ask them. Gourlay got up suddenly. "I really shouldn't stay," he said. "You want to rest, right? Come up to the top in about two hours and we'll go over things with you. You know where the tube is?"

We nodded, and Gourlay left. I turned to Lyanna. "What do you think?"

She lay back on the bed and considered the ceiling. "I don't know," she said. "I wasn't reading. I wonder why they've had so many administrators. And why they wanted us."

"We're Talented," I said, smiling. With the capital, yes. Lyanna and I have been tested and registered as psi Talents, and we have the licenses to prove it.

"Uh-huh," she said, turning on her side and smiling back at me. Not her vampire half-smile this time. Her sexy little girl smile.

"Valcarenghi wants us to get some rest," I said. "It's probably not a bad idea."

Lya bounced out of bed. "OK," she said, "but these twins have got to go."

"We could push them together."

She smiled again. We pushed them together.

And we *did* get some sleep. Eventually.

Our luggage was outside the door when we woke. We changed into fresh clothes, old casual stuff, counting on Valcarenghi's notorious lack of pomp. The tube took us to the top of the Tower.

The office of the planetary administrator was hardly an office. There was no desk, none of the usual trappings. Just a bar and lush blue carpets that swallowed us ankle-high, and six or seven scattered chairs. Plus lots of space and sunlight, with Shkea laid out at our feet beyond the tinted glass. All four walls this time.

Valcarenghi and Gourlay were waiting for us, and Valcarenghi did the bartending chores personally. I didn't recognize the beverage, but it was cool and spicy and aromatic, with a real sting to it. I sipped it gratefully. For some reason I felt I needed a lift.

"Shkeen wine," Valcarenghi said, smiling, in answer to an unasked question. "They've got a name for it, but I can't pronounce it yet. But give me time. I've only been here two months, and the language is rough."

"You're learning Shkeen?" Lya asked, surprised. I knew why. Shkeen is rough on human tongues, but the natives learned Terran with stunning ease. Most people accept that happily, and just forgot about the difficulties of cracking the alien language.

"It gives me an insight into the way they think," Valcarenghi said. "At least that's the theory." He smiled.

I read him again, although it was more difficult. Physical contact makes things sharper. Again, I got a simple emotion, close to the surface—pride this time. With pleasure mixed in. I chalked that up to the wine. Nothing beneath.

"However you pronounce the drink, I like it," I said.

"The Shkeen produce a wide variety of liquors and food-stuffs," Gourlay put in. "We've cleared many for export already, and we're checking others. Market should be good."

"You'll have a chance to sample more of the local produce this evening." Valcarenghi said. "I've set up a tour of the city, with a stop or two in Shkeentown. For a settlement of our size, our night life is fairly interesting. I'll be your guide."

"Sounds good," I said. Lya was smiling too. A tour was unusually considerate. Most Normals feel uneasy around Talents, so they rush us in to do whatever they want done, then rush us out again as quickly as possible. They certainly don't socialize with us.

"Now—the problem," Valcarenghi said, lowering his drink and leaning forward in the chair. "You read about the Cult of the Union?"

"A Shkeen religion," Lya said.

"*The* Shkeen religion," corrected Valcarenghi. "Every one of them is a believer. This is a planet without heretics."

"We read the materials you sent on it," Lya said. "Along with everything else."

"What do you think?"

I shrugged. "Grim. Primitive. But no more than any number of others I've read about. The Shkeen aren't very advanced, after all. There were religions on Old Earth that included human sacrifice."

Valcarenghi shook his head, and looked toward Gourlay.

"No, you don't understand," Gourlay started, putting his drink down on the carpet. "I've been studying their religion for six years. It's like no other in history. Nothing on Old Earth like it, no sir. Nor in any other race we've encountered.

"And Union, well, it's wrong to compare it to human sacrifice, just wrong. The Old Earth religions sacrificed one or two unwilling victims to appease their gods. Killed a handful to get mercy for the millions. And the handful generally protested. The Shkeen don't work it that way. The Greeshka takes *everyone*. And they go willingly. Like lemmings they march off to the caves to be eaten alive by those parasites. *Every* Shkeen is Joined at forty, and goes to Final Union before he's fifty.''

I was confused. "All right," I said. "I see the distinction, I guess. But so what? Is this the problem? I imagine that Union is rough on the Shkeen, but that's their business. Their religion is no worse than the ritual cannibalism of the Hrangans, is it?"

Valcarenghi finished his drink and got up, heading for the bar. As he poured himself a refill, he said, almost casually. "As far as I know, Hrangan cannibalism has claimed no human converts."

Lya looked startled. I felt startled. I sat up and stared. "What?"

Valcarenghi headed back to his seat, glass in hand. "Human converts have been joining the Cult of the Union. Dozens of them are already Joined. None of them have achieved full Union yet, but that's only a question of time." He sat down, and looked at Gourlay. So did we.

The gangling blond aide picked up the narrative. "The first convert was about seven years ago. Nearly a year before I got here, two and a half after Shkea was discovered and the settlement built. Guy named Magly. Psi-psych, worked closely with the Shkeen. He was it for two years. Then another in '08, more the next year. And the rate's been climbing ever since. There was one big one. Phil Gustaffson."

Lya blinked. "The planetary administrator?"

"The same," said Gourlay. "We've had a lot of administrators. Gustaffson came in after Rockwood couldn't stand it. He was a big, gruff old guy. Everybody loved him. He'd lost his wife and kids on his last assignment, but you'd never have known it. He was always hearty, full of fun. Well, he got interested in the Shkeen religion, started talking to them. Talked to Magly and some of the other converts too. Even went to see a Greeshka. That shook him up real bad for a while. But finally he got over it, went back to his researches. I worked with him, but I never guessed what he had in mind. A little over a year ago, he converted. He's Joined now. Nobody's ever been accepted that fast. I hear talk in Shkeentown that he may even be admitted to Final Union, rushed right in. Well, Phil was administrator here longer than anybody else. People liked him, and when he went over, a lot of his friends followed. The rate's way up now."

"Not quite one percent, and rising," Valcarenghi said. "That seems low, but remember what it means. One percent of the people in my settlement are choosing a religion that includes a very unpleasant form of suicide."

Lya looked from him to Gourlay and back again. "Why hasn't this been reported?"

"It should have been," Valcarenghi said, "but Stuart succeeded Gustaffson, and he was scared stiff of a scandal. There's no law against humans adopting an alien religion, so Stuart defined it as a nonproblem. He reported the conversion rate routinely, and nobody higher up ever bothered to make the correlation and remember just what all these people were converting *to*."

I finished my drink, set it down. "Go on," I said to Valcarenghi.

"I define the situation as a problem," he said. "I don't care how few people are involved, the idea that human beings would allow the Greeshka to consume them alarms me. I've had a team of psychs on it since I took over, but they're getting nowhere. I needed Talent. I want you two to find out *why* these people are converting. Then I'll be able to deal with the situation."

The problem was strange, but the assignment seemed straightforward enough. I read Valcarenghi to be sure. His emotions were a bit more complex this time, but not much.

Confidence above all: he was sure we could handle the problem. There was honest concern there, but no fear, and not even a hint of deception. Again, I couldn't catch anything below the surface. Valcarenghi kept his hidden turmoil well hidden, if he had any.

I glanced at Lyanna. She was sitting awkwardly in her chair, and her fingers were wrapped very tightly around her wine glass. Reading. Then she loosened up and looked my way and nodded.

"All right," I said. "I think we can do it."

Valcarenghi smiled. "That I never doubted," he said. "It was only a question of whether you *would*. But enough of business for tonight. I've promised you a night on the town, and I always try to deliver on my promises. I'll meet you downstairs in the lobby in a half-hour."

Lya and I changed into something more formal back in our room. I picked a dark blue tunic, with white slacks and a matching mesh scarf. Not the height of fashion, but I was hoping that Shkea would be several months behind the times. Lya slipped into a silky white skintight with a tracery of thin blue lines that flowed over her in sensuous patterns in response to her body heat. The lines were definitely lecherous, accentuating her thin figure with a singleminded determination. A blue raincape completely the outfit.

"Valcarenghi's funny," she said as she fastened it.

"Oh?" I was struggling with the sealseam on my tunic, which refused to seal. "You catch something when you read him?"

"No," she said. She finished attaching the cape and admired herself in the mirror. Then she spun toward me, the cape swirling behind her. "That's it. He was thinking what he was saying. Oh, variations in the wording, of course, but nothing important. His mind was on what we were discussing, and behind that there was only a wall." She smiled. "Didn't get a single one of his deep dark secrets."

I finally conquered the sealseam. "Tsk," I said. "Well, you get another chance tonight."

That got me a grimace. "The hell I do. I don't read people on off-time. It isn't fair. Besides, it's such a strain. I wish I could catch thoughts as easily as you do feelings."

"The price of Talent," I said. "You're more Talented, your price is higher." I rummaged in our luggage for a raincape, but I didn't find anything that went well, so I decided not to wear one. Capes were out, anyway. "I didn't get much on Valcarenghi either. You could have told as much by watching his face. He must be a very disciplined mind. But I'll forgive him. He serves good wine."

Lya nodded. "Right! That stuff did me good. Got rid of the headache I woke up with."

"The altitude," I suggested. We headed for the door.

The lobby was deserted, but Valcarenghi didn't keep us waiting long. This time he drove his own aircar, a battered black job that had evidently been with him for a while. Gourlay wasn't the sociable type, but Valcarenghi had a woman with him, a stunning auburn-haired vision named Laurie Blackburn. She was even younger than Valcarenghi—mid-twenties, by the look of her.

It was sunset when we took off. The whole far horizon was a gorgeous tapestry in red and orange, and a cool breeze was blowing in from the plains. Valcarenghi left the coolers off and opened the car windows, and we watched the city darken into twilight as we drove.

Dinner was at a plush restaurant with Baedurian decor—to make us feel comfortable, I guessed. The food, however, was very cosmopolitan. The spices, the herbs, the *style* of cooking were all Baldur. The meats and vegetables were native. It made for an interesting combination. Valcarenghi ordered for all four of us, and we wound up sampling about a dozen different dishes. My favorite was a tiny Shkeen bird that they cooked in sourtang sauce. There wasn't very much of it, but what there was tasted great. We also polished off three bottles of wine during the meal: more of the Shkeen stuff we'd sampled that afternoon, a flask of chilled Veltaar from Baldur, and some real Old Earth Burgundy.

The talk warmed up quickly; Valcarenghi was a born storyteller and an equally good listener. Eventually, of course, the conversation got around to Shkea and Shkeen. Laurie led it there. She'd been on Shkea for about six months, working toward an advanced degree in extee anthropology. She was trying to discover why the Shkeen civilization had remained frozen for so many millennia.

"They're older than we are, you know," she told us. "They had cities before men were using tools. It should have been space-traveling Shkeen that stumbled on primitive men, not the other way around.

"Aren't there theories on that already?" I asked.

"Yes, but none of them are universally accepted," she said. "Cullen cites a lack of heavy metals, for example. A factor, but is it the *whole* answer? Von Hamrin claims the Shkeen didn't get enough competition. No big carnivores on the planet, so there was nothing to breed aggressiveness into the race. But he's come under a lot of fire. Shkea isn't all *that* idyllic; if it were, the Shkeen never would have reached their present level. Besides, what's the Greeshka if not a carnivore? It *eats* them, doesn't it?"

"What do you think?" Lya asked.

"I think it had something to do with the religion, but I haven't worked it all out yet. Dino's helping me talk to people and the Shkeen are open enough, but research isn't easy." She stopped suddenly and looked at Lya hard. "For me, anyway. I imagine it'd be easier for you."

We'd heard that before. Normals often figure that Talents have unfair advantages, which is perfectly understandable. We do. But Laurie wasn't resentful. She delivered her statement in a wistful, speculative tone, instead of etching it in verbal acid.

Valcarenghi leaned over and put an arm around her. "Hey,"

he said. "Enough shop talk. Robb and Lya shouldn't be worrying about the Shkeen until tomorrow."

Laurie looked at him, and smiled tentatively. "OK," she said lightly. "I get carried away. Sorry."

"That's OK," I told her. "It's an interesting subject. Give us a day and we'll probably be getting enthusiastic too."

Lya nodded agreement, and added that Laurie would be the first to know if our work turned up anything that would support her theory. I was hardly listening. I know it's not polite to read Normals when you're out with them socially, but there are times I can't resist. Valcarenghi had his arm around Laurie and had pulled her toward him gently. I was curious.

So I took a quick, guilty reading. He was very high—slightly drunk, I guess, and feeling very confident and protective. The master of the situation. But Laurie was a jumble-uncertainty, repressed anger, a vague fading hint of fright. And love, confused but very strong. I doubted that it was for me or Lya. She loved Valcarenghi.

I reached under the table, searching for Lya's hand, and found her knee. I squeezed it gently and she looked at me and smiled. She wasn't reading, which was good. It bothered me that Laurie loved Valcarenghi, though I didn't know why, and I was just as glad that Lya didn't see my discontent.

We finished off the last of the wine in short order, and Valcarenghi took care of the whole bill. Then he rose. "Onward!" he announced. "The night is fresh, and we've got visits to make."

So we made visits. No holoshows or anything that drab, although the city had its share of theaters. A casino was next on the list. Gambling was legal on Shkea, of course, and Valcarenghi would have legalized it if it weren't. He supplied the chips and I lost some for him, as did Laurie. Lya was barred from playing; her Talent was too strong. Valcarenghi won big; he was a superb mindspin player, and pretty good at the traditional games too.

Then came a bar. More drinks, plus local entertainment which was better than I would have expected.

It was pitch-black when we got out, and I assumed that the expedition was nearing its end. Valcarenghi surprised us. When we got back to the car, he reached under the controls, pulled out a box of sober-ups, and passed them around.

"Hey," I said. "You're driving. Why do I need this? I just barely got up here."

"I'm about to take you to a genuine Shkeen cultural event, Robb," he said. "I don't want you making rude comments or throwing up on the natives. Take your pill."

I took my pill, and the buzz in my head began to fade. Valcarenghi already had the car air-borne. I leaned back and put my arm around Lya, and she rested her head on my shoulder. "Where are we going?" I asked.

"Shkeentown," he replied, never looking back, "to their Great Hall. There's a Gathering tonight, and I figured you'd be interested."

"It will be in Shkeen, of course," Laurie said, "but Dino can translate for you. I know a little of the language too, and I'll fill in whatever he misses."

Lya looked excited. We'd read about Gatherings, of course, but we hardly expected go see one on our first day on Shkea. The Gatherings were a species of religious rite; a mass confessional of sorts for pilgrims who were about to be admitted to the ranks of the Joined. Pilgrims swelled the hill city daily, but Gatherings were conducted only three or four times a year when the numbers of those-about-to-be-Joined climbed high enough.

The aircar streaked almost soundlessly through the brightly-lit settlement, passing huge fountains that danced with a dozen colors and pretty ornamental arches that flowed like liquid fire. A few other cars were airborne, and here and there we flew above pedestrians strolling the city's broad malls. But most people were inside, and light and music flooded from many of the homes we passed.

Then, abruptly, the character of the city began to change. The level ground began to roll and heave, hills rose before us and then behind us, and the lights vanished. Below, the malls gave way to unlit roads of crushed stone and dust, and the domes of glass and metal done in fashionable mock-Shkeen yielded to their older brick brothers. The Shkeen city was quieter than its human counterpart; most of the houses were darkly silent.

Then, ahead of us, a hummock appeared that was larger than the others—almost a hill in itself, with a big arched door and a series of slit-like windows. And light leaked from this one, and noise, and there were Shkeen outside.

I suddenly realized that, although I'd been on Shkea for nearly a day, this was the first sight I'd caught of the Shkeen. Not that I could see them all that clearly from an aircar at night. But I did see them. They were smaller than men—the tallest was around five feet—with big eyes and long arms. That was all I could tell from above.

Valcarenghi put the car down alongside the Great Hall, and we piled out. Shkeen were trickling through the arch from several directions, but most of them were already inside. We joined the trickle, and nobody even looked twice at us, except for one character who hailed Valcarenghi in a thin, squeaky voice and called him Dino. He had friends even here.

The interior was one huge room, with a great crude platform built in the center and an immense crowd of Shkeen circling it. The only light was from torches that were stuck in grooves along the walls, and on high poles surrounding the platform. Someone was speaking, and every one of those great, bulging eyes was turned his way. We four were the only humans in the Hall.

The speaker, outlined brightly by the torches, was a fat, middle-aged Shkeen who moved his arms slowly, almost hypnotically, as he talked. His speech was a series of whistles, wheezes, and grunts, so I didn't listen very closely. He was much too far away to read. I was reduced to studying his appearance, and that of other Shkeen near me. All of them were hairless, as far as I could see, with softish-looking orange skin that was creased by a thousand tiny wrinkles. They wore simple shifts of crude, multicolored cloth, and I had difficulty telling male from female.

Valcarenghi leaned over toward me and whispered, careful to keep his voice low. "The speaker is a farmer," he said. "He's telling the crowd how far he's come, and some of the hardships of his life."

I looked around. Valcarenghi's whisper was the only sound in the place. Everyone else was dead quiet, eyes riveted on the platform, scarcely breathing. "He's saying that he has four brothers," Valcarenghi told me. "Two have gone on to Final Union, one is among the Joined. The other is younger than himself, and now owns the farm." He frowned. "The speaker will never see his farm again," he said, more loudly, "but he's happy about it."

"Bad crops?" asked Lya, smiling irreverently. She'd been listening to the same whisper. I gave her a stern look.

The Shkeen went on. Valcarenghi stumbled after him. "Now he's telling his crimes, all the things he's done that he's ashamed of, his blackest soul-secrets. He's had a sharp tongue at times, he's vain, once he actually struck his younger brother. Now he speaks of his wife, and the other women he has known. He has betrayed her many times, copulating with others. As a boy, he mated with animals for he feared females. In recent years he has grown incapable, and his brother has serviced his wife."

On and on and on it went, in incredible detail, detail that was both startling and frightening. No intimacy went untold, no secret was left undisturbed. I stood and listened to Valcarenghi's whispers, shocked at first, finally growing bored with the squalor of it all. I began to get reckless. I wondered briefly if I knew any human half so well as I now knew this great fat Shkeen. Then I wondered whether Lyanna, with her

Talent, knew anyone half so well. It was almost as if the speaker wanted all of us to live through his life right here and now.

His speech lasted for what seemed hours, but finally it began to wind up. "He speaks now of Union," Valcarenghi whispered. "He will be Joined, he is joyful about it, he has craved it for so long. His misery is at an end, his aloneness will cease, soon he shall walk the streets of the sacred city and peal his joy with the bells. And then Final Union, in the years to come. He will be with his brothers in the afterlife."

"No, Dino." This whisper was Laurie. "Quit wrapping human phrases around what he says. He will be his brothers, he says. The phrase also implies they will be him."

Valcarenghi smiled. "OK, Laurie. If you say so. . ."

Suddenly the fat farmer was gone from the platform. The crowd rustled, and another figure took his place: much shorter, wrinkled excessively, one eye a great gaping hole. He began to speak, haltingly at first, then with greater skill.

"This one is a brickman, he has worked many domes, he lives in the sacred city. His eye was lost many years ago, when he fell from a dome and a sharp stick poked into him. The pain was very great, but he returned to work within a year, he did not beg for premature Union, he was very brave, he is proud of his courage. He has a wife, but they have never had offspring, he is sad of that, he cannot talk to his wife easily, they are apart even when together and she weeps at night, he is sad of that too, but he has never hurt her and . . ."

It went on for hours again. My restlessness stirred again, but I cracked down on it—this was too important. I let myself get lost in Valcarenghi's narration, and the story of the one-eyed Shkeen. Before long, I was riveted as closely to the tale as the aliens around me. It was hot and stuffy and all but airless in the dome, and my tunic was getting sooty and soaked by sweat, some of it from the creatures who pressed around me. But I hardly noticed.

The second speaker ended as had the first, with a long

praise of the joy of being Joined and the coming of Final Union. Toward the end, I hardly even needed Valcarenghi's translation—I could hear the happiness in the voice of the Shkeen, and see it in his trembling figure. Or maybe I was reading, unconsciously. But I can't read at that distance—unless the target is emoting very hard.

A third speaker ascended the platform, and spoke in a voice louder than the others. Valcarenghi kept pace. "A woman this time," he said. "She has carried eight children for her man, she has four sisters and three brothers, she has farmed all her life, she . . ."

Suddenly her speech seemed to peak, and she ended a long sequence with several sharp, high whistles. Then she fell silent. The crowd, as one, began to respond with whistles of their own. An eerie, echoing music filled the Great Hall, and the Shkeen around us all began to sway and whistle. The woman looked out at the scene from a bent and broken position.

Valcarenghi started to translate, but he stumbled over something. Laurie cut in before he could backtrack. "She has now told them of great tragedy," she whispered. "They whistle to show their grief, their oneness with her pain."

"Sympathy, yes," said Valcarenghi, taking over again. "When she was young, her brother grew ill, and seemed to be dying. Her parents told her to take him to the sacred hills, for they could not leave the younger children. But she shattered a wheel on her cart through careless driving, and her brother died upon the plains. He perished without Union. She blames herself."

The Shkeen had begun again. Laurie began to translate, leaning close to us and using a soft whisper. "Her brother died, she is saying again. She faulted him, denied him Union, now he is sundered and alone and gone without . . . without . . ."

"Afterlife," said Valcarenghi. "Without afterlife."

"I'm not sure that's entirely right," Laurie said. "That concept is . . ."

Valcarenghi waved her silent. "Listen," he said. He continued to translate.

We listened to her story, told in Valcarenghi's increasingly hoarse whisper. She spoke longest of all, and her story was the grimmest of the three. When she finished, she too was replaced. But Valcarenghi put a hand on my shoulder and beckoned toward the exit.

The cool night air hit like ice water, and I suddenly realized that I was drenched with sweat. Valcarenghi walked quickly toward the car. Behind us, the speaking was still in progress, and the Shkeen showed no signs of tiring.

"Gatherings go on for days, sometimes weeks," Laurie told us as we climbed inside the aircar. "The Shkeen listen in shifts, more or less—they try terribly to hear every word, but exhaustion gets to them sooner or later and they retire for brief rests, then return for more. It is a great honor to last through an entire Gathering without sleep."

Valcarenghi shot us aloft. "I'm going to try that someday," he said. "I've never attended for more than a couple of hours, but I think I could make it if I fortified myself with drugs. We'll get more understanding between human and Shkeen if we participate more fully in their rituals."

"Oh," I said. "Maybe Gustaffson felt the same way."

Valcarenghi laughed lightly. "Yes, well, I don't intend to participate *that* fully."

The trip home was a tired silence. I'd lost track of time but my body insisted that it was almost dawn. Lya, curled up under my arm, looked drained and empty and only half-awake. I felt the same way.

We left the aircar in front of the Tower, and took the tubes up. I was past thinking. Sleep came very, very quickly.

I dreamed that night. A good dream, I think, but it faded with the coming of the light, leaving me empty and feeling cheated. I lay there, after waking, with my arm around Lya and my eyes on the ceiling, trying to recall what the dream had been about. But nothing came.

Instead, I found myself thinking about the Gathering, running it through again in my head. Finally I disentangled myself and climbed out of bed. We'd darkened the glass, so the room was still pitch-black. But I found the controls easily enough, and let through a trickle of late morning light.

Lya mumbled some sort of sleepy protest and rolled over, but made no effort to get up. I left her alone in the bedroom and went out to our library, looking for a book on the Shkeen—something with a little more detail than the material we'd been sent. No luck. The library was meant for recreation, not research.

I found a viewscreen and punched up to Valcarenghi's office. Gourlay answered. "Hello," he said. "Dino figured you'd be calling. He's not here right now. He's out arbitrating a trade contract. What do you need?"

"Books," I said, my voice still a little sleepy. "Something on the Shkeen."

"That I can't do," Gourlay said. "Are none, really. Lots of papers and studies and monographs, but no full-fledged books. I'm going to write one, but I haven't gotten to it yet. Dino figured I could be your resource, I guess."

"Oh."

"Got any questions?"

I searched for a question, found none. "Not really," I said, shrugging. "I just wanted general background, maybe some more information on Gatherings."

"I can talk to you about that later," Gourlay said. "Dino figured you'd want to get to work today. We can bring people to the Tower, if you'd like, or you can get out to them."

"We'll go out," I said quickly. Bringing subjects in for interviews fouls up everything. They get all anxious, and that covers up any emotions I might want to read, and they *think* on different things, too, so Lyanna has trouble.

"Fine," said Gourlay. "Dino put an aircar at your disposal. Pick it up down in the lobby. Also, they'll have some keys for you, so you can come straight up here in the office without bothering with the secretaries and all."

"Thanks," I said. "Talk to you later." I flicked off the viewscreen and walked back to the bedroom.

Lya was sitting up, the covers around her waist. I sat down next to her and kissed her. She smiled, but didn't respond. "Hey," I said. "What's wrong?"

"Headache," she replied. "I thought sober-ups were supposed to get rid of hangovers."

"That's the theory. Mine worked pretty well." I went to the closet and began looking for something to wear. "We should have headache pills around here someplace. I'm sure Dino wouldn't forget anything that obvious."

"Umpf. Yes. Throw me some clothes."

I grabbed one of her coveralls and tossed it across the room. Lya stood up and slipped into it while I dressed, then went off to the washroom.

"Better," she said. "You're right, he didn't forget medicines."

"He's the thorough sort."

She smiled. "I guess. Laurie knows the language better, though. I read her. Dino made a couple of mistakes in that translation last night."

I'd guessed at something like that. No discredit to Valcarenghi; he was working on a four-month handicap, from what they said. I nodded. "Read anything else?"

"No. I tried to get those speakers, but the distance was too much." She came up and took my hand. "Where are we going today?"

"Shkeentown," I said. "Let's try to find some of these Joined. I didn't notice any at the Gathering."

"No. Those things are for Shkeen about-to-be-Joined."

"So I hear. Let's go."

We went. We stopped at the fourth level for a late breakfast in the Tower cafeteria, then got our aircar pointed out to us by a man in the lobby. A sporty green four-seater, very common, very inconspicuous.

I didn't take the aircar all the way into the Shkeen city, figuring we'd get more of the feel of the place if we went through on foot. So I dropped down just beyond the first range of hills, and we walked.

The human city had seemed almost empty, but Shkeentown lived. The crushed-rock streets were full of aliens, hustling back and forth busily, carrying loads of bricks and baskets of fruit and clothing. There were children everywhere, most of them naked; fat balls of orange energy that ran around us in circles, whistling and grunting and grinning, tugging at us every once in a while. The kids looked different from the adults. They had a few patches of reddish hair, for one thing, and their skins were still smooth and unwrinkled. They were the only ones who really paid any attention to us. The adult Shkeen just went about their business, and gave us an occasional friendly smile. Humans were obviously not all that uncommon in the streets of Shkeentown.

Most of the traffic was on foot, but small wooden carts were also common. The Shkeen draft animal looked like a big green dog that was about to be sick. They were strapped to the carts in pairs, and they whined constantly as they pulled. So, naturally, men called them whiners. In addition to whining, they also defecated constantly. That, with odors from the food peddled in baskets and the Shkeen themselves, gave the city a definite pungency.

There was noise too, a constant clamor. Kids whistling. Shkeen talking loudly with grunts and whimpers and squeaks, whiners whining and their carts rattling over the rocks. Lya and I walked through it all silently, hand in hand, watching and listening and smelling and . . . reading.

I was wide open when I entered Shkeentown, letting everything wash over me as I walked, unfocused but receptive. I was the center of a small bubble of emotion—feelings rushed up at me as Shkeen approached, faded as they walked away, circled around and around with the dancing children. I swam in a sea of impressions. And it startled me.

It startled me because it was all so familiar. I'd read aliens before. Sometimes it was difficult, sometimes it was easy, but it was never pleasant. The Hrangans have sour minds, rank with hate and bitterness, and I feel unclean when I come out. The Fyndii feel emotions so palely that I can scarcely read them at all. The Damoosh are . . . *different*. I read them strongly, but I can't find names for the feelings I read.

But the Shkeen—it was like walking down a street on Baldur. No, wait—more like one of the Lost Colonies, when a human settlement has fallen back into barbarism and forgotten its origins. Human emotions rage there, primal and strong and real, but less sophisticated than on Old Earth or Baldur. The Shkeen were like that: primitive, maybe, but very understandable. I read joy and sorrow, envy, anger, whimsy, bitterness, yearning, pain. The same heady mixture that engulfs me everywhere, when I open myself to it.

Lya was reading, too. I felt her hand tense in mine. After a while, it softened again. I turned to her, and she saw the question in my eyes.

"They're people," she said. "They're like us."

I nodded. "Parallel evolution, maybe. Shkea might be an older Earth, with a few minor differences. But you're right. They're more human than any other race we've encountered in space." I considered that. "Does that answer Dino's question? If they're like us, it follows that their religion would be more appealing than a *really* alien one."

"No, Robb," Lya said. "I don't think so. Just the reverse. If they're like us, it doesn't make sense that *they'd* go off so willingly to die. See?"

She was right, of course. There was nothing suicidal in the emotions I'd read, nothing unstable, nothing really abnormal. Yet every one of the Shkeen went off to Final Union in the end.

"We should focus on somebody," I said. "This blend of thought isn't getting us anywhere." I looked around to find a subject, but just then I heard the bells begin.

They were off to the left somewhere, nearly lost in the city's gentle roar. I tugged Lya by the hand, and we ran down the street to find them, turning left at the first gap in the orderly row of domes.

The bells were still ahead, and we kept running, cutting through what must have been somebody's yard, and climbing over a low bush-fence that bristled with sweethorns. Beyond that was another yard, a dung-pit, more domes, and finally a street. It was there we found the bell-ringers.

There were four of them, all Joined, wearing long gowns of bright red fabric that trailed in the dust, with great bronze bells in either hand. They rang the bells constantly, their long arms swinging back and forth, the sharp, clanging notes filling the street. All four were elderly, as Shkeen go—hairless and pinched up with a million tiny wrinkles. But they smiled very widely, and the younger Shkeen that passed smiled at them.

On their heads rode the Greeshka.

I'd expected to find the sight hideous. I didn't. It was faintly disquieting, but only because I knew what it meant. The parasites were bright blobs of crimson goo, ranging in size from a pulsing wart on the back of one Shkeen skull to a great sheet of dripping, moving red that covered the head and shoulders of the smallest like a living cowl. The Greeshka lived by sharing the nutrients in the Shkeen bloodstream, I knew.

And also by slowly—oh so slowly—consuming its host.

Lya and I stopped a few yards from them, and watched them ring. Her face was solemn, and I think mine was. All of the others were smiling, and the songs that the bells sang were songs of joy. I squeezed Lyanna's hand tightly. "Read," I whispered.

We read.

Me: I read bells. Not the sound of bells, no, no, but the *feel* of bells, the *emotion* of bells, the bright clanging joy, the hooting-shouting-ringing loudness, the song of the Joined, the togetherness and the sharing of it all. I read what the Joined felt as they pealed their bells, their happiness and anticipation, their ecstasy in telling others of their clamorous contentment. And I read love, coming from them in great hot waves, passionate possessive love of a man and woman together, not the weak watery affection of the human who "loves" his brothers. This was real and fervent and it burned almost as it washed over me and surrounded me. They loved themselves, and they loved all Shkeen, and they loved the Greeshka, and they loved each other, and they loved us. They loved us. They loved *me,* as hotly and wildly as Lya loved me. And with love I read belonging, and sharing. They four were all apart, all distinct, but they thought as one almost, and they belonged to each other, and they belonged to the Greeshka, and they were all *together* and linked although each was still himself and none could read the others as I read them.

And Lyanna? I reeled back from them, and shut myself off, and looked at Lya. She was white-faced, but smiling. "They're beautiful," she said, her voice very small and soft and wondering. Drenched in love, I still remembered how much I loved *her,* and how I was a part of her and her of me.

"What—what did you read?" I asked, my voice fighting the continued clangor of the bells.

She shook her head, as if to clear it. "They love us," she said. "You must know that, but oh, I felt it, they *do* love us. And it's so *deep*. Below that love there's more love, and below that more, and on and on forever. Their minds are so deep, so open. I don't think I've ever read a human that deeply. Everything is right at the surface, right there, their whole lives and all their dreams and feelings and memories and oh—I just took it in, swept it up with a reading, a glance. With men, with humans, it's so much work, I have to dig, I have to fight, and even then I don't get down very far. You know, Robb, you know. Oh, *Robb!*'' And she came to me and pressed tight against me, and I held her in my arms. The torrent of feeling that had washed over me must have been a tidal wave for her. Her Talent was broader and deeper than mine, and now she was shaken. I read her as she clutched me, and I read love, great love, and wonder and happiness, but also fear, nervous fear swirling through it all.

Around us, the ringing suddenly stopped. The bells, one by one, ceased to swing, and the four Joined stood in silence for a brief second. One of the other Shkeen nearby came up to them with a huge, cloth-covered basket. The smallest of the Joined threw back the cloth, and the aroma of hot meatrolls rose in the street. Each of the Joined took several from the basket, and before long they were all crunching away happily, and the owner of the rolls was grinning at them. Another Shkeen, a small nude girl, ran up and offered them a flask of water, and they passed it around without comment.

"What's going on?" I asked Lya. Then, even before she told me, I remembered. Something from the literature that Valcarenghi had sent. The Joined did no work. Forty Earth-years they lived and toiled, but from First Joining to Final Union there was only joy and music, and they wandered the streets and rang their bells and talked and sang, and other Shkeen gave them food and drink. It was an honor to feed a Joined, and the Shkeen who had given up his meatrolls was radiating pride and pleasure.

"Lya," I whispered, "can you read them now?"

She nodded against my chest and pulled away and stared at the Joined, her eyes going hard and then softening again. She looked back at me. "It's different," she said, curious.

"How?"

She squinted in puzzlement. "I don't know. I mean, they still love us, and all. But now their thoughts are, well, sort of more human. There are levels, you know, and digging isn't easy, and there are hidden things, things they hide even from themselves. It's not all open like it was. They're thinking

about the food now and how good it tastes. It's all very
vivid. I could taste the rolls myself. But it's not the same.''

I had an inspiration. 'How many minds are there?''

"Four," she said. "Linked somehow, I think. But not
really." She stopped, confused, and shook her head. "I
mean, they sort of feel each other's emotions, like you do, I
guess. But not thoughts, not the detail. I can read them, but
they don't read each other. Each one is distinct. They were
closer before, when they were ringing, but they were always
individuals."

I was slightly disappointed. "Four minds then, not one?"

"Umpf, yes. Four."

"And the Greeshka?" My other bright idea. If the Greeshka
had minds of their own . . .

"Nothing," Lya said. "Like reading a plant, or a piece of
clothing. Not even yes-I-live."

That was disturbing. Even lower animals had some vague
consciousness of life—the feeling Talents called yes-I-live—
usually only a dim spark that it took a major Talent to see.
But Lya *was* a major Talent.

"Let's talk to them," I said. She nodded, and we walked
up to where the Joined were munching their meatrolls.
"Hello," I said awkwardly, wondering how to address them.
"Can you speak Terran?"

Three of them looked at me without comprehension. But
the fourth one, the little one whose Greeshka was a rippling
red cape, bobbed his head up and down. "Yesh," he said, in
a piping-thin voice.

I suddenly forgot what I was going to ask, but Lyanna
came to my rescue. "Do you know of human Joined?" she
said.

He grinned. "All Joined are one," he said.

"Oh," I said. "Well, yes, but do you know any who look
like us? Tall, you know, wth hair and skin that's pink or
brown or something?" I came to another awkward halt,
wondering just how *much* Terran the old Shkeen knew, and
eyeing his Greeshka a little apprehensively.

His head bobbled from side to side. "Joined are all different, but all are one, all are shame. Shome look ash you. Would you Join?"

"No, thanks," I said. "Where can I find a human Joined?"

He bobbed his head some more. "Joined shing and ring and walk the shacred city."

Lya had been reading. "He doesn't know," she told me. "The Joined just wander and play their bells. There's no pattern to it, nobody keeps track. It's all random. Some travel in groups, some alone, and new groups form every time two bunches meet."

"We'll have to search," I said.

"Eat," the Shkeen told us. He reached into the basket on the ground and his hands came out with two steaming meatrolls. He pressed one into my hand, one in Lya's.

I looked at it dubiously. "Thank you," I told him. I pulled at Lya with my free hand and we walked off together. The Joined grinned at us as we left, and started ringing once more before we were halfway down the street.

The meatroll was still in my hand, its crust burning my fingers. "Should I eat this?" I asked Lya.

She took a bite out of hers. "Why not? We had them last night in the restaurant, right? And I'm sure Valcarenghi would've warned us if the native food was poisonous."

That made sense, so I lifted the roll to my mouth and took a bite as I walked. It was hot, and also *hot*, and it wasn't a bit like the meatrolls we'd sampled the previous night. Those had been golden, flaky things, seasoned gently with orangespice from Baldur. The Shkeen version was crunchy, and the meat inside dripped grease and burned my mouth. But it was good, and I was hungry, and the roll didn't last long.

"Get anything else when you read the small guy?" I asked Lya around a mouthful of hot roll.

She swallowed, and nodded. "Yes, I did. He was happy, even more than the rest. He's older. He's near Final Union, and he's very thrilled about it." She spoke with her old easy manner; the aftereffects of reading the Joined seemed to have faded.

"Why?" I was musing out loud. "He's going to *die*. Why is he so happy about it?"

Lya shrugged. "He wasn't thinking in any great analytical detail, I'm afraid."

I licked my fingers to get rid of the last of the grease. We were at a crossroads, with Shkeen bustling by us in all directions, and now we could hear more bells on the wind. "More Joined," I said. "Want to look them up?"

"What would we find out? That we don't already know? We need a *human* Joined."

"Maybe one of this batch *will* be human."

I got Lya's withering look. "Ha. What are the odds?"

"All right," I conceded. It was now late afternoon. "Maybe we'd better head back. Get an earlier start tomorrow. Besides, Dino is probably expecting us for dinner."

Dinner, this time, was served in Valcarenghi's office, after a little additional furniture had been dragged in. His quarters, it turned out, were on the level below, but he preferred to entertain upstairs where his guests could enjoy the spectacular Tower view.

There were five of us, all told: me and Lya, Valcarenghi and Laurie, plus Gourlay. Laurie did the cooking, supervised by master chef Valcarenghi. We had beefsteaks, bred on Shkea from Old Earth stock, plus a fascinating blend of vegetables, that included mushrooms from Old Earth, groundpips from Baldur, and Shkeen sweethorns. Dino liked to experiment and the dish was one of his inventions.

Lya and I gave a full report on the day's adventures, interrupted only by Valcarenghi's sharp, perceptive questioning. After dinner, we got rid of tables and dishes and sat around drinking Veltaar and talking. This time Lya and I asked the questions, with Gourlay supplying the biggest chunk of the answers. Valcarenghi listened from a cushion on the floor, one arm around Laurie, the other holding his wine glass. We were not the first Talents to visit Shkea, he told us. Nor the first to claim the Shkeen were man-like.

"Suppose that means something," he said. "But I don't know. They're *not* men, you know. No, sir. They're much more social, for one thing. Great little city builders from way back, always in towns, always surrounding themselves with others. And they're more communal than man, too. Cooperate in all sorts of things, and they're big on sharing. Trade, for instance—they see that as mutual-sharing."

Valcarenghi laughed. "You can say that again. I just spent the whole day trying to work out a trade contract with a group of farmers who hadn't dealt with us before. It's not easy, believe me. They give us as much of their stuff as we ask for, if they don't need it themselves and no one else has asked for it earlier. But then they wanted to get whatever *they* ask for in the future. They expect it, in fact. So every time we deal we've got a choice; hand them a blank check, or go through an incredible round of talks that ends with them convinced that we're totally selfish."

Lya wasn't satisfied. "What about sex?" she demanded. "From the stuff you were translating last night, I got the impression they're monogamous."

"They're confused about sex relationships," Gourlay said. "It's very strange. Sex is sharing, you see, and it's good to share with everyone. But the sharing has to be real and meaningful. That creates problems."

Laurie sat up, attentive. "I've studied the point," she said quickly. "Shkeen morality insists they love *everybody*. But they can't do it, they're too human, too possessive. They wind up in monogamous relationships, because a really deep sex-sharing with one person is better than a million shallow physical things, in their culture. The ideal Shkeen would sex-share with everyone, with each of the unions being just as deep, but they can't achieve that ideal."

I frowned. "Wasn't somebody guilty last night over betraying his wife?"

Laurie nodded eagerly. "Yes, but the guilt was because his other relationships caused his sharing with his wife to diminish. *That* was the betrayal. If he'd been able to manage it without hurting his older relationship, the sex would have been meaningless. And, if all of the relationships have been real love-sharing, it would have been a plus. His wife would have been proud of him. It's quite an achievement for a Shkeen to be in a multiple union that works."

"And one of the greatest Shkeen crimes is to leave another alone," Gourlay said. "Emotionally alone. Without sharing."

I mulled over that, while Gourlay went on. The Shkeen had little crime, he told us. Especially no violent crime. No murders, no beatings, no prisons, no wars in their long, empty history.

"They're a race without murderers," Valcarenghi said, "which may explain something. On Old Earth, the same cultures that had the highest suicide rates often had the lowest murder rates, too. And the Shkeen suicide rate is one hundred percent."

"They kill animals," I said.

"Not part of the Union," Gourlay replied. "The Union embraces all that thinks, and its creatures may not be killed. They do not kill Shkeen, or humans, or Greeshka."

Lya looked at me, then at Gourlay. "The Greeshka don't think," she said. "I tried to read them this morning and got nothing but the minds of the Shkeen they rode. Not even a yes-I-live."

"We've known that, but the point's always puzzled me," Valcarenghi said, climbing to his feet. He went to the bar for more wine, brought out a bottle, and filled our glasses. "A truly mindless parasite, but an intelligent race like the Shkeen are enslaved by it. Why?"

The new wine was good and chilled, a cold trail down my throat. I drank it, and nodded, remembering the flood of euphoria that had swept over us earlier that day. "Drugs," I said, speculatively. "The Greeshka must produce an organic pleasure-drug. The Shkeen submit to it willingly and die happy. The joy is real, believe me. We felt it.''

Lyanna looked doubtful, though, and Gourlay shook his head adamantly. "No, Robb. Not so. We've experimented on the Greeshka, and . . ."

He must have noticed my raised eyebrows. He stopped.

"How did the Shkeen feel about that?" I asked.

"Didn't tell them. They wouldn't have liked it, not at all. Greeshka's just an animal, but it's their God. Don't fool around with God, you know. We refrained for a long time, but when Gustaffson went over, old Stuart had to know. His orders. We didn't get anywhere, though. No extracts that might be a drug, no secretions, nothing. In fact, the Shkeen are the *only* native life that submits so easily. We caught a whiner, you see, and strapped it down, and let a Greeshka link up. Then, couple hours later, we yanked the straps. Damn whiner was furious, screeching and yelping, attacking the thing on its head. Nearly clawed its own skull to ribbons before it got it off.''

"Maybe only the Shkeen are susceptible?" I said. A feeble, rescue attempt.

"Not quite," said Valcarenghi, with a small, thin smile. "There's us."

Lya was strangely silent in the tube, almost withdrawn. I assumed she was thinking about the conversation. But the door to our suite had barely slid shut behind us when she turned toward me and wrapped her arms around me.

I reached up and stroked her soft brown hair, slightly startled by the hug. "Hey," I muttered, "what's wrong?"

She gave me her vampire look, big-eyed and fragile. "Make love to me, Robb," she said with a soft sudden urgency. "Please. Make love to me now."

I smiled, but it was a puzzled smile, not my usual lecherous bedroom grin. Lya generally comes on impish and wicked when she's horny, but now she was all troubled and vulnerable. I didn't quite get it.

But it wasn't a time for questions, and I didn't ask any. I just pulled her to me wordlessly and kissed her hard, and we walked together to the bedroom.

And we made love, *really* made love, more than poor Normals can do. We joined our bodies as one, and I felt Lya stiffen as her mind reached out to mine. And as we moved together I was opening myself to her, drowning myself in the flood of love and need and fear that was pouring from her.

Then, quickly as it had begun, it ended. Her pleasure washed over me in a raw red wave. And I joined her on the crest, and Lya clutched me tightly, her eyes shrunk up small as she drank it all in.

Afterwards, we lay there in the darkness and let the stars of Shkea pour their radiance through the window. Lya huddled against me, her head on my chest, while I stroked her.

"That was good," I said in a drowsy-dreamy voice, smiling in the star-filled darkness.

"Yes," she replied. Her voice was soft and small, so small I barely heard it. "I love you, Robb," she whispered.

"Uh-huh," I said. "And I love you."

She pulled loose of my arm and rolled over, propping her head on a hand to stare at me and smile. "You do," she said. "I read it. I know it. And you know how much I love you, too, don't you?"

I nodded, smiling. "Sure."

"We're lucky, you know. The Normals have only words. Poor little Normals. How can they *tell*, with just words? How can they *know*? They're always apart from each other, trying to reach each other and failing. Even when they make love, even when they come, they're always apart. They must be very lonely."

There was something . . . disturbing . . . in that. I looked at Lya, into her bright happy eyes, and thought about it. "Maybe," I said, finally. "But it's not that bad for them. They don't know any other way. And they try, they love too. They bridge the gap sometimes."

"Only a look and a voice, then darkness again and a silence," Lya quoted, her voice sad and tender. "We're luckier, aren't we? We have so much more."

"We're luckier," I echoed. And I reached out to read her too. Her mind was a haze of satisfaction, with a gentle scent of wistful, lonely longing. But there was something else, way down, almost gone now, but still faintly detectable.

I sat up slowly. "Hey," I said. "You're worried about something. And before, when we came in, you were scared. What's the matter?"

"I don't know, really," she said. She sounded puzzled and she *was* puzzled; I read it there. "I *was* scared, but I don't know why. The Joined, I think. I kept thinking about how much they loved me. They didn't even *know* me, but they loved me so much, and they understood—it was almost like what we have. It—I don't know. It bothered me. I mean, I didn't think I could ever be loved that way, except by you. And they were so *close*, so together. I felt kind of lonely, just holding hands and talking. I wanted to be close to *you* that way. After the way they were all sharing and everything, being alone just seemed empty. And frightening. You know?"

"I know," I said, touching her lightly again, with hand and mind. "I understand. We do understand each other. We're together almost as they are, as Normals can't ever be."

Lya nodded, and smiled, and hugged me. We went to sleep in each other's arms.

Dreams again. But again, at dawn, the memory stole away from me. It was all very annoying. The dream had been pleasant, comfortable. I wanted it back, and I couldn't even remember what it was. Our bedroom, washed by harsh daylight, seemed drab compared to the splendors of my lost vision.

Lya woke after me, with another headache. This time she had the pills on hand, by the bedstand. She grimaced and took one.

"It must be the Shkeen wine," I told her. "Something about it takes a dim view of your metabolism."

She pulled on a fresh coverall and scowled at me. "Ha. We were drinking Veltaar last night, remember? My father gave me my first glass of Veltaar when I was nine. It never gave me headaches before."

"A first!" I said, smiling.

"It's not funny," she said. "It hurts."

I quit kidding, and tried to read her. She was right. It *did* hurt. Her whole forehead throbbed with pain. I withdrew quickly before I caught it too.

"All right," I said. "I'm sorry. The pills will take care of it, though. Meanwhile, we've got work to do."

Lya nodded. She'd never let anything interfere with work yet.

The second day was a day of manhunt. We got off to a much earlier start, had a quick breakfast with Gourlay, then picked up our aircar outside the tower. This time we didn't drop down when we hit Shkeentown. We wanted a human Joined, which meant we had to cover a lot of ground. The city was the biggest I'd ever seen, in area at any rate, and the thousand-odd human cultists were lost among millions of Shkeen. And, of those humans, only about half were actually Joined yet.

So we kept the aircar low, and buzzed up and down the dome-dotted hills like a floating roller-coaster, causing quite a stir in the streets below us. The Shkeen had seen aircars before, of course, but it still had some novelty value, particularly to the kids, who tried to run after us whenever we flashed by. We also panicked a whiner, causing him to upset the cart full of fruit he was dragging. I felt guilty about that, so I kept the car higher afterwards.

We spotted Joined all over the city, singing, eating, walking—and ringing those bells, those eternal bronze bells. But for the first three hours, all we found were Shkeen Joined. Lya and I took turns driving and watching. After the excitement of the previous day, the search was tedious and tiring.

Finally, however, we found something: a large group of Joined, ten of them, clustered around a bread cart behind one of the steeper hills. Two were taller than the rest.

We landed on the other side of the hill and walked around to meet them, leaving our aircar surrounded by a crowd of Shkeen children. The Joined were still eating when we arrived. Eight of them were Shkeen of various sizes and hues, Greeshka pulsing atop their skulls. The other two were human.

They wore the same long red gowns as the Shkeen, and they carried the same bells. One of them was a big man, with loose skin that hung in flaps, as if he'd lost a lot of weight recently. His hair was white and curly, his face marked by a broad smile and laugh wrinkles around the eyes. The other was a thin, dark weasel of a man with a big hooked nose.

Both of them had Greeshka sucking at their skulls. The parasite riding the weasel was barely a pimple, but the older man had a lordly specimen that dripped down beyond his shoulders and into the back of the gown.

Somehow, this time, it *did* look hideous.

Lyanna and I walked up to them, trying hard to smile, not reading—at least at first. They smiled at us as we approached. Then they waved.

"Hello," the weasel said cheerily when we got there. "I've never seen you. Are you new on Shkea?"

That took me slightly by surprise. I'd been expecting some sort of garbled mystic greeting, or maybe no greeting at all. I was assuming that somehow the human converts would have abandoned their humanity to become mock-Shkeen. I was wrong.

"More or less," I replied. And I read the weasel. He was genuinely pleased to see us, and just bubbled with contentment and good cheer. "We've been hired to talk to people like you." I'd decided to be honest about it.

The weasel stretched his grin farther than I thought it

would go. "I am Joined, and happy," he said. "I'll be glad to talk to you. My name is Lester Kamenz. What do you want to know, brother?"

Lya, next to me, was going tense. I decided I'd let her read in depth while I asked questions. "When did you convert to the Cult?"

"Cult?" Kamenz said.

"The Union."

He nodded, and I was struck by the grotesque similarity of his bobbing head and that of the elderly Shkeen we'd seen yesterday. "I have always been in the Union. You are in the Union. All that thinks is in the Union."

"Some of us weren't told," I said. "How about you? When did you realize you were in the Union?"

"A year ago, Old Earth time. I was admitted to the ranks of the Joined only a few weeks ago. The First Joining is a joyful time. I am joyful. Now I will walk the streets and ring my bells until the Final Union."

"What did you do before?"

"Before?" A short vague look. "I ran machines once. I ran computers, in the Tower. But my life was empty, brother. I did not know I was in the Union, and I was alone. I had only machines, cold machines. Now I am Joined. Now I am"—again he searched—"not alone."

I reached into him, and found the happiness still there, with love. But now there was an ache too, a vague recollection of past pain, the stink of unwelcome memories. Did these fade? Maybe the gift the Greeshka gave its victims was oblivion, sweet mindless rest and end of struggle. Maybe.

I decided to try something. "That thing on your head," I said, sharply. "It's a parasite. It's drinking your blood right now, feeding on it. As it grows, it will take more and more of the things *you* need to live. Finally it will start to eat your tissue. Understand? It will *eat* you. I don't know how painful it will be, but however it feels, at the end you'll be *dead*. Unless you come back to the Tower now, and have the surgeons remove it. Or maybe you could remove it yourself. Why don't you try? Just reach up and pull it off. Go ahead.''

I'd expected—what? Rage? Horror? Disgust? I got none of these. Kamenz just stuffed bread in his mouth and smiled at me, and all I read was his love and joy and a little pity.

"The Greeshka does not kill," he said finally. "The Greeshka gives joy and happy Union. Only those who have no Greeshka die. They are . . . alone. Oh, forever alone." Something in his mind trembled with sudden fear, but it faded quickly.

I glanced at Lya. She was stiff and hard-eyed, still reading. I looked back and began to phrase another question. But suddenly the Joined began to ring. One of the Shkeen started it off, swinging his bell up and down to produce a single sharp clang. Then his other hand swung, then the first again, then the second, then another Joined began to ring, then still another, and then they were all swinging and clanging and the noise of their bells was smashing against my ears as the joy and the love and the feel of the bells assaulted my mind once again.

I lingered to savor it. The love there was breathtaking, awesome, almost frightening in its heat and intensity, and there was so much sharing to frolic in and wonder at, such a soothing-calming-exhilarating tapestry of good feeling. Something happened to the Joined when they rang, something touched them and lifted them and gave them a glow, something strange and glorious that mere Normals could not hear in their harsh clanging music. I was no Normal, though. I could hear it.

I withdrew reluctantly, slowly. Kamenz and the other human were both ringing vigorously now, with broad smiles and glowing twinkling eyes that transfigured their faces. Lyanna was still tense, still reading. Her mouth was slightly open, and she trembled where she stood.

I put an arm around her and waited, listening to the music, patient. Lya continued to read. Finally, after minutes, I shook her gently. She turned and studied me with hard, distant eyes. Then blinked. And her eyes widened and she came back, shaking her head and frowning.

Puzzled, I looked into her head. Strange and stranger. It was a swirling fog of emotion, a dense moving blend of more feelings than I'd care to put a name to. No sooner had I entered than I was lost, lost and uneasy. Somewhere in the fog there was a bottomless abyss lurking to engulf me. At least it felt that way.

"Lya," I said. "What's wrong?"

She shook her head again, and looked at the Joined with a look that was equal parts fear and longing. I repeated my question.

"I—I don't know," she said. "Robb, let's not talk now. Let's go. I want time to think."

"OK," I said. What was going on here? I took her hand and we walked slowly around the hill to the slope where we'd left the car. Shkeen kids were climbing all over it. I chased them, laughing. Lya just stood there, her eyes gone all faraway on me. I wanted to read her again, but somehow I felt it would be an invasion of privacy.

Airborne, we streaked back toward the Tower, riding higher and faster this time. I drove, while Lya sat beside me and stared out into the distance.

"Did you get anything useful?" I asked her, trying to get her mind back on the assignment.

"Yes. No. Maybe." Her voice sounded distracted, as if only part of her was talking to me. "I read their lives, both of them. Kamenz was a computer programmer, as he said. But he wasn't very good. An ugly little man with an ugly little personality, no friends, no sex, no nothing. Lived by himself, avoided the Shkeen, didn't like them at all. Didn't even like people, really. But Gustaffson got through to him, somehow. He ignored Kamenz' coldness, his bitter little cuts, his cruel jokes. He didn't retaliate, you know? After a while, Kamenz came to like Gustaffson, to admire him. They were never really friends in any normal sense, but still Gustaffson was the nearest thing to a friend that Kamenz had.''

She stopped suddenly. "So he went over with Gustaffson?" I prompted, glancing at her quickly. Her eyes still wandered.

"No, not at first. He was still afraid, still scared of the Shkeen and terified of the Greeshka. But later, with Gustaffson gone, he began to realize how empty his life was. He worked all day with people who despised him and machines that didn't care, then sat alone at night reading and watching holoshows. Not life, really. He hardly touched the people around him. Finally he went to find Gustaffson, and wound up converted. Now . . .''

"Now . . . ?"

She hesitated. "He's happy, Robb," she said. "He really is. For the first time in his life, he's happy. He'd never known love before. Now it fills him.''

"You got a lot," I said.

"Yes." Still the distracted voice, the lost eyes. "He was open, sort of. There were levels, but digging wasn't as hard as it usually is—as if his barriers were weakening, coming down almost . . .''

"How about the other guy?"

She stroked the instrument panel, staring only at her hand. "Him? That was Gustaffson . . .''

And that, suddenly, seemed to wake her, to restore her to the Lya I knew and loved. She shook her head and looked at me, and the aimless voice became an animated torrent of words. "Robb, listen, that was *Gustaffson*, he's been Joined over a year now, and he's going on to Final Union within a week. The Greeshka has accepted him, and he wants it, you know? He really does, and—and—oh Robb, he's *dying!*"

"Within a week, according to what you just said.''

"No. I mean yes, but that's not what I mean. Final Union isn't death, to him. He believes it, all of it, the whole religion. The Greeshka is his god, and he's going to join it.

But before, and now, he was dying. He's got the Slow Plague, Robb. A terminal case. It's been eating at him from inside for over fifteen years now. He got it back on Nightmare, in the swamps, when his family died. That's no world for people, but he was there, the administrator over a research base, a short-term thing. They lived on Thor; it was only a visit, but the ship crashed. Gustaffson got all wild and tried to reach them before the end, but he grabbed a faulty pair of skinthins, and the spores got through. And they were all dead when he got there. He had an awful lot of pain, Robb. From the Slow Plague, but more from the loss. He really loved them, and it was never the same after. They gave him Shkea as a reward, kind of, to take his mind off the crash, but he still thought of it all the time. I could see the picture, Robb. It was vivid. He couldn't forget it. The kids were inside the ship, safe behind the walls, but the life system failed and choked them to death. But his wife—oh, Robb—she took some skinthins and tried to go for help, and outside those *things*, those big wrigglers they have on Nightmare—?"

I swallowed hard, feeling a little sick. "The eater-worms," I said, dully. I'd read about them, and seen holos. I could imagine the picture that Lya'd seen in Gustaffson's memory, and it wasn't at all pretty. I was glad I didn't have her Talent.

"They were still—still—when Gustaffson got there. You know. He killed them all with a screechgun."

I shook my head. "I didn't think things like that really went on."

"No," Lya said. "Neither did Gustaffson. They'd been so—so *happy* before that, before the thing on Nightmare. He loved her, and they were really close, and his career had been almost charmed. He didn't have to go to Nightmare, you know. He took it because it was a challenge, because nobody else could handle it. That gnaws at him, too. And he remembers all the time. He—they—" Her voice faltered. "They thought they were *lucky*," she said, before falling into silence.

There was nothing to say to that. I just kept quiet and drove, thinking, feeling a blurred, watered-down version of what Gustaffson's pain must have been like. After a while, Lya began to speak again.

"It was all there, Robb," she said, her voice softer and slower and more thoughtful once again. "But he was at peace. He still remembered it all, and the way it had hurt, but it didn't bother him as it had. Only now he was sorry they weren't with him. He was sorry that they died without Final Union. Almost like the Shkeen woman, remember? The one at the Gathering? With her brother?"

"I remember," I said.

"Like that. And his mind was open, too. More than Kamenz, much more. When he rang, the levels all vanished, and everything was right at the surface, all the love and pain and everything. His whole life, Robb. I shared his whole life with him, in an instant. And all his thoughts, too . . . he's seen the caves of Union . . . he went down once, before he converted. I . . ."

More silence, settling over us and darkening the car. We were close to the end of Shkeentown. The Tower slashed the sky ahead of us, shining in the sun. And the lower domes and archways of the glittering human city were coming into view.

"Robb," Lya said. "Land here. I have to think a while, you know? Go back without me. I want to walk among the Shkeen a little."

I glanced at her, frowning. "Walk? It's a long way back to the Tower, Lya."

"I'll be all right. Please. Just let me think a bit."

I read her. The thought fog had returned, denser than ever, laced through with the colors of fear. "Are you sure?" I said. "You're scared, Lyanna. Why? What's wrong? The eater-worms are a long way off."

She just looked at me, troubled. "Please, Robb," she repeated.

I didn't know what else to do, so I landed.

*   *   *

And I, too, thought, as I guided the aircar home. Of what Lyanna had said, and read—of Kamenz and Gustaffson. I kept my mind on the problem we'd been assigned to crack. I tried to keep it off Lya, and whatever was bothering her. That would solve itself, I thought.

Back at the Tower, I wasted no time. I went straight up to Valcarenghi's office. He was there, alone, dictating into a machine. He shut it off when I entered.

"Hi, Robb," he began. "Where's Lya?"

"Out walking. She wanted to think. I've been thinking, too. And I believe I've got your answer."

He raised his eyebrows, waiting.

I sat down. "We found Gustaffson this afternoon, and Lya read him. I think it's clear why he went over. He was a broken man, inside, however much he smiled. The Greeshka gave him an end to his pain. And there was another convert with him, a Lester Kamenz. He'd been miserable, too, a pathetic lonely man with nothing to live for. Why *shouldn't* he convert? Check out the other converts, and I bet you'll find a pattern. The most lost and vulnerable, the failures, the isolated—those will be the ones that turned to Union."

Valcarenghi nodded. "OK, I'll buy that," he said. "But our psychs guessed that long ago, Robb. Only it's no answer, not really. Sure, the converts on the whole have been a messed-up crew, I won't dispute that. But why turn to the Cult of the Union? The psychs can't answer that. Take Gustaffson now. He was a strong man, believe me. I never knew him personally, but I knew his career. He took some rough assignments, generally for the hell of it, and beat them. He could have had the cushy jobs, but he wasn't interested. I've heard about the incident on Nightmare. It's famous, in a warped sort of way. But Phil Gustaffson wasn't the sort of man to be beaten, even by something like that. He snapped out of it very quickly, from what Nelse tells me. He came to Shkea and really set the place in order, cleaning up the mess that Rockwood had left. He pushed through the first real trade contract we ever got, *and* he made the Shkeen understand what it meant, which isn't easy.

"So here he is, this competent, talented man, who's made a career of beating tough jobs and handling men. He's gone through a personal nightmare, but it hasn't destroyed him. He's as tough as ever. And suddenly he turns to the Cult of the Union, signs up for a grotesque suicide. Why? For an end to his pain, you say? An interesting theory, but there are other ways to end pain. Gustaffson had years between Nightmare and the Greeshka. He never ran away from pain then. He didn't turn to drink, or drugs, or any of the usual outs. He didn't head back to Old Earth to have a psi-psych clean up his memories—and believe me, he could've gotten it paid for, if he'd wanted it. The colonial office would have done anything for him, after Nightmare. He went on, swallowed his pain, rebuilt. Until suddenly he converts.

"His pain made him more vulnerable, yes, no doubt of it. But something else brought him over—something that Union offered, something he couldn't get from wine or memory wipe. The same's true of Kamenz, and the others. They had other outs, other ways to vote no on life. They passed them up. But they chose Union. You see what I'm getting at?"

I did, of course. My answer was no answer at all, and I realized it. But Valvarenghi was wrong too, in parts.

"Yes," I said. "I guess we've still got some reading to do." I smiled wanly. "One thing, though. Gustaffson hadn't really beaten his pain, not ever. Lya was very clear on that. It was inside him all the time, tormenting him. He just never let it come out."

"That's victory, isn't it?" Valcarenghi said. "If you bury your hurts so deep that no one can tell you have them?"

"I don't know. I don't think so. But . . . anyway, there was more. Gustaffson has the Slow Plague. He's dying. He's been dying for years."

Valcarenghi's expression flickered briefly. "That I didn't

know, but it just bolsters my point. I've read that some eighty percent of Slow Plague victims opt for euthanasia, if they happen to be on a planet where it's legal. Gustaffson was a planetary administrator. He could have *made* it legal. If he passed up suicide for all those years, why choose it now?"

I didn't have an answer for that. Lyanna hadn't given me one, if she had one. I didn't know where we could find one, either, unless . . .

"The caves," I said suddenly. "The caves of Union. We've got to witness a Final Union. There must be something about it, something that accounts for the conversions. Give us a chance to find out what it is."

Valcarenghi smiled. "All right," he said. "I can arrange it. I expected it would come to that. It's not pleasant, though, I'll warn you. I've gone down myself, so I know what I'm talking about."

"That's OK," I told him. "If you think reading Gustaffson was any fun, you should have seen Lya when she was through. She's out now trying to walk it off." That, I'd decided, must have been what was bothering her. "Final Union won't be any worse than those memories of Nightmare, I'm sure."

"Fine, then. I'll set it up for tomorrow. I'm going with you, of course. I don't want to take any chances on anything happening to you."

I nodded. Valcarenghi rose. "Good enough," he said. "Meanwhile, let's think about more interesting things. You have any plans for dinner?"

We wound up eating at a mock-Shkeen restaurant run by humans, in the company of Gourlay and Laurie Blackburn. The talk was mostly social noises—sports, politics, art, old jokes, that sort of thing. I don't think there was a mention of the Shkeen or the Greeshka all evening.

Afterwards, when I got back to our suite, I found Lyanna waiting for me. She was in bed, reading one of the handsome volumes from our library, a book of Old Earth poetry. She looked up when I entered.

"Hi," I said. "How was your walk?"

"Long." A smile creased her pale, small face, then faded. "But I had time to think. About this afternoon, and yesterday, and about the Joined. And us."

"Us?"

"Robb, do you love me?" The question was delivered almost matter-of-factly, in a voice full of question. As if she didn't know. As if she really didn't know.

I sat down on the bed and took her hand and tried to smile. "Sure," I said. "You know that, Lya."

"I did. I do. You love me, Robb, really you do. As much as a human can love. But . . ." She stopped. She shook her head and closed her book and sighed. "But we're still apart, Robb. We're still apart."

"What *are* you talking about?"

"This afternoon. I was so confused afterwards, and scared. I wasn't sure why, but I've thought about it. When I was reading, Robb—I was in there, with the Joined, sharing them and their love. I really was. And I didn't want to come out. I didn't want to leave them, Robb. When I did, I felt so isolated, so cut off."

"That's your fault," I said. "I tried to talk to you. You were too busy thinking."

"Talking? What good is talking? It's communication, I guess, but is it *really?* I used to think so, before they trained my Talent. After that, reading seemed to be the real communication, the real way to reach somebody else, somebody like you. But now I don't know. The Joined—when they ring—they're so *together,* Robb. All linked. Like us when we make love, almost. And they love each other, too. And they love us, so intensely. I felt—I don't know. But Gustaffson loves me as much as you do. No. He loves me more."

Her face was white as she said that, her eyes wide, lost, lonely. And me, I felt a sudden chill, like a cold wind blowing through my soul. I didn't say anything. I only looked at her, and wet my lips. And bled.

She saw the hurt in my eyes, I guess. Or read it. Her hand pulled at mine, caressed it. "Oh, Robb. Please. I don't mean to hurt you. It's not you. It's all of us. What do *we* have, compared to *them*?"

"I don't know what you're talking about, Lya." Half of me suddenly wanted to cry. The other half wanted to shout. I stifled both halves, and kept my voice steady. But inside I wasn't steady, I wasn't steady at all.

"Do you love me, Robb?" Again. Wondering.

"Yes!" Fiercely. A challenge.

"What does that mean?" she said.

"You know what it means," I said. "Dammit, Lya, *think*! Remember all we've had, all we've shared together. *That's* love, Lya. It is. We're the lucky ones, remember? You said that yourself. The Normals have only a touch and a voice, then back to their darkness. They can barely find each other. They're alone. Always. Groping. Trying, over and over, to climb out of their isolation booths, and failing, over and over. But not us, we found the way, we know each other as much as any human beings ever can. There's nothing I wouldn't tell you, or share with you. I've said that before, and you know it's true, you can read it in me. *That's* love, dammit. *Isn't it?*"

"I don't know," she said, in a voice so sadly baffled. Soundlessly, without even a sob, she began to cry. And while the tears ran in lonely paths down her cheeks, she talked. "Maybe that's love. I always thought it was. But now I don't know. If what we have is love, what was it I felt this afternoon, what was it I touched and shared in? Oh, Robb. I love you too. You know that. I try to share with you. I want to share what I read, what it was like. But I can't. We're cut off. I can't make you understand. I'm here and you're there and we can touch and make love and talk, but we're still apart. You see? You see? I'm alone. And this afternoon, I *wasn't.*"

"You're not alone, dammit," I said suddenly. "I'm here," I clutched her hand tightly. "Feel? Hear? You're not alone!"

She shook her head, and the tears flowed on. "You don't understand, see? And there's no way I can make you. You said we know each other as much as any human beings ever can. You're right. But how much can human beings know each other? Aren't all of them cut off, really? Each alone in a big dark empty universe? We only trick ourselves when we think that someone else is there. In the end, in the cold lonely end, it's only us, by ourselves, in the blackness. Are you there, Robb? How do I know? Will you die with me, Robb? Will we be together then? Are we together *now?* You say we're luckier than the Normals. I've said it too. They have only a touch and voice, right? How many times have I quoted that? But what do *we* have? A touch and two voices, maybe. It's not enough anymore. I'm scared. Suddenly I'm scared."

She began to sob. Instinctively I reached out to her, wrapped her in my arms, stroked her. We lay back together, and she wept against my chest. I read her, briefly, and I read her pain, her sudden loneliness, her hunger, all aswirl in a darkening mindstorm of fear. And, though I touched her and caressed her and whispered—over and over—that it would be all right, that I was here, that she wasn't alone, I knew that it would not be enough. Suddenly there was a gulf between us, a great dark yawning thing that grew and grew, and I didn't know how to bridge it. And Lya, my Lya, was crying, and she needed me. And I needed her, but I couldn't get to her.

Then I realized that I was crying too.

We held each other, in silent tears, for what must have been an hour. But finally the tears ran out. Lya clutched her body to me so tightly I could hardly breathe, and I held her just as tightly.

"Robb," she whispered. "You said—you said we really

know each other. All those times you've said it. And you say, sometimes, that I'm *right* for you, that I'm perfect."

I nodded, wanting to believe. "Yes. You are."

"No," she said, choking out the word, forcing it into the air, fighting herself to say it. "It's not *so*. I read you, yes. I can hear the words rattling around in your head as you fit a sentence together before saying it. And I listen to you scold yourself when you've done something stupid. And I see memories, some memories, and live through them with you. But it's all on the surface, Robb, all on the top. Below it, there's more, more of *you*. Drifting half-thoughts I don't quite catch. Feelings I can't put a name to. Passions you suppress, and memories even you don't know you have. Sometimes I can get to that level. Sometimes. If I really fight, if I drain myself to exhaustion. But when I get there, I know—I *know*—that there's another level below *that*. And more and more, on and on, down and down. I can't reach them, Robb, though they're part of you. I don't know you, I can't know you. You don't even know yourself, see? And me, do you know me? No. Even less. You know what I tell you, and I tell you the truth, but maybe not all. And you read my feelings, my surface feelings—the pain of a stubbed toe, a quick flash of annoyance, the pleasure I get when you're in me. Does that mean you know me? What of *my* levels, and levels? What about the things I don't even know myself? Do *you* know them? How, Robb, how?"

She shook her head again, with that funny little gesture she had whenever she was confused. "And you say I'm perfect, and that you love me. I'm so right for you. But *am* I? Robb, *I read your thoughts*. I know when you want me to be sexy, so I'm sexy. I see what turns you on, so I do it. I know when you want me to be serious, and when you want me to joke. I know what kind of jokes to tell, too. Never the cutting kind, you don't like that, to hurt or see people hurt. You laugh *with* people not *at* them, and I laugh with you, and love you for your tastes. I know when you want me to talk, and when to keep quiet. I know when you want me to be your proud tigress, your tawny telepath, and when you want a little girl to shelter in your arms. And I *am* those things, Robb, because you want me to be, because I love you, because I can feel the joy in your mind at every *right* thing that I do. I never set out to do it that way, but it happened. I didn't mind, I don't mind. Most of the time it wasn't even conscious. You do the same thing, too. I read it in you. You can't read as I do, so sometimes you guess wrong—you come on witty when I want silent understanding, or you act the strong man when I need a boy to mother. But you get it right sometimes, too. And you *try,* you always try.

"But is it really *you?* Is it really *mè?* What if I wasn't perfect, you see, if I was just myself, with all my faults and the things you don't like out in the open? Would you love me *then?* I don't know. But Gustaffson would, and Kamenz. I know that, Robb. I saw it. I know *them.* Their levels . . . vanished. I *KNOW* them, and if I went back I could share with them, more than with you. And they know me, the real me, all of me, I think. And they love me. You see? *You see?*"

Did I see? I don't know. I was confused. Would I love Lya if she was "herself"? But what was "herself"? How was it different from the Lya I knew? I thought I loved Lya and would always love Lya—but what if the real Lya wasn't like my Lya? *What* did I love? The strange abstract concept of a human being, or the flesh and voice and personality that I thought of as Lya? I didn't know. I didn't know who Lya was, or who I was, or what the hell it all meant. And I was scared. Maybe I couldn't feel what she had felt that afternoon. But I knew what she was feeling then. I was alone, and I needed someone.

"Lya," I called. "Lya, let's try. We don't have to give up. We can reach each other. There's a way, our way. We've done it before. Come, Lya, come with me, come to me."

As I spoke, I undressed her, and she responded and her

hands joined mine. When we were nude, I began to stroke her, slowly, and she me. Our minds reached out to each other. Reached and probed as never before. I could feel her, inside my head, digging. Deeper and deeper. Down. And I opened myself to her, I surrendered, all the petty little secrets I had kept even from her, or tried to, now I yielded up to her, everything I could remember, my triumphs and shames, the good moments and the pain, the times I'd hurt someone, the times I'd been hurt, the long crying sessions by myself, the fears I wouldn't admit, the prejudices I fought, the vanities I battled when the time struck, the silly boyish sins. All. Everything. I buried nothing. I hid nothing. I gave myself to her, to Lya, to *my* Lya. She had to know me.

And so too she yielded. Her mind was a forest through which I roamed, hunting down wisps of emotion, the fear and the need and the love at the top, the fainter things beneath, the half-formed whims and passions still deeper into the woods. I don't have Lya's Talent, I read only feelings, never thoughts. But I read thoughts then, for the first and only time, thoughts she threw at me because I'd never seen them before. I couldn't read much, but some I got.

And as her mind opened to mine, so did her body. I entered her, and we moved together, bodies one, minds entwined, as close as human beings can join. I felt pleasure washing over me in great glorious waves, my pleasure, her pleasure, both together building on each other, and I rode the crest for an eternity as it approached a far distant shore. And finally as it smashed into that beach, we came together, and for a second—for a tiny, fleeting second—I could not tell which orgasm was mine, and which was hers.

But then it passed. We lay, bodies locked together, on the bed. In the starlight. But it was not a bed. It was the beach, the flat black beach, and there were no stars above. A thought touched me, a vagrant thought that was not mine. Lya's thought. We were on a plain, she was thinking, and I saw that she was right. The waters that had carried us here were gone, receded. There was only a vast flat blackness stretching away in all directions, with dim ominous shapes moving on either horizon. *We are here as on a darkling plain,* Lya thought. And suddenly I knew what those shapes were, and what poem she had been reading.

We slept.

I woke, alone.

The room was dark. Lya lay on the other side of the bed, curled up, still asleep. It was late, near dawn I thought. But I wasn't sure. I was restless.

I got up and dressed in silence. I needed to walk somewhere, to think, to work things out. Where, though?

There was a key in my pocket. I touched it when I pulled on my tunic, and remembered. Valcarenghi's office. It would be locked and deserted at this time of night. And the view might help me think.

I left, found the tubes, and shot up, up, up to the apex of the Tower, the top of man's steel challenge to the Shkeen. The office was unlit, the furniture dark shapes in the shadows. There was only the starlight. Shkea is closer to the galactic center than Old Earth, or Baldur. The stars are a fiery canopy across the night sky. Some of them are very close, and they burn like red and blue-white fires in the awesome blackness above. In Valcarenghi's office, all the walls are glass. I went to one, and looked out. I wasn't thinking. Just feeling. And I felt cold and lost and little.

Then there was a soft voice behind me saying hello. I barely heard it.

I turned away from the window, but other stars leaped at me from the far walls. Laurie Blackburn sat in one of the low chairs, concealed by the darkness.

"Hello," I said. "I didn't mean to intrude. I thought no one would be here."

She smiled. A radiant smile in a radiant face, but there was no humor in it. Her hair fell in sweeping auburn waves past her shoulders, and she was dressed in something long and gauzy. I could see her gentle curves through its folds, and she made no effort to hide herself.

"I come up here a lot," she said. "At night, usually. When Dino's asleep. It's a good place to think."

"Yes," I said, smiling. "My thoughts, too."

"The stars are pretty, aren't they?"

"Yes."

"I think so. I—" Hesitation. Then she rose and came to me. "Do you love Lya?" she said.

A hammer of a question. Timed terribly. But I handled it well, I think. My mind was still on my talk with Lya. "Yes," I said. "Very much. Why?"

She was standing close to me, looking at my face, and past me, out to the stars. "I don't know. I wonder about love, sometimes. I love Dino, you know. He came here two months ago, so we haven't known each other long. But I love him already. I've never known anybody like him. He's kind, and considerate, and he does everything well. I've never seen him fail at anything he tried. Yet he doesn't seem driven, like some men. He wins so easily. He believes in himself a lot, and that's attractive. He's given me anything I could ask for, everything."

I read her, caught her love and worry, and guessed. "Except himself," I said.

She looked at me, startled. Then she smiled. "I forgot. You're a Talent. Of course you know. You're right. I don't know what I worry about, but I do worry. Dino is so perfect, you know. I've told him—well, everything. All about me and my life. And he listens and understands. He's always receptive, he's there when I need him. But—"

"It's all one way," I said. It was a statement. I knew.

She nodded. "It's not that he keeps secrets. He doesn't. He'll answer any question I ask. But the answers mean nothing. I ask him what he fears, and he says nothing, and makes me believe it. He's very rational, very calm. He never gets angry, he never has. I asked him. He doesn't hate people, he thinks hate is bad. He's never felt pain, either, or he *says* he hasn't. Emotional pain, I mean. Yet he understands me when I talk about my life. Once he said his biggest fault was laziness. But he's not lazy at all, I know that. Is he really that perfect? He tells me he's always sure of himself, because her *knows* he's good, but he smiles when he says it, so I can't even accuse him of being vain. He says he believes in God, but her never talks about it. If you try to talk seriously, he'll listen patiently, or joke with you, or lead the conversation away. He says he loves me, but—''

I nodded. I knew what was coming.

It came. She looked up at me, eyes begging. ''You're a Talent,'' she said. ''You've read him, haven't you? You know him? Tell me. Please tell me.''

I was reading her. I could see how much she needed to know, how much she worried and feared, how much she loved. I couldn't lie to her. Yet it was hard to give her the answer I had to.

''I've read him,'' I said. Slowly. Carefully. Measuring out my words like precious fluids. ''And you, you too. I saw your love, on that first night, when we ate together.''

''And Dino?''

My words caught in my throat. ''He's—funny, Lya said once. I can read his surface emotions easily enough. Below that, nothing. He's very self-contained, walled off. Almost as if his only emotions are the ones he—*allows* himself to feel. I've felt his confidence, his pleasure. I've felt worry too, but never real fear. He's very affectionate toward you, very protective. He enjoys feeling protective.''

''Is that all?'' So hopeful. It hurt.

''I'm afraid it is. He's walled off, Laurie. He needs himself, only himself. If there's love in him, it's behind that wall, hidden. I can't read it. He thinks a lot of you, Laurie. But love—well, it's different. It's stronger and more unreasoning and it comes in crashing floods. And Dino's not like that, at least not out where I can read."

"Closed," she said. "He's closed to me. I opened myself to him, totally. But he didn't. I was always afraid—even when he was with me, I felt sometimes that he wasn't there at all—"

She sighed. I read her despair, her welling loneliness. I didn't know what to do. "Cry if you like," I told her, inanely. "Sometimes it helps. I know. I've cried enough in my time."

She didn't cry. She looked up, and laughed lightly. "No," she said. "I can't. Dino taught me never to cry. He said tears never solve anything."

A sad philosophy. Tears don't solve anything, maybe, but they're part of being human. I wanted to tell her so, but instead I just smiled at her.

She smiled back, and cocked her head. "You cry," she said suddenly, in a voice strangely delighted. "That's funny. That's more of an admission than I ever heard from Dino, in a way. Thank you, Robb. Thank you."

And Laurie stood on her toes and looked up, expectant. And I could read what she expected. So I took her and kissed her, and she pressed her body hard against mine. And all the while I thought of Lya, telling myself that she wouldn't mind, that she'd be proud of me, that she'd understand.

Afterwards, I stayed up in the office alone to watch the dawn come up. I was drained, but somehow content. The light that crept over the horizon was chasing the shadows before it, and suddenly all the fears that had seemed so threatening in the night were silly, unreasoning. We'd bridged it, I thought—Lya and I. Whatever it was, we'd handled it, and today we'd handle the Greeshka with the same ease, together.

When I got back to our room, Lya was gone.

"We found the aircar in the middle of Shkeentown," Valcarenghi was saying. He was cool, precise, reassuring.

His voice told me, without words, that there was nothing to worry about. "I've got men out looking for her. But Shkeentown's a big place. Do you have any idea where she might have gone?"

"No," I said, dully. "Not really. Maybe to see some more Joined. She seemed—well, almost obsessed by them. I don't know."

"Well, we've got a good police force. We'll find her. I'm certain of that. But it may take a while. Did you two have a fight?"

"Yes. No. Sort of, but it wasn't a real fight. It was strange."

"I see," he said. But he didn't. "Laurie tells me you came up here last night, alone."

"Yes. I needed to think."

"All right," said Valcarenghi. "So let's say Lya woke up, decided she wanted to think too. You came up here. She took a ride. Maybe she just wants a day off to wander around Shkeentown. She did something like that yesterday, didn't she?"

"Yes."

"So she's doing it again. No problem. She'll probably be back well before dinner." He smiled.

"Why did she go without telling me, then? Or leaving a note, or *something?*"

"I don't know. It's not important."

Wasn't it, though? *Wasn't it?* I sat in the chair, head in my hands and a scowl on my face, and I was sweating. Suddenly I was very much afraid, of what I didn't know. I should hever have left her alone, I was telling myself. While I was up here with Laurie, Lyanna woke alone in a darkened room, and—and—and *what?* And left.

"Meanwhile, though," Valcarenghi said, "we've got work to do. The trip to the caves is all set."

I looked up, disbelieving. "The caves? I can't go there, not now, not alone."

He gave a sigh of exasperation, exaggerated for effect. "Oh, come now, Robb. It's not the end of the world. Lya will be all right. She seemed to be a perfectly sensible girl, and I'm sure she can take care of herself. Right?"

I nodded.

"Meanwhile, we'll cover the caves. I still want to get to the bottom of this."

"It won't do any good," I protested. "Not without Lya. She's the major Talent. I—I just read emotions. I can't get down deep, as she can. I won't solve anything for you."

He shrugged. "Maybe not. But the trip is on, and we've got nothing to lose. We can always make a second run after Lya comes back. Besides, this should do you good, get your mind off this other business. There's nothing you can do for Lya now. I've got every available man out searching for her, and if they don't find her you certainly won't. So there's no sense dwelling on it. Just get back into action, keep busy." He turned, headed for the tube. "Come. There's an aircar waiting for us. Nelse will go too."

Reluctantly, I stood. I was in no mood to consider the problems of the Shkeen, but Valcarenghi's arguments made a certain amount of sense. Besides which, he'd hired Lyanna and me, and we still had obligations to him. I could try anyway, I thought.

On the ride out, Valcarenghi sat in the front with the driver, a hulking police sergeant with a face chiseled out of granite. He'd selected a police car this time so we could keep posted on the search for Lya. Gourlay and I were in the back seat together. Gourlay had covered our laps with a big map, and he was telling me about the caves of Final Union.

"Theory is the caves are the original home of the Greeshka," he said. "Probably true, makes sense. Greeshka are a lot bigger there. You'll see. The caves are all through the hills, away from our part of Shkeentown, where the country gets wilder. A regular little honeycomb. Greeshka in every one, too. Or so I've heard. Been in a few myself, Greeshka in all of *them*. So I believe what they say about the rest. The city, the sacred city, well, it was probably built *because* of the caves. Shkeen come here from all over the continent, you know, for Final Union. Here, this is the cave region.'' He took out a pen, and made a big circle in red near the center of the map. It was meaningless to me. The map was getting me down. I hadn't realized that the Shkeen city was so *huge*. How the hell could they find anyone who didn't want to be found?

Valcarenghi looked back from the front seat. ''The cave we're going to is a big one, as these places go. I've been there before. There's no formality about Final Union, you understand. The Shkeen just pick a cave, and walk in, and lie down on top of the Greeshka. They'll use whatever entrance is most convenient. Some of them are no bigger than sewer pipes, but if you went in far enough, theory says you'd run into a Greeshka, setting back in the dark and pulsing away. The biggest caves are lighted with torches, like the Great Hall, but that's just a frill. It doesn't play any real part in the Union.''

''I take it we're going to one of them?'' I said.

Valcarenghi nodded. ''Right. I figured you'd want to see what a mature Greeshka is like. It's not pretty, but it's educational. So we need lighting.''

Gourlay resumed his narrative then, but I tuned him out. I felt I knew quite enough about the Shkeen and the Greeshka, and I was still worried about Lyanna. After a while he wound down, and the rest of the trip was in silence. We covered more ground than we ever had before. Even the Tower—our shining steel landmark—had been swallowed by the hills behind us.

The terrain got rougher, rockier, and more overgrown, and the hills rose higher and wilder. But the domes went on and on and on, and there were Shkeen everywhere. Lya could be down there, I thought, lost among those teeming millions. Looking for what? Thinking what?

Finally we landed, in a wooded valley between two massive, rock-studded hills. Even here there were Shkeen, the red-brick domes rising from the undergrowth among the stubby trees. I had no trouble spotting the cave. It was halfway up one of the slopes, a dark yawn in the rock face, with a dusty road winding up to it.

We set down in the valley and climbed that road. Gourlay ate up the distance with long, gawky strides, while Valcarenghi moved with an easy, untiring grace, and the policeman plodded on stolidly. I was the straggler. I dragged myself up, and I was half-winded by the time we got to the cave mouth.

If I'd expected cave paintings, or an altar, or some kind of nature temple, I was sadly disappointed. It was an ordinary cave, with damp stone walls and low ceilings and cold, wet air. Cooler than most of Shkea, and less dusty, but that was about it. There was one long, winding passage through the rock, wide enough for the four of us to walk abreast yet low enough so Gourlay had to stoop. Torches were set along the walls at regular intervals, but only every fourth one or so was lit. They burned with an oily smoke that seemed to cling to the top of the cave and drift down into the depths before us. I wondered what was sucking it in.

After about ten minutes of walking, most of it down a barely perceptible incline, the passage led us out into a high, brightly-lit room, with a vaulting stone roof that was stained sooty by torch smoke. In the room, the Greeshka.

Its color was a dull brownish-red, like old blood, not the bright near-translucent crimson of the small creatures that clung to the skulls of the Joined. There were spots of black, too, like burns or soot stains on the vast body. I could barely see the far side of the cave; the Greeshka was too huge, it towered above us so that there was only a thin crack between it and the roof. But it sloped down abruptly halfway across the chamber, like an immense jellied hill, and ended a good twenty feet from where we stood. Between us and the great bulk of the Greenshka was a forest of hanging, dangling red strands, a living cobweb of Greeshka tissue that came almost to our faces.

And it pulsed. As one organism. Even the strands kept time, widening and then contracting again, moving to a silent beat that was one with the great Greeshka behind them.

My stomach churned, but my companions seemed unmoved. They'd seen this before. "Come," Valcarenghi said, switching on a flashlight he'd brought to augment the torchlight. The light, twisting around the pulsing web, gave the illusion of some weird haunted forest. Valcarenghi stepped into that forest. Lightly. Swinging the light and brushing aside the Greeshka.

Gourlay followed him, but I recoiled. Valcarenghi looked back and smiled. "Don't worry," he said. "The Greeshka takes hours to attach itself, and it's easily removed. It won't grab you if you stumble against it."

I screwed up my courage, reached out, and touched one of the living strands. It was soft and wet, and there was a slimy feel to it. But that was all. It broke easily enough. I walked through it, reaching before me and bending and breaking the web to clear my path. The policeman walked silently behind me.

Then we stood on the far side of the web, at the front of the great Greeshka. Valcarenghi studied it for a second, then pointed with his flashlight. "Look," he said. "Final Union."

I looked. His bean had thrown a pool of light around one of the dark spots, a blemish on the reddish hulk. I looked closer. There was a head in the blemish. Centered in the dark spot, with just the face showing, and even that covered by a thin reddish film. But the features were unmistakable. An elderly Shkeen, wrinkled and big-eyed, his eyes closed now. But smiling. Smiling.

I moved closer. A little lower and to the right, a few fingertips hung out of the mass. But that was all. Most of the body was already gone, sunken into the Greenshka, dissolved or dissolving. The old Shkeen was dead, and the parasite was digesting his corpse.

"Every one of the dark spots is a recent Union," Valcarenghi was saying, moving his light around like a pointer. "The spots fade in time, of course. The Greeshka is growing steadily. In another hundred years it will fill this chamber, and start up the passageway.

Then there was a rustle of movement behind us. I looked back. Someone else was coming through the web.

She reached us soon, and smiled. A Shkeen woman, old, naked, breasts hanging past her waist. Joined, of course. Her Greeshka covered most of her head and hung lower than her breasts. It was still bright and translucent from its time in the sun. You could see through it, to where it was eating the skin off her back.

"A candidate for Final Union," Gourlay said.

"This is a popular cave," Valcarenghi added in a low, sardonic voice.

The woman did not speak to us, nor us to her. Smiling, she walked past us. And lay down on the Greeshka.

The little Greeshka, the one that rode her back, seemed almost to dissolve on contact, melting away into the great cave creature, so the Shkeen woman and the great Greeshka were joined as one. After that, nothing. She just closed her eyes, and lay peacefully, seemingly asleep.

"What's happening?" I asked.

"Union," said Valcarenghi. "It'll be an hour before you'd notice anything, but the Greeshka is closing over her even now, swallowing her. A response to her body heat, I'm told. In a day she'll be buried in it. In two, like him—" The flash found the half-dissolved face above us.

"Can you read her?" Gourlay suggested. "Maybe that'd tell us something."

"All right," I said, repelled but curious. I opened myself. And the mindstorm hit.

But it's wrong to call it a mindstorm. It was immense and

awesome and intense, searing and blinding and choking. But it was peaceful too, and gentle with a gentleness that was more violent than human hate. It shrieked soft shrieks and siren calls and pulled at me seductively, and it washed over me in crimson waves of passion, and drew me to it. It filled me and emptied me all at once. And I heard the bells somewhere, clanging a harsh bronze song, a song of love and surrender and togetherness, of joining and union and never being alone.

Storm, mindstorm, yes, it was that. But it was to an ordinary mindstorm as a supernova is to a hurricane, and its violence was the violence of love. It loved me, that mindstorm, and it wanted me, and its bells called to me, and sang its love, and I reached to it and touched, wanting to be with it, wanting to link, wanting never to be alone again. And suddenly I was on the crest of a great wave once again, a wave of fire that washed across the stars forever, and this time I knew the wave would never end, this time I would not be alone afterwards upon my darkling plain.

But with that phrase I thought of Lya.

And suddenly I was struggling, fighting it, battling back against the sea of sucking love. I ran, ran, *ran*, *RAN* . . . and closed my minddoor and hammered shut the latch and let the storm flail and howl against it while I held it with all my strength, resisting. Yet the door began to buckle and crack.

I screamed. The door smashed open, and the storm whipped in and clutched at me, whirled me out and around and around. I sailed up to the cold stars but they were cold no longer, and I grew bigger and bigger until I *was* the stars and they were me, and I was Union, and for a single solitary glittering instant I was the universe.

Then nothing.

I woke up back in my room, with a headache that was trying to tear my skull apart. Gourlay was sitting on a chair reading one of our books. He looked up when I groaned.

Lya's headache pills were still on the bedstand. I took one hastily, then struggled to sit up in bed.

"You all right?" Gourlay asked.

"Headache," I said, rubbing my forehead. It *throbbed,* as if it was about to burst. Worse than the time I'd peered into Lya's pain. "What happened?"

He stood up. "You scared the hell out of us. After you began to read, all of a sudden you started trembling. Then you walked right into the goddamn Greeshka. And you screamed. Dino and the sergeant had to drag you out. You were stepping right in the thing, and it was up to your knees. Twitching, too. Weird. Dino hit you, knocked you out."

He shook his head, started for the door. "Where are you going?" I said.

"To sleep," he said. "You've been out for eight hours or so. Dino asked me to watch you till you came to. OK, you came to. Now get some rest, and I will too. We'll talk about it tomorrow."

"I want to talk about it now."

"It's late," he said, as he closed the bedroom door. I listened to his footsteps on the way out. And I'm sure I heard the outer door lock. Somebody was clearly afraid of Talents who steal away into the night. I wasn't going anywhere.

I got up and went out for a drink. There was Veltaar chilling. I put away a couple of glasses quick, and ate a light snack. The headache began to fade. Then I went back to the bedroom, turned off the light and cleared the glass, so the stars would all shine through. Then back to sleep.

But I didn't sleep, not right away. Too much had happened. I had to think about it. The headache first, the incredible headache that ripped at my skull. Like Lya's. But Lya hadn't been through what I had. Or had she? Lya was a major Talent, much more sensitive than I was, with a greater range. Could that mindstorm have reached *this* far, over miles and miles? Late at night, when humans and Shkeen were sleeping and their thoughts dim? Maybe. And maybe my half-remembered dreams were pale reflections of whatever she had felt the same nights. But my dreams had been pleasant. It was waking that bothered me, waking and not remembering.

But again, had I had this headache when I slept? Or when I woke?

What the hell had happened? What was that thing, that reached me there in the cave, and pulled me to it? The Greeshka? It had to be. I hadn't even time to focus on the Shkeen woman, it *had* to be the Greeshka. But Lyanna had said that Greeshka had no minds, not even a yes-I-live . . .

It all swirled around me, questions on questions on questions, and I had no answers. I began to think of Lya then, to wonder where she was and why she'd left me. Was this what she had been going through? Why hadn't I understood? I missed her then. I needed her beside me, and she wasn't there. I was alone, and very aware of it.

I slept.

Long darkness then, but finally a dream, and finally I remembered. I was back on the plain again, the infinite darkling plain with its starless sky and black shapes in the distance, the plain Lya had spoken of so often. It was from one of her favorite poems. I was alone, forever alone, and I knew it. That was the nature of things. I was the only reality in the universe, and I was cold and hungry and frightened, and the shapes were moving toward me, inhuman and inexorable. And there was no one to call to, no one to turn to, no one to hear my cries. There never had been anyone. There never would be anyone.

Then Lya came to me.

She floated down from the starless sky, pale and thin and fragile, and stood beside me on the plain. She brushed her hair back with her hand, and looked at me with glowing wide eyes, and smiled. And I knew it was no dream. She was with me, somehow. We talked.

Hi, Robb.

Lya? Hi, Lya. Where are you? You left me.

I'm sorry. I had to. You understand, Robb. You have to. I didn't want to be here anymore, ever, in this place, this awful place. I would have been, Robb. Men are always here, but for brief moments.

A touch and a voice?

Yes, Robb. Then darkness again, and a silence. And the darkling plain.

You're mixing two poems, Lya. But it's OK. You know them better than I do. But aren't you leaving out something? The earlier part. "Ah love, let us be true . . ."

Oh, Robb.

Where are you?

I'm—everywhere. But mostly in a cave. I was ready, Robb. I was already more open than the rest. I could skip the Gathering, and the Joining. My Talent made me used to sharing. It took me.

Final Union?

Yes.

Oh, Lya.

Robb. Please. Join us, join me. It's happiness, you know? Forever and forever, and belonging and sharing and being together. I'm in love, Robb, I'm in love with a billion billion people, and I know all of them better than I ever knew you, and they know me, all of me, and they love me. And it will last forever. Me. Us. The Union. I'm still me, but I'm them too, you see? And they're me. The Joined, the reading, opened me, and the Union called to me every night, because it loved me, you see? Oh, Robb, join us, join us. I love you.

The Union. The Greeshka, you mean. I love you, Lya. Please come back. It can't have absorbed you already. Tell me where you are. I'll come to you.

Yes, come to me. Come anywhere, Robb. The Greeshka is all one, the caves all connect under the hills, the little Greeshka are all part of the Union. Come to me and join me.

Love me as you said you did. Join me. You're so far away, I can hardly reach you, even with the Union. Come and be one with us.

No. I will not be eaten. Please, Lya, tell me where you are.

Poor Robb. Don't worry, love. The body isn't important. The Greeshka needs it for nourishment, and we need the Greeshka. But, oh Robb, the Union isn't just the Greeshka, you see? The Greeshka isn't important, it doesn't even have a mind, it's just the link, the medium, the Union is the Shkeen. A million billion billion Shkeen, all the Shkeen that have lived and Joined in fourteen thousand years, all together and loving and belonging, immortal. It's beautiful, Robb, it's more than we had, much more, and we were the lucky ones, remember? We were! But this is better.

Lya. My Lya. I loved you. This isn't for you, this isn't for humans. Come back to me.

This isn't for humans? Oh, it IS! It's what humans have always been looking for, searching for, crying for on lonely nights. It's love, Robb, real love, and human love is only a pale imitation. You see?

No.

Come, Robb. Join. Or you'll be alone forever, alone on the plain, with only a voice and a touch to keep you going. And in the end when your body dies, you won't even have that. Just an eternity of empty blackness. The plain, Robb, forever and ever. And I won't be able to reach you, not ever. But it doesn't have to be . . .

No.

Oh, Robb. I'm fading. Please come.

No. Lya, don't go. I love you, Lya. Don't leave me.

I love you, Robb. I did. I really did . . .

And then she was gone. I was alone on the plain again. A wind was blowing from somewhere, and it whipped her fading words away from me, out into the cold vastness of infinity.

In the cheerless morning, the outer door was unlocked. I ascended the tower and found Valcarenghi alone in his office. "Do you believe in God?" I asked him.

He looked up, smiled. "Sure." Said lightly. I was reading him. It was a subject he'd never thought about.

"I don't," I said. "Neither did Lya. Most Talents are atheists, you know. There was an experiment tried back on Old Earth fifty years ago. It was organized by a major Talent named Linnel, who was also devoutly religious. He thought that by using drugs, and linking together the minds of the world's most potent Talents, he could reach something he called the Universal Yes-I-Live. Also known as God. The experiment was a dismal failure, but *something* happened. Linnel went mad, and the others came away with only a vision of a vast, dark, uncaring nothingness, a void without reason or form or meaning. Other Talents have felt the same way, and Normals too. Centuries ago there was a poet named Arnold, who wrote of a darkling plain. The poem's in one of the old languages, but it's worth reading. It shows—fear, I think. Something basic in man, some dread of being alone in the cosmos. Maybe it's just fear of death, maybe it's more. I don't know. But it's primal. All men are forever alone, but they don't want to be. They're always searching, trying to make contact, trying to reach others across the void. Some people never succeed, some break through occasionally. Lya and I were lucky. But it's never permanent. In the end you're alone again, back on the darkling plain. You see, Dino? *Do you see?*"

He smiled an amused little smile. Not derisive—that wasn't his style—just surprised and disbelieving. "No," he said.

"Look again, then. Always people are reaching for something, for someone, searching. Talk, Talent, love, sex, it's all part of the same thing, the same search. And gods, too. Man invents gods because he's afraid of being alone, scared of an empty universe, scared of the darkling plain. That's why your men are converting, Dino, that's why people are going over. They've found God, or as much of a God as they're ever likely to find. The Union is a mass-mind, an immortal mass-mind, many in one, all love. The Shkeen don't die, dammit. No wonder they don't have the concept of an afterlife. They *know* there's a God. Maybe it didn't create the universe, but it's love, pure love, and they say that God is love, don't they? Or maybe what we call love is a tiny piece of God. I don't care, whatever it is, the Union is it. The end of the search for the Shkeen, and for Man too. We're alike after all, we're so alike it hurts."

Valcarenghi gave his exaggerated sigh. "Robb, you're overwrought. You sound like one of the Joined."

"Maybe that's just what I should be. Lya is. She's part of the Union now."

He blinked. "How do you know that?"

"She came to me last night, in a dream."

"Oh. A dream."

"It was *true*, dammit. It's all true."

Valcarenghi stood, and smiled. "I believe you," he said. "That is, I believe that the Greeshka uses a psi-lure, a love lure if you will, to draw in its prey, something so powerful that it convinces men—even you—that it's God. Dangerous, of course. I'll have to think about this before taking action. We could guard the caves to keep humans out, but there are too many caves. And sealing off the Greeshka wouldn't help our relations with the Shkeen. But now it's my problem. You've done your job."

I waited until he was through. "You're wrong, Dino. This is real, no trick, no illusion. I *felt* it, and Lya too. The Greeshka hasn't even a yes-I-live, let alone a psi-lure strong enough to bring in Shkeen and men."

"You expect me to believe that God is an animal who lives in the caves of Shkea?"

"Yes."

"Robb, that's absurd, and you know it. You think the Shkeen have found the answer to the mysteries of creation.

But look at them. The oldest civilized race in known space, but they've been stuck in the Bronze Age for fourteen thousand years. We came to *them*. Where are their spaceships? Where are their towers?''

"Where are our bells?" I said. "And our joy? They're happy, Dino. Are we? Maybe they've found what we're still looking for. Why the hell is man so driven, anyway? Why is he out to conquer the galaxy, the universe, whatever? Looking for God, maybe. . . ? Maybe. He can't find him anywhere, though, so on he goes, on and on, always looking. But always back to the same darkling plain in the end.''

"Compare the accomplishments. I'll take humanity's record.''

"Is it worth it?''

"I think so.'' He went to the window, and looked out. "We've got the only Tower on their world,'' he said, smiling, as he looked down through the clouds.

"They've got the only God in our universe,'' I told him. But he only smiled.

"All right, Robb,'' he said, when he finally turned from the window. "I'll keep all this in mind. And we'll find Lyanna for you.''

My voice softened. "Lya is lost,'' I said. "I know that now. I will be too, if I wait. I'm leaving tonight. I'll book passage on the first ship out to Baldur.''

He nodded. "If you like. I'll have your money ready.'' He grinned. "And we'll send Lya after you, when we find her. I imagine she'll be a little miffed, but that's your worry.''

I didn't answer. Instead I shrugged, and headed for the tube. I was almost there when he stopped me.

"Wait,'' he said. "How about dinner tonight? You've done a good job for us. We're having a farewell party anyway, Laurie and me. She's leaving too.''

"I'm sorry,'' I said.

His turn to shrug. "What for? Laurie's a beautiful person, and I'll miss her. But it's no tragedy. There are other beautiful people. I think she was getting restless with Shkea, anyway.''

I'd almost forgotten my Talent, in my heat and the pain of my loss. I remembered it now. I read him. There was no sorrow, no pain, just a vague disappointment. And below that, his wall. Always the wall, keeping him apart, this man who was a first-name friend to everyone and an intimate to none. And on it, it was almost as if there were a sign that read, THIS FAR YOU GO, AND NO FARTHER.

"Come up," he said. "It should be fun." I nodded.

I asked myself, when my ship lifted off, why I was leaving.

Maybe to return home. We have a house on Baldur, away from the cities, on one of the undeveloped continents with only wilderness for a neighbor. It stands on a cliff, above a high waterfall that tumbles endlessly down into a shaded green pool. Lya and I swam there often, in the sunlit days between assignments. And afterwards we'd lie down nude in the shade of the orangespice trees, and make love on a carpet of silver moss. Maybe I'm returning to that. But it won't be the same without Lya, lost Lya . . .

Lya whom I still could have. Whom I could have now. It would be easy, so easy. A slow stroll into a darkened cave, a short sleep. Then Lya with me for eternity, in me, sharing me, being me, and I her. Loving and knowing more of each other than men can ever do. Union and joy, and no darkness again, ever. God. If I believed that, what I told Valcarenghi, then why did I tell Lya no?

Maybe because I'm not sure. Maybe I still hope, for something still greater and more loving than the Union, for the God they told me of so long ago. Maybe I'm taking a risk, because part of me still believes. But if I'm wrong . . . then the darkness, and the plain . . .

But maybe it's something else, something I saw in Valcarenghi, something that made me doubt what I had said.

For man is more than Shkeen, somehow; there are men like Dino and Gourlay as well as Lya and Gustaffson, men who fear love and Union as much as they crave it. A dichotomy, then. Man has two primal urges, and the Shkeen only one? If so, perhaps there is a human answer, to reach and join and not be alone, and yet to still be men.

I do not envy Valcarenghi. He cries behind his wall, I think, and no one knows, not even he. And no one will ever know, and in the end he'll always be alone in smiling pain. No, I do not envy Dino.

Yet there is something of him in me, Lya, as well as much of you. And that is why I ran, though I loved you.

Laurie Blackburn was on the ship with me. I ate with her after liftoff, and we spent the evening talking over wine. Not a happy conversation, maybe, but a human one. Both of us needed someone, and we reached out.

Afterwards, I took her back to my cabin, and made love to her as fiercely as I could. Then, the darkness softened, we held each other and talked away the night.

Chicago
January–February, 1973